PRAISE FOR *Gracianna*

"*Gracianna* is a riveting and remarkable narrative. The characters come alive through their unassuming but compelling stories, as Nazi-occupied Paris unfolds before our eyes. We come to care deeply about the characters, which makes putting down the book almost impossible. Highly recommended."

—**STACEY KATZ BOURNS**, Director of Language Programs, Department of Romance Languages and Literatures, Harvard University

"While wine is obviously a significant part of life's enjoyment, the story behind the wine can be even more gratifying. You will be fixated on this thrilling story written by Trini Amador, which was inspired by Gracianna, his great-grandmother, the French Basque namesake of his family's award-winning winery in Sonoma County."

—**BOB CABRAL**, Director of Winemaking and General Manager, Williams Selyem Winery

"Debut novelist Trini Amador sparkles as this riveting story unfolds. His characters are deeply endowed with vibrant features and flaws and his evocative descriptions allow readers to experience each environment as though they had been there themselves [. . .] The story is carefully crafted, flowing smoothly and constantly, with impressive purpose and inspiration. More than a tale of good and evil, *Gracianna* is spun from convincing and memorable scenes and vivid personalities—a compelling and inspiring novel whose chronicle and characters will remain in the reader's memory long after."

—**CHARLES WEINBLATT**, New York Journal of Books

Gracianna

DEAR

KIM — WITH A

ENJOY GLASS OF

GLASS WINE

Gracianna

A novel inspired by true events

TRINI AMADOR

IRENE

HAPPY BIRTHDAY

FROM

ALX
+
CLAUDETTE

RIVER GROVE
BOOKS
www.rivergrovebooks.com

SUMMER 2022

This book is a work of fiction inspired by true events. Names, characters, businesses, organizations, places, events, and incidents are either a product of the author's imagination or are used fictitiously.

Published by River Grove Books
Austin, TX
www.rivergrovebooks.com

Distributed by River Grove Books

Design and composition by Greenleaf Book Group LLC
Cover design by Greenleaf Book Group LLC
Cover images: Woman on train tracks by ©iStockphoto.com/Rubén Hidalgo and gun by ©iStockphoto.com/titelio. Interior images courtesy of Angelsoft.

Publisher's Cataloging-in-Publication data is available.

Print ISBN: 978-1-63299-255-0

eBook ISBN: 978-1-60832-571-9

First Edition

With gratitude to my family: Lisa, Ashley, and Trini
who put the meaning in my life.

ACKNOWLEDGMENTS

I wish to thank my aunt, Kathy Prow, for the wonderful stories, background, and her recollections of her grandmother Gracianna. Thanks to brilliant early readers, Janet Verlander and Sherry Wright, who gave the author "real reader" direction and some realistic advice. Yvonne Shu, in her usual no-nonsense style, offered early expert proofing and copy support. Elizabeth Roggeveen sat at the kitchen table and read "Gracianna" to me and helped me realize how to sharpen dialogue that brought the book to life. She pushed and pulled aggressively and worked through those revisions. Thanks very much, Liz. Courtney Kolos offered support with continuous line editing, while Diana Imhoff Brown and Aaron Broughton, along with Kevin Anderson and Andy from A.I. Writing gave excellent copy edits and proofing. Thanks to Gunnar for translations. Lisa, Ashley, and T4 took the task seriously and read the book while on vacation and gave loving feedback. Thanks to Greenleaf Book Group for their effort and professionalism. Well done, everyone!

Hillel Black was my "tough-love" editor. He served as editor-in-chief of William Morrow, publisher of Macmillan, and executive editor of Sourcebooks. He has edited (and was the publisher of) no less than twenty *New York Times* best-selling books, including the likes of Sidney Sheldon's *Other Side of Midnight*, George Plimpton's *Curious Case of Sidd Finch*, and Richard Hooker's *M*A*S*H*, as well as every variety of nonfiction.

Much gratitude to Hillel who took me to school on writing something that was "well worth reading." His professional objective was clear: getting to a story that was not just readable but also enjoyable and meaningful, one that reflected my voice as a first-time author. We eventually spent hours working at his apartment on the Upper East Side of New York. Our time was filled with sometimes incredulous looks followed by laughter and momentous stories. I look forward to repeating the process with you again my dear friend, Hillel. [Update, Summer 2019: Sadly, Hillel has passed away as of this reprint. He would be proud of the fact that we have a second edition. As a seasoned "book man," he would gush at the thought. My time with Hillel is a "life" highlight. I can only hope to be as sharp and insightful as he was. I honor him for the work we did together and for his lifelong commitment to the craft, but I am missing my dear friend, Hillel Black.]

Finally, thank you very, very much to my friend and partner, Danny Gromfin who is always there. A jack of all trades, he sings, dances, proofs, builds websites, project manages, thinks marketing and sales, and has always been here through thick and thin—he does it all. We talk a million times a day on a million different subjects. He's one of the smartest cats I know. Thank you so much, Jack (not a typo).

Gracianna

PROLOGUE

Odds are I was the only four-year-old to have ever freely fumbled a loaded German Luger.

I was barely able to lift it. How could I know it was a real gun?

That was years and years ago at my great grandmother's house in California. It was stuffy inside, with muted light, full of old-world furniture. I remember being fascinated by the side and dining tables filled with intricate hand carvings. The dark and oily wood spoke of an important past. The sofas and chairs, with pale green skin of curlicued print, sported shouldered arms topped with hand-woven lace doilies. I was unable to comprehend the past I would later learn about.

We were alone in the house.

Innocently, I strolled out of my grandma Gracianna's bedroom carrying the heavy gun and faced her, O.K. Corral-style. I can still remember the weight of the Luger; feel the scratchiness of the crosshatched grip on the handle, the smoothness of the worn parts.

Although I didn't quite point it at her, I remember how her smile faded and she looked at me very calmly. I will never forget—as if I were about to touch a hot stove—she ordered, "Put it down," in her thick and French-sounding accent.

Instantly she was standing over me.

"Put it there."

She did not touch it.

All these years later, that moment still lives within me. Her calm, her controlled smile. I remember what I believed to be her burden, "Always be thankful," she had *always* said to me. It stayed with me.

The Luger—"from the war," I learned—was very real. Over the years it roiled inside me, in my little-boy dreams, my uninitiated young-man imagination, and my grown-up suspicions and research. I was sure I had it all figured out; I knew exactly the job that this gun had done and how she carried its weight. This story is the sum of my beliefs inspired by the facts that I learned about my great-grand-mère Gracianna and why she was so grateful.

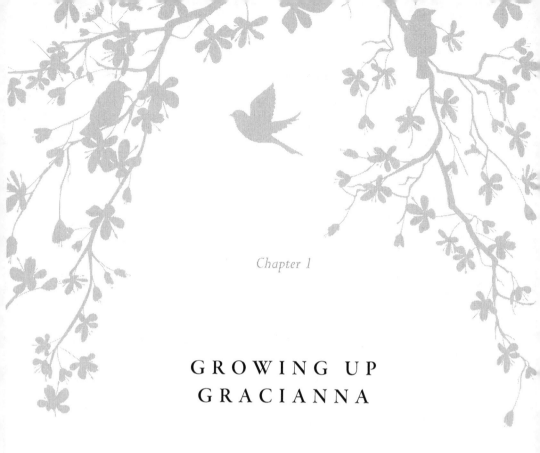

GROWING UP
GRACIANNA

*H*er name was Gracianna Arrayet. Her mother was Ann. Her birth certificate read, "Father Unknown." Her people were Basque. *Her* grandmother, Grand-mère Anastasia, was a staunch Basque woman.

Gracianna was born in the Pyrenees—the daunting, green-granite and limestone mountains that form the border between France and Spain. They wind like a fickle sea snake drinking from the cold Atlantic's Bay of Biscay in the west, stretching its body overland for 300 miles with a flicking tail that warms in the Mediterranean Sea to the east at Cap de Creus.

Growing up in the Pyrenees after the turn of the century, Gracianna came to enjoy excellent health, her muscles conditioned by walking the steep hills and valleys of her mountain kingdom, and performing endless chores at home. Chores were what Gracianna remembered and she enjoyed doing most of them. She did not enjoy doing outside chores however because the yard was filled with chickens, pigs and sheep. There was just too much going on around her and she had to watch her step, too.

Of course, she never complained. Grand-mère Anastasia would have none of that. "And neither would God!" Grand-mère would be sure to point out, her woolly brows scrunching as she crossed herself with three fingers.

No, Gracianna much preferred other domestic "tidying" chores and the long walks to attend church or share goods with neighbors. Most of all, though, it was books that she loved.

Books were always with her, borrowed from her teachers, the Catholic rectory, the neighbors. Late at night, long after everyone in the village was fast asleep, Gracianna was still reading by candlelight in the quiet of the bedroom she shared with her little sister, Constance. Of course, she made sure to flex the carelessly dripped hardened wax off the worn pages that she'd consumed before she returned the books, sometimes walking on auto-pilot, reading or de-waxing, her feet knowing the path, each rock, each gnarl and dip.

Her favorite subject was world history, but her favorite story was the folk-story of Pyrene, the princess from whom the Pyrenees' tragic name was born. She had heard the tale fireside many times as local festivals died down. Juan was a local boy she knew whose grandfather was her favorite at telling the story. An elder from the area, most everyone called him "Big Juan," and she'd heard him tell that tale in at least three languages, depending on which foreigners were visiting. Most of the people who live in the region spanning parts of north-central Spain and southwestern France are tri-lingual, speaking French, Spanish, and Basque and usually some Portuguese depending on their nationality. But above all she loved her native Basque, the language unrelated to any other European languages, more isolated, more ancient.

"Pyrene," Big Juan would begin, his warm voice mysterious, "was the young, beautiful virgin daughter of Bebryx, a king in Mediterranean Gaul. Once, King Bebryx hosted Hercules, who was on a quest to steal the whole herd of cattle from Geryon, the giant, three-headed war-mongering monster!" That usually got some attention.

"Now, Hercules was known for his strength and heroism, but he was less known for his drinking, boisterousness, lust, and indiscretion, like some other people you should watch out for."

There was a solemn pause.

"Apparently, all of Hercules' vast strength was useless against his own weakness because he violated the most inviolate rules of hospitality." Then, after spitting in the fire, Big Juan would explain to the mostly-child audience how Hercules had forcibly defiled his host's 15-year-old daughter, how Pyrene ended up giving birth to an ugly, vicious serpent that represented all that was evil and sadistic about the "hero" Hercules, and how she was then unable to face the horror-struck villagers and, most of all, her father. The children's eyes would be wide by now and their parents, most in festive moods and not paying attention, were unaware of the nightmares Big Juan was spawning. Finally he told his small audience that the young mother Pyrene ran away into the outer forest. In her grief and all alone she lamented, sobbing out her story.

"Why me?" Big Juan would wail dramatically playing the role of Pyrene. "I feel so very alone and afraid," he would whisper, "but Pyrene was not alone, and soon her fear turned to terror!" And he would describe the many eyes that were watching her from the darkness.

Big Juan explained that instead of gaining the consolation from the forest and feeling the wispy touch of the worried weeping willows, "She drew the attention of a score of wild beasts in nature's trick of seduction. The coarse-haired musty black wolves, the grizzled brown bear, and the muscled mountain lion chased her past the hot springs and through the craggy rocks toward a cliff where she could have jumped. But with a twisted sense of guilt Pyrene turned to face the animals," he paused for the effect, "and then . . . she punished herself." He looked toward the parents looking on, and he smiled and nodded toward them as he amused himself. "And then . . . Pyrene allowed the animals to tear her tiny body from limb to limb." Some of the children backed up. "And as the first bite sunk into her flesh, she went inside herself, into her head and into a place where she knew heaven was not far. The dumb-eyed ancient ibex stood by watching but did not know what to do. The blind insects common to our high meadows could not see anything, but tears formed in their eyes nonetheless."

Waiting a moment for the children who had tears in their eyes to absorb the terror, he went on with even more details.

"Pyrene could then hear the animals tearing and growling and gnawing and gnarling into her and understood that this was better treatment than when Hercules stole her 'self' from herself. For a moment her will to live was revived in a flicker, but she died," his stuttered inflection deepened, "Seven . . . minutes . . . later."

He would allow the children to look at each other in disbelief and then would explain, as if it were the moral of the story, how Hercules, victorious over Geryon despite the rain and now on his exultant march homeward, had passed through the kingdom of Bebryx and happened to stumble upon his conquest's shredded body! "Pyrene!" Hercules picked up the pieces of her little body and held them close and lamented.

Big Juan loved to lament as Hercules! He told of how Hercules wanted to jump with Pyrene's tattered remains into the abyss, how he finally recognized his corruption, how he howled in sorrow and rage, and finally, he placed Pyrene's body on a soft bed of peat moss. When it began to rain, as it often does in that moist region of swirling bulbous clouds that form in the Atlantic over the Bay of Biscay, Hercules turned to face Mother Nature, who was human nature, too, in all of her glory and weakness.

"Mourn with me!" Big Juan would shout as Hercules had shouted at the valleys, the rivers, and the lakes. He quickened the story here because some parents were catching on since the children had not made a sound for nearly thirty minutes. "Pyrene is your own!" And on Big Juan would go.

"But the gentle rain and mist did not ease his pain, and he, with Herculean voice, shouted, 'Pyrene! Pyrene! Pyrene! Pyrene! Pyrene!' The name echoed through the mountains, and her name haunts the region still.

"And the story finishes with this quote from a famous book," Big Juan would swoon, looking into the eyes of each and every petrified child, "'Struck by Herculean voice, the mountaintops shudder at the ridges; he keeps crying out with a sorrowful noise "Pyrene!" and all the rock-cliffs and wild-beast haunts echo back "Pyrene!" The mountains hold on to the wept-over name through the ages.' And that's how our mountains got the name the Pyrénées."*

Even though it was terrifying, Gracianna loved the story because it told of how her birthplace had been named.

While she enjoyed local lore, Gracianna branched out with her reading. Any subject was open for study and scrutiny, and Gracianna would eventually know most subjects cold.

"If you don't apply yourself, you won't get anywhere," she would insist while standing on her toes, always nearly a head shorter than the next child, to any who were jealous of her ability to quote verses from poems and entire passages of history. They just didn't seem to be like her—"ambitious and curious," as her mother, Ann, had once boasted.

Gracianna, with her broad face and always-thin wetted lips, was naïve

---

* Ben Tipping, Exemplary Epic: Silius Italicus' Punica (Oxford University Press, 2010), pp. 20–21.

but wickedly aware like her mother and grand-mère. So aware, that all the other children were wary of her and adults were initially surprised at her ability. She saw and heard everything. And, remembered everything she saw. Although not outgoing, she had a natural social nuance. Her mother chalked up any awkwardness to the white streak in her prematurely turning hair (Gracianna's brown hair had already started turning white by her sixth birthday). Once she decided to engage with anyone on a given subject, they would become transfixed by her confidence, and the grasp and depth of her knowledge. Her sureness came from her strong core.

Close to the ground, with strong legs planted, her wisdom was delivered from roots steeped below the earth. Earthly nutrients seeped self-assurance and knowledge into her from a young age. It was conceived that she would be invited to become a nun—even at this early age—since the best and brightest were invited to be closer to the church and God.

However, there was something gnawing at her. It was her drive to make everything clean, bright, and right, all the time. It was in her and it would haunt her throughout her life.

More and more, Gracianna began to notice that there didn't seem to be any people in the village who were like her.

Gracianna thought: *At least my mother understands me.*

THE STORY OF ANN

Gracianna still thought of her now and then. *Mère [mother]* . . .

"We're not carefree, but we're happy," Ann would say with a toothy smile, tucking Gracianna and her little sister, Constance, into the sleeping cupboard near the kitchen, the warmest room in the house. And she would sing soft and low as she cleaned and swept a half step away and tended to the heat of the fireplace. Her favorite was a sailor's song of hope and love and life and equality:

> *I go away to provide for the family*
> *I go away to clear my mind*
> *I go away to make for the new*
> *I go away to come home for love*

But that was all over now.

Ann had died in childbirth when Gracianna was eight and Constance was six. Sometimes, it was impossible for Gracianna not to think of that night.

The screaming had been horrific. The long silences worse.

Gracianna had been hiding behind the pulled curtain, too afraid to even peek. She'd heard birth before. It was painful. It could mean death as well. She had tucked that knowledge away. The low birth moans had become a hush, and now there was only screaming. Suddenly, Grand-mère's soothing tones had turned into frantic prayer, the kind of prayer that is blurted at the moment of truth when you know there is no alternative but to beg a higher power to intercede.

The priest just appeared. Gracianna still didn't know who had sent for him or when, but he was there, standing right at the bedside as if following a familiar path.

The praying and screaming grew louder and then it became quiet . . . for too long . . . life and maybe death was all happening too fast. Little Constance had fallen asleep in the long lull, unable to keep her eyes open waiting for the baby, and now she was mercifully oblivious to the brink of loss. As if from the core of the earth, there was a last powerful but quiet push. Then, more silence. Gracianna had heard this before, too—a final push with a growling grunt and then nothing—it meant the baby was stillborn. It had happened to Ann a year before. Last time, her mother had started to cry.

But there is no crying this time—it is silent . . . a dead baby—could it be? Dead?

Gracianna flung open the curtain that had obscured her eyes and saw it all.

"No!"

The priest reached to cover her eyes but she saw a bloody butchering. There was the bloody baby and her bloody mother, both still, the baby blue; her mother, just gone. No glinting eyes. No lilting smile. No reaching of the hardworking hands with the softest wrists that always caressed her face.

Now nothing. Just nothing.

Gracianna rushed into the bloody mess, pouncing on her mother's bed like she had a hundred times before. The priest barely held her back, weak with self-guilt for his miscarried effort. An exhausted Grand-mère Anastasia had crumpled into the chair beside her dead daughter's bed.

Gracianna flung her tiny bony elbows around her mother's neck, not noticing that she scraped her knees on the bedside. Then it was Gracianna's turn to beg.

"*Oh! Dieu! S'il vous plaît! Maman! Dieu! Reste avec moi reste avec moi Reste avec moi reste avec moi reste avec moi reste avec moi reste avec moi reste avec moi reste avec moi reste avec moi! oh! Dieu!*" [Oh! God! Please! Mommy! God! Stay with me stay with me stay with me stay with me stay with me stay with me stay with me stay with me stay with me oh! God]!"

But Ann was already gone. Nothing. Her mother's sweet songs were forever stricken from Gracianna's memory, forever replaced with the drawling, paining, echoing death.

Finally, Gracianna's prayers became quieter.

Fallen, she whispered the Lord's Prayer into her mother's cooling soft ear over and over desperate to try to get her mother to stay. It began, "*Notre Père* [Our Father]. . . ."

She repeated the prayer over and over as the cleanup began, crossing herself each time.

"*Notre Père,*" as one by one the birth team left under the mountain moon and the auntie who had helped deliver Gracianna years before bowed out in tears with an armful of red linen.

"*Notre Père,*" when the midwives gave way to the incoming neighbor, Jacque, who would help clean the wreckage and bury the lifeless players after their valiant struggle for life.

"*Notre Père,*" again as the neighbor lady, who had a seven-child brood, left to feed them.

"*Notre Père,*" as the priest departed patting Gracianna's stay-with-me-Mommy bowed head. *Oh, Notre Père. . . .*

And each time, she made the sign of the cross, over and over until she finally wept . . . then slept.

Gracianna was left to grieve twice for the brother not-to-be and the mother who had been her every being. Her mother was unable to grieve the death of her just-born still-child since she was now dead herself. Like Gracianna's father, the father of the blue boy was "unknown," and so never spoken of. The village children were taught the code of polite silence, and Gracianna obeyed as well. She figured her father was likely a mariner, one of the local men who went to sea to escape the herding life. She would never know. Now with no mother, her father, whom she'd never missed, was missed.

"*Mon Père* [My Father]. . . ."

Lifting her head from her mother's cooling face, Gracianna panicked.

Who will take care of Constance and me?

*I*nto her grandmother's care she had gone, along with Constance. She had no idea what an influence Anastasia would have.

Over time, Gracianna tried to be grateful for the eight short years of mothering she'd received from Ann.

But it wasn't really eight was it?

It was only four, because she couldn't remember anything before the age of four years old. There were many days that she couldn't remember anything specific happening.

So it was really three years wasn't it?

She realized that of her eight years she could only recall a handful of days that were *truly* meaningful.

So mother was really only my mother for about fifteen days?

It was hard to be grateful when their time together had been so short, the memories so sweet, the parting so bitter. In the end, Gracianna could not recall her mother's memory without feeling the pain of tragic loss; loss so painful it hindered her or hampered or blotted out any memory of the good.

Now I think the fear of losing someone dear is greater than my need to love again.

INDOCTRINATION

Despite the loss of her mother, with her grandmother and aunts and uncles and little sister close by, Gracianna had plenty of love and plenty of chores to keep her busy, Grand-mère Anastasia made sure of that.

Her grand-mère made sure of a lot of things.

"You are Basque," was Anastasia's familiar homily, always only speaking Basque at home. "In ancient Roman, that means 'proud mountain people.'

These are your people: fierce, independent, free. Even the Romans knew not to be rough with us, especially with the women. Even Basque men respect their women—where else? That's because strong women equal a strong culture. Plus, women do a perfect job of running the household and tending the gardens, that's why we pass everything to our daughters. Let the men tend the sheep and we'll welcome them home! Now eat your potatoes, you have to sweep." Even though there was no man who would be coming home.

"Yes, Grand-mère," Gracianna and Constance would say.

"Yes, Anastasia," many of the villagers would say.

Anastasia made sure she was respected and visible and somewhat feared by all outside the home and in, being careful to ensure that Gracianna and Constance got a thorough dose of Basque/Catholic indoctrination year after year. The only things Anastasia feared were lack of cleanliness and God.

Perfection is the only way.

AMERICANS AT THE INN

Because of Anastasia's influence and training, and after years of "perfection indoctrination," at seventeen Gracianna immediately landed a live-in job, cooking, cleaning, and caring at the biggest sheep ranch in the region. After all, she had finished school and she was expected to have a proper job. The ranch wasn't far, right in the heart of the verdant Aquitanian highlands.

So Gracianna left her little village of Baigorri. Her grandmother was proud to see her go.

Everyone knew Gracianna got the job not just because of her family's longtime standing in the area, but also because of the sheer presence of the imposing Anastasia. No one was surprised that Gracianna ended up at a sheep ranch. If you were Basque, you either "sheeped" or "sailored." One way or another, Basques were drawn to pioneer the land or sea. "Against a thousand valleys and a million waves, our people have struggled, fallen, and risen again," Anastasia would say while straightening Gracianna's collar. "Be proud. Proud and perfect."

On her very few days off from the ranch kitchen, Gracianna would walk down to an inn at the bottom of the valley to work even more in *their* kitchen, waiting tables, cleaning to perfection. Then walking back up the hill again, strong thighs working, barely breathless, and then down and back up again the next day. She loved walking down the winding path between the series of cascading, terraced earthen breaks peaking and jutting and piercing the sky.

Gracianna talked her shy and somewhat lazy ranch-roommate, Bettina, into taking the second job at the inn. Then, they would walk together.

"Basque living is not flat," she would joke with the foreigners. "'Nearby' is approximately five kilometers and that's an easy walk. Well, downhill."

"Not uphill! That would defeat a mere mortal!" One bow-tied gentleman visitor had declared. Gracianna and Bettina had bowed proudly and crossed themselves privately.

At the inn one evening as dark was falling, Gracianna met an American doctor and his wife. The adventuresome couple had been out hiking and were windswept and tired as they returned to the inn. Gracianna immediately took their coats, made from exquisite wool. She couldn't help but notice their towering height and distinguished looks.

"Tenk you," the lady said, her response businesslike but genuine. Her blue eyes were beautiful and Gracianna sensed that the woman was friendly beneath her cool courtesy. Gracianna was barely able to reach the lady's shoulders when taking her gorgeous coat. Her husband was tall and handsome, distinguished looking even with his windy hair. She was definitely Eastern European with that accent—somehow she must have found this American doctor, married him. . . . *Did he take her away to America?*

"You're so very welcome," Gracianna almost forgot to say in French-sounding English.

It was rare to see Americans, but Gracianna refused to pester them with questions. She would just watch and listen and be helpful, of course.

Gracianna had a highly developed sense of other people and herself. She was empathetic, keenly aware of her feelings and of those belonging to neighbors and strangers. She figured the Mrs., who was Coolish-on-the-Outside, was quite warm and could be affectionate toward her husband and to other people when she got to know them.

Bettina, who was only sixteen when she left school, also lived on the ranch as Gracianna's bunk and kitchen-mate. She occasionally worked as a helper at the inn with Gracianna. Bettina often gave Gracianna a hard time about her "helpfulness," so it was no surprise when she teased Gracianna about taking the American's coats "so quickly."

"But you must be a receptive hostess," Gracianna protested as they strode up the hill after working at the remote mountain inn. "You must look for ways to help others, in no matter what small way, even if it is simply to say a kind word. It's called having 'social grace' . . . one small favor returns many."

Bettina had just laughed and shrugged in her distant and shy way.

"And what about you?" Gracianna continued. "You do just enough work to get by but you appear to be working very hard. But I have to do the *real* work because I like it to be perfect!" They both laughed.

"I work two jobs," Bettina held up two fingers, "and not perfectly, but good enough is good enough for me. But you! You are destined for great things, Gracianna, like perfectly doing dishes for an even bigger inn—a hotel that is fifty kilometers to walk to!"

"As long as it is on top of the mountain!" And they both laughed some more.

That night, however, when Bettina again awoke to Gracianna reading by candlelight, she thought, *Why does she do that? Reading never got anyone anywhere.*

Bettina just knew the world out there was too much to handle. She shrugged and soon went back to sleep.

THE RIVIERA PROPOSAL

The following night, Gracianna was surprised to see the Americans were still at the inn. She watched them closely, discreetly, as they ate and drank.

"*Bonsoir* [Good evening]," they finally said from the small lounge area by the fireplace after the dinner rush had died down. The hopeful fire crackled and glowed casting its own ember light dance.

"My dear," the lady said to Gracianna in a thick European accent, "you are a hard worker. Isn't she, Herbert?" She turned to her husband, who was reading a book.

Herbert peered over his glasses that covered his finely lined eyes framed by crow's feet, and in a voice ever-so-slightly slurred, he said, "Yes, I believe she is darling. We could use her, you think?"

Gracianna's heart jumped and she nearly tripped over herself as she curtsied before them, and began to graciously reassure them what a fine worker she was. The Mrs. was studying her every move with those cool blue eyes.

Gracianna was pleased to demonstrate how attentive she could be, how professional, how perfect. And that her name was Gracianna.

"I am called Gracianna. Gra-see-ahnna."

"Oh, lovely," the lady said and took a sip of wine. "Hmmm. . . ."

"Well, Gracianna," Herbert piped up, raising his voice, "would you like to come to the U-nited States of Ame-ri-ca to work at our house?"

"Mmm-hmmm," the Mrs. agreed, gesturing for him to be quiet. "It's in the California Riviera. Of course, you've never heard of it," she chuckled forgivingly.

"The Riviera? Why, yes I've heard of it. I'm quite a reader, I . . . "— Gracianna stopped herself, not wanting to sound too excited, not believing what was happening, and so fast. She couldn't get too attached. These people were a little tipsy, she reminded herself. They could not know that no one had ever said anything to her that had so much meaning.

Herbert continued, quieter now, more nostalgic, "The breeze is always warm, so your kids can play at the beach when they come home from school. . . ."

My kids. Gracianna's mind wandered to her mother.

"If you think about it hard enough," her mother had said, "if you believe, and pray hard enough, and take some action, you can actually move in the direction of that hope. Your wishes can all come true!"

Grand-mère had reinforced Gracianna's sense of capability.

The Mrs. said something about California, then the Mr. went on about the weather but she couldn't hear a word they said.

Gracianna wanted to pass this capability and belief along, when she became a mother and grandmother. Like her mother Ann, she could help others see the future and she wanted to give this gift of belief in oneself to generations to come. She would teach them to have the discipline, to have belief in their own thoughts, and to work harder than others every day in every way to make those thoughts come to life. She had been taught that others want to help those that want to be successful.

There are swimmers and floaters and I am a swimmer.

So far, Gracianna had been able to make small things come true—but this was big, this was now, immediate, and real. She snapped her focus on the Mrs., who was talking again.

"Ugh, there is so much work to do at home. I just cannot find anyone that has my sensibilities and work ethic. But you, my dear," she pointed her glass at Gracianna, "are perfect. Don't you think, Herbert?"

The word at the inn was that Herbert was Doctor Herbert Newsome, a well-known and admired general practitioner posted in Santa Barbara, his family a longtime California clan that had come west. He had been schooled in the East. He was a bit of a swashbuckler, traveling into Mexico with friends on drinking, hunting, and whoring binges. He was living the big life, laughing, backslapping, and doing right by his patients, wife, and children for the most part.

"Yes, yes, Marie, she is perfect."

Gracianna tried to smile.

Herbert kissed his wife's forehead, murmured something into her ear, and then asked for Gracianna's address. She gave it to them, in her best handwriting.

I'm going to America. My dream has come true!

BETTINA

Gracianna was bursting to talk by the time she headed uphill with Bettina that evening. Hardly missing a breath, Gracianna raved, "I've always dreamed of seeing the world, but now I know it."

"Know what?"

"Of course, I should move to America! Oh, I expect that life would be just wonderful in America. I've read that anyone can start a business, and there are plenty of people to buy from you. And all the schools and libraries! What an opportunity! And I have a year to prepare because I am sure the Americans will send for me. . . ."

Bettina was more skeptical. "They were a little drunk, didn't you see?"

Gracianna shot a don't-you-dare-ruin-my-moment look at her, "But, this is my dream! God has brought the Americans to me to take me away!"

Bettina rolled her eyes as she always did when Gracianna started talking about God.

"Wouldn't it be great, just imagine if I met a man there?"

"A man!"

They giggled.

"We'd have a big house with a cellar to store food and make wine and have three children, two girls and a boy, and have our own business and it will be on the California Riviera! Oh, Bettina, I've had dreams about the French Riviera, but this. . . ."

Gracianna never told Bettina that her mother had told her bluntly one day, "I was never able to get away from these mountains. I wanted to go to America to live and learn and be alive. I never had the chance to be myself; I had to be too perfect for your grand-mère."

"I want to hear about the Rivieras," Bettina encouraged.

Gracianna longed to see California, but the beautiful Santa Barbara? She had read of it in a single line in a travel review and just happened to commit it to memory. "North of Los Angeles, with smiling Mediterranean-looking hillsides that drop to the sea." It had sounded to Gracianna like the French Riviera. The French Riviera . . . she had heard about it on the radio and read about it in newspaper articles. It was the site of one of her favorite fantasies, and she found herself surprised to be telling Bettina how sometimes at night she'd imagine working there in a hotel, catering to wealthy Europeans who were there on holiday. And how, one night, an especially kind, handsome and intelligent son of one of the guest families would catch her eye and, with real good intentions, ask her to meet him after work.

Of course she could never go out with a guest as it was strictly forbidden. In her dream, he persisted and sent her a note through one of the bartenders and she met him off the property. No one at the hotel could know because she would be fired. They walked by the water at night and laughed and laughed every night for three nights. She loved his smile and his nice teeth. He would be very gentle and gentlemanly and eventually, on the fourth night, the last night before his vacation with his wealthy family would end and before he left, he would take her in his strong arms and kiss her even though she was not ready. But she secretly wanted him to and had longed for it and he promised to come for her when he graduated from the university in Paris where he studied law.

Bettina was dumbstruck as she listened to Gracianna speeding up to tell the rest of her dream.

One day a cable came to the hotel. He was coming back! He wanted to see her! The day he arrived he brought flowers and still had his quick familiar smile but was wearing a pressed white linen suit and was a bit older than she remembered and his mildly Latin shade told her he had recently been in the sun somewhere—somewhere that he would take her on their honeymoon! Then they would embrace and she could not believe that he had finally come back; she had only slept a little for the few days prior to his arrival and was haggard and afraid he would see that she had aged too much while they had been apart . . . .

Bettina laughed at that part, unable to contain herself anymore. "You are a silly, silly girl, Gras'! What would a handsome, wealthy, educated man want with a mountain girl? A rock will have to fall from the heavens to wake you up and the chances of that is nothing!"

Yet, all week, Gracianna stubbornly held on to hope that the Americans had left word for her.

They had not come back.

The rumor was that maybe they would be back next year, or the year after.

Walking with Bettina, Gracianna fumed. Bettina just tried to make things better but made them worse. "They were just drunks—"

"Don't!" Gracianna didn't like that kind of talk, then she relaxed and said, "Well, I could wait a year standing in sheep dung, I just know it!"

Bettina laughed at the thought of standing in the barn with a shovel and the sheep dung at Gracianna's ankles for one year.

"Look, Gras', forget the Americans. You are the one who has to make it happen, if that's your dream. Maybe God just wanted to give you the idea and it's really up to you."

Crushed, Gracianna said nothing. Later, as Bettina fell off to sleep, Gracianna lay awake remembering what her grandmother Anastasia had said a thousand times before: *The more you expect, the more you will gain.*

DECISION

The next morning at the ranch, Gracianna was back to her bright self, making breakfast as usual—a slice of cheese, a fried egg—for herself and Bettina. Then they cooked for the men who worked the land and tended the sheep in the faraway hills. The men worked in herding shifts and would be away for weeks at a time.

After their chores were done, Gracianna disappeared briefly and then reappeared in her Sunday outfit. "Bettina, I am leaving," she announced, trying to sound confident. "I am going to get to America somehow. I have already arranged a ride to my village to say goodbye to Grand-mère, and then I'll get dropped off part of the way to the San Sebastian station. Then I am going to Paris tonight. For work."

"What? You can work here! And there is talk of war in France." Bettina had gone pale. "I'm sorry for what I said. Come, Gras' you are being too hasty."

"I know someone in Paris who will give me work," Gracianna half-stretched. "And even the ranchers say, 'In Paris, with hard work, the saving is easy.' I am a hard worker. I will be out of Paris in no time. I hope I will see you again someday, Bettina. I am glad you were my roommate and good friend but I must go. Thank you." She kissed Bettina twice on her cheek and then she left quickly, before the urge to hug Bettina overpowered her, before she confessed the fear she wanted to hide.

Bettina, stunned, throat tightening, watched her only friend walk out the door and get into the ranch manager's wagon, which was filled with a noisy racket of lambs in the back.

In a cacophony of bleats, Gracianna was down the path, her head swaying back and forth with the wagon's motion, rocking along with the ranch owner's broad stocky shoulders and with the blaring lamb bleats of an old song that was now her new song of hope.

For a second, Bettina considered calling out, "Wait!" The word in her heart was in her mouth like cotton, her throat choked. Her thin, pale lips could not open. But tears fell, tears of blessing and envy.

As the pair rolled out of sight, Bettina could still hear the bleating. As the hopeful song faded, it occurred to Bettina how miraculous the whole affair had been. Last night, they were talking about the dream. The next morning, it was done.

This is Gracianna's way.

Bettina had begun learning about how careful and responsible Gracianna could be from the first day they had met. Every single thing always *needed* to be in its place with her. In the tiny room they shared, each blanket was folded crisply, her personal effects perfectly set out, her hairbrush with not a hair in it, her toothbrush, worn but upright, her shoes always cleaned every night, and her three simple cotton dresses always fresh and folded. In the kitchen, each spoon was shined as it was dried. Bettina dried things in a hurry, but Gracianna dried *and* shined.

Bettina didn't know about the time that Gracianna's grandmother made her clean the tub with a very tiny brush, right after her mother had died. Every small spot and mineral deposit was to be removed.

Why do I have to do this?

With each inspection, Grand-mère Anastasia would stand at the door, barely entering, and point out a spot, a discoloration here, and an imperfection "right there, can't you see it?" Finally, exasperated that Gracianna would call her in before she was "finished," Anastasia grabbed a handful of Gracianna's young, white hair and pushed her face down to a spot.

"Why can't you see what you are missing?" she had growled.

A bit later, lithe little Constance had tried to help. She'd come in without a word, kneeled and just started brushing alongside her "big sister." It was always funny when Constance would call her that since Gracianna was at least a head shorter than Constance even at their young ages. Constance had found her own tiny brush somewhere. But Gracianna chased her away out of embarrassment and rage at her grandmother. It had nothing to do with the love that Gracianna felt for Constance. They shared a bond of love born from the loss of their mother. It would never die.

Bettina had to admit that Gracianna's extra efforts had made her resentful, and she wasn't the only coworker who felt that way. They were all resentful of the acknowledgment and special treatment that Gracianna received from their supervisors, making them feel second rate, as if they were not caring, detailed, or hardworking enough. Gracianna was oblivious to this resentment, or had seemed to be.

Bettina resented her now. It was a wonder how someone at Gracianna's young age, nearly eighteen, could be so serious and so smart and so determined and so—well, in control of everything. Bettina realized what annoyed her to the point of distrust about Gracianna was also what she truly admired and would miss. That structure, that damned incessant chiding, that comfort, that perfection was gone.

She also missed Gracianna's unique combination of her grandmother's strict upbringing; her innate interest in reading and learning; plus her unbridled, sometimes silly but always big, imagination—and she was tough to the core.

Bettina had seen Gracianna's fearlessness once before. It had happened in the kitchen. Bettina remembered she had once seen Gracianna stand down a grown man at least three times her size in the kitchen when he picked food out of the pot she was preparing for dinner. Her temper had been hot and quick and she had slapped his hand as if he were a child. Yes, Gracianna was like a miniature poodle or dachshund that might fiercely lash out at a German shepherd or other dog two to three times its size on the street. No, she had never seen such fearless determination.

Bettina's enlightenment was that some "small" souls only have belief in the size of their destiny not the size of their container. "Go get 'em!" Bettina finally whispered after Gracianna, breaking her silence. It was Bettina's final acceptance and blessing in one. Bettina knew she would never be able to make a decision like that. Never would. Never could.

What Bettina didn't see and what Gracianna would never say out loud was that she was scared to death to make this move. *I wish my mother were here; she would support me. She would know this was the right thing. She would say, "Go."* Gracianna was compelled to act because to be perfect meant she always had to try harder and move forward. *This is a curse. Being good enough isn't good enough. Lord, see me through.*

As Bettina looked at the empty road, she had a sinking feeling that she would never see Gras' again. She was gone.

Bettina suddenly wondered, *But what about Juan?*

Chapter 2

JUAN

*J*uan Laxague (*Lox-ag*) was nineteen, from the nearby village of Laxia. Like most Basque males, Juan had dark, wavy hair and olive skin that was somewhat fair in the long winters but tanned easily. Like most Basque males, Juan was stocky, strong, and not so tall. He had been working at the ranch for six months before Gracianna had arrived. Gracianna had recognized him right away by his big goose smile. Their families had been sharing and swapping goods for generations, Baigorri and Laxia being near enough to each other. She remembered how, when she was probably ten and he thirteen, Juan had helped her when she stumbled on some rocks.

"Mountain goat," she'd called him.

He had smiled and told her that he loved climbing rocks and running in the hills. She would try to chase after him, then give up and get upset. Then he would chase her but not catch her right away. That was much more fun.

He was just hairier now and a little more handsome. How could she forget his smile?

Juan thought that little Gracianna was cute, but at the time, he was really in love with his schoolteacher.

Catholic nuns of the Benedictine Order of Basses, France, taught Juan. The mother superior, Mother Immaculada, had moved two of the most hardworking nuns up to the Basque hills, forming a satellite enclave because Mother Immaculada believed the immaculate mountain air was "God actually entering your body with every breath."

"I can actually see the immaculate air of hell from here," Sister Timothy Marie had remarked once from one of the higher hills (she had the advantage, being rather tall). "But it *is clean* air!"

Sister Timothy Marie . . . Her eyes were perfectly bathtub-blue.

Juan's crush had been a big worry to him.

Isn't it a sin to be in love with a nun AND my teacher?

He would cross himself twice, but it didn't seem to have any lessening effect on his crush. So, with some variation, he would pray for his contradiction, "Please God, allow me to be a priest someday. And please, please make sure I am handsome and smart, so that Sister Timothy Marie will love me. Thank you, God. Good night."

Somewhere along the way, Juan had decided he didn't want to be a priest. After all, one day the farmstead in Laxia would belong to him, so that's where he knew he needed to stay.

The farmstead was a beautiful piece of land that had become a sort of compound over the generations. Five families now were scattered across the property—each worked a piece of land and lived in a traditional, deep-cellared dwelling.

Juan liked to look out from the porch.

Someday.

For now, it belonged to his grandfather, and then would pass to his father. Who knew what would happen after that? Still, he loved the place as his own.

Thousands of sheep were everywhere in the Basque Country but especially in the hills of Laxia. They were hardy, short-legged, longhaired, and in the spring became nobody-is-really-there-if-you-really-look-them-in-the-eye sheep. All were well watched. Juan could always be seen reclining on the hillsides alone, as if occupied by silent yet tumbling thoughts.

He kept to himself but was smart, and when he was with others had a quick smile. He literally was one of those "when you get to know him . . ." types and Oh!, when you got to know him, his warmth and belief in goodness and the good in people were contagious. He laughed with his head back and his eyes in the stars. When he really laughed he went away to another place to revel in the joy he was feeling.

He fancied Gracianna and teased her tirelessly even though he was nearly four years older. She knew this was a game and played back coyly although tiredly. His teasing episodes seemed endless. What especially annoyed her were his jokes about the premature evolution of her hair from light brown at six to perfectly white at sixteen. It was neither blond-white nor ivory-white. It was snow white, just like her grandmother's and her great-grandmother's and even one more before her. *That* grandmother had been burned at the stake for her white hair. So Gracianna had little-girl concerns about her hair and did not like the references spoken out loud, especially in front of others. Gracianna knew this was fancy play, though; her grandmother told her when a boy or man teases you, he is trying to tease you into his life. Gracianna was not sure if this was the life she wanted to be teased into, but she appreciated the attention. The only attention from men she had gotten before Juan was in her dreams or during rare, private in-her-head moments.

Laxia itself was beautiful; a land of vast hills and fields of green, green grass in the spring, the valley so wide you could barely hear a gunshot from one side to the next. Water ran everywhere; the runoff came from snowy, Alp-like peaks, some of which were so tall the locals had never been able to conquer them.

Nearly fifteen hundred summers earlier, the Romans had built an ingenious rock wall fashioned after the aqueducts in order to run water to residences, develop certain areas, and transport growth. They supposedly conquered Basque inhabitants who were very stubborn, but in time even the indigenous came to enjoy the bathhouses.

"You see what the Romans can do with some vision," they would say. "Too bad they are trying to conquer us Basques," they would laugh. "It will never work!" Then they would relax in the steamy waters.

The aqueducts still crisscrossed the region, and the one in Laxia on Juan's land still worked. Remote Basque families would come to take a look at the Laxagues' water system. It was a sound model. The setup had been updated for a few modern-day generations. Unfortunately, a "still working system" proved the Romans knew something after all, but this was never openly discussed nor acknowledged. Occasionally, Juan and his grandfather would travel to other parts of the region to teach other families about the water system.

Extra money was always good.

Especially good since Juan's great-aunt Marie lived in an old house on the property with a grown daughter. Marie's husband had died of fever, so of course her brother took her in. She didn't have much money, but she was a great baker and she brought her sourdough to the compound.

"It dates back to Caesar's time," she claimed, always saving a ball of the dough to start the next batch. It was not believable, really, but who could prove otherwise? Others would come and trade for her Caesar-breads, leaving the family rich in fruits and vegetables they didn't have to raise. The beets, roots, and seeds were stored in the large, cool basement that ran the length of the house along with the river-clay vat full of fermenting wild grapes.

Juan's grandfather, "Big Juan," or "The Storyteller" as most of the village knew him, was the perfect shepherd and the pride of the Laxague family. Juan's father, called "Juan Senior" by most everyone, was a more reluctant shepherd. Like Juan, his father, Juan Sr. was often alone with his shepherd's thoughts, but Senior felt burdened by the sheep like a casket of black-headed souls to watch over. Senior had tired of the mountain life and, like many others, had sold his sheep and become a sometimes seaman. Already married, he was caught between two worlds, never satisfied. He would move back and forth between the hills and sea, seeking satisfaction and trying to not be like Big Juan.

Juan loved his grandfather, Big Juan! He was a striving man, a family man, articulate, strong, gracious, well liked, and kind. He had a twinkle in his eyes and a saying for everything. His gracious toasts were always on the spot. After Juan's first solo shepherding initiation, his grandfather had welcomed him back with a party of family and friends. With open arms, he started the party with a boisterous shout, "*Adiskidegabeko bizitza, auzogabeko heriotza* [A life without friends means death without company]!"

It was uncanny how Big Juan always said the right thing at the right time. Some whispered that it was as if he had practiced each greeting or conversation beforehand, always having the just-right Basque proverb on the tip of his tongue. They admitted that many such situations couldn't have been planned for.

In contrast, Juan's father, Juan Sr., shouldn't have talked so much and he knew it but couldn't stop. He was flighty and fidgety, unable to focus, prone to storytelling, always angling to know what you were looking for and adept at playing back just what you needed, telling you what you wanted to hear—not from caring but from trying to please. He was easily swayed, unable to stand for something. It felt like he was always trying to accept your position in the hope you would like him. Most people wanted to like him and tried to give him a chance at redemption, especially for Big Juan's sake.

"I'll come over and help you clean out your barn on the weekend, of course!" Juan Sr. would say. He would never show up.

It was not long before people grew tired of Juan's father.

When he was away from home, he would find himself proving his weakness in shallow places over and over with carnal relations partaking of his failing whenever he could.

"It is too bad he is not like *his* father," the villagers would say.

Juan Sr. just did not believe in himself, maybe the shadow of Big Juan was too long. Senior never sat still. He strayed and wandered, not living up to what folks wanted to believe in him. He knew they knew it. It was a weight on him.

But Juan Sr. had his good side, of course. Like Juan's grandfather, he was courageous. Both were able with their hands. They could do anything, fix anything. Also, like most Basques, all three Laxagues could speak several languages, their native tongue mixing with Spanish, Catalan, and French. But Juan Sr., who had spent time on the seas, also spoke Portuguese, the language of the waves and the new world, and picked up North African speech patterns that always made themselves apparent as he yelled words and stuttered syllables when he was drunk. Other times, he would patiently translate what he was saying with foreigners for young Juan's sake. It seemed that Juan Sr. could talk to any foreigner!

A STRANGER ARRIVES

Unlike the men in his family, Juan was shy. This trait came from his mother, who some said was "too timid." Others said she was simply close to God, devoted to her family, and "preferred to stay inside," doing everything to make the household run. She even took on the mantle of both parents when Juan's imperfect guiding light was beckoned to the sea so that he could earn the living the family needed to survive.

As in Gracianna's family, Juan's mother taught the values of hard work and belief in God and the right way between a man and a woman.

"In the Basque culture, equality is central," she would explain. "A man and a woman come together and then they make decisions for their family and the community. Both sexes are called upon to contribute to the right decision. Decisions large and small are based on facts and opinions expressed by both sides."

Since his father was "on the sea," she would often call upon the eleven-year-old Juan to help make "decisions," to show him "how to do it."

Although the Laxague's environment was in difficult terrain, there were merchants from various cultures who came to trade. The Portuguese, Spanish, and French were always present; others, like Germans, Eastern Europeans, and North Africans, would come to the area to learn ways to better tend their flocks.

Late in the fall a windswept, tiny man ended up on their front porch when Juan Sr. was away. He did not look like anyone Juan had ever seen. *He was Chinese!*

Of course he was offered a meal. At the kitchen table it took hours for him to communicate what he wanted through a series of drawings and pictograms mustered together with five or six French and Spanish words he knew and many hand gestures and book-pointing and lots of high-pitched Chinese words. He spoke in a very loud way with intonations that sang from the bottom of his throat, the likes of which no one in these parts had ever heard before. The foreigner was quite excitable.

"Maybe he wants to buy some sheep. Or, he might just be lost. He's . . . difficult to understand," Juan told his mother.

His name was Shen, a small man with tiny eyeglasses.

Juan was transfixed and a little afraid of the man. He had rarely seen a stranger, and never one who looked and sounded so different.

Finally, Juan and his mother figured out that Shen was a professor who wanted to live with them in the mountains for the length of a lambing season to study and write about the experience—both shepherding techniques and his immersion in the shepherding lifestyle.

"What do you think if a Chinaman boards with us for some extra money, Juan? I think he is here to study shepherding."

It was not so unusual to take someone in during the winter but a

Chinaman? It made Juan feel pretty important, even though they didn't have many sheep.

Juan's mother was incredulous, wondering when the other shoe would drop.

At dawn the next morning, the professor awoke with them, helped to bring in wood and milk the cow, all the while using many gestures. He immediately began taking on some chores that Juan or his mother usually did. Just like that, he was suddenly and implausibly part of the family.

Still, he was a bit unusual.

Shen—the only name he would give, pointing to himself with a wide grin—turned out to be a spectacle not just in the household, but also in the village. Slight, pale, with dainty eyeglasses, he seemed so gentle. Until one night, when he broke into song and laughter and then pulled a knife on Big Juan, calling him "Old Man Laxague" in broken Euskera, the Basque language, and pinned him on the ground in a death-hold as Juan held his breath. *I'm going to jump on him!* Juan thought. Suddenly, Shen rolled over onto his back laughing hysterically about something that had to do with a child's poem (no one ever figured that part out). The next day, he acted as if it had never happened. From then on, Juan's grandfather always had an eye out and locked the wine cellar.

Fortunately, most of Shen's "surprises" were good ones.

Once, during Juan's twelfth birthday party, Shen produced a present wrapped in gold paper and a red ribbon. (Juan's mother reused both a few weeks later.) Who knew where he'd gotten it? He never went to the village by himself. The gift itself was a ram horn, intricately carved. It turned out the carving was a whistle that could be played like a small piccolo. Shen had carved it!

Shen carved several of these instruments in his time with them because there were plenty of horns lying around, and everyone wanted a carved one that played music, especially the shepherds. Shen would take many notes about this, in strange writing, and try to interview them about it, before and after he gave them the horn. He never asked for any money.

Juan's favorite times occurred when Shen used the back porch of the house for his "exercises." They were subtle and sometimes dramatic movements, gracefully stretching then shunting his whole body as if into another dimension; somehow it looked like slow-motion fighting, too.

Juan was not the only one hypnotized by this strange dance that Shen performed every day around noon for an hour, but the most mesmerized was surely Shen, going through the motions, deep in his own world, or in another land far from reality. The look on Shen's face when he was dancing reminded Juan of how his grandfather would stare off into the distant, high meadows where he had known many days of long herding.

Shen had such concentration!

For some reason, this skill seemed important, so Juan tried to ask Shen about it one day when they were alone on the deck. Luckily, Shen was picking up conversational Euskera pretty quickly. (By the end of his stay, his Spanish and French were better, too.) So, it did not take very long before they understood each other: Juan wanted to be more like Shen, so Shen would teach him how to "meditate."

As instructed, Juan would sit on the porch motionless next to Shen for a while every day. He wasn't sure what he was supposed to do, besides nothing. So mostly he did a lot of thinking. He imagined his boy-thoughts must be very small next to Shen's. Over the months, with Shen's encouragement, Juan was able to occasionally "let go" of the world and listen to himself.

Shen could also do magic tricks. To Juan's disappointment, no matter how much he bothered Shen for the year he was there (and he bothered him all year, aside from when he was off herding sheep), Shen would never tell him how it was possible to make a string seemingly pass directly through your hand right in front of everyone's eyes.

Having accepted the bespectacled spectacle that was Shen, it was not too long before the family was showing him off as their "educated traveler" to any guest who came for a meal, and to all the Spanish cowboy "vaqueros" who came for the lambing and ewe roundup.

Juan's mother liked having Shen around. He was like the exchange students she had heard about who came from wealthy families in Paris to experience the mountain life. Shen was just older and not from Paris. She hoped Juan's appreciation for different kinds of people and cultures was enhanced by his interactions with Shen. She hoped Shen would leave a mark on him, like exchange students were supposed to. Even though he was a bit mysterious he was very intelligent and genuinely liked Juan.

"What do you think of *you* being an exchange student—to the *city*?" she had asked Juan once.

He had heard about students going to live with families and doing interesting things far—very far—away, but Juan liked being a shepherd and thought the city was, well, for city folks and not for him. He was already able to spend more than two months with a herd in the hills—*by himself!*

ABOUT SHEPHERD LIFE
Shen tried to ask him about "sheeping" before Juan left with the herd.

"*Adiskidegabeko bizitza, auzogabeko heriotza* [A life without friends means death without company]," Juan said.

Shen didn't understand.

"It's the loneliest," Juan said.

Even though he might be in the company of up to 900 souls out in the hills including his hardworking dogs, it was still utterly solitary. There was only persistent loneliness.

Long moments would pass where the chortle of the robin came forward fast and loud followed by the faint late afternoon cricket performing his scratchy song. Juan could hear things like other herders could. These were all he could hear now. At night he could hear a grass blade bend since it was in his interest to ensure every ewe and lamb make it back in shape to be counted. His interest was also in hearing the fleece grow, for the number of souls he brought in and the weight their pelts delivered determined the small incentive he earned at the end of the lonely season. Juan was accustomed to listening to things on the range. "Fleece growth" was his favorite sound he would joke.

Juan tried to put it simply, "Imagine months with no one to talk to."

When Juan returned from helping on a short lambing season, Shen had better language skills and more questions about shepherding life.

Juan explained how everything on the mountain range began at dawn. The sheep would leave their hillside bedding grounds and begin to graze. Juan would wake up blanketed in his heavy wool bedroll inside his canvas tent, take care of business, and leave camp to count the sheep. "Camp" consisted of the tent, bedroll, some food supplies, and a tin Dutch oven over a fire pit. He took his trusty canteen, sheep hook, and flinty rifle with him long before daylight to check on his band and to protect them from wild dogs, mountain lions and bobcats.

His grandfather had taught him to use the black sheep, the *beltzas*, to do the headcount; otherwise, he would be there all morning counting heads.

If the beltzas were accounted for, it was safe to assume the whole herd was too. If one of the beltzas was missing, then Juan and his dogs would immediately search for the black sheep and the others likely with it.

The sheep would graze downhill all the way to water, fill their bellies, and then head for shade, resting during the heat of the day until late in the afternoon. The herd would then get up and start to graze uphill until dark. Juan and his canny dogs would position the band on an open hillside for the night, and then he'd head for his tent in the dark; or, if there had been night killings, he would stay with his band with his bedroll, rifle and dogs. He did this seven days a week. Ewes and lambs never took a minute off and he could not take his eyes off them either. Every few days he would move them to the next grazing area.

Herders would use salt if necessary to coax the sheep to move to different areas, especially if they were getting too skittish or unruly.

Otherwise, every day, it was the same. Lonely.

"You can't lose track of the days, though," Juan warned Shen, "or you can end up very hungry." The supply wagons came to specific locations on specific dates according to pre-season agreements. Juan's provision list included salt, cured bacon, wine, a little whiskey, peppered jerky (his favorite), and dried nuts and fruits.

The wagon driver would stay only for one or two hours if he arrived early enough, but he often arrived late and would stay overnight. It was never enough. Just when they were having a nice time, the driver had to get along since there were other herders to seek out. He could not stay longer than absolutely needed.

Once, Juan had "missed" his provision wagon by a day. By then, animals had pilloried his store. The supply driver had just left his food on a rock near where they were supposed to have met. Unfortunately, the wrapping wasn't very effective and most of the goods were consumed or scattered over the mountainside. Juan was angry with himself when he realized he was on his own for another ten days. This had only needed to happen once. After that, he met the provisions on time every time, and was usually early, no matter how late the driver came—which happened often.

Once, the wagon never came. Two weeks later, Juan had finally caught up to the driver.

"Where were you two Mondays ago?" Juan had demanded.

"Where I was supposed to be! Where were *you?*"

Juan had gotten the timing right and the location wrong. Another mistake he never made again.

"And you have to speak at least three languages, the more the better," Juan told Shen for the hundredth time. This mistake had taken a little more time to correct.

As a boy, Juan had resented how the nuns forced him to practice speaking and writing French instead of Euskera, his native Basque, but he was grateful now, even if he still pronounced the silent French "s" now and then.

"Your Euskera is classic but your French pronunciation is just so-so," one nun had said.

After weeks away, herders were starved for news and the sight of another human being from anywhere was much welcomed. Both sides were happy to figure out the other's language if either needed, and they always had something to share whether food, shelter, water or warming spirits. It was a bleat-filled brotherly community of unspoken respect and gracious hospitality.

"But a lot of times," Juan continued, "you may see each other and never even get to talk. I might see you far off on another hill. You have your sheep and I have mine. How am I supposed to know where you're going with your sheep? Hopefully not where I'm going with mine! And we cannot shout at that distance."

Shen grunted but didn't look up, too busy taking notes.

"Well, that is when you must know how to whistle properly."

The whistling was another curious Basque herding language. It had developed over time, by necessity, to supplement communication needs not met by the mother tongue. Whistling required breath control—one thing Basque herders were not short of, with their lifetime of brisk walks up and down hills. Whistling was like breathing: easy and essential.

"But be careful about the wind," Juan warned. The wind played funny tricks on the voice over the distance. A word called this way was heard that way on the other side. To get around the wind problem, the herders had linked short and long whistles into a series of meaningful messages. One long whistle: headed north. Two long: headed south. One short: headed east. Two short: headed west. They tried to keep it simple.

It was more important to the herders to know where others were headed than where they were currently.

"These signals allow them to manage mountain meadow feed areas and any feed conflicts," Juan said.

"There are conflicts?" Shen asked, looking up sharply.

Juan laughed and finally confessed that, during the pre-season planning, food management routes for the herds were mapped out extensively. In general, they knew where everyone was going. They had to. Because mistakes were rare, conflicts were rare.

"So whistling is just to double-check locations?" Shen clarified.

Actually, whistling was for a lot of things. Among the specific short sharp and longer whistle programs for north, south, east, and west, was a notable, long low whistle: "Trouble, come immediately." This would be followed by another long, low whistle, and then another, until help arrived.

There were other courtesies and professional considerations to uphold with the whistling. Friends and families often had special codes, signals and salutations, even inside jokes told by whistle.

"So, you like being sheeper?" That was Shen's last question.

Juan sighed. "I think so. Yes. It makes you smart. You always need to think so far ahead, not just one or two moves but three or four." Shen smiled to himself.

IN THE HILLS

Up there, long after Shen had left, Juan still thought of many things. Now twenty years old he mostly thought of the past and the future. Sometimes he thought of Gracianna.

She had visited him once while he was out sheeping, with the provisional driver, to bring him a book. While the driver snored, she and Juan had talked by the fire for two hours about Basque and Roman history and gotten a little drunk.

All Basque children are raised on the oppression and independence story, and appreciate—no, pride themselves on—their history of fiercely protecting their land, strategically surviving encroachments. Juan was being dramatic, "Reconquista! We fought that war for seven hundred years, all beginning with Pelayo's victory at Covadonga! They tried, but no one ever conquered us, and that is why we are free to practice our faith! So practice! Cross yourself for Pelayo three times!"

But Gracianna, now nearly seventeen, hadn't laughed. Instead, she said, "I would have hurt those Romans somehow if they had come to *our* village."

Then she had laughed, and he had also, even though he didn't think it was so funny. He realized he believed her. He found himself wondering if he was nearly as tough as she was, and how, in the face of a Roman invasion of his property, he would react.

Silently and gratefully, he agreed with himself that he would never need to know and found solace in the fact that he might not be the most coura-geous or brave Basque but he gave it a lot of thought and appreciated those who could fight well.

Juan, like Bettina, had somehow sensed Gracianna's distance. Gracianna seemed to have one foot in the Pyrenees and one foot someplace else. He guessed that he would probably enjoy a trip to America, but here is where he needed to be. Once, he had stopped himself from saying he would take her there. He had learned from his mother that you couldn't earn love by lies and false promises.

Finally, he had figured she had her own way to go, wherever that was, and his home was here.

Wasn't it?

Sometimes, all he could think of was how *c-c-cold* it was.

Luckily, he grew up to be hairy and, like most Basque men, had a furry pelt on his face, chest, arms, and legs. Perfect for when sleeping under the stars on cold nights, especially if caught in the mountains with early snow. Luckily, there were also small, cabin-like structures for sleeping in along the routes. Then there was the thick wool, and his mind wandered to the ancient times when there were steamy Roman bathhouses in the mountains.

The bathhouses were legendary. Some of these Roman cathedrals of washing could hold up to 3,000 people at a time, doubling in function as social gathering holes. Most had at least four rooms: the unctuarium, the exercise room where a sweat was worked up; the tepidarium, the room with the warm, tepid pool; the caldarium, which was the hot sauna and massage area where oils were rubbed into the skin by slaves; and the frigidarium, the cold pool for the brisk plunge before returning to life. There were also changing rooms, too. Often, brothels attached to the bathhouse for extra relief.

Juan tried not to think about those women.

Yes, a hot bath sounded nice.

Instead he unfurled his bedroll on the grassy knoll, checked the blank-faced sheep, and thought some more.

Through the seasons he pondered the future among an occasional random bleat up on the high meadow in the cool darkness and sea of silence.

There was a shiver up the back of his neck and then he dreamed.

A hot bath—that would be nice.

AN EPIPHANY

One rainy night: "I don't think I can do this forever," he told the sheep. It was not their fault.

Stares were all he ever got in return. His dog seemed to understand with a knowing look but this was only a dog-response learned from thousands of years of learning how to crook the head perfectly just to get an extra scrap. He wondered what it might be like: life after herding. He would have a family, of course. Who would he marry? She would be just right for him. What would his children's names be? They would be familial names. Where would he work? He could do anything with his hands. *And please God, I know I can be shy but let my work include more people!*

Where would he live? He never wanted to live in the big city. Or, not for long anyway.

"I'm not a city man," he promised the sheep.

Blank stares.

His dog covered his head with his paws.

Would he have a small farm? Yes, but he wanted the kind of things that money could not buy, freedom, unconditional love and self-respect. It was nice to have fresh vegetables and some plants around. Would it be his father's land? *No, even though it is rightfully mine.*

Juan stood abruptly, surveying the sheep that were not his own. He had nothing that was truly his own, and he suddenly and rather fiercely wanted it.

"I want to strike out on my own and be my own man, find *my own way!*" he declared to the herd. "I want a life that is *close* to me—it does not have to be a *big* life!"

He did not want to have to wish for faraway things like his father did, and Gracianna, too. He wondered if maybe he could raise just a *few* sheep—and this smell would go away! He tried to smile at that.

These were the thoughts in Juan's mind, kaleidoscopic thoughts that gently tumbled, night after night, in his pre-dream driftings. He dreamed of an emerald-colored good life. He saw the thoughts like a play unfolding and refolding on the inside of his eyelids, in vivid colors with his own mountaintop sound. These were his young man musings. Sometimes he would gaze skyward with his lonely imaginative eyes at the end of his night-play thoughts and sense the way the moist air would invisibly layer dew all over his bedroll cover and cap. Juan would grin, warmed because he knew his well-trimmed beard was impervious to the droplets.

Chapter 3

PARIS ARRIVAL

The train trip from San Sebastian, the Village of One Glimmering Light, to the City of Lights, was long and Gracianna had only a few francs tinkling in her pocket.

The train track ahead was exactly eight feet, four-and-one-half inches wide—the exact width that represented the axle of a Roman chariot, the ancient dimension made to fit exactly behind the two horses that pulled it. The irony was that, as the single-minded Romans had rolled, so did the contemporary Gracianna, she now on the track that they had laid centuries before.

"I'm leaving, Grand-mère," Gracianna had announced only yesterday.

Her grandmother, Anastasia, sitting by the fire, had looked surprised to see Gracianna come in the door during the week.

Gracianna had offered her a small woolen satchel heavy with coins.

Anastasia had taken it and, as usual used a proverb to answer, "*Hartuak, emana zor* [That which is taken is owed]."

"And this is for Constance," Gracianna said, giving Anastasia a sealed letter.

"To where are you leaving?"

"To La Maison Cossette in Paris. Tomorrow morning, I—"

"How do you know this place? You are just like your mother." Anastasia's mouth had tightened. "Do not come back in trouble."

"Mother told me when I was little. I remembered." She paused and said, "I'm not coming back, Grand-mère. I'm going to America." Deep breath.

"*Aurrera begiratzen ez duena, atzean dago* [Well, those who don't look forward, stay behind]."

A snort in response—it was not clear if the old woman was jealous, sad, or scornful. Gracianna thought it was all wrapped into one—*Since I'm just like my mother. This must be good.*

"I will send my address when I get where I am going."

"*Arrotz-herri, otso-herri* [A foreign land is a land of wolves]."

"Yes, Grand-mère, I understand how you feel—I will be careful."

"Isn't there a boy you like here?"

Gracianna just shook her head, *no.*

"*Azken gaizto egingo duk, txoria, gazterik egiten ex baduk habia* [You will have a sad end, bird, if you don't make your nest while you're still young]."

"Yes, Grand-mère."

Silence.

Finally: "I have pushed you too hard. So hard, that you leave me on your eighteenth birthday."

Gracianna had tried to protest but Anastasia had waved her hand impatiently toward the door. "So go then. Happy birthday," she said, her voice condescending.

Awkwardly, Gracianna had lurched forward toward the old woman, and her grandmother had embraced her tightly, briefly. There were no more words until Gracianna had skated out.

"Do not go with men after they have been drinking!" Anastasia called after her . . . but Gracianna discounted it as worn advice and understood it as the only way the old woman could say, *I love you.*

Finally, Gracianna arrived in Paris at the grand station, Gare d'Orsay, on the left bank of the Seine. She had to sit down on a bench for a moment to take it all in.

Her over-read books had come breathtakingly alive.

Once, the impressive Beaux-Arts station had been a palace—the Palais du Quai d'Orsay, built by Napoleon in 1810, the crown of the City of Lights. There was no proverb, Basque or otherwise, no language, no words to capture the moment, to satirize it, to build on it, to encapsulate it. For sixty years, it had stood. Then, in the midst of the terrible "Paris Commune" riot, the entire neighborhood was overrun with fire.

Émile Zola had described the conflagration in *La Débâcle*: "An immense fire, the most massive, the most appalling—a giant cube of stone, with two-story porticoes, was spewing flames. The four buildings, which surrounded the great inner courtyard, had caught fire at once; and then the oil poured down the stairs. . . ."*

The grand Palais had taken two days to burn and break. The embers themselves had actually smoked for the next thirty years, a daily reminder of the tragedy. Finally, the French government had given the Orléans railroad company the site to build a central terminus.

Sitting on the bench, Gracianna suddenly felt very small. She was overwhelmed by the history and majesty, and by the well-dressed people bustling everywhere. She realized that there had been safety in her reading of books but now, in the middle of it, everything was too real, too big, too bright, too loud, too. . . .

I'm afraid.

Gracianna caught herself, swallowing the fear that she felt welling up, holding back the threat of tears. She always caught herself.

Three times, she said: "*Ezina, ekinez egina* [Through effort and sacrifice, the impossible can be done]."

She reminded herself how much she had already achieved; already catapulting past thousands of others who believed in their own hearts that moving so far away shouldn't be done. She'd felt fear a hundred times, but choked back the embarrassment of her "silly" dream *a million times*. She'd walked the last three miles past all anxiety to the San Sebastian station after the ranch manager dropped her; she had click-clacked a total of thirty-one miles from the mountains that she had called home. And now standing on her own two feet in the City of Lights, she knew she was alive because her heart beat forty-five times per minute as she felt life coursing through her body. All she wanted was to shine, to share her shining unique self with others.

* Émile Zola, *La Débâcle*, Paris: Charpentier, 1892.

For a moment, she missed Bettina and Constance.

I am a hard worker and I will find my way.

Sitting there, she resolved to be courageous. To stay. To open herself to the experience of many new things and people. To follow her heart all the way to America. To learn and grow—and to share herself. Her mother always told her (and she even remembered her grandmother saying once when she was very young): "You are a light in the world, Gracianna, like a gift."

She would be kind and helpful, spread warmth, work hard, and have wine and laughter, of course, being always watchful for wolves. Eventually, she would find her way. She might even find her handsome university man!

Feeling better, she smiled and said, "Bonjour" to a businessman passerby.

He stopped. "*Bonjour, excusez-moi mademoiselle? Vous cherchez un endroit* [Hello, excuse me miss? Are you looking for a place]?"

He was handsomely dressed and seemed concerned.

"*Merci beaucoup, je suis nouve à Paris* [Thank you so much, I am new to Paris]." She beamed at him.

Then, Gracianna wasn't sure she liked the way he looked at her dark wool dress and scarf, and that he suddenly seemed to be in a rush. Her smile dissolving, she quickly said, "*Excusez-moi monsieur. Je cherche la Maison Cossette près du Louvre* [Excuse me, sir. I am looking for La Maison Cossette near the Louvre]."

He pointed her in the right direction, wished her luck, and they parted ways. Looking back, she imagined she saw him shake his head.

Turning, she accidentally ran into a tall, fancy woman who looked at her sharply.

Gracianna blushed, began to apologize, was nodded at, and continued on her way, forcing herself to smile confidently, with chin high.

She was thrilled as she stole glances at the throng of Paris passing her by. They were so tall, well dressed and coiffed, and *smelling* so new. None of them smiled back.

On she walked toward La Maison, guided by the powerful beating energy that told her she was alive and not to miss the next thing that would get her to the next place. That energy drove her past her fears to the sense of adventure, to the next blocky step.

She tried to not to worry about the troubling fact that Monsieur

Dominique wasn't expecting her. Or that it had been many years ago since her mother had dropped his name and the name of his establishment.

MEETING MONSIEUR DOMINIQUE

Two blocks later, she saw the sign: *La Maison Cossette*, above large dark windows.

There was a group of friendly-sounding gentlemen speaking out front, and Gracianna inquired of them about Monsieur Dominique.

The men grinned.

One man said: "I am Monsieur Dominique!"

Laughter.

"No, pay no attention to him—*I* am Monsieur Dominique!"

More laughter. One man had to lean on another.

Gracianna put her hands on her hips. It did not stop the laughter.

"Mademoiselle, I beg forgiveness for my fat friends. I am Monsieur Dominique. And how can I help you please?"

She regarded him suspiciously. *Is this the real Monsieur Dominique?* He was an older gentleman, pale, with a bulbous nose, heavyset. His belt buckle was hidden by his belly-paunch. He seemed very French with his beret and cigarette. She could practically smell the wine, bread, and cheese on his clothes and hands. But what she saw and felt from him was bright eyes and a warm old soul. She instantly felt she could trust him.

Even still, she asked for proof of his identity. He laughed and held his belly as he guided her toward the building.

He pointed to the picture in the window of the café—one of himself with the former mayor of Paris, who had signed it: "*Vive la France, mon ami Dominique* [Long live France, my friend Dominique]."

Then it was Gracianna's turn to prove herself. She told him that she was Basque. He answered with his eyebrows, *"I figured."* She told him that her mother had mentioned his name and the name of his business to her a long time ago. "My mother's name was Ann."

Dominique seemed nonplussed and just looked at her flatly as if to say, *"So?"*

Quickly, she got to the point about working for him in order to go to America.

Dominique scratched his beret. "How is Ann?"

"I am so sorry to tell you. She died many years ago," and he seemed surprised and very sorry to hear it as he furrowed his brow again and looked up toward the café sign. Despite her curiosity, Gracianna did not ask for information about how Dominique had known her family, it did not seem her business and she was single-minded on her objective.

"And you traveled all this way?"

"Yes. I want to work. But if you don't have work, it is a big city at least," Gracianna reassured him with a smile and a shrug. No one wanted someone who was needy, so she tried to act casual.

"I cannot pay you much."

Tantaka-tantaka upela bête [Drop by drop, the barrel fills].

"The waitressing and cleaning is not easy work."

Ez da ogirik neke gaberik [There is no bread without pain].

"And the hours are long. It is best to clean once everything is closed for the night. It is always very late work."

Silence.

"I hope you have a place to stay?"

"No."

It was clear to him that she was right from the mountains, so trusting!

She is expecting everyone, anyone, me, to take her in!

He suggested the women's dormitory a few blocks away and, with a great, big clap on her shoulders and flash of bright, wrinkled eyes, told her she was hired. "I'll write you a letter of introduction for your lodging." The owner introduced her to Marceau, a handsome man in his forties. He was "the bartender who has been working here always." She was to report to Marceau on her first day. Tomorrow!

I have a job! America is very, very soon!

THE WOMEN'S DORMITORY

The women's dormitory was a long, busy place set above a storefront. Many of the windows had clothing hung out to dry, and some stray men stood on the other side of the street, which probably belonged to the men's dormitory. Some were on the women's side of the street, talking up to their windows like tomcats in the ancient dance.

After standing in line, Gracianna found out from the large desk woman that there weren't "any beds available" and no, she didn't have any suggestions about where else Gracianna could find lodging "at this time of year."

"Please." Gracianna stood firmly at the desk.

The woman had gone back to reading a yellowed newspaper.

"Please, I have a bedroll. I have money for you now and I have a job—here is the letter. A bed, I'm sure will open. I am a good cleaner, too, and a cook for help in the cafeteria. Please, even in an old room I can clean out. I promise I am an excellent tenant, never any problems. *Please mademoiselle. . . .*"

It turned out there were only four rooms with eight beds each. Each bed had its own private floor space and closet. However for Gracianna, there was not even a cupboard to spare.

Then, from behind her, a whisper: "You can share my bed until a room opens," so the attendant could not hear her above the din of the radio.

She felt a flood of relief.

That was how Gracianna met Siobhan. Siobhan knew the ropes. She said, "We'll have to keep this between us and you will have to be scarce for a while. But I know a girl who is moving out next week."

THE LETTER TO BETTINA

A bed did open after a few days, and Gracianna sent a letter home with her new address.

Gradually, she settled into the routine of working at the café from the late afternoon into the middle of the night, waiting tables and then the cleaning, from top to bottom, all by herself. She missed Bettina beside her even if she only worked at half the speed. Sometimes Gracianna could earn a half-night's worth of free rent by working at the dorm's cafeteria on her day off.

One afternoon, a postcard arrived from Bettina. She was curious how things were going, and if Gracianna had walked slowly by the university yet, and if there was more news about the war expanding elsewhere in Europe, namely in France and Paris.

Gracianna splurged just a little on some nice stationary, carved out some time, and lay down on her bed with the paper and pen. She wrote:

Dear Bettina-

Yes, I have gotten a job working in a bar café—the first step in my plan to be discovered by a young university graduate . . . but the dream seems farther away. Hours are long, and the work is very hard—since I am the only one cleaning the café, and it is such a new, big city it is a bit scary, I must admit! And I have no place of my own, no privacy. I am living in a drafty room with ten other girls in a female dormitory. There are some men in a dormitory across the street. Sometimes I see some of them during meals at the cafeteria (breakfast is free and dinners are cheap, but if I work a day a week there, then I can eat any time for free). Occasionally, a man tries to get into the women's dorm, always at night, always after 2 a.m. when the bars close. But we are always safe.

And I like the girls at the dorm. Some of them share a single bed. There is a nice Spanish girl, Montserrat, who is quiet but don't be fooled—she loves the men! And a Russian girl. What I don't understand is why I see her flirting with any man at any time. All these girls think of is men! But, she has taught me to do my hair more fashionably—I like it because it's still very sensible. I cannot scrub floors with complicated barrettes in my hair!

Sometimes, there are squabbles among the girls in the house—some others are Eastern European, Polish, Jewish. Also, a girl who is a "gypsy" or Romani (the word gypsy comes from "Egyptian" you know—but who knows where they are from, they may also be from India from a long time ago, there is some question—I would love to go there someday! So different, so much to learn. . . .) But it is mysterious because I've heard they stay close to their own—so why is a gypsy girl living with us? Maybe she is hiding. Or I think that she is just trying to find her way like me—trying to go forward.

But mostly, I am curious about the Jewish girl since others seem to find Jews curious. I quite like her! She is funny but very smart, she has read a lot of the same books as me and has some that I am reading now and I quite like them. She loves to read,

Bettina! She has a funny crooked smile and a crooked eyebrow too, and her name I've never heard: Siobhan (pronounced "show-von"). Except there are some problems with discrimination that sometimes make her sad and angry.

Gracianna sighed and rubbed her writing hand. It was too difficult to explain. The other day, Gracianna could tell Siobhan had been crying.

She had asked, "Is something—?"

"You cannot believe!" Siobhan had exploded. "Today I was thrown out of a restaurant. I sat, prepared to pay, and they told me to get out, I'm a pig! Things have happened before, but. . . ." She turned away, holding back a sob.

Gracianna had listened, unsure what to say except, "But why—?"

"Because I'm Jewish?! Maybe they can tell by looking at my hair or skin or the way I dress or the way I say things? Sometimes, if they are not paying attention, they smile at me—until they realize . . . and then I see that look coming over their face, like *they* have made a mistake and that *I* am a mistake."

Gracianna felt a surge of sympathy. She herself had sensed the stares from strangers regarding her own not fitting in. They were not particularly nice stares. Pity. Impatience. Sometimes, dislike. But discrimination like Siobhan described? No!

"I am kind and look at my curly hair, who could not like me? And I had been prepared to pay!"

Gracianna felt it—a surge of deep-rooted anger, a heat on her neck in the front and in the back. It was hard to have compassion for such small-minded people with their small thoughts.

Then, Gracianna had tried to offer some wisdom: "What they need to learn is what my grandmother told me: *"Arranoak lumak behar, txepetxak ere bai* [The eagle needs feathers, and the wren does too]."

Siobhan had paused, already accustomed to struggling with Gracianna's proverbs. Finally she said: "So! What you are saying is we all have the same needs, all of the eagles and even a lowly wren like me?"

That had made Gracianna laugh.

For a second, there had been a flash of Siobhan's crooked smile. Then, a sigh. "Because that is how I feel and how I am treated—like a wren, and everyone else thinks they are such eagles."

"They are fools," Gracianna said evenly. "Listen, it means that despite our superficial differences, of *any* kind, we have more similarities. Listen, God didn't even make our fingers all the same."

That made Siobhan laugh, even if she didn't understand it. Gracianna smiled at the memory and returned to writing her letter to Bettina.

Like Siobhan, you know we were raised not to like arrogant people. It must be so different, being a gypsy or a Jew, without a deep sense of establishment, not able to be rooted to a land of their own the way our people are rooted in the mountains Bettina. Well, like you are rooted. Can you imagine if this made us arrogant against those less fortunate?

Now that I am mixed with girls from other places, I see how much variety we lacked. Even from my books, I never realized how different the world is. There are many kinds of wine; there are other faiths than Catholicism, so many other peoples than the Basque, the French, the Spaniards, and Portuguese, so many many many others! Oh!

Even though we did not learn much about other kinds of people, I am glad how we learned to be tolerant of others no matter their difference. Do you remember Gill? The girl in my village neighborhood who was "different?" She seemed slower than the other kids and not as adaptable to the games, or as agile as the other children. Some of them teased her, but I did not participate in it. I liked her! Gill had a sweet smile and a genuine interest in seeing new things. I came to understand that she was seeing and hearing and experiencing the world in a way like no one else. She saw beauty, the way things were interconnected, the newness of every little thing. She was special to me. I will always remember her.

Gill gave me this gift; I try to see beyond the everyday, to see what is really all around me—the wonder of God's creation. There is the daintiness and pure energy of the butterflies that appear each spring in our mountains, and there is a grove of trees whose leaves will turn fiery yellow and orange in the fall and drop only to be replaced by green the very next season, and there is the coarseness and muskiness of the fleece of the ewe but the pure purity and soft softness of it too. I miss all that. We are surrounded by gifts and miracles of the environment around us. I think that God put Gill near me so I could take this lesson for myself. I am a version of her in Paris, I think.

So many things are new to me now. This is what I always craved—to explore. So it is hard work, but I am screaming inside myself with wide wonder to be here. I wonder what else is in store and how fast I could start learning about them. I know I am naïve about so many subjects, but I am determined to understand as fast as I can these and other things I am not yet aware of. I vow to continue to experience new things and to learn to see things from beyond my little view—to try to see what they really are and not to forget them.

The last thing and this broke my heart Bettina, Siobhan lowered her voice and spoke her final thought on the subject, "I was waiting in line at the grocery store last evening and a little girl tugged on my coat and said, 'Do you live in the Jewish building?' And Siobhan said, "What do you mean?" And then she pointed to the two buildings and the little girl said, 'I live in the Jewish one. Jews are dirty and we can't live anywhere else. Where do you live?' Tears welled up in my eyes, Gras'—they did." That is what she told me. I am still trying to understand it all. I have to go now. I miss you.

Gracianna

A CHILDHOOD MEMORY

Lying there on her bed during a rare daylight rest, Gracianna let her mind wander back to Basque Country, to the time when her grandmother had taught her a lesson about arrogance and tolerance.

Gracianna was ten or twelve years old. Her family had been invited to the next village of Urdos (with all of its 309 inhabitants) by her village of Baigorri (2,100 inhabitants) near the Nive des Aldudes River to visit Josie, who was Anastasia's old friend.

Josie, a widow, had recently and spontaneously married a Frenchman while visiting Paris, returned home with him, and now was proud to show him off.

"I will try to like your husband, and try to be happy for you, Josie," Gracianna had heard Anastasia say to Josie before the trip. "But you know what I think about hasty decisions, especially in marriage." Anastasia peppered their conversation with several proverbs on the subject, which tired Josephine instantly.

"But he is rich, and I think he's wonderful, too!"

Anastasia added, "*Aberats izatea baino, izen ona hobe* [It is better to have a good name than to be rich]." She raised a bony finger in warning. "Already, they are saying he is boastful, crude, and drinks too much. 'It is too bad,' they *already* say!"

"Yes, but if you were to put in a good word for him! You must understand that he is a Frenchman! So he can improve in some areas, just give him a chance! Who is perfect? Even Gracianna is not perfect—look, there she is hiding and listening to us!"

"Little pitchers have big ears," her grandmother said and then Gracianna was assigned "chicken duty" for eavesdropping.

Considering the situation and despite Anastasia's promise to try to accept the hurried-husband, Gracianna was not surprised that her grandmother's lips were drawn tight the entire walk to Urdos.

They arrived at Josie's family mountain home and were warmly welcomed by the newlyweds and their guests. Both the husband and Anastasia were polite but took an instant dislike of one another. He, for her eyeballing him, and her, for his shifty eyes. Later, as they all sat at supper together, the pleasant conversation quickly took a turn for the worse. This happened because the husband made it clear he did not like anyone who was not like him and started right in making a tasteless and inappropriate comment about the few Negroes in the area and how they shouldn't be here.

"You should know," Anastasia said to him, "that today there is an influx of migrant workers from North Africa, but many of the Negroes you see are actually true natives of the region, and also partly Spanish. You see, for many years before the Romans, there was a—"

"Fine! Let the natives stay, but at least get rid of the migrant workers!" he interrupted. It seemed he was making a joke.

When everyone gasped—not only because of the husband's sustained attack on the Negroes that each of them had grown up to value, but also because he had been so dismissive and interrupted *Anastasia* with an even ruder comment than the one she had been addressing—he hardly noticed because he was pouring himself more wine and was spit-talking all the while.

Josie laughed nervously and beamed at the man putting him in the very best light possible. But it wasn't working. "Dear, you really cannot mean what you said. Who cares if some migrants come to work the vineyards in the summer—that is when the Burgundy settles. Oh, wait until you see how the mountains change color!"

"They are not just 'some' migrants, and they are not just vineyard work-ers," Anastasia had said warningly to Josie. Then, to the small-minded man, "They also work on some ranches as hands, and a few women do housework for the few who are able to pay. All of these services are welcome."

What followed was a lengthy and passionate lecture by Anastasia about the value of diversity and interconnection and harmony that would have put a sermonist to shame.

The husband couldn't have cared less. During the lecture, he looked everywhere but at her and sipped his wine while forcibly biting his tongue.

Finally, Anastasia had serenely finished by pointing out, "You must keep in mind, Monsieur, that our green hills and the abundant western running water of our Basque land is in stark contrast to the North African arid topography." Gracianna, who had studied all this, was sure her grand-mother was right. Although she knew better than to nod on the outside, Gracianna was surely nodding on the inside.

Anastasia finished on how, throughout time and nature, peoples have had migratory routes, and some of the people ended up staying for the winter and then settled.

"Settled?!"

That was too much for the man, and he hadn't been able to control his laughter. He tried to apologize. "Sorry, I agree with your migration path argument Madame, I *do* think they are like the animals—and animals migrate! I'm sorry, can't you see the humor?"

He laughed and laughed and laughed until he wiped his eyes as he cried.

Josie had subtly shaken her head at her husband, her eyes full of warning.

Anastasia's face was blotchy now.

Gracianna knew to get ready to grab Constance.

Josie could see it coming. "How about some pie. . . ."

Then, the flustered man finishing half a glass of wine in one motion added, "The problem is," he shouted, dangerously, "*Ils volent des emplois des Français De plus, les nègres volent et ne jamais* [They are stealing jobs from the original Frenchman plus, niggers steal and never]. . . ."

"*S'IL VOUS PLAÎT* [PLEASE]!," Anastasia interrupted, red-faced, "*Ne dis pas cela devant les enfants* [Do not say this in front of the children]."

It was his last chance at redemption. Gracianna had been tempted to cross herself. She could feel Anastasia's temper radiating like a sun about to explode.

The husband had started laughing again and said, with a wave of his hand, "See that is the problem with you! You take everything too seriously. Besides, even children should know that niggers are the—"

He was unable to finish his sentence—then in shock—when the entire loaf of bread hit him square on the forehead.

Anastasia stood slowly and the look in her eye left no doubt that she was in the right. No need to ask, she would tell you. "Never," she said, visibly shaking, "have I ever thrown my own food at someone, someone who I came to visit! What the villagers say is true! You are arrogant and crude—and you drink too much!"

Then the man had stood and roared, "How dare you treat me this way in my own house, old woman! Who do you think you are? Get out, and take your little peasant children with you! You are no longer welcome here! And you, Josie—I forbid you to be a friend to this woman any longer!"

Anastasia roared back, "*Vous êtes un mauvais homme* [You are a bad man]!" As she scooped up Gracianna and her sister Constance, she went on the attack with, ". . . *et Dieu vous punira de votre petit cerveau pour toujours* [. . . and God will punish you and your little mind forever]! It is our pleasure; we leave your company, Monsieur." Gracianna and her sister Constance were at their grandmother's side in a second. It was time to leave.

He laughed, mildly embarrassed, as Anastasia burst out of the house with an astonished Gracianna and Constance. By dessert, the man again forbade Josie from ever seeing or talking to Anastasia again.

Villagers knew that he was a boor but being a successful businessman and landowner seemed to excuse his behavior.

*O*ne year later, Josie had come to talk with Anastasia. Gracianna listened, carefully hidden.

"Josephine," Anastasia had said in greeting. It was unusual, because she had always called her Josie since Gracianna could remember.

Josie looked uncomfortable, twisting her dress between her fingers. It was a pretty dress, fancy with green ribbons. "Anastasia, I wanted to thank you . . . for not telling anyone about the bread incident."

Anastasia grunted.

"And I just want you to know I am happy with him," Josie said. "He is a good provider. I want for nothing. And he has gained some status in the community because of this."

"Do you love him?"

Josie went on to say that she needed him because he provided for her and she had grown to appreciate the status even though she admitted she had never *truly* loved him—not like she had hoped she would.

"That's because you two are incompatible."

"No, it's because there's no such thing as compatibility or *true love*." Josie sounded so sure, but Gracianna thought she sensed a hint of sadness, resignation. "My first husband, it was the same," Josie said. "Incompatibility is normal. Managing that incompatibility is the real work in marriage. Cope-ability is the issue! Besides, how can two people be compatible when they are different people? And you know I am from a family with our centuries-old East Indian roots where it's traditional to marry without even meeting the man until the wedding day, because there are other considerations in marriage. So, Louis and I may not truly love each other like a girl might hope in her silly dreams, but we need each other and try to meet each other's needs, and it seems to work out most of the time."

"Most of the time," Anastasia had repeated thoughtfully.

"Well, he drinks more in the winter, and then . . . he is not himself." Josie shrugged.

"But when he is not himself, well, there are other things to worry about or do to pass the time. It is really not my concern, since I cannot change him and my needs are taken care of for the most part. So what, really, do I have to complain about? I have a very nice house and do not want for anything material really. I have my prayers to help."

Anastasia thought the prayers just helped rationalize away the bad times.

"It is a good life all in all," Josie argued. "I hope that, someday, you also find happiness with a man." Josie had smiled sweetly at Anastasia then.

"I could never be happy with such a man as your coarse husband," Anastasia had said firmly. "Now, if you have nothing more to say. . . ."

"Ana!" Josie had said, strongly. "Listen to this. Maybe my husband is right about you—you live life too hard, always expecting so much of yourself and others, being so serious, teaching your children, and now your grandchildren, teaching them to strive so hard. You are a dreamer! Never satisfied, always wanting for more, nothing ever good enough, never truly happy—and don't you know how people say you are too 'uppity'? You complain of his arrogance, but look at your own! I try to explain my point of view, but it is not good enough for you." Josie took a deep breath and said softly, "I thought you would understand me, Ana. You have been my friend for forty years."

"I could say the same!" Anastasia had shouted.

In the end, they had said the same: "*Amen—zu hor eta ni hemen* [Amen—you there and me here]." They had agreed to disagree, each feeling their own side was right.

All of this had taught Gracianna how different people were and how differently they could see things. "Truth" was more personal than she had thought. Who was to say who was right, but each person for herself? Josie had always been good to Gracianna though and for that she was always grateful. In Gracianna's heart, the encounter sealed the impression that there are those who understand God's will and those whose mind is not open enough to understand the world as it should be.

It changed her forever. Afterward, Anastasia made a wonderful remark to Gracianna, "We will never speak of it again," which meant, "there is a lesson in this somewhere and I expect you have learned it."

Gracianna wondered about the shopkeeper who'd kicked Siobhan out of his business. *What was he thinking? Why would he do such a thing? He could not be right! Could he? What was he suffering from? How can people be like that?*

The sun was going to go down soon, Gracianna noticed, looking back at her unfinished letter to Bettina. She signed it and then reread it. And then reread it two more times.

She sighed at the imperfect way she had written, how much better it could be, how much more she wanted to say. She had even messed up the "G" when she had signed her own name, making her flourish look foolish.

She should rewrite it.

But I do not have time! Everything seemed to take so much *time* to get it just the way she wanted it. Briefly, she considered not sending the letter. Maybe it could wait until she had time.

No, she should send it. It was just Bettina. And there were important things in the letter.

Finally, Gracianna wrote a postscript apologizing for her imperfect letter. Then she added: *I would also like some news of how you are and what you are thinking?* After a long pause, she wrote, *Has anyone asked about me?*

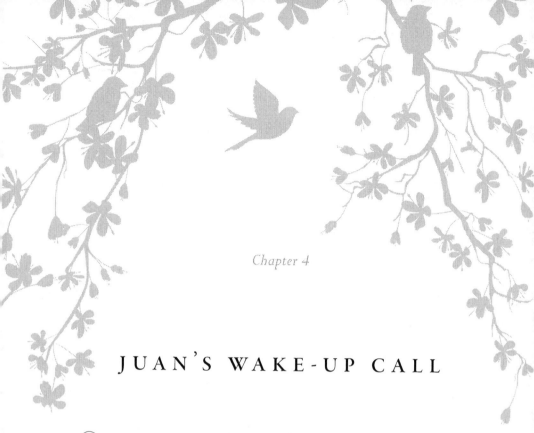

Chapter 4

JUAN'S WAKE-UP CALL

*A*fter Juan heard the news from Bettina about Gracianna's departure—
and that she had asked specifically about *him* in her very first letter—he had
something new to think about while out in the hills. But it is hard to think
when feelings are so raw and confusing; *she* was the only thing he could
think about.

He wondered what she was doing now. According to Bettina, *Juan* was
all Gracianna could think about. He imagined that Gracianna was probably scrubbing a floor wearing a pretty barrette. He was sure that it would
look nice with her now-full head of mystical white hair. Bettina knew she
could never go to Paris but she could do the very next best thing—send
Juan!

Juan felt emboldened by Gracianna's move—not to just leave, himself,
but to be with her wherever she was.

But what if she won't have me?

Because of this, when he returned to the ranch from the high meadows,
he made some inquiries with the ranch manager, Mikolaus. They had a long
conversation. Ultimately, Mikolaus pointed to an article in the local paper.

Juan picked it up from the rough-hewn desk and read it—an editorial about the growth of sheep ranching in America. He had to sit down, then.

"I cannot believe it!" said Juan. "They are offering," he mouthed the words, "room and board when not on the pasture. Shepherding in ninety-day shifts. A 'starter herd,' and even dogs, to begin his own flock. Aid in securing pasture land."

He could be the owner of the land and the sheep!

"And all they want is a two-season contract, and for me to find my own way to America? I cannot believe it!"

"It's a new land, son," said Mikolaus, "anyone can make it if they have enough belief."

"How long would it take for me to earn enough to pay my way to America?" Juan wondered, half to himself.

"If you have nothing saved, you would have to work here for about, oh, four years or so. Or, in Paris, two, maybe less."

Juan cursed under his breath. He had about half of what he needed, which meant he'd be serving here for two more years or for a year or more in Paris. Oh!, and Gracianna was already ahead of him. Then, adding it all up, he would still have at least two more years on an American contract before he could make his own way.

"Well, I am obligated to finish the lambing season with you at least," Juan finally said. "I will think about it, but maybe I will go to Paris in the spring."

Mikolaus nodded. These kinds of things were said all the time. But he thought Juan meant it and had a real motivation to make his decision stick.

Before he left, Juan paused in the doorway. He had already taken up so much time—how could he ask about the day Gracianna had left? It was not his business.

Swallowing hard, he asked anyway, "Uh, sir. . . ." Unfortunately, Mikolaus did not have much information besides that Gracianna had been pleasant company, full of questions and appreciative of any answers. Mikolaus also mentioned that Gracianna had been a good friend to Bettina, because he had watched Bettina for two years now, and Gracianna had helped to make her a better person.

"Bettina smiles more now," he said simply.

Watching Juan leave down the road toward the barns, Mikolaus smoothed his beard. He had taken Juan's meaning, even if Juan did not know what he meant. Mikolaus smiled to himself, a romantic who fancied that he could see things before others. It was just a matter of time before Juan would follow Gracianna, and then they would marry and have children and a better life. The ranchman was a seer, he foresaw the good, the bad, and the lesser of sorts—like Gracianna, he could feel things in people and he felt the goodness in both of these "kids." His time was past but he knew as the clock ticked that this was their time. Being a ranchman, having spent so much time with the volumes of sheep over the years, he had come to feel the animals' souls. Somehow, this empathy transferred to knowing men and their innermost feelings.

Being alone as much as he was, Mikolaus had come to a certain sense of himself, which was in contrast to how he felt when he was around other people. He felt peoples' emotions as plain as day. And he knew Gracianna was an energy mass that attracted like a gravitational pull—she was constantly moving ahead, gathering energy and emotions along the way. He felt that this drive was something she would pass to the generations that followed her. If they built their nest together, Juan would add gentleness to those generations.

At that moment, a hard shiver came over the old rancher, up the back of his neck, like a sign that a spirit is near or a threshold is about to be crossed. It was settled. During the next season-change, Mikolaus told Juan that it was okay to consider marrying Gracianna when he went to Paris. It wasn't like he was in any position to offer permission but it was knowing advice. He kept it simple.

For Juan, although the support boosted his twenty-two-year-old confidence, it was more complicated than that. She, well, was already complicated enough at eighteen.

Now, on the hillside, Juan was a jumble of jelly thoughts and newfound feelings—about his life, his past, his family and people, his future, his skills, his finances, and possibilities for marriage! Oh!, and Gracianna—all a tumbling turmoil. He wondered, *Is this how Gracianna felt, before she left?* And, *Is her dream to marry an American? Or anyone but me?* This was the worst thought he had to face, that it was a possibility. It was bothersome—so he steered away from it.

For years, he had teased Gracianna as he watched her grow. He liked her, yes, but he had never allowed himself to *really* like her. Somehow, he had sensed she wasn't the kind of girl to just settle down and get married and live in the community, like most of the other girls.

He'd been right.

She was a troubadour.

Now, especially after Mikolaus' suggestion about marriage, Juan had to admit how much he had come to really like Gracianna, since her strength was undeniable and attractive to him. She was pretty, he thought. This was troubling because it would muddle matters if he went to Paris. He could not have two dreams—being *both* a sheep ranch owner and Gracianna's husband would be too good to be true, and also impossible. Impossible because he was pretty sure that Gracianna was not interested in a Basque shepherd for a husband, even if the hills were warmer in some places in America.

He wondered if there was a pretty girl in America that might want him to be her husband. The thought of *marriage* was a strange one to put on; it felt odd but perfectly honest. *Am I old enough to make that commitment? Do I know what I want? Do I want an American wife?* It was hard to imagine a foreign girl would understand him and the sheeping way of life, and rise to the occasion like Gracianna could. *No one, he thought, knows me like Gracianna does.*

THE ANCIENT DANCE

That night, as he drifted to sleep, his mind wandered back a few years to the only private time he'd spent with Gracianna on the high meadow one evening.

The women who made the meals at the ranch—Gracianna, Bettina, and one older woman—would occasionally make the trek up the hills in place of the regular provisioners for various reasons. Mostly, they did it just to get out of the monotonous, heavy routine of cooking for the men in that hothouse called the kitchen.

The fresh-air trip usually took most of a day on horseback with a trailing ass to carry the provisions. Occasionally, the regular provisioners would stay overnight to visit and break the silence of the shepherd's life. They were not so rushed as some of the provisional drivers in the past, and made the drop-off more of a visitation ritual. Mikolaus went to some lengths to ensure that the isolated herders got at least two visits per sheep turn.

Sure, they'd had meals together, the two of them, but Gracianna rarely took a break. Maybe she and Juan would walk together for a minute or two on the way to church. They'd see each other on the ranch nearly every day, exchange a nice glance, but barely speak. It seemed to everyone there was an underlying attraction; maybe it was just a respect. This visit, however, was their time. It was Mikolaus' idea to send her—he knew fascination when he saw it and conjured this trip to stir it up. After all, he fancied himself a man of emotion. Just as she had when they were young, Gracianna had brought a book for Juan.

Juan remembered that book when he recognized Gracianna coming up the hill, his heart filled with a remarkable happiness. He hoped she would stay and visit.

However, she was very businesslike and went through her checklist. "Here is your this, your that, your this," she had skipped on quickly, handing him the blankets, beans, cheese, and more.

She had arrived punctually at the spot where he was supposed to be, the predetermined location organized in advance of the season. He feared it was not late enough in the afternoon and that she might actually have time to start the trek back to camp.

As his list was being checked off, Juan could feel these important private moments too quickly slipping away. He desperately wanted to just sit and talk with her! He wanted to hear her Basque voice—which was sounding so guarded and stilted, turn softer, sweeter, and more personal.

Just then, she reached into the bag and produced, almost surprised, ". . . and your whiskey."

Juan knew this was his chance. With a relaxing smile, he said, "Wonderful! Just so you know, my provisioner and I celebrate our meeting with two quick drinks, and you must follow the traditions set before you, or . . ."

"Or what?"

". . . or, or, you will . . . dishonor my family." He *was* desperate.

She hadn't said anything, which meant she didn't object.

Juan plunged on, "I will go stoke the fire. It is sure to be a cool evening."

Gracianna started to object.

"It is no trouble," Juan assured her. "Look, I brought extra wood for the company." He lamb-smiled at Gracianna. He did not know that she had seen in his smile and his hazel eyes at that moment, a glint of innocence.

So as not to imply that his intentions were anything but wholesome he needed to make it clear that he only sought the company of another person. His sheepishness persisted.

He could see by her shifting eyes that Gracianna was deciding whether to stay or not.

"I'm so sorry, Juan," she looked at him plainly and flatly for the first time ever and he could see her face, open and practical. Their eyes locked. Deep. This was their moment. He was overcome.

"I was hoping to start back to the ranch early. There is so much work to do there." She made moves to ready her horse for the long way back, even though it was late afternoon now and the sun on the horizon was too low for her to go far. It was silly of her to start the trek back—he knew it, she knew it—but her motions of closing and tying her saddle packs, settling and petting her horse, retying her shoes, were all acts signaling Juan that she was making a run for it.

"All right," he said and shrugged. "Who would want to spend time with a lonely shepherd? And who am I to force anyone to stay when they do not want to?"

Then he looked at her directly, in an honest moment and whisper-pleaded, "But Gracianna, you are welcome to stay if you change your mind. I wish you would. . . ."

She felt the truth of the compliment.

"And I can protect you from the wolves." Even Juan was unsure where the words were coming from. He really wanted this. "I can protect you."

Juan was not looking at her but began to stoke the fire and settle the camp.

She, preparing for departure—he, preparing for settlement.

Her actions shouted what she wanted him to hear so he responded in unspoken signals meant to quell her, flow with her, cajole her. Juan acquiesced into a sympathetic silhouette that answered her moves. She was leading and he was following toward an agreement. Neither had danced this dance before but each knew what to do. Here they were, miles from nowhere in a ballet of opposing body language.

It was an ancient dance of innocence. Ceremoniously, Juan moved some stump seats into place for a long evening, swept the earth for a smooth conversation pit, placed the coffee pot as sentry for the next morning, shook and then carefully laid out his thick, wool bedroll—like a Turkish carpet man rolls out his wool for a buyer to inspect and admire—careful not to look her in the eye, but using motions and hand gestures to trick her eye into looking at the welcoming spot on the ground.

Gracianna was now thoroughly adjusting the tack, with occasional rattles of buckles, snaps of leather straps, plus some light horse whispering thrown in.

Her whispering in the ear of the horse intensified his interest.

Juan leaned forward. Gracianna leaned back. Each finding a reason to circle back to the other.

No words.

He now felt her wanting to flow with him. More and more, the tension built as the inevitable moment of choice came closer.

Finally, the crack-opening of the ranch-stilled whiskey, the tinny sound of two small cups being set atop the uneven log between the stumps, set tentatively, set just right, set with the smallest of a wood-pewter clink to signal the final moment of truth and set out the evening's field of intrigue.

Gracianna turned to look at Juan, her hand curled into the horse's mane with the reins, nearly ready to mount.

Neither knew it, but only the late afternoon cricket, with his hypersensitive saw-legs could feel the vibe-pitch of the intense duel; cleverness, wonder, and anxiety from deep inside both souls. They were closer than ever and mate-dancing so perfectly. It was hardwired. Not knowing that we know how, we just do it, involuntarily the first time. "Just one drink is fine, if you don't want to stay for two." Juan began to pour.

Gracianna said nothing, which meant she did not object.

Juan poured the second cup. When he was done, Gracianna had not moved, so he brought the cups to her.

But, coming closer, he'd read the truth in her eyes.

"You'll stay won't you?"

They both knew she could not leave but her look told him she wanted him to know she was not *that* interested—whether she was or not, even if she was interested—it did not matter; his concern or interest was inconsequential.

She seemed so indifferent. She wanted Juan to know she was free to decide. But decision was already made.

He held the cup out to her. Evening light skipped off her white hair.

Once his eyes told her that he could accept her leaving—only then did Gracianna take the cup.

"*Oui.*"

His heart pounded.

"Maybe one sip, then, since you poured it," she said with a genuine smile.

Just one sip.

GRACIANNA'S SURPRISE

As Gracianna and Juan settled into a conversation of reflection, the salve of her "*Oui*" still reverberated in his ears.

He was relieved beyond words. In the moments between his question and her answer he wondered what his action would be if she had said she was to go. He considered running to her and begging or running away but realized that running could be construed poorly. Some Basque men were known to flee rather than fight for France or Spain in their colonial wars.

There was, after all, a long-standing and warm feeling between them; they had known each other since they were children and their families were friendly, but not so familiar. Plus, it was nice to talk with someone else who also questioned the future.

By the third drink, they had talked a lot about their jobs. They had tried to laugh a couple times about certain aspects, but Juan was not so funny. He was nervous and realized he was dying a little since things weren't going so smoothly.

She coolly said, "Well, I took this job to save enough money to get to America."

It came out curt. Not meaning to sound above him, "We all deserve what we want, don't we, Juan?"

"Yes, I think we do."

She told him that her ranch chores were a step toward to the next level and that this would soon give way to moving forward. The job was intended to help her launch herself onto the world. This hillside and campfire and conversation, mundane as it was, was just another step to a life where she felt she belonged. He had no idea what she was talking about.

He knew she loved putting things in order. "It sounds like a lot of hard work," Juan said of Gracianna's work.

"It sounds so quiet," Gracianna said of Juan's job. They both knew she meant that it sounded so *lonely.*

It was a bit too raw, so they tried to bandage it.

"But it sounds like you enjoy making everything so perfect."

"Yes, and it sounds like you enjoy—" Gracianna would have finished her sentence, but just then, somehow, the stump she was sitting on rolled forward and she spilt completely backwards, heels over her head, short legs and small boots flailing into the air, giving Juan a great view of her white woolen socks tipped with her own handcrafted frill-finish leafing over the ankle tops—arms flapping to the side to catch her fall, and catching only Juan. She let him go immediately, attempted to sit up and right herself. But the way the stump was, and her legs were, and the hill was, she had no chance of getting up gracefully without a hand from Juan, and there was also no way to cover her socks.

She glared at him wishing it were not so, as he desperately looked away so as not to make her feel the subject of embarrassment. Meanwhile, Juan gently pulled her up, being careful to not make eye contact. In the distance, the crickets could be heard and could be expected to continue.

After she resettled on the log, Juan took his time to lean across and re-pour Gracianna's spilled drink. He handed it to her with a brief glance and a nod, and she took it and they sipped their drinks.

Unable to hold it anymore, Juan burst out laughing.

"I think you fell," he said with that grin.

She held back as long as she could but she finally burst out as well—even louder than he had. The ice broke, causing them to connect as the cool craggy hillside became a warm familiar campsite. He fell in love at that moment and she realized in the same moment that she could not achieve what she needed to do all alone.

He inadvertently touched her on her wrist as he helped her onto her horse the next morning. "I'm glad you stayed," he said.

"Me too."

His glancing touch had been soft and caring and true and she touched her wrist at the same spot as she crossed over the hilltop. She drifted into her long ride, realizing that she would be unable to lift herself every time. His presence was appreciated.

How could another memory be sweeter?

JUAN'S BIG PLAN

When Juan woke up the day after Gracianna had left, he had an idea: finish the lambing season, go to Paris, and find Gracianna—just to help her to get to America.

Well yes, I would be open to marriage if she wanted, he thought.

Meanwhile, he would work and save money. He knew he could do anything with his hands, or with animals. Even if things did not work out romantically with Gracianna, maybe they could go overseas together, if the timing was right, just to help each other.

I'll save everything until we make it.

After all, a foreign land is a land of wolves, and sometimes a person needs a hand, as Gracianna had already shown.

I am just the man to be there.

Just in case Gracianna did want to marry him, Juan's first step was obvious: he had to talk to Anastasia. She would understand, and he wanted her blessing. Of course, he would have to be very careful about which details he included, and which he left out of the courtship story. The stories he told of the times Juan and Gracianna spent together would have to demonstrate that his love was pure, that he was wholesome, that he was capable of providing, and that there was no hint or even an inflection of bad faith. He had all season to think of the elements that represented their love.

The stories would be sincere. He hoped that Gracianna might have some romantic feelings for him, as well (even if they seemed only to be superficial), and his goal was for her grandmother to see it and approve. The final story he would tell her was about Gracianna's "dance" visit that season. He would make it clear that his concern for keeping her overnight was for her safety, of course, and that the whiskey was purely for warmth . . . *no*, the whiskey part was definitely out. He would emphasize the cold and loneliness, and his desire for warmer mountains like those in America—even though they were not as beautiful as the Pyrenees. He would be sure to point out that he was still going to be a shepherd, and this would cause Anastasia to judge his leaving for America less harshly.

Juan hoped this story would do the trick to ensure that Gracianna's grandmother would approve of his intentions. He hoped that he could be on his way the next morning to San Sebastian to catch the train to Paris to start the search for what he believed was his life's partner. Quite easily, he could get Gracianna's address from Bettina, and he would. But he thought Anastasia might like to give it to him, so he would ask her, too. He must be sure to ask about Gracianna's sister, Constance, just to be polite.

Yes, he would go to Paris, the City of Lights, after this season. He would walk—no, Mikolaus would give him a ride—to Gracianna's grandmother's house in Baigorri. He would respectfully knock on the door, and make sure he brought some bread and cheese. She would not appreciate wine at this serious moment.

After the elaborate storytelling ritual, Juan would directly explain his love for her granddaughter, show his great-grandparents' wedding rings, and then ask for Gracianna's hand in marriage—"if she wants to."

Any answer except "No," should be received equally well.

Then a hungry lamb's bleat startled Juan, and reality set in. The craggy hillside, the cold of morning mist, and the slap of alone reminded him that an entire season was yet ahead, and many more years ahead after that—with or without Gracianna. He should not get too attached to the idea.

As Big Juan had said, "*Lehenean barka, bigarrenean urka* [Before, things were that way; now, this way; and it is not known how they will be later]."

Besides, chances were, she had met a wealthy university man by now.

The embers of last night's solitary fire smoldered like a symbol of the small love that was growing inside him.

Chapter 5

LA MAISON

$\mathcal{G}$racianna thought La Maison Cossette was a fascinating place to work. It was more upscale and kind of a crossroads for people from many walks of life and from different places and—Oh!, it was wonderful. It was nestled perfectly in the heart of Paris on the Right Bank of the River Seine, in the shadow of the Saint Germain l'Auxerrois Church—you could find Gracianna there every Sunday. This area was known as the 1st arrondissement of Paris, or Louvre arrondissement, or just "the Louvre," sometimes.

On the way to work, Gracianna liked to cross the Pont Neuf [New Bridge]. She would watch the old and the young stroll across it and admire the architecture.

"The first stone was laid in 1578," a man had said after noticing she did not look like a local and inquiring if she spoke French. "It is Henry the IV's labor of love—and of necessity, today, as it is the widest bridge in the city—and the most heavily trafficked, you will see all sorts of people for all reasons. Commerce, frivolity, mischief, and love." Then he had tried to charge Gracianna some money for the information, after making sure that she appreciated it. In the end, he had become so rude that Gracianna had to nearly run-walk away from him.

Another time, some passersby had asked directions to La Maison Cossette. Gracianna had been happy to tell them: "Yes, I know La Maison! It is a café and bar that serves wine and appetizers. Sometimes, it is a nightclub. After the sun goes down, it can get very busy with lively music, mostly American dance tunes and very popular but hard-to-find ones, like Glenn Miller, Artie Shaw, and the Andrews Sisters. Most of the customers are international guests and expatriates from England, Spain, and even American tourists too—but always some locals and couples."

Gracianna was a virtual information center and her excitement was infectious. But all the passersby had wanted was directions.

She did not even get to tell them about the owner and manager, Monsieur Dominique—how he was a true French patriot and a good man. This did not stop her from thinking about all the other attributes of Maison. Yes, the Monsieur preferred to be called "Dom'" by those he came to know. The music was from M. Dom's personal collection—American and embargoed most of them. His favorite record was the new vinyl grooves of the French "overnight" sensation Edith Piaf, and they might be lucky enough to hear her.

"They call her *La Môme Piaf* [The Waif Sparrow]," he had told her, smoothing his hand over the picture on the record. "She got the nickname because her health was not so good—she was a little sickly and gangly. And she may be popular now, but she had to earn her success, starting as a street singer at any cabaret that would have her."

He looked side-to-side and low-whispered, "She would even play at garage-door openings, for any money or even just bread and sometimes wine." Then he winked and laughed to himself.

He would pause to see Gracianna's wide eyes and laugh out loud at his own joke.

Dom' had paused, solemnly and then looked at Gracianna intensely. "For twelve years, this went on, this schlepping around. But Edith had a talent, Gracianna—a gift. It was undeniable, unrestrainable. France could not help but embrace her. And look how popular she is today! Still, her songs can be so sad—heartbreaking! Sometimes, I think she is like the heart of France singing." His voice quavered, and he quickly went on to talk about how the radio played such an important part in music.

Then they had been interrupted by some men who Gracianna had come to realize were not simply customers. There were four and sometimes five of them. A couple times or more per week they would come, usually arriving in pairs. They would greet Dom', who was usually behind the bar; they would have a quick drink of wine and then settle into one of the back booths. There, they would crouch and crowd in, and talk in quiet voices.

One man's behavior seemed very odd. He would fidget, often looking around, worried-like. Gracianna wondered how he could actually pay attention to the conversation since all he seemed to do was look around the entire time. He looked at her strangely as well. He really looked at her. He would watch her closely as she served them, as if he were trying to figure her out. But she was just there to do her job, and do it efficiently.

Still, she would steal glances at them as she worked serving and cleaning up after the other customers.

They would have cheese and bread and fruit, the wine freely flowing. Over the next hour or two, the language would get a little harsher and rougher. They seemed to get upset about things easily, and argued, and then—a toast! And their voices would fall and spike and fall and then more toasts, and most of the men's chests became puffed—much more than when they walked in.

Dom's nose always got redder when he drank. His tongue thickened, his words wandered and shorted and stronged. He was a bit dramatic, with exaggerated moves—especially cocking his head and looking from side to side slowly and purposefully.

Always, at the end of the meeting, a final toast: "*Vive la France* [Long live France]!"

Always, they stopped talking when she or anyone else would come around. It seemed strange behavior to her.

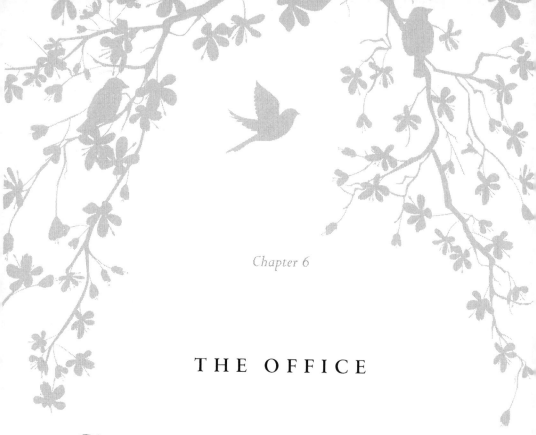

Chapter 6

THE OFFICE

Not long after Gracianna had settled into the routine at Maison, M. Dom' asked her before he left for the night to put a broken chair "in the *petit placard.*"

"Petit placard?"

"Yes, the small closet upstairs. It is a small storage room. I have used it as an office from time to time."

"Of course, the closet," Gracianna hid her embarrassment that, somehow, she had not known there was a closet upstairs. She had never been invited upstairs.

When she started up the stairs, Dom' said, "Gracianna, the chair."

Gracianna turned, cheeks burning bright pink for her mistake. Avoiding eye contact, she took the chair.

Dom' chuckled. "Goodnight, Gracianna."

"Goodnight, M. Dom'!" With the chair firmly in hand, she started again up the stairs.

"Gracianna." Dom' had paused at the doorway. "I am concerned for you walking home alone so late at night."

She tried to laugh lightheartedly. "It is only a few blocks away. Besides, I am Basque." She preferred not tell him that the dark walk home sometimes made her more cautious in the empty streets but that she had no fear. What could he do about it?

"You may be brave and a little dangerous Basquo, but you are also just a pretty young woman who is not very big and I," he paused, "I want to make sure you are protected. I am very fond of you."

"I am okay," Gracianna said with a smiling shrug as she averted her eyes from his. Leaving the chair on the steps, she reassured Dom' and shooed him out, locking the door behind him.

She loved to have the place to herself at the end of the night. And tonight, there was a mysterious closet to break up the long cleaning routine. For some reason, this was exciting.

She drew the blinds, turned on some loud, beautiful music, and performed the lengthy routine cleaning the counters, tables, and floors, always careful to set things just so. Finally, she was done, and the place looked just right, everything back in its place.

So she brought the chair all the way up the stairs. She could not help but notice that the stairs needed to be cleaned, even though Dom' had not requested it.

She found the closet-office. It was locked.

The next night, after her long routine, key in hand, broken chair nearby, Gracianna opened the closet. It was dark, and she found a light switch by hand.

Broken chairs seemed to be the favorite throwaway in the room. Stacked. Very high. Who could have placed the ones on the top? They were very old chairs with rips and tears with parts and pieces missing—chinked and chunked, standing and limping without limbs, legs and arms, just chattel that was chittered away so only dust could sit, set, and settle on them.

Beneath the ascension of chairs were dishes. Dishes everywhere. Chipped, chapped, and chancily placed. A meal of dust could be served from these platters. And the glasses! How many different types of glasses could one café have? There were piles of towels and soaps randomly placed. To top it off, a broom was thrown right in the middle of the floor.

Gracianna shook her head. Some people see a mess like this and are drawn to it. Others close the door and look for what they were looking for somewhere else. Her assessment was that someone or many someones had looked somewhere else for years and years.

Looking more closely, Gracianna realized there was a small desk and bed amid the clutter and a dusty window that was closed. So this is where Dom' comes for his naps and getaways when he is a little drunk! She could hardly believe it.

She stepped into the closet and was hit by the smell. Mice or rats—she knew that smell. Her mind went instantly to the time her grandmother had discovered a mouse infestation in the old house's cupboard and ordered Constance to clean it to Anastasia's exacting standards. Constance had leaned into the cupboard with a little broom, started sweeping, but with her delicate, weakish constitution, she nearly vomited. Gracianna had watched Constance run from the room very upset and nearly in tears, as if her hair were afire at the thought of touching anything close to mouse droppings.

If Constance hadn't been so upset, Gracianna would have laughed. It was just mouse droppings! So what if there were hundreds of them? Constance promised Gracianna she would do anything if she would clean up the mess for her, and Gracianna expected she would hold her to account for it someday. But it never happened. An hour later, you could have eaten off the floor of the cupboard. The old woman praised Constance broadly for the job "she" had done.

Constance embellished her version of the incident over the years, saying she had fallen ill and was unable to tend to her chore and that Gracianna "had done it because she is obsessive, when it comes to cleaning" and "after all Gracianna just likes it."

Gracianna never did ask Constance to do anything in return.

Now, droppings surrounded her. The mice, or maybe rats, had found some old cans of rice and a sad flaccid sack of flour. Water had compromised the tins and over time, and with very little pecking the uncanny animals created a small rusty hole. The jagged entrance in one large empty container was well-worn from hundreds of vermin comings and goings. Hair was stuck to the edges and feces were everywhere, most old and dried, but revolting just the same.

Gracianna's grandmother had taught her, demanded really, that she be a perfectionist in everything—a detail that Mr. Dominique did not know when he hired her, but a trait that he, over time, came to rely on.

So, there they were, the droppings all these years later, still strewn on the floor of her memory.

Slowly, Gracianna realized that the place was not just disorganized and rodent-infested, but deeply filthy. This was a big problem, a big project.

She grinned. It will be beautiful in here when I am finished and Dom' will be grateful—if I don't get in trouble for changing things around. . . . Her smile faded. She must be careful not to overstep the bounds.

She sighed and cautiously placed the broken chair in the pile of others, careful not to cause them to topple. She should leave now. The project should wait until she was more established. Besides, it was late—too late for a project this big, and she had done so much work already, and she had to work in the cafeteria for breakfast in just a few hours.

Still, her hand would not leave the doorknob. Maybe she could do at least a little bit tonight. Why wasn't she tired? It was almost as if the mess had energized her. Maybe she could do the closet in the next few hours and go straight to the cafeteria at the dormitory, and then go to sleep. Tomorrow night, she would be back.

The next night, she wondered how Dom' would react to really changing the closet—his sometimes bedroom and office—around so much. Really, the bed would be better if it were moved under the little window. Gracianna tested the weight of the bed. It was not so difficult, and she could pivot it; she did not want to scratch the floors by dragging it.

After looking around a little more, she sat on the bed to get a better feel for the room. Sitting, she realized her back ached—just a little. Yes, she should walk away from this tonight, walk home, sleep, and wait for the right time and spring. Still, she looked around, planning and plotting the room's potential. Something had to be done about the broken chairs taking up so much room. She did not have much skill with carpentry, she hated to admit.

To sleep or not to sleep? To clean or not to clean? The struggle was a constant rotisserie. Is there something wrong with me? The demon went round and round, over and over again in her head.

Finally, she crossed herself and left.

By the end of a week, all on her own time, she had done what she could with the closet. On the last night, she ended up falling fast asleep in the bed.

She was awoken very early in the morning with a loud, "What is this?"

It was Dom', standing in the doorway of the petite office with a broken chair in hand, looking wide-eyed at Gracianna in his bed and the room rearranged.

Gracianna sprang out of the bed. The worst mistake!

"Who told you to do this?" Dom' demanded. He did not look as pleased as she had hoped he would.

Her cheeks were burning again and she could not look at him. She knew she had gone too far—just doing what she thought was right. Instantly, she regretted all she had done and swore to herself never to do it again. But she could not tell Dom' it was as big of a mistake as she felt it was. She tried to be brave: "It needed some tidying up." She shrugged, as if it didn't matter much.

"Tidy? This is not just tidy! Gracianna, I cannot pay you for this!"

Gracianna shook her head, "I did not do this for the money."

"Then why did you do this—you have moved everything?"

It was a difficult question to answer, and Gracianna was glad Dom' didn't wait for one. Instead, he declared he hadn't seen this place sparkle so brightly in the past forty years. The tiny window's blind was opened for the first time, the floor consisted of black and white tile, which he did not even know, the rows of glasses were perfect and they shined. The shelves were orderly. Somehow she had moved some furniture and repaired the chairs—and it even appeared she had dealt with the rat infestation! Not just that, but there was something pleasant about the rearrangement. It was truly lovely. He could not imagine it could ever be any cleaner, any more perfect, and he told her so.

Gracianna was torn between pride and shame, and just stood there awkwardly, realizing she should be working at the cafeteria at this very moment. Another mistake! What is going on?

Suddenly M. Dom' broke into a broad smile and laughed so loud as he said, "Perfection, perfection *absolue!* You have made this office so beautiful and I appreciate it and it must be yours from now on.

"And you may come in here and do as you please until you go home. It will be your place to store your supplies and do your work. It will be your office!"

After that it had officially become "Gracianna's office" to everyone, even though she had only cleaned it—it was a source of pride to her and sometimes on her break, she would go up there and tidy things. Even though he sometimes snuck away to nap there in the small bed during the day, it was a place that she could own in her work and she was proud. She was able to control something in this wilting city. M. Dom' once joked that she was the Princess of the Office and all had laughed. Gracianna swelled with pride for her initiative.

"This place is now your work office!" he kept saying. And he gave her his key and would not take it back.

Then he noticed the painting hanging near the window and could not control his good spirits anymore. "I have not seen that painting in a hundred years!" He laughed a lot, looked like he wanted to hug her, and then he was gone down the hallway, still chuckling.

Gracianna had hung the painting on the wall because it was so empty there, and she had unearthed a piece of art along the way. The painting was of a man smoking on a tall horse as he looked over a horizon. He was snappily dressed, wearing a uniform of sorts, epaulets and a cross-ribbed vest with buttons that could not be described. There was a dog at horse's feet, standing and inquisitively looking up at his owner, and a small smoky fire in the background. The man looked like a handsome American cowboy but maybe more Spanish-like, what the Spaniards call a vaquero.

She loved the little room. She had never had a work space she called her own.

A couple times, when she was feeling lonely, she would write to Bettina from the small desk in her shared room in the dormitory. Once, she got a letter back. It seemed that Bettina had taken an interest in Mikolaus' son (who was taking over the ranch manager job, because his father had, unfortunately, become ill). They were in love! But, with Mikolaus being ill, it was mixed news. Bettina never mentioned Juan, Gracianna noticed.

In her response, Gracianna told Bettina all about her Parisian adventures on her one day free (rarely two days free, but one was always spent in church). Sometimes, she would go to places with her roommate Siobhan and she told Bettina how she was still waiting to be discovered by a man with whom she could fall in love—but maybe she would not meet him until she got to America—and maybe never! How could she be found living in a girl's dorm?—she would joke. It was a possibility she had to accept. In fact, it seemed that the only thing she could ever control was her own destiny. She decided right then that her goal was not marriage—because who wanted to be married to a husband who was no good, and good ones seemed to be hard to find. No, her goal was to get to America.

Money is not as easy to get as I expected, and America . . . it seems so far away still.

A SEASON OF PERFECT WORK

"Relax and eat your dinner; there is nothing much to do," the kitchen staff would say after the customers left, but Gracianna was always bustling about Maison.

The work was meant to help her slowly fill the small jar she kept to hold the money she needed to complete her American dream. Some came in and then more went out because she had needed to buy shoes and a coat for the winter; even then, she would only shop at a thrift shop.

I just planned on saving not spending.

She reasoned that a restaurant at closing is an exaggerated dinner table after a large family meal on a Sunday—thrown napkins, food bits on plates dried in place like the sun had baked it hard for days, spilled pepper and salt from fallen porcelain standards, chairs askew scattered like dominoes, and half-empty emerald wine bottles and standing clear glasses shining in a medley of colors when the light skips through their varying glassy paths.

Gracianna would guide the last customers out, and the rest of the staff followed as soon as possible. Then the entire place was hers to do what should be done—and no one was there to see her on her hands and knees scrubbing the floor that Dom' had told her only needed to be scrubbed once a week even though it only took an hour, sweating, and for some reason thoroughly enjoying herself. There was nothing like good, hard work, executed with precision, and leaving something beautiful.

Six nights a week it was this way; she was left in peace to resurrect her palace from the damage of the evening.

"*Au revoir.*"

"*Bonsoir.*"

Lock the door.

Draw the shades.

Tie hair back and out of the way into a bun, fastened securely with one of Siobhan's clever barrettes.

Replace the service apron with the cleaning apron.

Put the Victrola on. Loud. Louder.

Go upstairs to the office for supplies: mop, broom, sponge, bucket, duster, and towels.

Pause at the top of the stairs and let the music take her away. The music was the only thing that broke the monotony of the work. She'd turn it up and she could soar anywhere.

But Gracianna's biggest concern was the sticky floor. Of all the chores, she disliked her floor duty the most. Dom' told her to lighten up because what he considered "clean," was "good enough," but Gracianna did not agree that "good enough" and "clean" could ever go in the same sentence. The job never felt finished if the floors weren't perfect. *I have to get this back in order. Start low and work my way back up.* "The top is easy. Always do the bottom and the 'bend-over' work first," her grandmother had taught her. The bend-over work was the worst because the position of it could be somewhat degrading, being subservient on your knees, under the world and seeing things from a place most never see. If it needed to be done she would do it and do it well. So doing the bend-over work first was especially good advice after a long day because she was dead-tired by the time she walked out on the drawn streets of Paris in the cape of the early mornings.

Every night was the same.

Clear, dust, wipe, sweep, mop, stairs, replace, pull, push, and straighten.

Clear the tables and bar top.

Dust the window shades, tabletops, railings, and chair and barstool underbellies.

Wipe anything anyone could touch and shine up the dusting trail she'd left in the preceding step.

Sweep the bathroom, back room, front room, front entrance, stairs, back-bar, kitchen, and the back alleyway entrance.

Mop the sticky; this gave her the most pleasure because it was righting something that was terribly wrong. She could see the filth disappear before her eyes and it was satisfying.

Stairs. Up and down, to get whatever supplies were needed to replace.

Replace towels, napkins, glasses, salt, pepper, wine, beer, and light food-stuff for the kitchen and bar-back.

Pull the tables back into place.

Push the chairs and barstools back into place.

Straighten anything that was out of place.

"Perfection must be a heavy cross to bear," she overheard one of the kitchen staff remark to another once.

There. Done. Lights out.

MYSTERIOUS MEETINGS

Lights out. Except, it seemed that they were more frequent now. The mysterious meetings. One by one, men that Gracianna had never seen before came in and greeted Dom'.

Dom'? He is never here this late at night.

One night she stood on her tiptoes to peek through the kitchen window to see the men huddled around the cooking island. They seemed to be gathered round pouring wine and talking quietly. Gracianna recognized a face: the fidgety man who visited Dom'. The sentry.

As if on cue, he crossed toward the closed blinds, right in front of Gracianna, and chinked them open.

It had been a close call.

Gracianna had been relieved to hear the sound of Dom's laughter at that moment. He was teasing his nervous friend for peeking through the blinds; they called him *Oeil de Faucon.* [Hawkeye].

Now more and more frequently they would come and the blinds would be closed and the lights turned down low. They stopped waiting for her to leave. As she did her chores, they would be there with their talking that sounded like whispering, the clink of glasses, cigarettes delivering shadowy wisps that disappeared into the ceiling and wafted into her office.

She wondered what they were up to. But it was none of her business. Still, a few days later, she asked one of the mediocre cooks—whom she found to be nosy and aware of everything—about it.

"What do you know about their meetings here, late at night?" Gracianna asked.

"I do not know anything about secrets like that. I think they are just dreamers or drunks—or else, they are just political schemers," he had said, but then he added, "but aren't those the same? Unless you are in office, politics is just all talk, right?"

THE LATOURS

The dancing was Gracianna's favorite part of the job. She would pause her serving duties in the evening—just for a moment, sometimes a few—to watch the couples swaying as they danced at Maison. Now and then people would sing along with the records. Occasionally, at the end of the night, when married couples really see each other, after a few drinks and the fog of their early romance casts over them once again, they see the side of their partner they never see during the busy week.

Of all the dancers, Gracianna especially loved watching the Latours who, in their forties, really seemed to still be in love. They would come in with smiles and greet everyone.

The cook had explained who the Latours were: Monsieur Latour was a butcher and supplied meat to Monsieur Dominique; he was a patron of the café to be visible out of respect and to protect his business relationship. Gracianna, despite her relative youth, knew that this quid pro quo behavior was expected and was the way of the world. And Mrs. Latour, with her lovely clothes and posture, was like a fashion model seasoned by age, refined in manners and always perfectly put together, with a luxuriously tall frame enhanced by her high heels. Gracianna felt especially short next to her. Still, Gracianna sensed a slight sadness in her. Again, the cook explained: M. Latour wanted children, but for some reason they had never had any. Gracianna was never sure why. She had heard that some women were unable to have children and that some women did not want them which was unbelievable.

One time, Gracianna had poured M. Latour's favorite drink for him— actually several of the civilized aperitifs—as the couple danced in the shadow of the visible Bonal aperitif billboard on the building across the street.

The Bonal drink was an after-dinner aperitif infused with quinine and gentian that was "gentled" by rocks. The drink seemed to help M. Latour smooth into a gentile *homme français de la soirée* [Frenchman of the evening] and fueled the monsieur's hazy contentment.

Once, while approaching the couple, Gracianna was surprised to hear a tense word cross their marriage table, and she slowed, trying not to be obvious. She had not heard exactly what was said. But then, quickly and tenderly, M. Latour said, "Well, forget it then. I will never speak of it again." Gracianna could see the tears in Mrs. Latour's eyes, so she had looked away.

Ever since then, Gracianna suspected that the argument was about "the subject" and figured she knew something intimate, that their relationship was not free of pain and was not all it appeared to be. She believed she knew something that most didn't, and she resolved she would never tell anyone.

But, oh how they danced—so easily.

The Latours would stroll in the shadow of the Bonal billboard.

Mr. Latour always danced very very close to Mrs. Latour, unlike the other couples. In most cases, diners and onlookers might glance disapprovingly, if knowingly, at a couple that was dancing so close because it was not appropriate to press your waists so closely together. "So crude and tasteless," some would say. The way the Americans danced so close was the worst though.

But when the Latours danced, it seemed natural and no one would ever say anything negative about them. They pressed together like a perfect gladness. They were, after all, in love wholeheartedly, with nothing left to prove, and anyone who had been in love could see it and respected their ability to express their love so freely, the perfect blend of closeness and distance.

Gracianna made this mental note: if her university boy would finally arrive, they would be free to dance in public at a café late at night and sway to the slow music as easily and as dreamily as the Latours. It made her blush and feel fluttery in her middle. She saw this love and wanted her future love to be as sweet and free.

Sometimes, they would be very affectionate. Mr. Latour would look around to see if anyone was looking—Gracianna would steal a glance—as he kissed his tall wife on the neck. Sometimes he licked or bit it (!) a little but the Mrs. would never pull back (!), even though she was (or pretended to be) embarrassed when others could see. Gracianna witnessed it several times over the winter. This behavior made her absolutely tingly inside, like the jump of the dancing lambs in the spring. The lambs would prance in front of their mother when they wanted to play, their knobby knees barely able to sustain their newborn weight. Gracianna could feel this excitement inside and liked the feeling.

She thought Mr. Latour was very handsome with his trimmed beard and blue eyes. Sometimes, Gracianna would dare to imagine that she was Mrs. Latour as the lovely lady laid her head back with her eyes closed and swayed to the music in her husband's arms. And Mr. Latour would lean into her ear, his beard against her neck. Gracianna would peek and imagine his stubbled face scratching her own neck. Yes, she liked him. He seemed charming and a bit outward and friendly, plus he always looked happy and was finely put together.

Once, after a close dance, Gracianna heard Mr. Latour tell Dom' that he thought the best things in life were free, and Mrs. Latour had smiled at Mr. Latour. But then Dom' had joked back that Mrs. Latour probably thought the best things in life were very, very expensive. They had all laughed. Gracianna noticed that the Latours laughed with their heads back. The "Latour Laugh" is what Gracianna called it in her head.

One night was very magical, when they were dancing together to Edith Piaf's *La Vie en Rose* [A Life in Pink] with that magical voice singing:

> *When he takes me in his arms*
> *He speaks to me softly*
> *I see life in pink*
> *He speaks to me words of love*
> *These words every day*
> *And this does something to me*
> *He has entered my heart*

After that night, during her solo cleaning routine, if Dom' and his late-night friends were not around, Gracianna would sweep the broom across the dance floor with her eyes closed, listening to that song, imagining what it might be like to feel so deeply in love. It was silly, she knew.

At least, Siobhan seemed to understand her feelings. She understood even though she had her own troubles. Her run-ins with discriminatory episodes seemed to be increasing. Gracianna could not understand why. Were the rumors of war true?

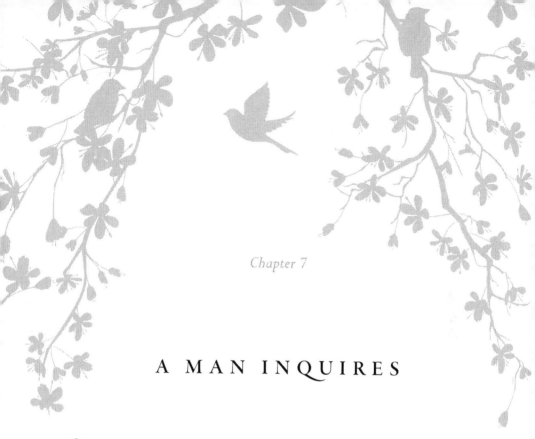

Chapter 7

A MAN INQUIRES

*O*ne morning, when Gracianna was on her way out of the dormitory to do errands before she started work, the pretty Russian girl told her, quite nonchalantly, that someone, "*un homme* [a man]," had inquired about her. And then she winked and said she knew no more.

It left Gracianna with a hundred imaginings and distraction. But she couldn't be late for work and left wondering. She almost walked down the wrong street, she was unable to bargain with her usual skill with the sellers, and her mind wandered at work through the evening.

Gracianna immediately thought that bad news had come from home. Anxious thoughts pinged from side to side in her head. She tried to focus but they kept on.

Her worried mind swirled all evening. It was an eternity to get back to the dorm to see if there was word. She knew she would get home around 2:30 a.m., like most nights, after cleaning the bar café. Tonight would be no different, and the Russian girl would probably be sleeping, or be out with a man, or be stubbornly silent on the subject. Gracianna felt a little angry with her, unable to get the issue out of her mind.

Who could be calling?

The anticipation was killing her. Absorbed in thought she dried one glass five times.

Was there more news? Was it bad news?

She had been contemplating it all night, unable to let her mind drift to romance or school in America or other easy thoughts. On and on and on, the worst possible news came flooding over her.

Who could be looking for me, unless my grandmother is dead?

Who is looking for me?

Why do I feel so afraid?

She hated the feeling.

Tonight, even the dancing seemed to take too long.

It had never even occurred to her to ask to leave early—before everything was spotless.

Finally finished, she walked fast but arrived at her building later than usual.

This is the time of night all bad news is delivered.

ARRIVAL

As Gracianna unlocked the oversized dormitory door, she heard a commotion inside. Her hand paused, the key was still in the lock, half turned. *When in doubt, distrust.*

She decided to open the door expecting bad news. It overwhelmed her, that oozing feeling. She tried to brace herself, be brave and go on—but her hand trembled on the key and she could not press the door forward. She felt tired. Suddenly, all the hard work did not seem to be paying off. Living as she was, always so busy, unable to rest consistently and not sleeping well; she had some difficulty trying to be grateful for her situation. And there it was—the weight of the ominous, dark blanket that overshadowed Paris had fallen on her. It whispered, *"Things are no good."*

Maybe I need to go back where I belong?

She wanted to cry. Maybe it was because of lack of sleep. She promised herself she would get more sleep, somehow. Maybe this was her worst mistake. For now, it was time to face the news.

With a firm hold, she cautiously opened the dormitory door—*Grand-mère, I will never forget what you taught me. Never.*

There was a man sitting crouched against the wall in the dimly lit entry.

Gracianna had never noticed the light before. *Men are not allowed in here.* It was a bare dim bulb dangling with cause and the cause was deliverance. Seeing her, the visitor stood, brushing himself off. He was not so tall, but he looked very strong, like an ox. Gracianna felt a surge of fear. She had still not bought herself the knife that she had promised herself she would.

His dark hair was ruffled, his coat wrinkled. It seemed he had been sleeping, the way he rubbed his eyes. Yes, his hands looked very strong. Her helplessness made her angry with him.

Gracianna took a step back—afraid. "No men are allowed in this dormitory," she said loudly. Just as she was about to exclaim again, she recognized that goose smile and friendly beard.

"Juan!"

"Gras'!"

Even though she had not seen him for six months he looked exactly the same, except for the beard. They did not embrace but moved closer to each other—he reached for her but she did not reciprocate for some reason bracing for the news. *Is this who they sent to tell me?*

"What is the matter?"

"Nothing is the matter," he said.

Really, everything is fine?

"I like your hair," he said.

"Why are you here?"

"I like your hair," he said.

Gracianna blushed all the way from her roots to the tips of her ears, suddenly thankful for the dim lighting.

He likes my hair.

SHOWING JUAN THE ROPES

Until Juan had come, Gracianna did not realize how lonely she had been. At nineteen she took him under her wing in the big city, and liked to show off while showing the twenty-three-year-old the ropes, whenever her work would allow. A couple times, she had to say no to Dom' if he asked her to stay a bit late for extra work. Doing so made her feel in control of her life.

She introduced Juan to the neighborhood she already knew so well. The bridge, the church, the shops.

"*Bonjour, Gracianna*," the neighbors would call out to her along the market road. She loved picking up fresh vegetables at the stands on the way to work in the afternoons for the chef. Of course, Gracianna noticed her market acquaintances were now aware that she had a "friend," and she noticed they could tell he was not from Paris. Some of the looks from strangers were not so nice, but the good people she knew responded with pleasure.

Everyone knows her, Juan thought.

"He is from the hills?" one vendor offered.

Gracianna waved off the vendor, nodding, but it was a bit embarrassing. "The Pyrenees are no mere hills," she had said and resisted the urge to cross herself.

Juan loved to watch her interact with her world. It was natural for him to observe. That was his way to live—to perceive life differently than his own predictable orientation. He found himself more curious than he had expected and was glad to experience new things. He thought Gracianna's world was so full of . . . people.

Many many people.

She was an excellent negotiator. He watched and learned as she interacted with the butcher and the fishmonger and produce men, angling for the value she deserved for her own hard-earned money, never mind that this shopping money belonged to Dom'.

Gracianna would categorically refuse the first, second, *and* third offer of the wriggling fishmonger, a man who knew she was more slippery than his trawl.

The merchant recognized he was going to lose but playfully tried, as entertaining as it was, to parry with her. If he was going to lose anyway, or at least break even, he wanted to at least enjoy it, and he wanted her out as quickly as possible so as not to allow the others to see him lose face to the smallest of retail adversaries.

Oh! She is maddening!

In the background, Juan would smile, offering solace to the bent fish seller, the butcher, and the produce man like some sort of consolation prize when they would wave her off with a disbelieving half-smile. The merchants, as much as they would tense when she approached, hoped she would come back because they knew she sent enthusiastic referrals, always mentioning their prized products—but never the weakness of their incompetent haggling. It was worth it to take a small beating because she helped them recoup their individual loss of face through the praise she paid them as men and purveyors to any and all that would listen. It was right to deliver them a quid for her quo.

For her, negotiating was not just acting or playing. She felt she deserved to get the most perceived value for what she received. She felt, rightly or wrongly, that she could set the value of a product—what she thought it was worth and a fair price, considering the supply-demand ratio. If they did not have the same value, she would not negotiate with them in the future and it was their loss. Otherwise, she reasoned she was offering them a win-win and they could take it or leave it.

Once, she caught Juan smiling sympathetically at one of the losers, and her eyes had told him not to do that anymore. "Let them have their pride," she had murmured, and let us take ours, too.

She never crowed about her "win," even to people who would not think badly of the merchants. The way Juan saw it she just went about her day and wouldn't give it another thought.

Another time, the baker wrapped up the day-old bread in return for her hard-earned money. Gracianna silently pushed it back to him and straightened her jacket. Apparently, they had met before because, with a quick glance at the other buyers, the baker had reached for the hottest bread, re-wrapped it, pushed it to her, and gave the old bread to the next customer, who had not noticed.

At first, Juan would praise her for her gamesmanship, but he came to realize that this was not a game to her—this was her life. He could accept it.

She was so gracious, speaking with the other hardworking ladies she would see at church or the café about news, the war-whispers, her street observations, her proverbs—always shying away from repeating gossip but never straying from listening to it.

Gracianna happily introduced Juan to everyone, especially to Dom', and Juan could see their affection. To Juan, Dom' seemed like the father Gras' had never had.

"He needs work," Gracianna said, though, she and Juan had already agreed he should find a job of his own while he stayed in the men's dormitory. They agreed it would be awkward but not impossible, if only for a short time, for him to work at La Maison Cossette.

With pride she showed Juan the little room upstairs where she organized her work, the one that everyone called her "office."

A BASQUE-STYLE COURTSHIP

In his heart, Juan wanted to help Gracianna to be happy. He thought she objected too much, but he could accept that for now. She sometimes allowed him to walk her to the dormitory where she lived with Siobhan and the girls after work. This dance of allowing and not allowing was their courtship way. Sometimes, she accepted small gifts from him.

Her role was to allow small things to occur to him, to help him please her. Once, seeing an elderly couple walking together, Gracianna quipped, "That is nice how they are holding hands."

The next time Juan walked her to the dormitory, he took her hand in his. It was warm and fit just right. From then on, he would take her hand sometimes—not too often, but more often than not—by her little finger. *He is sweet.*

Gracianna remembered the Latours and their carefree romantic ways, and she wanted to emulate them. Even though Juan was not as comfortable with affection, he forced himself to open up to please her and she knew he would do or say anything to do so. He was usually romantically awkward, whatever it was she asked for . . . it had never occurred to him to provide it until she asked.

Sometimes, their hands said things to each other that their eyes and mouths were too shy to say. But Gracianna was still unsure and this was understood and accepted.

At times they were quiet, at times full of laughter and talking during their walks. Gracianna saw that Juan was an easy talker—just a little shy at the onset. This was probably held over from his years of isolation in the mountains. Sometimes, she felt shy, too, even though she knew her heart was brave when it came to many things. After all, shyness aside, he seemed so relaxed!

He understood her candor when she would be direct about some difficult things—other things, she would never mention. For example, she was curious about Juan's feelings for the Russian girl at the dormitory, who had been asking many questions about him and had winked at him at least three times now.

"I give you my blessing," Gracianna had said, only to find out he did not want or need it, having no interest in the pretty Russian girl. Gracianna had learned to be candid by listening to her grandmother's romance stories—always ending with the lesson that a healthy marriage calls for "open lives" lest things build up and then you find yourself unable to talk about other, more important things. "It's the more important subjects that are necessary to talk about," she would say, but oddly they were the ones most marriages don't broach.

Since Juan and Gracianna lived across from each other at the dorms there would be times when they could see each other at night from window to window. Gracianna's curtain was always pulled closed, but when there was a small crack that her roommates surely left, she would peer toward Juan's, thinking what a man he could be. He would often hang something in the window to amuse her: a flower, a small sign he made saying, "*bonjour*," or something simple just to let her know he was thinking of her.

She would never acknowledge his thoughtfulness.

He would have to ask her if she had seen his window gift.

If he asked, glancingly she would say, "I saw it the moment you put it up." She expected that it was good to keep him wondering, because she was still wondering, too. This way, both were able to keep their balance and position.

There he was, peering across the street through swirling framed glass at his girl, who was "A handful," as his friends would put it artfully.

He joked that Gracianna, being Basque, was much more than those men could manage, strong and opinionated, a force, but in a quiet way. Juan had a friend from the train station who always said, "Any man who wanted to be with her would have to have the strength of an ox."

"Or be brainless," another said. They all chuckled, but feared he might tell her what they said.

Her will was what impressed any onlooker. It seemed as if she always got what she wanted in her own way, but he apparently profited as well. It was a solid match.

In the end, they both loved the way they had figured out how to herd each other—their needs were met simply by being themselves and following their individual hearts.

Juan and Gracianna knew they would marry if they ever both felt the time was right. There is a time with most couples when the man signals to the woman that the right time is coming and she pretends not to notice. There are gestures or knowing smiles or looks when he sees something that pleases him, or the knowing look when they are together and see a couple holding hands, or in a million little ways he says, "I want you to be my wife—if you want."

Their affection grew. This was unsettling again for Gracianna, who had not expected this strange change in things. The presence of Juan made her question some of her dreams. She thought, perhaps, that she might be a little in love with him. She could not let him know it though. *It would not be right. I don't want to pressure him.*

She also could not get the Latours out of her mind's eye or Edith Piaf out of her heart. To *see in pink* was what she wanted! Or—was that just a silly dream? Juan could tell her thoughts by the way she watched the Latours, and once, he had accidentally seen Gracianna swaying to the music by herself.

He will come, or he will not come. It will be Juan or it will not be Juan. Only time will tell, and meanwhile I must keep on living and working toward what I believe in.

Still, Juan gently wooed, and Gracianna did not object.

"Yours is an unusual courtship," some would say to them.

"Not if you are Basque," they would smile back, holding hands a little more often.

Not if you're Basque.

DOM'S AFFECTION

One night, Dom' was a little drunk as Juan and Gracianna ate their soup.

"I have come to love you both!" He said after a long, quiet spell. "I have never had much luck with help; sometimes it is just plain nepotism! Situations are foisted upon me, whether it's my doing or my wife's. I should know better! I have to keep her in the background or it would be chaos around here. Did I say too much?"

Juan and Gracianna were staring at each other.

Dom' shouted, "Yes, I know better but just can't say no, and it rarely works out."

When they tried to respond graciously, he waved his chubby hand impatiently. "Only when there is complete trust and belief in a common goal are there the makings of a family business! But I no longer expect this from my own. No one in my family is hardworking or sober enough to do the work." Long pause accentuated with a sip of wine. "I have felt very alone with my responsibilities, until you came along, Gracianna—and then you, Juan. Juan! You have helped me with these important jobs I have wanted done here for years! Thank you for coming in and helping here and there. They are not so small, no, not so small. This is just until you find something, yes. . . ."

Juan nodded. Soon after Juan arrived, Dom' had him repairing the plumbing, the roof, the boiler, and everything else broken at the café—it felt like full-time work but it was sporadic. The café disrepair was a source of embarrassment for Dom' and it weighed heavily on the proud man.

"I wish I could slow down and work less, just play cards with my men, the ones I affectionately call my friends! *Le tabagisme, la tricherie, se plaignant, le mensonge, et les hommes paresseux* [The smoking, cheating, complaining, lying, and lazy men]."

"I would give more responsibilities to someone if they would take it! And they would if I could pay for it! You cannot understand what it takes to run a business. It seems there is no way to relieve the pressure."

As a boy, M. Dom's father, also Monsieur Dominique, used to say, "*La pression est un privilège* [Pressure is a privilege]." Monsieur Dominique Junior believed that to be true.

Noticing how Juan and Gracianna were sadly looking at him, Dom' seemed to snap out of it. "Oh, it's not so bad," he said quickly. "I have lessened the stress over the years only because I am good at what I do, and I know the business so well. But the place takes all I have . . . but you two," he smiled at them, "It runs so much smoother with you two helping me."

"Juan!" Dom' said, clapping him on the back. "I wish I had a son like you! You're straightforward, sensible, good-hearted, with a can-do attitude and hands always handy. And Gras'," as M. Dom' now affectionately called her, "you, you my girl, you must be so tired!"

Gracianna stiffened, torn between staring silently at her soup and giving Dom' a warning look to say no more. Out of the corner of her eye, she noticed Juan was staring at his soup.

"You are so willing and self-directed in your work ethic!" he continued, patting her. "But it is a waste for you to scrub the floors every night—it is too much! Let me see your hands, Gras'!" She instantly hid them under the table.

Dom's shoulders slumped. "I am sorry, I should not get drunk and talk so much but this has been on my mind. And to be honest, there is something sad I feel when I see you two in love, because *I* have loved but it long gone." He wiped away a tear, angrily.

"Don't you lose this love!" He shook his finger at them, rising with his wine glass. "You will not know love like this again—do you hear me?" He pointed at them once more for good measure and stumbled away.

Juan and Gracianna finished their soup in silence.

Without a word Juan and Gracianna walked back to the dormitories that night.

Juan noticed that Gracianna did not want to hold hands and knew it was because Dom' had embarrassed her. Yes, maybe they were a little rough. Maybe he would get her some hand cream.

No, not a good idea, but a good thought.

Outside the dormitory, he said: "Good night, Gras'."

"Goodnight Juan."

Their eyes shared a brief kiss before they parted.

Juan waited to make sure she was safe inside the door and then he caught his breath.

Someday she'll be mine. Can I wait? I'm not made of steel, after all.

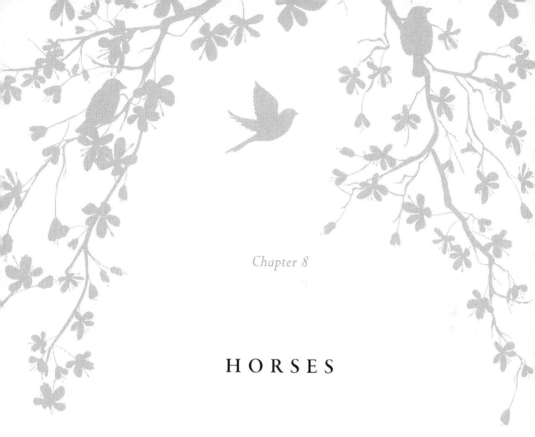

Chapter 8

HORSES

*O*ne quiet afternoon, Juan burst into La Maison.

Gracianna was serving coffee to Dom's friends in the back booth and not many others were around.

"My God!" he shouted.

Gracianna looked up sharply. Juan was angry? She watched him cross himself, shaking some newspaper, barely able to speak.

Gracianna felt a chill run down her spine.

Everyone else was looking at him too. Quickly, she pulled him aside, ending up in the garden behind Maison.

"What is it?" She was embarrassed that he had upset the café patrons.

Juan sat on a stump. "I am sorry, Gracianna, I am so angry. Read this," he said as he handed her the paper. "The Germans—they have massacred an entire infantry of horsemen! Horsemen!" he said, looking at Gracianna, "like our Basque vaqueros." Shaken, he looked directly at Gracianna and said, "They killed the men and then they shot every one of the horses. They left them dead in the road. Hundreds of them!"

Gracianna read—and saw the picture. There were hundreds of horses dead on the road—just stiff with bloated stomachs, long legs, and long faces. The French mounted militia had been attempting to fight against the Nazis, but the Nazis had killed all of them—even their French horses. Then the closed-mouthed tanks had driven right over them!

She gasped when she looked at the picture.

"Gras'." Juan's eyes were intent. "The whispers of war are no longer whispers. The entire German army is coming—everywhere, this news says! It's all over the railroad, I keep hearing it."

Another chill.

But now he had to go back to work. Between "small work" here and there he seemed to be called back to a railroad job more and more often. He had told Gracianna just the day before that anything worth anything eventually passes through the station.

Gracianna could not help but think of the vaqueros from home. She remembered one of the gentle cowboy vaqueros who came to help round up livestock each spring. He had the most beautiful chestnut horse that Gracianna had ever seen. He had probably been teasing, but he had let her name the horse.

"Babieco," she said.

"He loves you," the tall cowboy would say after that.

He had promised her a foal, when Babieco successfully sired. Gracianna had held that hope for several years and still thought he might have followed through—but now she had moved away, before he could come back.

News of the massacre spread swiftly throughout Paris and beyond. The mood was tense.

Walking to the dormitory alone that night, she remembered the hundreds of horses dead alongside the road—and it made her sick to her stomach.

The horse-chestnut trees lining the Parisian streets had bloomed early this spring. Nearly twenty thousand of them line the city's streets. The branches turn up, like the arms of candelabra, each tipped with a white blossom-cluster, pointed with a flower-candle flame. Each flower of the pyramid has its throat-dashes of yellow and red, and the curving yellow stamens thrust far out of the dainty ruffled border of the petal. Gracianna believed the tree roots could feel the molten onslaught coming through earthly vibrations that forced the blossoms to explode early out of the winter bark. A

Dead horses along the road outside Paris.

newspaper blew down the dark street. "*NAZI INFERNO,*" the headline in the newspaper read, with a picture of a burning building.

She caught the newspaper with her tiny foot and stepped on it. She could not even feel sad for the horses, the horsemen, or the people on the roof of the burning building. She was too angry.

Dear God, save us.

THE FALL OF FRANCE

Gossip and stories rushed through the country like wildfire. But Hitler knew what was true.

At Maison, Dom' had finally included Juan and Gracianna in some of his "meetings" with his "friends." And they all followed Hitler's "progress" as the German army advanced toward Paris.

"Let's hope it stays far away, darling," Mrs. Latour would say with troubled eyes. "Otherwise. . . ." Before you knew it, they had stopped coming around anymore.

"The Nazis are coming," everyone was saying. "Haven't you heard?"

But not everyone could leave like the Latours. Gracianna talked to Siobhan, concerned because many Jews were starting to flee. Siobhan had cried and said she had no place to go. Later, Gracianna told Juan, "The Latours have fled, and Siobhan might need a place to hide." She was in a fearful state. And then the mood shifted.

"France is fighting back," people began to say hopefully, then more proudly, and then more passionately. There was news about how the eastern border of France, the one adjoining Germany, was well protected by French troops that were ready for a battle with Hitler's advancing army.

War at any age is wrong; I am sure of it. Gracianna had been in Paris a year now and was turning twenty. The café and shops were buzzing with the news. Dom' started to smile again.

Then, there was a terrible, terrible mistake. Many people didn't believe it when they heard the news: "Surprise attack from the northern border!" The Nazis had battled their way through Luxembourg and entered at a border that France had considered safe. Paris had been left undefended. French had made a strategic error. Their entire army was waiting for a battle with Germany on its own border, which would never occur. The mistake had proved fatal.

"The Germans are moving swiftly!" became the cry.

"They are slicing through France with glee, like a soft sheep's cheese," Juan said. Gracianna and Juan were not originally from Paris but they were from here now. They held each other's hands as they heard the news. Still, they could not help but think of the Basque people facing the Roman invasions, wave after wave. For hundreds of years they had fought.

As they followed the news, resistance seemed futile, even Dom' would admit. Then Dom's wife had abandoned him. One day, she was just gone without even leaving a letter. It did not seem much of a loss to anyone, including Dom,' because she didn't love him anyway.

"Gras', we should leave," Juan said one night. "Let's go back home. We can take Siobhan, shouldn't we? Maybe we can come back when the war is over."

However, after accidentally seeing Dom' drunk-weeping about his loss and the oncoming war and his life and every weight he probably felt, Gracianna told Juan that he could always go, but she had to stay.

"I will not run away, like Basque men have done for years," she had snapped when Juan tried to insist. She had apologized immediately. Juan knew she was referring to the time when Spain and France needed troops. They would come to the mountains looking for Basque men, the "fierce fighters." But they did not want to fight for a country or a cause they did not belong to or believe in, so they would hide. It sounded much worse than it was and it was a sore point for every Basque man.

"*Vive la Résistance* [Long live the Resistance]!" Gracianna began to say. Dom' told her to hush, and she stopped saying it publicly after that.

Onward, the German army thundered south, sullying, bullying, pushing and pulling the French army apart for several weeks—forcing them to retreat alongside civilians in overwhelming numbers. Not thousands, nor tens of thousands, nor hundreds of thousands—but millions, over ten million left Paris for its countryside or for relatives in nearby countries, North Africa, anywhere but the occupied city. Citizens were abandoning their French life. Siobhan refused to become a gaunt wandering-eyed refugee or a prisoner. She wanted to hide, but no place seemed safe.

And so Paris was declared an "open city" and the Germans waltzed in with their weapons and their shiny boots like they owned the place.

Parisians were in horror.

French soldiers guarded by German soldiers after capture in 1940.

German officers in France during the invasion in 1940

So on June 14, 1940, five weeks after the start of the Battle of France, an undefended Paris fell to German occupation forces. The Germans marched past the Arc de Triomphe on the 140th anniversary of Napoleon's victory at the Battle of Marengo.

The news only brought Gracianna and Juan closer. There was more news that resistance was continuing as the Germans overran the remaining French soldiers. But it was over. Even Dom' said so, but Gracianna could not believe it.

A SHAMEFUL SURRENDER

On June 17, the various people in the café were huddled around the radio as the blooming street lilacs went unnoticed. Juan read in the news that in Vichy, literally in the middle of nowhere in the south of France, and miles from an "A" French city, a new French government was being hastily formed.

Marshal Pétain, a proud and beloved Frenchman and war hero from World War I, spoke to the French people in a sad radio broadcast. The aging warrior announced, to the French people, "*C'est avec le coeur lourd que je vous dis aujourd'hui qu'il faut cesser le combat* [It is with a heavy heart that I tell you today that we must stop fighting]."

"Stop fighting?" said Gracianna disdainfully. She threw her hands up in the air in disgust.

The invasion was complete. The French government buckled and the French asked the Germans for it to be over. The blitzkrieg had invaded with the force of hell. It was hard to accept.

SIOBHAN

One day, Juan insisted that Gracianna come to the cinema with him to get away from the tension of the war. Finally, with a lot of charm and patience, he had talked her into taking a break with him, getting dressed up, and seeing a movie. Gracianna immediately realized that going to the movies was a way for Parisians to escape the revulsion—there were crowds of people, almost twice as many as she had ever seen there. For a little while, she allowed herself to be happy with Juan, for both of their sakes.

After the movie Gracianna walked into her dormitory room feeling a bit distracted as Juan had intended.

She saw Siobhan hurriedly packing her belongings, her eyes full of tears when she glanced up. They both knew that the Jews were especially worried and fleeing the murderous treatment that was to descend upon them.

"Gras', I must go; it is not safe," Siobhan said, as she continued to fold and pack.

Gracianna sunk down on the bed next to her. Many of the beds were empty now. "What are you going to do?"

"I have heard there are some Jews living in the forests. I have no place else to go, so I must find them." She turned to Gracianna with sudden anger. "You are lucky you have a family and a *place* you can return to!"

"Why don't you go to my family?" Gracianna blurted out. The thought had not occurred to her earlier.

"It is too far. There is no time. It is not safe. I must go now; I have one person I can travel with. This offer is too late."

"I'm sorry," said Gracianna, looking away.

"What are you sorry for? That I am Jewish? You cannot help that."

"No. I am sorry for the situation."

"Do not be so helpless!" Siobhan practically shouted. "You must be practical and do what you must to survive. You should marry Juan. That is what you should do!" She was serious. "Gracianna, it is not safe to be Jewish or, even a single woman in Paris with these pigs. You know what I mean, don't you? Married or not, you are not safe. You are a duck sitting alone! You think it's bad what they did to those horses and men, but you don't know what they do to women. I have heard stories. Do you understand?"

Gracianna nodded, suddenly feeling ill.

"What will you do to be safe?" Siobhan wanted to know. She closed her suitcase. "Can't you go to America now?"

"No," Gracianna said in disappointment, "I do not have enough money to do that. But I will soon. It is all I can think about. I am so close." Actually it would take at least another year to collect enough francs and she did not want to burden her friend with that knowledge.

"Will Juan go with you?"

"I'm sure he will come."

"He loves you very much. I'm sure you two will be fine and take care of each other. As for me, like many Jews, I must accept that whatever happens to us is God's will. I have to go now."

Gracianna declared, "The rumor that the camps are not so bad is just bad information. It cannot be believed. Even if you see a letter saying it is not so bad, do not believe it. Juan knows the truth from working at the railroad."

Siobhan was grateful for the tip—she had heard that rumor, too. "They are just lying bastards." Siobhan could not admit she had been tempted by the rumors, tempted to end the struggle of wondering where she could go to be safe.

They hugged briefly, intensely, kissed on both cheeks, and then Siobhan tugged her suitcase off the bed.

Gracianna walked her friend down the stairs.

The *thunk, thunk, thunk* accompanied Siobhan's suitcase, as it dropped down each step.

God be with you Siobhan.

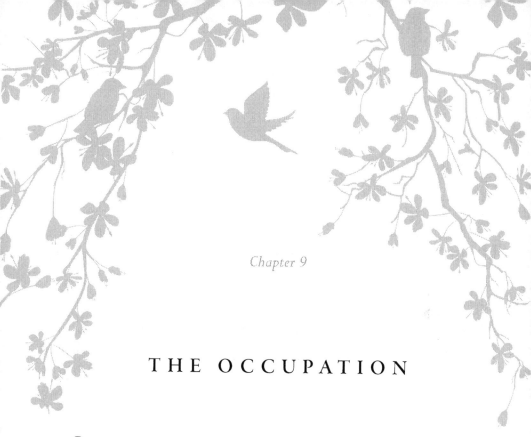

Chapter 9

THE OCCUPATION

$\mathscr{S}$iobhan had fled just in time, because suddenly a waterfall of soldiers appeared in the neighborhood. The officers, in their pressed uniforms and shiny boots, were not shy.

The French hunkered down inside themselves and tried to look away.

Gracianna heard the bartenders talking one night. The Nazi command had set up a high-level strategy office just down the street from La Maison at the rue de Rivoli in the Le Meurice Hotel.

"Not Le Meurice!" Gracianna had interrupted. One Sunday, it seemed so long ago, Siobhan had suggested that she and Gracianna visit the grande dame Le Meurice. Their original Sunday plans had changed because Gracianna's church was wary about letting Siobhan enter; the Nazis had stormed it earlier in the week looking for asylum seekers.

So they had gone to Le Meurice, which was opposite the Tuileries Garden, between Place de la Concorde and the Musée du Louvre.

"This is like a French palace, not a hotel!" Gracianna had exclaimed as they stood admiring the architecture. It was a vast place of great beauty and prestige.

A gravelly-voiced French tour man had given them a free leaflet. It felt right for Gracianna to hand it Siobhan to read.

As they had stood admiring the architecture (they could not go in), Siobhan, whose reading was animated, pretended to be the tour operator, and summarized the leaflet. Apparently, Le Meurice was the recognized Parisian pied-à-terre [apartment] of the privileged, known for extravagant dining and entertainment. "The supper seating," Siobhan read, "began at 8 p.m., and lasted twelve hours, until near the middle of the next morning!"

She looked over her glasses, feigning the tour man, and continued speaking slowly like he had, "At the luncheons they only served hard-boiled eggs from the rarest of birds—quail eggs, partridge eggs, swan eggs, to ball-sized ostrich eggs. Our international reputation is sparkling," she paused and looked directly at Gracianna with her hand waving as if presenting the magnificent hotel, "impressive, and elaborate, with its breathtaking Louis XVI décor."

Both young women burst into laughter at Siobhan's display and her near-perfect intonation and enunciation of the cartoon-character tour operator.

Then, Gracianna's eye settled on the leaflet's central photograph featuring Le Meurice's rooftop garden peacefully overlooking the glamour and glint of nighttime Paris.

"*Le ventre de la bête* [the belly of the beast]," Gracianna whispered. It was the perfect location. The hotel of kings and queens was now the hotel of killers and questionables.

Even the symbol of the greyhound on the leaflet made Gracianna irritated. The story said that, a hundred years ago, during one of many renovations, the workers had taken in a stray dog, a greyhound. Soon, the higher personnel were so in love with the dog that they made him the official mascot of the hotel.

But now, wolves had come, turning the palace into their lair with a new symbol: the swastika. Gracianna hated all that it stood for. She could not help but wonder about the hotel workers, and how the hotel was so close to Maison. To think! Nazi headquarters right in her backyard. *The cold wolves have moved the greyhounds out.*

Chapter 10

THE FIGHT

*A*ll the letter said was, "I'm coming to join you and work." But why was she coming *now*?

Constance arrived in Paris to great fanfare. She was the smartest eighteen-year-old in the world; just ask her and she would tell you. Constance was set to take over Paris.

"Oh! Gras', I had to come; it was all I could think about, you here and me there. You blazed the trail for me. And I am here now to work and, oh! I don't know what I will do, go to America with you or go home but I wanted to have this experience with you . . . and with Juan?"

"Juan and I are just fine, but it is hard here now with the war. What were you thinking?"

"I did see people fleeing, but I was called here, I think. It just seemed right," was all she said, "and Grand-mère was happy that I left."

"I bet she was. . . ."

Gracianna understood now. It was just a rash move, typical Constance and what was there to be done?

Constance moved into the dorm and started looking for work.

"Juan, this just isn't a good time for Constance to come to Paris. Doesn't she know there is a war going on?"

For the thousands of refugees who were still leaving Paris to escape the occupation, few souls wanted to come *into* the city and expose themselves to potential abuse at the time.

As distracted as Gracianna was with work she was nonetheless happy to have Constance join her and hear news from home, the ranch, and Grand-mère, even though nothing had changed.

But the burden quickly became apparent.

"Constance needs work Juan. She is just a girl—what does she know? It was hard enough for you to find work. She needs a job, knows no one, and I don't know what to do." He agreed.

"I cannot afford to take a day off to help her!" Gracianna worried, "I am behind schedule and not there yet. I haven't saved nearly as much as I thought I would have for my, our, tickets to the United States. But who will help her if I don't? She is nearly helpless."

WAIT! Had Grand-mère given Constance some of MY money to get here? That was the "toll" I paid to get away from the mountains so I could feel right about leaving. This is just Grand-mère throwing my gift back in my face.

But Gracianna and Juan did help Constance. Gracianna introduced her to the owner of a nearby bar, M. Rousseau, the nephew of a friend of Dom. Gracianna and Juan knew him of course. Everyone just called him "Rousseau." He had come to Maison often and they had been to his establishment once or twice and had been warmly welcomed because of their relationship with Dom'.

After hiring Constance, a smitten Rousseau pleasantly surprised Juan one afternoon by saying, "She is glamorous and taller than I expected, compared, of course, to, uh, um, her sister's beauty. Constance is different from Gracianna in so many ways—but they are the same too."

Rousseau's bar was a popular bohemian place in the nearby neighborhood in le Marais [the Marsh]," the Jewish Quarter. With its proud architectural heritage, the quarter lay across both the 3rd and 4th arrondissement in Paris on the Rive Droite, or Right Bank, of the Seine. People enjoyed listening to music in this "fun neighborhood" and drank until late in the night.

"I'm getting married!" Constance shrieked.

"What?" Gracianna exclaimed in disbelief. She had only known Rousseau two weeks.

Before Juan and Gracianna knew it, Constance had quickly married the wealthy Rousseau and his family's money. It was a whirlwind.

Just like Constance, Gracianna thought.

Constance told Gracianna, "Rousseau loves me, he thinks. And I think I love him, I think, no, I am sure. He is so handsome and funny. He can help me and that helps you and Juan. No one needs to be worried about me. Maybe I can now help you two and Grand-mère too."

Gracianna had heard Constance say to Rousseau in the bar one night before the engagement, "Fun finds me," and she thought this was too forward but typically emblematic of Constance's cavalier attitude. She was different from anyone Rousseau had met, Gracianna reasoned, which was what attracted him to her.

The wedding reception was at Rousseau's well-appointed family home. There, Constance told Gracianna, "I plan to spend my days shopping while my husband works. He has insisted that I do not work, 'You have worked too hard in your life. I am going to take care of you my dear—I thank God for bringing you from the mountains to me,' he told me."

Gracianna rolled her eyes.

"He plans on spoiling me," she giggled.

Gracianna was angry about Constance's impetuous and immature behavior. It was grating on Gracianna now that her sister had followed her to Paris.

There is a war, after all.

Constance often said things that ladies of that era did not say. She spoke of her enjoyment of alcohol and even her monthly period easily in front of anyone and it made Gracianna very uncomfortable.

Constance would speak of her own failings and how she felt sickly sometimes, and Gracianna thought those things private and just did not take kindly those who spoke about themselves in this whiny way; Constance was oblivious to it. Constance never held back. She was just like Grand-mère in this way. But Constance really never thought she was good enough and had a low self-image, even though she would often say she was prettier than Gracianna, with a circus smile. Constance did not think herself as smart as her sister. "After all, Grand-mère treasured smarts above beauty," she announced to Juan one night after a few glasses of wine.

Constance was not as book smart as her older sister but considered her use of her looks as a game that required intelligence. It was self-styled and dramatic, though; Constance came to believe what her inner voice said. Gracianna liked Rousseau but thought Constance was taking advantage of him.

No one should be catered to like this; she has just given in to the easy life.

Just after closing one night Gracianna was not expecting the sudden knock at the door to the café, and could not see because the blinds were drawn, so she slipped around to peek through a different window.

It was some woman in a large fur coat—Constance(!) showing up out of the blue.

Gracianna flipped the blind closed and cursed silently.

What is she doing here?! This place is still a mess, I'm sweating and it is only Wednesday!

She wiped her brow, adjusted her barrette, peeled away her apron, flipped off the music, and opened the door for Constance, who gushed and embraced her with furry hugs.

"It is Wednesday! You said you were coming home on Thursday!"

"We came home a day early," Constance announced.

"I want to invite you and Juan to a party," she said, but Gracianna couldn't hold back any longer and said, "Why have you done this?"

"Done what? How about, 'How was the honeymoon?'" asked Constance innocently.

"You don't belong here. It is dangerous and you married a man you don't even know!"

"Well I have news for you. Rousseau and I have decided to rescue you— we are going to take you and Juan back home and buy us all a big place to live—a ranch and Juan can have. . . ."

"Stop it, you fool."

It quickly devolved into an epic argument.

Even Juan and Gracianna were speaking to each other mostly in French now, but anyone within 50 yards could now hear the two women shouting at each other in their Euskera native tongue.

"All you do is work. You are no fun Gracianna. We used to laugh and enjoy one another's company but you have changed since you moved here. This beautiful city—and you—you never have any fun. You don't like to go out—go dancing, go anywhere."

"You are throwing yourself away for just some passing fun."

That hurt a little because Constance knew it was true.

Puffing up her small frame, Gracianna said, "I am working my way to America . . . and soon." But Gracianna did not add that she was at least a year behind in her own aggressive American plan. Saving money was much harder than she had expected.

"It is not safe here!" they both yelled. Gracianna yelled about the murdered horses and the tricky Germans with their camps.

They argued about everything from years past.

That Constance was the pretty one and Gracianna was the smart one. How Gracianna had always had her nose in a book and Constance was always too interested in boys.

How they both felt abandoned.

And they yelled about money and Constance's ridiculous fur coat and Gracianna's chipped barrette.

"What about your university man?" Constance wanted to know.

"It is not all about men, Constance!" Gracianna shouted.

"Well, Juan then? What, what will you do with your Juan? He is your puppy dog and you don't even see it. He adores the ground that you walk on and you don't even know it."

Tears came to Gracianna's eyes.

Constance screamed more, ". . . but you have no room for Juan—he is the 'mountains' to you—he is 'Basque' and you are trying to be 'American'—you think he is holding you back."

"Holding me back!?" Gracianna shrieked. "Get out! You should never have come here! Get out. I do not want your gifts! Who do you think you are, prancing in here in the middle of a German occupation? And take me shopping with your husband's money? Go—with your new dress! You should not have come!"

"Well, it seems I am not good enough for you!" Constance shouted.

"And it seems I am not good enough for you!" Gracianna shouted back.

Juan and Rousseau were at the door now. They had walked together from the train station, and Constance—being so excited to see her sister—had run ahead of the men. As they neared Maison, the men had heard the yelling—and that told them everything they needed to know.

Neither sister looked at the men; their eyes locked and glared.

Constance burst into tears and huffed out. "UGH!"

Rousseau, of course, followed.

Gracianna's words bowled after her, ". . . and you leave Juan out of this! Go!!!"

Constance stopped and turned around, just far enough way, with her hands on her hips and shouted, "Good-bye 'Little American,' GOOD-BYE!" The words seared, as Gracianna peered at her with pursed lips.

"OH! She is so stupid!" she said with a sneer to Juan.

Gracianna turned on her heel without a word and marched up her stairs.

Juan was left holding some flowers, alone.

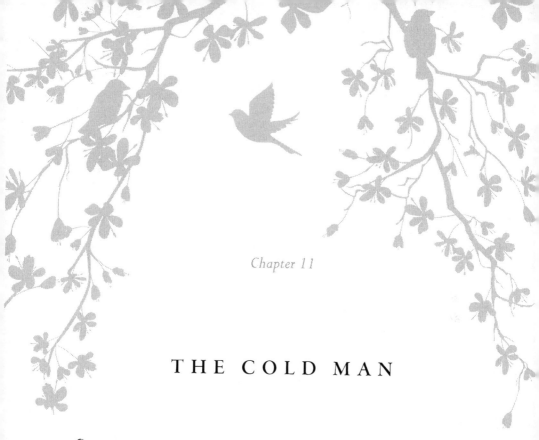

Chapter 11

THE COLD MAN

One morning, Gracianna was returning early from shopping—she always went very early now. She was grateful that some vendors Dom' had known for a long time delivered goods to Maison because, at the market and shops, there was now some difficulty with negotiating the price and quantity—regardless of the quality! Some of the keepers had been giving only small rations so that everyone could have some, and some people had been left out. Shopping, once pleasant, had become more tense and desperate. Even for Gracianna, who had shopped with them for many months to supply many things for Maison, sometimes there was no exception.

As she was nearing the café with her small grocery bag, she could not help but see a dark Mercedes staff car glide past her slowly. It looked brand new, direct from some immaculate factory in Stuttgart. And more followed, each slung sleek, long, and low with swastika flags on either side.

Gracianna could not help but slow down to watch as the first car slipped to a stop. She could see there were several officers inside.

The tall driver got out, opened the back door. The first officer emerged slowly, looked around as if to assess the field of battle, grabbed his jacket, and tugged on the front tails and then the back—hard, to straighten the one wrinkle in his perfectly pressed uniform.

That's when he saw Gracianna staring from across the street with some loaves of bread. Both of them stopped cold.

He looked right through her like an owl perusing a field mouse that gathers seeds in a predator-free field-market. Now the chance of being plucked had come. He seemed to be paying very close attention.

Gracianna knew she should look away, but she could not. And she knew that, if she insisted on looking she should at least not look at him so defiantly, but she could not look at him another way—submissive. All that was Basque blazed in her eyes. His eyes were so cold and stark. They both stared at each other each refusing to look away.

"But I *am* the owner of this café!"

The shout broke their attention.

Gracianna looked toward La Maison. Dom' was loudly complaining outside his car to German footmen who had stopped in the middle of the street, saying they were blocking the way and that he could not pass to get to his own café.

Gracianna hurried to Dom', who quit his complaining and took her by the arm with a warning look, pulling her toward the café. "You should not look that way at the officers," he whispered harshly. "I had to create a distraction. Who knows where you would be now? You are lucky I saw you."

"Your distraction was a little dangerous. You may have brought trouble for yelling at soldiers."

"It was what came to mind! Gras'. You must be careful! You must be small."

As they closed the door of Maison behind them, Gracianna looked back toward the officer, even though she knew she shouldn't.

He had not moved.

From the cars behind him, a gray-woolen sea of officers was spilling out in liquid and inky efficiency, as if they'd drilled disembarking.

Their eyes locked briefly before the officer turned away with a smirk.

The wolves live here now.

TO SERVE OR NOT

Early in the next afternoon, when Gracianna arrived there was already a meeting in progress in the kitchen between Dom' and the two main bartenders and cook. From behind the bar, Gracianna could hear them talking loudly and the discussion ended with angry voices and raised tempers.

"I will not serve them!" the chef said as he stomped out of the kitchen. He took off his apron, threw it to the floor, looked straight at Gracianna, and said, "I will not serve those dogs! I will not host them or be hospitable! Who knows what I will do instead? I will find my way!"

Storming headlong, he yanked open the door and slammed it shut behind him so hard that Gracianna flinched. The slam shook Maison. Glasses rattled and dust and crumbled plaster fell from the ceiling.

Gracianna tried to keep working, straightening, sweeping—only to realize how tense she was. Everything was happening too fast, too close. She could feel her jaw clenching and her arm muscles tightening. Her legs were heavy and did not move as freely.

Soon, Dom' emerged from the quiet kitchen with Marceau and the other bartender and miserably announced to her, "We *are* going to serve them."

Long pause. She looked at him quizzically.

"This morning, a German footman startled me in the kitchen—he came right into the kitchen! He told me, in broken French, that there will be officers here for dinner tonight, that they wanted wine and food, and would pay a fair price." Dom' looked at Gracianna gravely. "And he specifically asked for you to serve them, Gras'. He described you, in bad French, "*La petite aux cheveux blancs* [She small and white hair]."

Another chill.

"It must be the officer from yesterday?" Gracianna finally admitted. "This is my fault." She would not look at Dom'.

"And he told me it would not just be for tonight, but from now on."

It was quiet between the four of them.

"It is my choice to serve them," said Dom', "and you each must choose what you will. La Maison is all I have in this world. If I serve them, I will keep this place, keep my life, and keep much of my freedom, have a steady income, and we will not be molested, too much. You do not want to know what goes on in those prisons if you resist!"

"Is this what happened at Le Meurice Hotel?" Gracianna asked a moment later. "Is this how France became the Nazi's footstool?" Gracianna wanted to know, the familiar spark of anger burning again.

No one said anything for a long time.

"What if we poison them?" Gracianna asked quietly, "Just like we finally had to poison the rats to get rid of them."

"It would be too obvious," Dom' pointed out.

"Maybe just one here and there," Gracianna suggested. "We could coordinate with the new cook—"

"No," Dom' said. "If we serve, we do it right. We must be professional. I don't want any trouble. We do a good job, and we hope it goes fine."

Silence.

Gracianna looked at the men. "I will not run and hide. You understand that my heart, all of my instincts, rebel against the thought! I do not want to do it." To Dom', she said, "And you ask me to just serve them, and graciously? I shudder at this thought. It is difficult to see the dignity. And fighting an open battle with them, we would all be quickly killed—how I wish I could fight Hitler to the death—myself!"

Finally, Gracianna said, "I will serve them tonight and be professional, but I cannot do it permanently. Who knows what will happen tonight or what I will choose in the future?" She raised her finger at Dom', one of her two favorite people in the world, and said, "But, no matter what happens, I swear that I will not let them do harm or break our spirit. If Le Meurice can manage them—we can."

There was some mutual agreement about this statement. Then the attention shifted to Marceau and the other men who would give their decision.

One bartender simply said, "I am in, M. Dominique." The other, Marceau, an emotional bartender who had been with Dom' "always", stood up straight behind the bar from where he had been lean-listening, said, with his hand over his heart and tears in his eyes, "I will serve them too. I think they are mongrels, but I will stay to help you, Monsieur. You have been good to me and I love you and I love France."

"I must find Juan and tell him of this decision and tell him what has happened." Gracianna wanted him to hear about this decision from her and explain what she was going to do. She knew he would agree.

"We are going to serve these men and do it with dignity," she would say if he needed convincing.

So Gracianna left. Her centipede feet, tap tap tapping in handmade leather shoes—tapping on the street one after the other—fast because her gait was so small. For her, millions of steps are needed to get anywhere. She needed to get to Juan to tell him the news.

NEW JOBS

Soon, Juan had a few reference letters, including one from Mikolaus back at the ranch. They would help qualify him and were helpful in differentiating him from all the others looking for good paying work. It was Gracianna's idea. It seemed that Juan could do everything and had a certain freedom in not being too dependent on any one person or business. He was still roaming all over Paris working as a cook, as a bartender, or as handyman. Like other Basque shepherds, he was quick on his feet and friendly—and he had good hands, capable with all things mechanical. During the winters he'd had lots of time to repair things at the ranch house and was particularly good with just getting ahold of something that was broken, taking it apart, and then putting it back together—*voila!* He had even taken up weaving a local hemp-like material into rope to sell or trade at the market. His hands were wise and weathered beyond his years. Gracianna liked his strong, manly looking hands. She also appreciated his work ethic more than she let on.

Gracianna would still not let Juan in when she was working alone, late at night, scrubbing the sticky floor and listening to records. She had her pride and did not like for him to see her on her hands and knees, scrubbing. Instead, the thoughtful Juan decided to fashion a homemade scrubbing-mop for her.

She had blushed when he gave it to her, and never told him how much it helped. If the brush got used up, Juan would quietly replace it.

They both knew that he would like very much for Gracianna to be his "always" partner, and he would protect her from anything bad and give her only joy, if she wanted. Sometimes, he fantasized about what their life might be like—saving money, moving to a special place they both would love—a quieter place, but America—that part scared him a bit.

It's the unknown. But Paris is so noisy at night! And if we aren't going back home. . . .

Juan could never sleep because of the noise in the men's dormitory, especially, the drunken shouts toward the girls' dorm. Even though it was a dry dorm everyone knew that was really a joke because the landlord was an alcoholic himself. When Juan did sleep, he dreamed of owning hundreds of acres, somewhere, and running his herd on wax-shined fields of tall grass, hopefully with Gracianna.

He could accept her saying, "*No,*" for now, but who knew what might happen?

In the case where romance with Gracianna was possible, Juan looked very hard for steadier work, to show that he could be a responsible man. He also wanted to be that way for his own sake. And he was anxious to get a small room of his own or to share with one other man.

For months, for a day here and there, he would work at the Gare du Nord train station. It wasn't consistent work, mostly small repairs. But the foreman, André, liked Juan and always had him in mind for full-time work.

At the same time as Gracianna's meeting with Dom' and the staff, Juan was having a successful pair of interviews himself. He ended up with two solid jobs in the same day!

Along with now-permanent shifts at the train station, he was to manage a small apartment building for a customer of La Maison and friend of Dom's who was impressed with what Juan had done for him. The apartment's infrastructure was falling apart and needed repairs after years of neglect. The landlord was not renovating it because of loss of tenants—plus, there was a free flat for Juan!

Two real jobs *and* a place to live!

This is how things sometimes happen, Juan thought, *it is all coming together!*

Juan's new train job was as a railcar mechanic. He ended up responsible for the finicky Lafayette railcars run by the *Société nationale des chemins de fer français* (SNCF). He had already been working on them on and off and was now known as a "knuckle man," named after the "knuckles" or couplers that held the railcars together that were prone to needing constant care. He would wrestle and cajole and link and pull and jostle to get those steel horse couplers to perform the way they should. He would constantly oil and grease them to do the job they needed. Gracianna affectionately nicknamed him, "*Greasy*."

It was a funny story that had led Juan to the railway in the first place. A friend of a friend, Jean, was the driver for the Michelins—the well-known French tire family. The Michelins had been toying with the idea of adding their pneumatic tires to a train! Monsieur André Michelin, the enterprising young family leader, had the idea that railroads would be interested in a train that would give a very quiet ride, while adding tire sales for Michelin. Michelin had invented a steel flange for the wheels to keep them on the track and had been experimenting with the idea by running an old Citroën bus on a railroad track!

Juan landed his original part-time job at the station one day when Jean, the driver, was waiting for his consignment at the railway lot where he was chatting up the workers. Jean met Yves who told him that the railroad needed a skilled "knuckle man." Jean told Yves about a young man, Juan, who had been fixing Monsieur Michelin's Citroën and that he was an obvious choice. This impressed Yves and with Jean's (and implicitly Monsieur Michelin's) enthusiastic recommendation, Juan secured the well-paying position. He was unsure how long they would keep him but it was a foot in the door.

Juan now worked full time at one of the busiest and largest central train stations in all of Europe. It was cavernous and noisy and there was a lot going on. Even though the occupying command had control, there were many moving people and parts. It was often chaotic.

More often these days, a sad sight materialized. Standing listlessly out of nowhere would be hordes of shocked people waiting to be shipped to work camps the Nazis had set up. They would line up stoically and drifting between reality and inevitability. Guards were in good spirits because the station assignment was easy. Their large dormitory was nearby, many bordellos were closer, and the food was plentiful and good.

LIFE IS SPONTANEOUS

The work paid well and it was getting to feel more like real steady full-time work. And he had an apartment too? How grateful he was. This was the break he had been waiting for. He knew what to do.

He was so happy, he ran all over town searching for Gras' to tell her the good news—at Maison, he was told, "She is looking for you!" He ducked into the usual shops, the Bridge, the church. Finally, he arrived at the women's dormitory.

The Russian girl was hanging out the window with a Polish girl.

"Juan, what do you want? Gracianna is not here," the Russian girl winked at him and smiled, but Juan was oblivious to her.

"I wanted to tell Gracianna, I got a new apartment and a real job! Two!" he yelled. "I am working on the railroad and I am a manager now! Of a building with rooms to let right by the station!"

"I want, I want," he gulped hard, "to marry her!" he shouted to the world.

There was clamoring and giggling and giddiness from within and windows started flying open. Women were gushing except for one, who said, "Well, maybe you can manage an apartment, but good luck with Gracianna! She has her own way." All the girls laughed. "Don't mind her," the Russian said, uncharacteristically showing her soft side for a moment, "Ah, don't mind her, that maid is just jealous." To that all the girls boomed with laughter and 'she got you' catcalls.

Even some men across the street were clapping now as they heard the clamoring and realized the news. They were hanging out of their windows in their t-shirts with beer they had snuck into the dormitory.

Juan's takeaway from the girls' giddy reaction was that the word, "marry," no matter how loudly or softly spoken by a man, to any woman, was like a high-pitched sound to animals, they could hear it from miles away. He chuckled to himself at this grown-up insight.

Juan looked up at the well-wishers as everyone fell silent. The Russian girl disapprovingly pointed behind him. Wondering why, he turned to see Gracianna walking up. She whistled "hello" as they often did to keep their Basque roots alive. He smiled at the familiar greeting. He knew her whistle anywhere. She was happy to finally find him and said, "What's going on? What are you doing here?"

Surprised, he looked up for encouragement and there were plenty of *"go on"* motions and giggles and he blurted it out, "I got a full-time job. Two of them! *And* my own apartment!" he looked up for encouragement, the Russian, rolling her eyes at him and said, "Go on. . . ."

"Marry me!?" he finally exclaimed, to the squeals and delight of the audience above and to a muted lone clapper from across the street; one very drunk man among the lesser drunks hanging out the window. Other men were playfully making fun of him, mimicking, "Marry me," and another man imitated a blushing woman, "Who? Me? Oh, you are so romantic, Juan." The men slapped each other in a congratulatory manner as if saying, "Thank God it isn't me."

No matter the antics, Gracianna smiled and looked up at too much encouragement. "Say yes, say yes, say it Gracianna. . . ."

Is he the one? Am I betraying my dream? I love him so much and who knows what might happen. We need to go to America though. It has to be 'yes.'

She said, "Yes," with a twinge of doubt. Constance's words rang in her ears, *"You are going backward, back home, not moving forward."* And Siobhan echoed too, *"It is not safe without a man in this city."*

Gracianna was afraid. And she loved him.

Juan held out a ring. "It was my grandmother's ring."

Gracianna took it.

She wanted it now.

She smiled.

Juan teared up.

Gracianna teared and smiled, relieved.

There was thunderous applause from above.

"We need to go now," he said, pulling at her coat.

"Go where?"

"To get married silly!"

"Married!? Now!?"

"Yes," he took her hand. Gracianna laughed and smiled at the spontaneity, and she died a hundred times on the way to the civil bureau that was closing. In an unusual display of emotion Juan pleaded with his heavy Basque French accent to the brusque woman at the window, "Please Mademoiselle, allow us a license and marry us—we don't know what will happen in the future." She understood it and realized she could have a soft spot for pleading men. She *was* a civil-servant but *French* after all and romance was in her heart when she could find it. "Yes, now, I will do it. Fill this in quickly!"

"This is the happiest day of my life," he said to both women.

Juan filled in the forms for both of them. He was twenty-four and she was twenty; her birthday was in a few days.

Immediately after the simple ceremony Gracianna sort of woke up from the dream and said, "I have to go back to work right away. It is an important night." There had been so much commotion she forgot all about telling him anything about tonight's dinner service controversy.

"What? Why? Our wedding night!? We will go to dinner and have wine and. . . ."

"No. I'll tell you on the way. Let's go, quickly."

On the way back to their homes they stopped at a small café to share their happy news with a friend who worked there and accepted an espresso in celebration. It was there that Gracianna told Juan what was happening.

Juan had been living in Paris for nearly four months and now they both were speaking French nearly full time. Juan calmly sat at the bare wooden table waiting to hear what she had to say. The chair creaked because one leg had been broken, but he had fixed it for the shopkeeper weeks before. He was conscious that he could have done a better job. He was listening but simultaneously evaluating his workmanship, considering the news of the Nazi dinner service and pondering his at-risk wedding night all at once.

"The Nazis are going to begin coming to Maison for meals. Regularly. Starting tonight! It was my decision, I told Dom' I would work there and not quit like the stupid chef. He ran out saying 'I will not serve them' and he left Dom' short. . . ." He realized she was leaving something unsaid. Juan was floored, hearing all this for the first time, "A---n---d?" he said, drawing it out.

"And. . . ." she grimaced in light of their unplanned nuptial, "Dom' asked me to be there." She quickly added, "Remember the man I told you about . . . he knows me."

"What?!!!! Who? What man?"

She responded rapidly, "I said I would do it—we cannot let Dom' down. I am not afraid of them. That's it," she said sternly and abruptly.

It was done. She had made up her mind. He knew there was no changing it.

"No Gras', we could leave now. I don't want to sit by while you put yourself in danger. This is now a land of wolves and you have somehow come to their attention. It will be no good for you. For us. You can hide in my apartment, and we will figure out a plan to leave. You must be practical!"

"Please do not mention it again. I have made up my mind, Juan. Besides, it is not safe to leave—you have heard about the brutality that is happening to travelers—even the ones with much money, and we have little."

Juan looked at her in amazement. It was a wonderful remark.

He knew that in Grand-mère-like fashion Gracianna had efficiently thought of all the options to come up with the right decision.

For her that was the way to get things done.

Perfectly.

It did not occur to him that Gracianna was really *driving* the relationship. Someone needed to and no one better than Gracianna. He was in love with her, but she was stronger than he and he knew it. They never talked about what they both knew. He just went with the obvious and wondered, *why say that air is invisible?*

As they walked to Maison, he could not help but remember something Mikolaus had told him when he gave Juan his farewell wagon-ride to meet Anastasia and ask for Gracianna's hand in marriage.

"Every Basque marriage should have two elements," Mikolaus had said, his eyes sparkling. "One spouse must be a lover, and the other, a fighter. For years in our culture, this has worked well." Mikolaus had smiled broadly but had not explained further.

Now looking at Gracianna, with the fight in her eyes, Juan realized he was more of a lover. It was difficult to understand how such a relationship could work.

Gracianna looked at Juan and her blue eyes said *it* for the first time, "I love you."

He melted in understanding. Just like that, Juan understood Mikolaus' words.

They approached Maison, where Dom' was sitting at a table on the sidewalk enjoying his coffee. "While you try to save everyone, Gracianna," Juan said slowly, taking her hand even though Dom' was sitting right there, "I will try to save you. I will try to make you happy and keep you safe. I will do this. But you have to let me make you happier and let me help you more."

She half-nodded, ". . . and there is one more thing. . . ."

"What?"

"Please don't clean up tonight—it will make me too nervous. I will meet you after."

"No."

That was that.

"I will get a hotel then. We will stay together tonight. We are married!"

Surprised, at the words, "We are married," she realized it, and she smiled broadly, "Yes, yes, yes of course, my love."

"You called me my love," Juan beamed.

Dom' could hear them and was confused, "What is this talk of marriage? You two?"

Oblivious to Dom', she gathered herself and Juan said, "A hotel. The place next to our church, where the old man and woman sit on the rocking chairs outside, the hotel there . . . I did some work there. You know it. Let's go there. . . . Yes, I will be there. Late, but I will be there, wait for me."

Dom' stammered, "Wedding? There was a wedding?"

"You should see the apartment, Gras'," Juan whispered, "It needs a little work, but it will be ours." But she did not hear him as she turned her attention to Dom'.

"Apartment? Marriage? You have married haven't you?" Dom' laughed and he gathered and hugged them both, "Come here. I love you two. I am so happy for you." Sobering quickly, "Now go Gracianna, get busy. We will celebrate later."

"Remember, I will come to you Juan. See you tonight." She was happy.

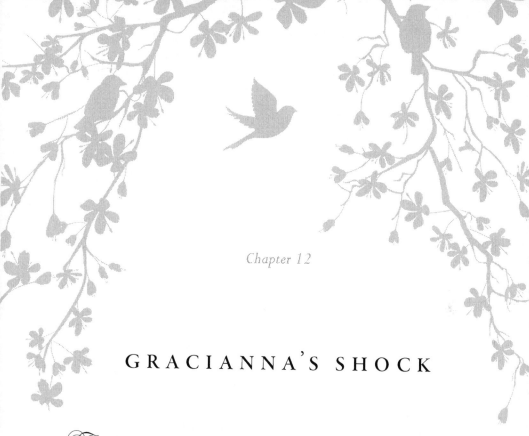

Chapter 12

GRACIANNA'S SHOCK

The Nazis arrived with efficiency at 8 p.m. sharp. Black ink had arrived in the dining room; their dark boots wrote evil words on the tiled floor as they cracked. Gracianna wondered how she would scrub the evil imprints of their footsteps off the floor.

Eyes flitted from host to host—Dom' to the bartenders, to the cooks peeking from behind a grate in the wall, and to Gracianna, who was looking at the floor. Everyone was nervous.

Through the night, the "guests" were mockingly unaware of any discomfort. To the contrary, they overextended their stay, drank nearly all the beer in the house, and then moved to wine. Finally, to the aperitifs.

On cue, they all stood up and exited as one man motioned to pay the bill.

As Gracianna took his money, they both knew he was the same man who had given her the once-over only the day before.

His eyes lingered on her face again.

She did not like the superior sentiment that exuded from him, and she looked away quickly.

Standing up, he slid a crooked smile across his face and then walked out, bumping into the doorframe on the way.

The staff smirked at that and did not dare to look at one another as he walked in front of the window, peering in to ensure no one had laughed at him behind his back. He stopped at the last windowpane, backed up, and cupped his hands on the glass and looked in, lingering on Gracianna for a long moment before disappearing into the night.

Gracianna gave Dom' the money. It was twice as much as anyone had hoped for.

"We are all getting a bonus!" Dom' whispered.

The work of war for the evening had been done as the soldiers' drink dried up. Not for lack of it—they just stopped ordering at some point and continued to speak in a haze. As orderly as possible, considering their condition, the soldiers filed out from lowest rank to highest.

Not long after, Gracianna shooed the rest of the restaurant staff out. It had been a long day and now everyone could let down from relief. She closed the door, to the last "*bonsoir*" from Marceau, the bartender, and she turned volume of the Billie Holiday music higher. They had tried to keep the volume dinnerly during the meal but as it got later, the music was turned quieter to encourage a winding down. After she was alone, she raised the volume probably louder than she should have. Then, she went to fetch some cleaning supplies from the office, bringing up a tray of clean glasses on the way. She thought it best to save a trip this way, looking for every opportunity to be efficient.

At the top of the stairs balancing her tray with some sense of pride, she placed a step stool, found the right shelf, and started to put the glasses away.

As Gracianna reached up, a striking match startled her and she jumped visibly, knocking the tray against the wall—the glasses crashed to the floor as she caught her fall from the step stool.

It was the cold-eyed officer. Somehow, he'd slipped up the stairs after everyone was marching out. Standing against the office doorway, Gracianna noted that he had appeared in her hallway as coolly as he had disappeared.

He leaned because he had to.

Shards and chunks of heavy glass had flown everywhere. His eyes were glazed. His crooked grin was ghastly. His uniform uncharacteristically askew. His jacket buttons were down with the long lapel hanging like a rag.

In that moment, Gracianna came to understand the significance of a man's weakness for a woman.

He lunged at her. For reasons that defy decency, an injustice began to unfold in the small office doorway.

In the background, Gracianna could not hear Billie singing from the Victrola downstairs any longer—the same song had been playing the last night the Latours had been in. They had swayed to the music, feeling almost American and as free as they could be.

All of me
Why not take all of me
Can't you see?
I'm no good without you
Take my lips I want to lose them
Take my arms
I'll never use them
Your good-bye left me with eyes that cry
How can I go on dear without you?
You took the part
That once was my heart
So why not take all of me?

Holiday's "back-phrasing," the technique that delays the entry of each song phrase, had no effect on delaying the actions taking place upstairs. The song's melody was loose and it offered no mercy from the soldier's rough and exacting movements.

Like the resilient melody, Gracianna struggled with the drunken onslaught as the officer grabbed at her body and woolen clothing. He was so tall!

There was a terrible fight. The drink had barely worn down his strength. Finally she managed to pull the gun from the holster at his side. There was no thought; she just pulled the trigger.

BANG!

He dumped to the floor.

Dead.

The record player, she could hear it now, it skipped, bounced, and

then skipped again, over and over, making the same sound . . . . . .
"shrumph" . . . . . . "shrumph" . . . . . . "shrumph" . . . . . . "shrumph" . . . . . .
"shrumph" . . . . . .

Out of nowhere there was a powerful but short rain burst and the rain,
rain, rain came to try to wash away the dust, the debris, the decay, and the
filth that etched itself into her without warning.

. . . . . . "shrumph" . . . . . . "shrumph" . . . . . . "shrumph" . . . . . .
"shrumph" . . . . . . "shrumph" . . . . . .

She was spent. Tired. Pale. Sweating. It was back to reality suddenly.
Done.

THE DISCOVERY

Juan was waiting at the hotel, not wanting to leave thinking she would
arrive any moment; he did not want to miss her. He had splurged and chosen the room with the fireplace.

The flowers drooped and the wine wasted.

Where is she? Maybe the rain is keeping her? He kept looking at the clock.
Unable to sit still anymore, he set out at 1:45 a.m. for La Maison.

He entered the café out of breath. He was drenched with worry as he
entered the bar downstairs; the door was open. He immediately felt ice
course down the nape of his neck.

"Gras'?"

. . . . . . "shrumph" . . . . . . "shrumph" . . . . . . "shrumph" . . . . . .
"shrumph" . . . . . . "shrumph" . . . . . .

She heard him checking in the kitchen, "Gras'?" The toilet, "Gras'?" The
back room, "Gras'?"

Juan lifted the needle on the Victrola with a scrAAAAAAAtch. . . . He
listened.

He knew then she was upstairs.

His eyes followed the railing. *Broken glass and cups have tumbled down
the stairs?* Instantly, he climbed the stairs two at a time.

"Gras'?" he said quietly.

He appeared at the door as a shadow. The dim light of the landing barely
embraced her as she sat at the desk with blood spatter on her hands and
face. Her long white hair, usually in a bun, was loose and in her face.

Juan found Gracianna collapsed in the half-dark, the gun in her hand still pointed right at the officer. Beside her, kicked away, was a man in a uniform, slumped and leaning against the thin-lipped bed. Broken glass and a broken tray surrounded them.

"Gras'!" Stopping himself from entering he reached toward her.

She would not look at him.

Juan looked at the man and cursed himself for being such a fool. He had seen the officer looking at her. He instantly felt sick with guilt. Could he have stayed or asked someone to stay? She was breathing deliberately as if she was trying to see her breath, with blood on her dress and apron, and some on her mouth.

Juan was overcome. "Are you all right?"

"Oui." She closed her wet eyes. She felt used like dishwater. She was busted up, just like her door.

Juan surveyed the shamble but did not cross the threshold. He wanted to come to her and touch her. It was obvious but he asked anyway, "What happened?"

"I shot this bastard." Her eyes flashed through her hair, looking right through him with a newfound coldness.

During the struggle neither participant knew they were not alone. The man in the painting on the horse was smoking and watching the entire time. He was smirking at the freedom of his role as "cowboy" with a bedroll behind his saddle. It meant he could go in any direction he pleased.

But the officer's foolish final act could not be seen because the light was dimmed somehow by the violent fight and it was now near pitch black in Gracianna's office. While he was in his throe, Gracianna had spotted and calmly and deliberately reached for his state-issued killing machine. Her hand roamed over the pebble-textured, black-leathered holster. She instinctively drew-pointed and pulled the hair trigger.

In the struggle for her virtue—in her own "office"—she had shot the officer with his own gun.

"Please!" she said, "Go get Dom'; he will know what to do. I am fine now. Please!"

Juan insisted on putting her on the little mattress in the office—but Gracianna's temper instantly flared. "Do not come through that door Juan," she said.

He stood there confused in the dim light from the hallway above. She refused to let go of the Luger.

Juan turned to go. "Yes, yes, yes, I will get Dom'."

As her eyes closed, she thought, *have I fallen in love with that man? This isn't the way love is supposed to happen.*

TO THE RESCUE

Juan ran into the rain and dark toward the home Dom' had mentioned. "Four kilometers southwest, about 15 Paris blocks, between the 8th and 9th arrondissement." Or, was it the 19th? He should have asked Gracianna to remind him!

Within ten minutes he knew he was lost.

But I am a herder, he thought as he collected himself. He was known for following a trail for the first time in the fall and then bringing his herd back on the same godforsaken thin trail, the same one he had only seen once. His sense of direction was keen. Calming himself for a moment and calling upon his mountain genes, he recalled every map and route of Paris that he'd ever seen in person or in a picture.

North—he ran some more. Then, there he was at *the* flat, the one with the shiny 1936 Hispano Pourtout next to the small copper-clad church between the 8th and 9th arrondissement. Dom' had told Juan that his Pourtout was like many that normally slid through the wide Parisian streets. Dom' was proudest because his car was perfectly carnauba-waxed by the North African who lived down the street. The man needed money and M. Dom' liked to feel conspicuously magnanimous because he had a "man" that took care of his car. He liked his car to flash his little success. He had affectionately nicknamed the car his "*Fierté*." It was the smallest of weaknesses, Juan thought.

M. Dom' was rousted by Juan pounding on his door. It must have been almost 2:30 in the morning.

M. Dom' was calm and resolute. He listened as Juan gulped out the words, "Gracianna. Maison. Nazi. Dead. Please come."

Dom' grabbed his jacket, while slipping on his wide pants, and he was out the door. He drove carefully but directly to La Maison. Dom' calmly said, "We will go to her and I will send you to get more help—to find a man, Fontaine. He is only ten minutes away from Maison. I will stay with her."

The stars glimmered off the hood and bounced into a jiggly lighted dance on the windshield. The fact that rain had started did not even occur to M. Dom', who was usually finicky about raindrops falling on his Fierté. His Fierté was wet and his star was in trouble, he reasoned, and he intended to fix everything.

Juan had never seen M. Dom' run anywhere. When they arrived at the café, however, Dom' ran up the creaky stairs, each foot and hand touching or pulling something at the same time, in a shoulder-rocking motion from side to side as he hurried up the stairs, rail, step, rail, step, rail, step.

The office door was open and he walked all the way in and saw what he'd expected. He had seen the officer staring at her. He instantly felt sick with guilt.

"*Çava* [Are you all right]?"

"*Oui* [Yes]."

"*Vous sûre* [Are you sure]?"

"*Oui.*"

He turned at the hips and said to Juan, "Go to Rue du Provence, 122, by the market—next to the church with the tall steeple—you know where that is?

"Yes."

"Knock boldly. Ask for M. Fontaine—he has wild gray hair in a pony-tail—and tell him only this: "Le ciel est rouge *[The sky is red]*!" He made Juan repeat the words.

"Now go!"

Juan sliced down the stairs dove into the Fierté and carefully pulled away. He drove agonizingly slow because he did not want to bring attention to himself. But he had started to cry, and the combination of streaks in his eyes and on the windshield made it all but impossible to see a street sign. Juan was turned around again. He pointed the car in the direction he knew was right and then turned right on the very next street and as if by miracle, again, he was at rue de Provence.

Back in the office, Gras' had settled. Dom' purposefully said, "Do not move," and he turned off the only light in the room. They all just waited there. Silently.

Even though the office bulb's filament was dark the witness-light was still hot. "That saved me," she nodded up at it.

The light had given her strength to reach for the gun.

Her breath had calmed. A car splashed by and she would start. Dom' put his fingers to his mouth and said, "shhhhhhhh . . ." and they both listened intently.

As they waited and waited Dom' knew what had happened to his hope of help coming quickly. He just knew Juan was too upset and lost.

But Juan was running up the three flights to 122. The door opened quickly to a large apartment of fully dressed men standing in the entry hall and beyond, like gargoyles.

Juan delivered his "red-sky" message to Fontaine. Fontaine and several men raced down the stairs and piled neatly into the Fierté. This time, Fontaine drove. Another car followed with the leftovers. During the ride, Fontaine wanted to know every detail from Juan, who was descriptive with his limited information, and Fontaine did not have to ask for more. It had been almost an eternity since Juan had left Gracianna. In another couple hours, it would be dawn. The glowing dash lit Fontaine's steeled face as they rode to within a block of Maison, where they glided to a crawl past the front of the café.

"We cannot park in front!" Fontaine whispered.

After parking in the alley, the men spilled onto the wet shiny street. It had been too long since Juan had originally left his wife. Fontaine and some of the men ran up the stairs crowding the door like birds in a mud nest, all craning to see. They pretended to be unimpressed but admired Gracianna's work with their mouths agape. A man in the back crossed himself. It was the first time he had seen a dead body. Gracianna recognized one man but not the four others.

Juan stood outside Gracianna's office. Something was odd.

They used military language Gracianna and Juan did not recognize. With German-like efficiency they unleashed a series of events she would not understand until years later.

ENTER FONTAINE

One man introduced himself to Gracianna as "Monsieur Fontaine." With a quick and slight "madame-bow" introduction, he took control. She had seen him at some news meetings at the café. He had never seemed very important—perhaps that had been intentional.

When he spoke, he e-n-u-n-c-i-a-t-e-d everything and was speaking authoritatively to all and no one. "You are in safe hands, Gracianna. We will fix all this. Now, we will deal with inquiries. Let's plant a man to say he saw an officer walking down the street going toward the train station with a prostitute at a specific time—it is very important that you tell me exactly what time this officer came to you—*THE EXACT TIME.*"

Gracianna guessed it had been 1:45 in the morning that he had returned, and he had originally left around one-thirty. She would not change her answer.

Fontaine turned to the thin French magpie wearing the purple beret and repeated the time, "Get it on the string and meet us at the river."

Gracianna understood the curious word, the "string" to mean some sort of communication network. She watched Fontaine long-look at the slumped body. He pointed to it while looking at the two burliest Frenchmen. "You know what to do. Get busy!"

"Now, mademoiselle—"

"I'm Gracianna."

"Yes, Gracianna," he smiled amused, "I need to have that gun and your bloody clothes."

She handed the Luger to Fontaine and he handed it to M. Dom', saying, "river." Dom' in turn handed it to one man at the door saying, "river," who then handed it to Juan. "River."

M. Fontaine continued, "Then get M. Le Blanc here in 15 minutes with his car and tell him we are going to the river near La Défense . . . then get M. Marchal here to clean this up," as he gestured broadly, "all of this." Let's get her home and wait . . . everyone listen to me carefully now. Gracianna," he looked at her. He was telling her and everyone at the same time, "*LISTEN TO ME VERY CAREFULLY.* This place will be filled with Nazis tomorrow looking for their officer. He left at 1:30 AM and you never saw him again. Investigators will come, but everything must be just as usual. You left at your typical time, 2:30 or so?" She nodded. "And no one at the café will know about this."

Gracianna realized by watching this precise action that there was a vast organization at work. M. Fontaine was talking about many people they did not even know. Resisters who were linked and eager to help make this go away very purposefully. Each had a specific job, and each an important one.

Juan understood that he and his new wife were both changed forever.

"M. Marchal, you clean this up. And somebody get this door fixed now!" M. Fontaine furrowed his brow exhibiting his displeasure as he looked at the broken door. "And we will have to do something about this office, a desk, the bed, all the supplies—make this room more disorderly—not the way I imagine it was, so perfect."

Gracianna stole a look at Dom'.

Fontaine paused before he turned to go and said to Gracianna, "You are a true *Française* and a hero. Now be sure to be on time to work at the same time tomorrow; avoid any car or anyone on your way tonight. Nothing changes. All of you do as I say—you *must* act as if nothing has happened. Say nothing to anyone. Do you understand?" Then turning to her, "And, I will be back to talk with you soon," he half-reached out toward Gracianna but respected the moment. "Someone give her a shirt and help her change. I want that blouse before she goes. Burn it."

He was very commanding, but Gracianna felt he was more protective than domineering, and he clearly was in control, so she nodded yes.

He said, "Now go and make sure you do not look at anyone on the way to your apartment." After she paused, he repeated, "Just go. . . ."

She regally stood up and with all eyes on her she drew herself up. When everyone turned back, Fontaine was gone.

She bent down to wipe something off the floor, but Dom' caught her and moved her along by her arm, crossing her over the door threshold toward Juan who wanted to reach out to her but could not. He said, "Let's go home."

She turned and said, "But my office—." Another man put an overcoat on her after unceremoniously removing her blouse and said, "Do not open your coat, and burn anything else with blood on it. Burn them one at a time through the night."

Gracianna wanted to walk down the stairs on her own. Juan followed, glancing back up to see Dom. His eyes were filled with tears.

Parched, Juan swallowed.

WEDDING NIGHT WALK

Juan and Gracianna had made the old walk a million times before. This time, they walked just past the dormitory to their new apartment, the one Juan had been preparing for them. He had wanted to surprise her. It was not remodeled yet but already filled with his loving touches. It would do for now.

Gracianna leaned against Juan's strong shoulders. He accepted her lean, knowing that he was usually leaning on her more. But they did not speak a word that night. For the first time he realized that now he was supporting her.

We are married now.

Cars passed them by, but they looked forward statue-like—she with pursed thin wetted lips, and he with head still but lava eyes roaming where they needed to see.

They both knew that they had to support each other when necessary.

Maybe I am not able to lift myself every time, she thought.

Up until now Juan had been excited to show the one-bedroom to her. There was no excitement now. In unison, in silence, they marched up the flights in the typical mountain way, with barely a heavy breath. Relative to most, at least.

The key slipped in the lock and the door opened to hopeful and new beginnings. Finally. Gracianna crossed the threshold and headed straight to find the bathroom. "Just leave me be," she said, shutting and locking the door.

There she stayed until dawn. Juan went out to fetch their things from the hotel including a still cold bottle of champagne and when he came back her skirt was on the bathroom door handle. He burned it. He sat. He looked out the window. He paced. He sat. He looked out the window. He had been staring at the ceiling for thirty minutes when the first ray of light peeked through the rattan shade before he finally went to the door to check on her.

"Are you okay?"

She let out an affirmative "Uh, huh." She was lying in the cast iron bathtub, which was nearly filled to the top; her teeth were chattering since the water had been freezing cold for at least an hour.

He could hear her get out. He opened the door and dutifully handed her a warmed towel that he had heated by the oven. She came out with his bathrobe on and, as if in a trance, walked to "her" bureau, opened it, looking for fresh clothes. It was empty. She turned to the bed where Juan had laid out the smallest shirt he had to replace the bloody blouse she'd left behind at Maison. She went into the bathroom to put on last-night's clothes again. She glanced at herself in the mirror while she held herself up against the sink for a moment.

When she came out, she said, "*Veux-tu des œufs avec ton café aujourd'hui mon mari* [Would you like eggs with your coffee today, husband]? It was odd because, in a moment like this, Juan would have expected her to speak to him in their native tongue. French was now her language and, he realized, *so it is mine.*

Husband. It rang in Juan's ears. The word was bittersweet. Finally his dream of them being together had come true, and now this had happened. Could they put it behind them, like Fontaine said, and just go on?

There was something between them now—*the tragedy*.

Oh, how she moved, though. Over the years, his romantic interest had grown and he knew she, too, had a spark that she revealed from time to time. For some reason, Juan was drawn to her.

We are man and wife?

Juan marveled at her effortless ballet through the kitchen. It wasn't hard to navigate around it, though; it was tiny, everything within arm's reach.

She reached for a small tin of olives.

"Can you open this?"

He reached in his pocket for his knife and pulled out their hotel room key instead. They both just looked at it—then at each other and then back at the key.

He returned the key to his pocket and fished the knife out of the other pocket and opened the can. She drained the olives, put them in a bowl and then into their tiny cooler without picking one or offering any to Juan.

He watched her on the other side of the room, as she folded the nearly frozen clothes that she had pulled in from the line outside the window—he thought it odd, but she folded them nonetheless. He wondered, *is this behavior right?*

Even though it had been unusually cold that night, after the rain the sun was streaming through the blinds, and Gracianna opened them with a clap.

"Stunning," was all she said.

Hmmm. Juan noticed that she was acting strangely—quiet, but agitated at the same time.

She is folding my nearly frozen clothes? Isn't this odd?

Yes, it will take some time for everything that happened last night to settle with her.

But how long could it take? Will we ever have our wedding night? What will tonight at the café be like? Should I wait for her at work to be close to her, no! M. Dom' and the other man said everything should be the same as before.

It doesn't matter how long it takes. I will be here for her.

It occurred to him right then that, if they wanted to, it would take about 45 minutes for them to gather their most important things and get out.

We can't run. But why fight?

THE FIRST
INVESTIGATION

She was right on time and, within minutes, they came looking. It was as if on cue and it was overwhelming, like the blackness of a locust swarm, except these men were in perfectly creased gray uniforms as they thundered in—at least 20 soldiers in the café searching. They took everyone into separate corners and outside to interrogate them.

Marceau came back from his "interview" badly bruised, but the swarm found that nobody seemed to know anything except some people close to the station neighborhood. Word had spread up and down the street that the German officer was seen last night with a prostitute walking away from Le Meurice, where he was headquartered, toward Les Halles, the large central wholesale marketplace, and toward the train station. "Let's see, I think, no, I am sure, it was 1:30 a.m.," was repeated twice. One yarn spun by a taxi driver and then another by a bartender getting off work from Le Meurice.

Just as M. Fontaine had promised, miraculously, the heat of intense interrogations and discussions and notes taken by Germans looking for their man lasted for only two days.

"*Er war ein huren liebhaber* [He was a whore lover]," one of the interrogating officers was overheard to say to the other investigator. Gracianna noticed that the officers, the young ones with few stripes, seemed to just be going through the motions. Just like that, the investigation ended.

The cover story had worked.

In the days after, Dom' hosted Fontaine and Company for more afternoon meetings, right under the Nazis' noses.

The meeting men were back, more frequently. Every few days, at different times, Gracianna watched as M. Dom' was quietly accommodating men, some of whom she did not recognize. Some had been there on the night of the shooting. They were reticent, some Basque beret-wearing men, all sitting far from the window in the darkest corner of Maison. There was no shout of "*Vive la France*" coming from the corner, no smiles, no laughter or typical diminutive arguments or banter about de Gaulle versus Vichy (de Gaulle was proclaiming himself to have more right to power than the current mantle owner, Pétain).

Gracianna crossed herself to think that this was all happening right in the shadow of Le Meurice's provisional headquarters, where staff cars dripped with pressed men and pressed flags and pressed gas pedals that whisked passed the café at all hours. Officers continued coming to the café at all hours but especially at night to drink and eat. They were none the wiser.

The only thing Gracianna could catch in one of these meetings was how unhappy these men were about Prime Minister Paul Reynaud's decision to surrender to the Nazis. Especially M. Dom'. De Gaulle had unsuccessfully opposed surrender, advocating instead that the government remove itself to North Africa and carry on the war as best it could from France's African colonies. He had "skin in the game," Dom' liked to say of de Gaulle, "because you know he was wounded twice in the First World War." He said this as if for the first time every time, and he talked of how the common Frenchman revered him for his bravery, versus Pétain whom they perceived as rolling over and kissing Hitler's ass.

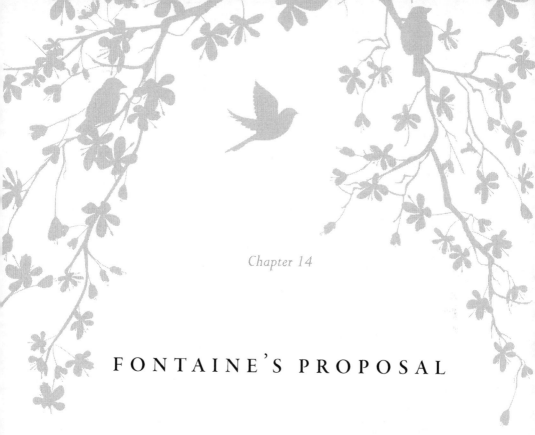

Chapter 14

FONTAINE'S PROPOSAL

*O*nce the investigation had gone ice cold, Fontaine showed up again. The café had closed early one night and M. Dom', who was uncharacteristically present at 11 p.m., twisted the sign so it read "CLOSED" as Fontaine approached. Fontaine nodded to Dom' and called to Gracianna and Juan. Juan was just arriving to join Gracianna on a small break before she started her nightly routine. Fontaine pointed to a dark corner of the café saying, "We need to talk."

Fontaine walked stiffly to the darkened back booth. Gracianna assumed it was serious because many followed—herself, Dom', Fontaine's miscellaneous corps of men, and now Juan. They all gathered around Fontaine like a meringue after its final whisk.

Gracianna was a petite woman who always stood out because her hair was nearly snow white. Her confidence was appealing. She was always in command of herself. Looking at her it would be inconceivable that she might be tied up in anything like this.

By the look on his face, though, she could see M. Dom' was neck deep. The choreographed assembly all knew the meeting's agenda it seemed, all except for Gracianna and Juan. She recognized men whom she had met from her very first day at La Maison. It seemed strange how everyone was gazing at her as they all sat crowding in or near her booth.

Looking at Gracianna, not Juan, Fontaine whisper-announced, "We are *La résistance française* [the French Underground]."

Juan looked at Gracianna. She looked straight at Fontaine and listened.

M. Dom' is more involved than I believed, Gracianna thought.

At the least, M. Dom' was a supporter and sympathizer. It was not apparent what his exact role was, but it was all coming together now—the meetings, the very short phone calls, M. Dom's connections and obvious efforts at the big cleanup. Gracianna could see it clearly now and she knew something important was going to happen.

M. Fontaine looked intensely at Gracianna and said something simple. "We want you to do it again."

Juan was confused and looked worriedly at Gracianna, then at Fontaine, and then to M. Dom'.

"What! Do what again?" Juan asked.

She understood exactly what he meant. He wanted her to kill again. Gracianna carefully studied Fontaine.

No one said anything. The group of men huddled around Gracianna and peered at her. Waiting.

Suddenly drawing on Fontaine, Juan exclaimed, "*IT?* No, not *it*! That was an accident. She won't do that again!" Turning to her, he implored, "Gras'?"

Fontaine said, "You are in it and you cannot be out. You are Basque and you are a fighter. We fight and you will fight with us. No one takes our freedom."

She just looked blankly at him. Unfazed. Gracianna knew it was idle patriotic nonsense designed to convince her, even if there was some truth to his words.

Fontaine continued, "There are high-value targets that will be around this extended neighborhood as a matter of course, and Dom' has already agreed to be the base operation. We want you to do what you did again."

A flicked dart toward him confirmed that Dom' was in agreement.

"And if you don't do this," the man called Hawkeye said, with his piercing eyes, leaning forward so she knew he meant it, "it is quite easy to leak word to the Nazis that you killed their man. We have your bloody blouse, don't forget. You and Juan would be taken to the camps. Have you heard of the camps and what goes on there?"

She knew that turning her in would never happen, that it was an empty threat. The moment the words escaped his stupid mouth, M. Dom' instantly gawped at him with disdain, as if he would slice the man in half. Dom' walked around to where the fidgety man sat and stepped on his toe.

Juan, however, fixed his eyes on the lackey. Not one to dislike or think or say ill against anyone, Hawkeye was now on Juan's "watch" list. The other men disregarded the pariah as well, and he retreated back into the group.

Fontaine instantly smoothed that mistake, salving the situation by saying, "It will be better after you do this. We will get a safe house for you and Juan and . . . if you do this well," he lowered his voice, ". . . we just need to eliminate these high-value targets—it is our assignment."

She stood there. Expressionless.

"Gracianna, look at me! You cannot imagine the outrages these men have committed against our people, our men, women, children, and even animals—I'm sure you have heard about the massacre of the cavalry, and many other bad things against refugees. You have not heard from your Jewish friend either, have you?"

Siobahn!

"Who knows what has become of her, and what these men might do if they caught her?"

Gracianna winced. He was on a roll, in full "sell" mode.

"We need you to take them out," he repeated, "they will be killed—with or without your help. You need to join us." All the men nodded.

"Of course, your safety is in our interest. We will have detailed plans for each assignment. All of these men, and more, to support you. The process is straightforward. We will be observing regulars who come to this and other cafés, then select a target and notify you. You will lure him to be alone, and then shoot the bastard."

Juan fatalistically added, "Using their own gun."

"Yes." Looking square at Gracianna's face, Fontaine said, "You can do it. You are the mouse and the lion, the bait and the hook, and you will make the call when it is time, when you have got a fish. Do not worry about the loud gunshot—we have a technician on our team to help us muffle it. You will have all the support needed."

Still, she said nothing.

Juan looked at her pleadingly.

"Gracianna," Fontaine said more softly, his eyes full of care, "this is a cause you can believe in, and you know it."

Her shoulders shrunk a little. No answer.

"And we can get you a bigger, nicer apartment close by—it would be very lovely—not like that tiny room you and Juan share." Fontaine knew no shame. "If you do this," he paused for effect before adding the jewel, "if you help us eliminate these 10 targets, I will also see your safe passage to America by Christmas—yours, and your husband's."

Gracianna shot a look at Juan again who threw up his hands, unable to overcome that ante.

"Of course, you are welcome to stay in our group for as long as you like, or head to America. You'll never have to scrub this sticky floor again."

Gracianna didn't like what he said, nor the way he had said it—the floor was not sticky, but she knew what he meant. It seemed he had found out a lot about her.

No one else said anything.

The group of men huddled around Gracianna and peered at her waiting for the mouse to choose the door with the cheese.

Gracianna stared at him, with his hundred reasons, some sound, many too personal to admit. She could feel the pressure. It was like sitting at the table with grand-mère again—the need to satisfy and the perfection expectation were always thick; Gracianna could feel the unwelcome push, push, push again. She also knew the Underground existed—she had heard her grand-mère speak of the mountain "Maquis" before. "There is always something to resist" she would say. Now, these lowlander, everyday plumbers and tobacconists and florists and lawyers—such as the ones gathered around her now—would have themselves known as 'La résistance française.' But there were many other resisters. 'Militants' were being executed in plain sight on the streets of Paris, and then hundreds, and thousands, and then eventually tens of thousands from France were imprisoned or deported to the death camps. Even everyday people were making trouble for the Germans, producing leaflets, having clandestine meetings, looking for a group to join, cutting telephone lines, even just letting air out of the tires of Nazi vehicles. Any act was better than nothing, they thought.

Gracianna was moved by Fontaine's plea, but did not give an inch.

She knew the stakes had been raised and it was maybe her, or Juan's, life or death.

With all of her four feet, eleven inches, Gracianna drew herself up to Fontaine and said quietly, "This is not my fight. I want to speak with Juan privately. We will do what we need to."

Sadly, Dom' looked at her knowing she was right, even though it was not clear what "do what we need to" meant for her.

Some of the men, taking "do what we need to" as an affirmative, mimed a celebration that she had agreed. Fontaine did not like what he heard as a rejection. Dom' knew her better and gave his assurances, "I think she will come around, but . . . I am not sure. She is stubborn."

As she and Juan left, Gracianna noticed a man fiddling with the café radio. In cooperation with the British authorities, de Gaulle and the other *Français á Londres* [French in London] broadcast two 5-minute programs, one in the morning and one in the evening. His provocations were filled with patriotic themes, including the past and future greatness of France and the value of continuing to struggle against the occupiers. Fontaine walked her toward the door and leaned toward her ear so Juan would not hear and said, "Now that you are with us I can tell you, we receive coded messages via these radio broadcasts."

She was a bit surprised by his assumption and openness but realized he was grooming her for "yes."

Then she heard the fresh-faced radio-boy ask Fontaine for permission to repeat one coded message. Fontaine nodded and the boy said, "*Les langoustines sont fraîches* [The prawns are fresh]." She had no idea what it meant.

She flashed Hawkeye a defiant look.

Distrust is a good instinct, Fontaine thought as he smiled to himself.

Dom' and Fontaine stood side by side as a show of expectation and solidarity as Gracianna said, "Juan and I will speak about it." They walked out.

"This will be harder for him, and on him, than on her . . ." Dom' trailed. "I'm not sure this is a good idea . . ."

Fontaine cut Dom' off, "We need her to do this. If she decides not to do it, we will put you in a skirt."

Dom' looked at him, surprised, not knowing the lengths Fontaine might go, but passed off his remark as dark humor.

The meeting went on in the shadow of the occupation headquarters for two more hours with some newfound gusto. Fontaine wanted his men to focus on what needed to be done and he allowed them to think that Gracianna's "do what we need to" comment was an indication that she was in.

There were smiles and smirks in the meeting as men glanced at one another in defiance—of the Germans down the street, of those in each Parisian whorehouse and at every checkpoint—indeed, even in defiance of Hitler himself. "We will show him" was on their faces, and they meant it.

Fontaine thought, *she'll do it.*

A SMALL BREAK

An unusual light rain caused Juan to shiver as goose bumps crossed his shoulders. He felt the same way as when he received a premonition or felt a spirit walk across his path: a shiver up his neck and back down again, electric and static.

Gracianna's strength was in always pressing forward, and his strength was to be her rock to press forward too. It did nothing to talk about it. As they walked home, the enormity of the insignificance of words dawned on Juan. For what could talk do, when they were only words? They would be just little words that would roll around in their mouths, a casserole of unimportant syllables to describe or complain or recount the Last Supper of events.

They did not need words between them. Besides, her curfew-lean told him everything he needed to know. Sometimes they had to dodge occupiers standing watch on street corners or driving, swerving down streets faster than needed. She would lean in and he held steady. The warmth and connection was familiar.

Juan knew about communication without words. He was Basque and the Basque were shepherds, experts at loneliness, whistle chats, and hand gestures on lonely high mountain meadows. The rub of her fabric against his fabric, the feel of her tiny, work-worn hand and her sort of miniature kaleidoscope-squeeze when they stepped off the curb or over a pothole let him know everything she was feeling. *I trust you, I know you and you know me. We are alive and we are in the right and I need you and I love you. I need you, don't leave me, don't talk to me about anything, just be here for me—for us. We are fine and we will be fine and I love you I love I love you I love you I love you I love you, Juan.*

Chapter 15

HORROR NIGHT

After the argument with Gracianna, Constance was more agitated and felt that maybe Gracianna was right.

Maybe I am taking advantage of Rousseau. What am I doing here? There is a war and maybe everything Gracianna said is true.

Constance decided to tell Rousseau that night—that their marriage was wrong—but he had insisted on taking her shopping that afternoon and she thought —well one more outfit couldn't hurt.

They began to argue in the department store. "What Gracianna said about you was not true," he said, sensing Constance's turn of heart toward him. But Constance knew her love was not true, and she realized that, although this was not the right place, it was the right moment to tell him.

"I have to go away now—back home. We can't do this anymore."

"What do you mean, home?"

"I'm leaving. This isn't going to work, Rousseau. You are a good man. I don't deserve all this, your love. . . . I am taking advantage of you."

"No!"

She knew what she had to say to get through to him, "It is true what she said, that I married you for your money."

It hurt him. She knew it would.

It hurt her to tell the truth.

He raised his voice, she raised her voice right in the middle of the store, where everyone could see and hear. The shopkeeper came to intervene and saw Constance put something in her pocket.

Just then two German soldiers shopping in another part of the store were also attracted by the ruckus. Both off duty, looking through lingerie—possibly for someone at home but likely for a new Parisian girlfriend—they just could not look away. The louder the words got, the more interested the soldiers became. The one, smoking, threw his butt to the ground and the other knew that meant there was going to be trouble.

Now Rousseau and Constance were full on arguing, the storekeeper was asking what was in Constance's pocket, thinking she had hidden something that belonged to the store, and now there were two soldiers there. One officer inquired in German and then in badly pronounced French, "*Problème?*"

Constance sneered at him, "*Ça ne vous concerne pas* [This is none of your business]!"

"But everything is our business," the other French-speaking soldier insisted, taking more of an interest in her.

The shopkeeper began to appeal to the soldier while pointing to her pocket as more angry words were spoken louder and louder. Under her breath, Constance said toward the German-speaking soldier, "Horse murderer," in French. And the shopkeeper reached toward Constance's pocket, shouting, "Shoplifter, shoplifter." Rousseau stretched over to slap him away even though both soldiers drew their weapons behind the shopkeeper. He kept at Constance's pocket and Rousseau, even knowing the soldiers had drawn, pushed the shopkeeper away anyway.

Rousseau's move was perceived as an act of defiance of their authority and one soldier said something about it. Rousseau pushed the shopkeeper again as he was trying to get to Constance, who was crying. Rousseau was only protecting her, but the shopkeeper nipped at both of them. Now the soldiers felt disrespected. With no apprehension one soldier raised his gun, aimed it at Rousseau and pulled the trigger.

The other German soldier, shocked, rushed to help Rousseau. He made the soldier who had shot him drag Rousseau to the street for help.

The shopkeeper ran.

Constance was trying to go with Rousseau, but the shooter held her back.

The shooter reached into her pocket and pulled out a small wallet that was obviously hers. It had her picture in it.

"You idiot. It was my wallet!"

Realizing he had made a fatal mistake, he was angry. He quickly turned to the closest sales shelf and picked up a scarf and put it in his pocket.

Constance was screaming, "What are you doing? You pig!"

He slapped her and she punched him back.

He pushed her to the floor and she was up and on him.

He knocked her down and was now pulling her by her jacket.

Something sharp like a red-hot poker entered Constance's side.

It felt like being hit by a car. She heard him say, "I am going to send you away, and I will see you back on the shelf of this fine store as a bar of soap." She had not heard the rumors that Nazis were making soap out of human bodies.

Constance was on the floor and the ceiling was a blur of swimming lights. Pain and tears clouded her vision. She could not catch her breath. Constance panicked and felt she was drowning on dry land.

She was terrified.

He picked her up like a rag doll as the nightmare continued.

She heard him asking something of the shopkeeper, but no one else was close by. Some shoppers had gathered on the other side of the store and were watching. The soldier picked her up and she was on his hip, flailing and gasping for breath.

She could think the words but they would not come out, *Rousseau! Rousseau? Why is this happening? Doesn't this pig know I am Catholic? I'm Basque? Rich? I'm with you, Rousseau!*

Constance realized a prediction had come true. "That mouth will get you in serious trouble someday young lady," her grandmother would say. This was serious trouble. Exactly the way her grandmother had said. Constance knew she was not very smart, and this time she was positive her looks were not going to help her. It then crossed her mind they would hurt her.

I'm in trouble and there is nothing anyone can do. No one knows where I am. Rousseau, is, is he dead? Oh God . . . help me.

She passed out.

Paris by now had spun out of control and the Germans were putting a tighter grip on her. Everyday Parisians were aghast that their way of life was being changed, pushed, pulled, frayed, undone—it was unthinkable that their world had shattered so fast.

When Constance woke up on the floor of the department store, she heard a surreal conversation accusing her of stealing something. The shopkeeper was making his case to have her prosecuted. Constance realized she had been rammed with a nightstick or something blunt that had been pushed so forcefully and deeply into her side that her wind had been nearly impossible to catch. She could hear herself gurgling as she tried to catch her breath. The shallowness of her breath led her to believe that she would die right there on the floor of a filthy department store with a lying shopkeeper and this filthy Nazi soldier dog-smiling over her.

"This was in her pocket. Yours?" was all the soldier said, as he produced the scarf from his pocket.

"Yes! I knew it," leered the vindicated proprietor. He looked at Constance ashamedly.

As the officer was taking details for his report he said, "I will take her but first I must interview her—where is there privacy?" The soldier was not distracted by another shopper, a Good Samaritan who knelt in front of Constance and said, "Your rib is broken. Get it wrapped soon and keep your head down. I fear for your life. I wish I could help more—whom can I contact?"

Constance, with every effort, looked up, blurry-teary eyed and was able to say, "Gracianna . . . Maison Cossette . . . Pont Neuf . . . sister . . . Gracianna. Maison."

Constance was dragged down the stairs by her hair, coming in and out of consciousness each stair step. Her back cracked, cracked, cracked as she went down, face up, headfirst. It took her mind off the chortling blood in her lungs and her lack of breath.

Her searing side beat was replaced with being rip-stripped and invaded by the man and anything else nearby. She was taken every way.

On her knees she looked down at the wooden floor, and with clarity she had never known, she could see a mixture of blood and sweat that was dripping off her nose. She could see her dignity puddling beneath her. Just above her one clear eye, she felt a vein in her forehead that was beading sweat. She knew she was sweating blood.

She could see the grain of the mahogany wood in the floor, with dust specs and dirt particles from years of being mashed into the wood. There had been a flood—she could see. A watermark was left years ago about six inches off the floor, uneven but with a dark line that represented the left-behind of a watery accident or storm. Constance smelled the mustiness of the basement as her nostrils flared from defiance for a moment. She could hear the heels click clack above her, click clack click clack click clack click, resuming business, click clack business, click clack click clack business being conducted above her. The register ringing, heels clicking, and laughter, and polite "*mercis*" and then heels clicking and clacking out the front door.

When she woke up it was done. How much time had gone? She awoke because she could feel her head, clonk, clock, clonk, clock, clonk, clock, clonking against each tread as she was dragged back up the stairs by one leg as her head and face graced each step.

Juan heard the news around noon the next day from someone at La Maison. A bartender from Rousseau's bar had called to tell Dom'. Rousseau had been shot. Juan said he would go to the hospital as Dom' got off the phone.

"Here take the Fierté."

Gracianna was at the market and nowhere to be found. By the time Juan got there, the news was grim. Rousseau, who had been hospitalized the evening before was not expected to last the night.

All Juan could think to ask the hospital was, "But what of Constance?" No one knew anything.

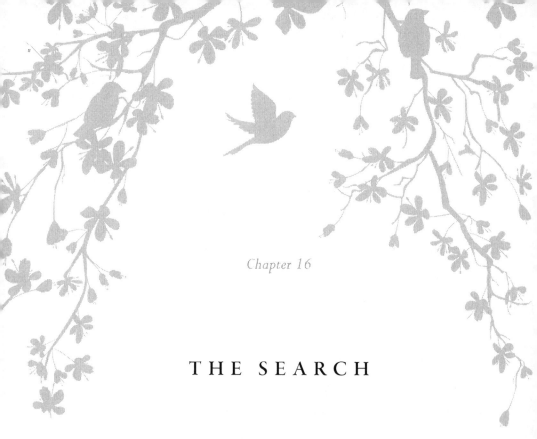

Chapter 16

THE SEARCH

$\mathcal{C}$onstance woke up again, a beaten prizefighter, on the floor of a Parisian jail cell with a warm, calm, kind blue-eyed woman attending to her as best she could. The comfort was worthless and Constance could not be blamed for not appreciating it.

This nightmare is real entered her swollen brain.

Her clothes had been tied back together, barely concealing her womanliness. Dried blood had run down her legs. The soldier who had framed her for theft the day before arrived at the jail during the late afternoon, after the morning shift was leaving. There were long shadows in the room. No one else was in the cell except for the woman attending to Constance when the soldier exposed himself to both of them and leered at the other woman. Constance did not recognize him through her swollen eyes but she could smell him. She knew she would never forget that cologne. It was rancid and overbearing like the old pastor from church when she was a child. It wafted into her nostrils and settled like fog that seeps into the lowest levels.

She vomited as he stood there wagging himself at the two women.

He grimaced and tidied himself and waddled away thinking how impolite she was.

It was afternoon before Gracianna got to Maison to find a waiting man. Everyone crowded around the Samaritan, "She told me to find you, your sister. They shot her husband. She was taken by the Nazis. They had beaten her. She had a broken rib. I am sure of it." He had no other details.

"But she was alive," she said it not asking. He nodded. That was all she needed to know.

And that was it.

Gracianna's insides were on fire and she was angry and afraid, but she instantly went to work to right the wrong. Without saying she was leaving the bar, she was away into the evening. Bread crumbs were left on the floor. Tiny splatters of wine dried in their spot. Forks were left across platters and knives touched them coldly. Lipstick and soup lip prints covered cloth napkins cloistered on tables. Other foodstuff congealed on chairs, seats, and tile for another time. Her work was no matter. She knew just what to do and her heart activated her feet to instant action.

"Where is she going?" asked one bartender.

"She is going to fix things. Better get Juan," said Marceau.

Gracianna had her own network, including the cleaning ladies. They often went to church together and had access to information. Some of them were sweet on German officers. Some just received gifts in return for favors and some were in actual relationships. Yet they always knew that, if someone had a need, they would do what they could to help, "relationship" or not. The cleaners knew they could get fired, beaten, or disappear for snooping through documents or passing along information. But they were generally in offices alone at night with free and ready access to information gathered from the communication rooms that ran 24 hours a day.

"I need to know everything about Constance's whereabouts and how she is, anything. . . ." Gracianna pleaded with two women she could trust.

In her favor, Nazis were efficient in their processing of all information—writing reports and ink-stamping everything, twice or more.

Gracianna fought for information for two days. "Please. Constance? Anything?"

She had not been to work.

She asked anyone and everyone she could trust to please help, to look further, and take any chance possible. Dom' was helping, of course. She knew Fontaine was helping. As a reward for information, she offered her cameo with dainty-chiseled Biedermeier relief flowers, the one that her grandmother had given her. No one would have taken it.

Juan tried his hardest at the train station, poring through many lists of passengers and getting his hands on any information about what was going out and coming into the main station. Everyone liked him after all, so getting ahold of bills of lading and passenger lists was pretty easy. The occupiers had not yet realized the strategic value of the information so they had not locked it down. There were plenty of supply lists as well. The human manifests were surprisingly openly available. But none of the lists named Constance.

Gracianna finally had to go to Fontaine and plead for more help. He agreed to do some looking.

Two days later Fontaine arrived at La Maison in the evening. He signaled her to the back.

"Voilà! Constance has been found!"

She shouted, "Alive?"

"Yes, she is in the jail system!"

"No!"

"And she is set to be sent away!"

"No!"

Sadly, "To Auschwitz," he trailed the "z."

"No—Auschwitz? Why?"

Hesitating, he said, "Constance is considered a criminal!?"

"No!"

Adding bleakly, "She will be there for hard labor."

"No!"

"Tomorrow. She is sent tomorrow, Gracianna. I am sorry. There is nothing we can do."

Instant tears formed in Gracianna's eyes, just like when she left home the first time, knowing she would never see her grandmother or the Pyrenees again. It came from the punch of unconditional love. Fontaine did not know what to say.

"But Constance is my very own flesh and blood," she said as she wept.

Constance was never far away from Gracianna's thoughts. Like the ironic Oktoberfest spoon in her sugar bowl that was given to her by her sister, a framed letter, the ribbon that hung from her bureau, all gifts from Constance. Constance was everywhere. Gracianna realized that this would be what it was like when someone close to her died.

She will not die if I can help it, Gracianna promised herself.

Juan promised to watch for Constance in days to come. He knew it was useless to try something stupid like breaking her out. Everyone knew she would be shipped right away to the camp. He had real access to the boarding area—not the holding area—so he had a good chance to see Constance. If he did, it would only be momentary. There was a very small chance he would be able to give Constance a letter or something. There was no way to save her, to keep her away from the wolves. Juan realized, having watched the Germans herding the prisoners, that there were too many rifles to try to save the lamb this time.

Then, like a dream, there it was. Constance's name was on a filched manifest. The man who passed it to Juan could have been shot. Juan smuggled a copy of the list home to his wife. With her own eyes Gracianna looked at the list written in some Nazi's hand: Constance Rousseau Arrayet, Criminal/Sympathizer, Le Marais, Paris, Basque; To: Auschwitz—Birkenau.

She was furious. Rousseau had been killed. Something, whatever it was that was left, broke in Gracianna.

This tragedy is my fault.

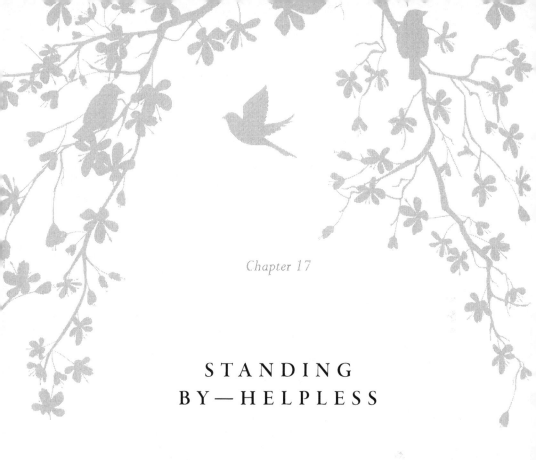

Chapter 17

STANDING
BY—HELPLESS

$\mathcal{C}$onstance arrived the next day at the station on a sunny afternoon. The departure time was on the manifest so Juan tried to catch a glimpse of Constance knowing they were supposed to load her in a car. He could only stand there as they shoved her on the train with the rest of "the criminals."

There she was. He was sickened.

He tried to make himself obvious to her without being obvious to anyone else. He had a letter for her. She was a zombie. Walking dead like the others. He could never tell Gracianna how badly she had been beaten. It was haunting. Just like that, Constance was going to be "*s'en va* [going away]," the term used for the many who were sent to the camps. It was always said stoically and meant death was inevitable—but only after starvation, gang rape, beatings, medical experimentation, gassing, strangulation, and a host of other bestial punishment.

Only the day before, one of Juan's coworkers, a Frenchman named Didier Simon, a trainmaster, had refused a German soldier's demand to force twelve more women into a railcar that was already overflowing with life. He was executed on the spot. The twelve were foisted anyway upon the humanity already humiliated. It was happening more and more now, visible acts of cruelty, some that had been ordered—no matter how brutal or inhumane. Occasionally, there were apparent willful insubordinations and open resistance by more and more railway workers. They were being killed for it. Some took their lunchboxes to work in the morning, but did not come home that night.

LOADED

Constance faded in an out of consciousness, coming to this time to the sound of wailing on the train.

The wail hurtled Constance to when she was 8 years old. She and Gracianna had been running in the hills and were stopped cold by the same sound. The girls ran toward the dark forest on the rim of the field toward the home of the neighbor Auguste Etchebarren.

"Etch'," as he was known, was a handsome man with a pretty wife and young children. As they came closer, they could hear the noise and saw that it was coming from a small building where the Mister would hang lambs to age after butchering.

Gracianna peered through the clapboard walls of the hang-shack as Constance just watched a butterfly fly by. Etch' had his wife spread out on the table and there was an unmistakable rhythm between their bodies. Mrs. Etchebarren looked like she was dream-sleep-smiling. They both had their eyes closed most of the time, then there was a wail.

"I wonder why they are in the lamb shed?" whispered Constance.

"They have to be in the lamb shed silly! She is so loud that they would wake the children if they played like that in the house!" and the girls laughed and Constance buried her face in her already long-fingered hands.

Constance faded back into reality, found her face once again—this time in bloody hands.

She did not know how many hours she had spent on the train. No food or water had been offered. She saw shock, loss, fear, hatred, and disgust in the eyes of the other few wretched people who made eye contact with her.

How could I be here? It was in every face. She knew and they knew, they would all die soon.

I am here and it was then and there that she resolved to make the very best of it and promised herself that she would do anything to stay alive, no matter what it took.

Constance knew they would all die, someday or soon, but if she could eke out two, three, four, or five more minutes of life . . . she would not dream in hours or days or, oh!, longer. Minutes must be her focus at the moment. This was going to be a fight—she knew it—but she had her grand-mère's spirit in her, despite not paying attention, not listening, and not minding her wishes in the past. It was bitter to realize that her grandmother had prepared Constance for life, and eventually death, at a concentration camp. She had already seen what she considered to be the war of her childhood. *Do I have to pass this long test all over again?*

She knew that, in order to live, all rules and conventions were out the window.

Clunk . . . clunk . . . clunk. The train. It sounded just like the train to the countryside she had taken so recently with her husband.

Rousseau! Oh Rousseau!

Constance wanted to see her husband again and feel his French arms holding her tight. She would eat glass if she could feel them around her just one more time. She would confess her thoughts. She would forsake any pleasure in life forever but to feel this one thing for one minute. She would even call upon the devil himself to offer her soul if that is what it would take to see Rousseau again. As a child, Constance had heard a monsignor talk of making a deal with the devil in church one time, quite by accident, and had been afraid of the thought.

Now, she welcomed it. She mouthed a forsaken prayer to herself.

GRACIANNA'S NEXT STEP

The dark days of Paris were like watching a colorful bunch of flowers die fast. Paris was being swallowed.

Thank goodness Siobhan was smart and had left.

On the bridge in dark Paris, Gracianna scratched her shoe on the ground and burst into tears thinking about her sister, blaming herself for everything. She was angry for not making Constance leave when she knew she should have.

All around her Parisians were disappearing. Jews were being rounded up. Criminals congregated. Ne'er-do-well's gathered. Homosexuals violated. Suspected sympathizers rooted out by the Gestapo. They were ruthlessly proficient. One Parisian lady who had been talking to Dom' outside the café said, "They busted the door down in the middle of the night." Everyone knew they would take whomever they targeted, bitch-slapping the women, often dislodging their eyeballs or worse. But it was the "or worse" stories that were ferried between Parisian women.

They would talk at coffee and whisper in passing and tell about Madame and Monsieur "So and so," who were targeted in the neighborhood last night. "They took him and they left her for dead after they took everything," they'd say. "All of them would take their turn with her in front of the children and in front of him, laughing, drunk," they would say.

Then they would just be gone. But Gracianna's own sister?

She knew what she must do. She decided right there on the bridge that nothing else mattered.

I must fight.

Now her only fear—that the Gestapo would somehow stop her from fighting for Fontaine and for France and for Constance. Now, the war was personal.

Gracianna heard the stories. She saw the victims on the street. Just last week, one of the girls Gracianna knew from the early dormitory days had been viciously beaten because she was an Armenian and a religious Chasid.

She also knew that Juan knew more than he would tell her. His eyes looked troubled. Nazis! Look what they were doing to the people she loved! It was clear he didn't approve of her going to the Underground. Gracianna convinced herself, he would tolerate her doing so for a little while. He must understand.

Because she could not get Constance out of her thoughts, she would do what she could against the Germans until her heart spoke otherwise. It all sickened Gracianna but bolstered and battened her resolve. She had told Fontaine that she would "talk to Juan" about his demand but Juan knew that was not true. She was going to decide on her own. Now.

Auschwitz. Fontaine. Juan. Gestapo. Constance. Auschwitz. Fontaine. Gestapo. Constance, Constance, Constance!

She surrendered to the fact that going to Fontaine was right—for now.

Thirty minutes later Gracianna found Fontaine briefing Dom' at Maison in the late afternoon. They were talking about the details of an upcoming operation but Dominique kept interrupting, always wanted to do more. He offered more of himself, his home, his little money, and his beloved car.

Fontaine waved him off. "You are doing enough, *mon ami*."

Bolstering himself, Fontaine turned to Gracianna, expecting her answer. "So, you are with us?"

"*Oui*. I am with you," she said and walked away quickly.

Fontaine asked Dom', "Now, do you think you will be doing enough, *mon ami*? You have given your place, your girl, and your life; just hold everything together for a bit longer. We will be moving the operation back and forth—from La Maison and to other venues, to keep it cool here."

Fontaine reassured Dom', who was looking even more concerned. Somberly, Fontaine said to his friend, "I know she is very special to you. La Résistance will take good care of her. I will watch over her. Don't worry."

Then Fontaine broke into a wide grin, rare for the serious Frenchman with the weight of Parisian operations on his shoulder. "What are we talking about *mon ami*? Maybe we should let her take care of us! She is tougher than you and me together, that is for sure," as he slapped Dom' on the back.

And both men laughed as they moved to leave the café. Dom' peeked into the kitchen as he left and asked Gracianna simply, "Are you all right?"

"Of course, I am fine."

She stood there alone and that was that.

"You are doing right, *ma fille, merci* [my girl, thank you]."

That was when Fontaine poked his head in and told Gracianna, "There is an operation shortly. You will get the details. Do as you are told. You will make us proud."

A SLICE OF MARRIED LIFE

During this confusing "cooling" time, Juan found himself reflecting on his newfound married life.

Even though they had never spoken of that night, he enjoyed watching his wife in the apartment whenever they got a chance to be together. Their schedules were nearly opposite. He didn't let his surveys of her be too obvious because he was afraid it would only make her self-conscious. He stole a look now and then. They slept in the same bed, well, he in it but she *on* it—or at least always a blanket between them. He would brush his teeth and get in bed first and then she would turn off the light, change in the tiny bathroom and then slip in the room and *onto* the bed in complete darkness.

Both just there. He could hear her breathe. She could hear him.

She always opened the blinds in the mornings. "Stunning," she would say when she saw the burst of sunlight.

Juan helped her move her things slowly from the dorms, a piece here and there. The dorm girls were oblivious to what she was experiencing and just wanted to talk about her new marriage and catch up on gossip, when they saw her. Gracianna always put everything in the best light. She'd smile and bite her always wetted lips.

He only insisted that she not walk home alone and, for now, she found this acceptable. So, they sat at the small table in their little apartment with big windows, watched the sun break over the nearby buildings, and accepted the slow pace of their unconsummated relationship.

THE SOUND OF GUNFIRE

Gunfire was often heard in the night in Paris. Because the apartments were so tall with so many artifices and reflective surfaces, the reverberation of gunfire could easily be masked, *if* you knew what you were doing.

One of the assigned Résistance team members was a professor and sound scientist who specialized in signal processing and signal response. His expertise was used in French military communications like radio and telephonic consulting. He wanted to serve La Résistance.

"*Le Professeur's*" hair was wavy and wild. His glasses sat on the tip of his nose. He appeared rumpled, exactly what you would expect. He was in a world of his own thoughts, with sound waves reverberating in his own head. He was summoned only once to "place" or prepare each room for killing. He would meticulously inspect the room where Gracianna was going to do her business. They had thought of everything, providing boxes filled with blankets and linens and other material that absorbed the sound of gunfire.

"*Non, là, plus à droite* [No, there, more to the right]."

To the eye—it would look like junk and just old storage boxes filled with innocuous stuff.

The principle was simple. He would say that sound absorption is "just an energy conversion process." The details were more complex—he would go on and on about how the kinetic energy of the sound is converted to heat energy.

"... *à la chaleur, à la chaleur* [to heat, to heat]," he would say over and over as if he could not believe it himself. Then, when the sound waves come in contact with the softness of an absorptive surface, "... *ils disparaissent, ils disparaissent* [they disappear, they disappear]!"

Just about this time, the room helpers would dream of other sounds they preferred, rather than his bouncy descriptions of sound wave reflexology—sounds of "*La Môme Piaf* [The Waif Sparrow]," or of a wine bottle being uncorked.

The Professor would apologize for his need to teach, shaking his head.

"I can't be in class during war time."

Gracianna could tell that he was heartbroken. This made him find every chance to teach. She listened with great care.

Finally—the test.

They closed the door, and Gracianna stood outside with the Professor and some others as one man inside her room fired a gunshot. The sound should have been piercing, jolting. But it had nearly disappeared after coming into contact with the Professor's well-placed and stacked-high-and-low blankets and boxes.

Many times, dogs bark at gunshots in the night, but a loud "pop"—even right across the street—might sound like an industrial "drop" or possibly as if it was coming from blocks or miles away, if properly masked.

The sound everyone mostly heard was that of the city alley cats fighting or mating in the night. A shroud had darkened Parisians' spirit. No one wanted any sound but the sound of an expelled German invasion. The occupation reality had sunk in now, and the Parisians' plan to expel the marauders had waned in a blanket of stifling humidity. The heated cover of stickiness, mixed with slack air, was converted into a dirty nail-grime feeling under every collar. The collective despair of Paris emasculated the desire to act against the Germans. It did not, however, deter destiny.

Chapter 18

SENTENCED

$\mathcal{B}$roken glass covered the floor of Constance's boxcar. The sun made the glass glittery through the winter-worn wooden walls. They reminded her of the clapboards of the Etchebarrens' lamb hang-shack.

The scattered glass was speckled and sprinkled at the feet of those standing, but it had cut her knees, drawing rivulets of blood.

The train slowed.

Screeeeeeeeeeeeeeeeeech.

Constance was on the ground and she either had to put her face against the urine-drenched trousers of a man she could not see or in the feces laden path of a child's dress.

Welcome to Auschwitz, Constance thought sardonically.

As the train growled to a crawl, gasps filled the car as people moved to one side to see what was happening. The pungent air was more apparent once body movement caused the stark stillness to swirl.

Please, I want the train to keep moving. As long as we are moving nothing worse could happen, except. . . .

The moment she heard voices in German, she knew it was the Devil all over again.

The car clunked to a stop, hitting the rail car ahead. Now she heard harsh commands and mayhem. The railcar doors opened and there was a rush for fresh air and the puddles in the road! Constance wished she had the strength to bend down and drink like the cattle that had once filled these cars.

Yet, Constance was able to fall off the car and lower herself to the muddy water. She felt someone pick her up by her hair, stand her upright, and shove her toward a line of people.

She was made to stand in the lineup while a "doctor" looked each person over and instantly assessed what line of labor he or she would join. Another soldier quizzed each person about his or her work skills. If you were a woman, "What skill?" If she was very attractive she was sent immediately to the camp whorehouse. If a man, and able, he went to the hard labor work pile. If you were a very strong and unattractive woman, you joined the men in hard labor. If a man and weak, you went "missing." The woman in front of Constance said, "Seamstress," and the interviewer pointed her in the standard direction.

Constance could not look him in the eye. "Chef," she announced with as much authority as she could muster through a wheeze from her broken ribs.

The man looked at Constance and said, "Chef? Preposterous!" The soldier looked at the "whore line" first since Constance had a nice figure, but it was longer than usual and he decided they needed a chef more than another whore.

Constance had learned early to be watchful. She had seen others who said, "Cook," and they were sent to one group. The private looked at "Chef Constance," then at another soldier, and pushed her toward him. "Chef," was all he said and nodded toward some buildings in the distance. Constance barely managed to get in the car in which he took her away to a building not far from the train drop.

They stopped after a bumpy ride, where they had driven past prisoners who seemed well dressed and who were walking two abreast, trance-like. He mechanically helped her out of the car and took her to the door that opened into a bright kitchen where several women were preparing food. He said something to them and they caught her as she was dropped to the floor.

Constance knew she was in a kitchen area. It was one of twelve kitchens at Auschwitz. She knew she had been saved for the moment and this was her first smile. "Chef," was the word she said aloud to the two who had rushed to her, not that she could see them very well. Luck was now a big part of her life, Constance realized, and she was determined to play her luck card. Kind arms were all she could feel.

Thank you. Thank you, so much.

ANJA, ANGEL

A thin woman, certainly Eastern European by her features and speech, was assigned to Constance. She took her to the kitchen pantry and laid her on some potato sacks. "There, stay there." She was Polish, Constance decided, judging from her accent.

She woke to the woman cleaning her face with a wet cloth. Constance's entire body was on fire.

The sun was streaming through the Pole's chestnut hair; her motherly eyes spoke to Constance and reminded her of the angel who had helped her in the jail in Paris. Constance did not know her name, for she was semi-conscious most of the time, but Constance finally managed, "*Nom* [Name]?"

"I am Anja." She sounded it out, "On'ya."

"Angel," Constance murmured with a tear, but her face hurt when she smiled. Something about the woman made her think of her sister. She moaned. *Oh, Gracianna. I should not have come. . . .*

Constance closed her eyes and gave herself to Anja, but she could not help but cry out with pain. "Shhhhhh . . . I will help you. We can keep you here until you are better—in a few days we will have you join us in the kitchen and work. You will be all right," she said as she lifted Constance's skirt to wipe her clean. While Constance was falling asleep, worry crossed Anja's face. When Anja saw Constance was waking, she came to attention. "You," she said, "you must eat something small, now."

Constance did not know how she could feel lucky in a place like this, with all that had happened, but that is what she felt as she ate her soup with the few carrots in it.

"Anja," said Constance, "*Merci.*"

In the morning, there was rattling in the kitchen—and the sound of birds. It was pots and pans banging, and voices of women speaking Polish and Russian, perhaps Romanian.

Anja was in the doorway and said, "We are cooking a special meal for the camp commander today, so I'll be in the kitchen all day. I will check in now and then." Anja gave Constance more of the broth she had been given the day before—it was chicken stock with small carrots and onions. It was light but full of just what Constance needed. *Love.*

The next day, she tried some bread, too, even though one of her incisors was sharply chipped. She remembered being dragged down—or was it up?—the stairs. . . .

"Try this."

"*Merci.*"

"Shhhhhh. . . ."

The kitchen was louder and then got quiet.

Constance listened.

Hush.

Their German supervisor, a slight man with round glasses and tiny eyes, had entered the kitchen and Anja, recognizing his voice, dropped Constance. Instantly, the light was turned off and the door to storage closed in the same move behind her. Outside, Constance could hear small laughs and then more laughter as the tension eased. Constance let out her breath a little, but it hurt. She could feel one of her ribs poking her insides. *I am getting used to being dropped now.* Suddenly she realized she was being hidden from the man.

Constance allowed the tears to roll down her face.

Rousseau was shot. I only assume he is dead—there was so much blood. I've been beaten, humiliated, taken. Now they say I'm a criminal in a concentration camp, a million miles from the only person who really loves me.

The kitchen staff were trying to make noise—a distraction!—and she could hear them laughing! The tension seemed to ease.

Yes, they are protecting me.

Constance wept freely.

And then Anja was back and Constance quickly wiped her wet face.

"I am so sorry for the sudden moves. That is our supervisor, Herr Meyer, he has come to check on dinner progress. He is a chef by nature and by training and not a soldier, even though he is a soldier now, a chef-soldier for the moment. Well, he is one of *them*, but agreeable and as long as we take good care of him," she winked, "then he is just happy and you are so lucky to have been assigned here. How did that happen?"

Constance had trouble following her quick talk.

Without taking a breath, Anja continued, "You must have had an angel smiling on you. Herr Meyer asked today where the new chef is and we knew he meant you, so we said you were in the infirmary but would be back tomorrow or the next day. He did not see you and he seems satisfied by that explanation so we have bought you a bit of time to get better. Can you sit up?"

She helped Constance sit in one fluid motion and before Constance could respond, she started talking again with her Polish accent. It was melodious, thought Constance. Anja, thin and tall with high cheekbones and penetrating eyes, sort of sang her words and never took a breath. "So we will get you all better and I have some new clothes for you. You probably will feel a bit woozy from your trip and long wait and lack of water and lying down so much, but I think I can help you and you should try to walk a little. I think you have a broken rib or two—it is not a problem. I checked while you were asleep—it is easier to check for cracked ribs when the patient is sleeping. . . . Oh, I said, patient? Yes, I did not tell you I am a nurse by training from Warsaw via, well, somewhere east of that but I was put here by accident because the line for nurses before me filled the soldier's truck, so he pointed me here. Me, a chef! Ha! Put these warm socks on. I have to go but I will be back. I suggest you walk from here to there 20 times. That is my prescription."

"*Merci*, doctor."

And Constance followed the doctor's orders and did walk back and forth in the small room. Five times. End to end. Six to eight feet. She could feel by the end of the day she did have her wits a bit and could sit up on her own. Her legs were miraculously under her and she could see in the reflection of a tin can that the swelling in her face was subsiding. It made her afraid, thinking that her beauty could return. She didn't want that to happen here. But Constance brushed her hair in front of her face a little more and waited for Anja as the cold draft of the room fell upon her. She knew she would never forget the smell of the potatoes. The brackish, cold mustiness from the rotted roots was sinewy in her nostrils; the room had an earthen aroma, like a cave or tunnel.

When Anja returned, Constance had put on her new clothes and neatly folded her bloody effects and placed them on the wooden box. The box had Polish writing on it. Constance was wearing her functional new shoes. She knew if she could last, her shoes would last her as well. They were comfortable and she thought of them because she caught Anja stealing a glance at them.

"They are nice, aren't they? I got them before my trip from Paris last week before . . . before . . . I was picked up." Her eyes drifted away.

Anja did not tell Constance that since her ordeal she was pretty sure more than two weeks had passed. "No need to tell me anything, dear. We try not to tell those stories. Let me introduce you to the girls."

One by one, the girls came in to meet Constance; they were all weathered but exuding life. Diana, an Eastern European, had the brightest smile of all. Constance was not accustomed to female friends. She had gotten closer to Bettina after her sister had left but she didn't realize until now how much she missed Gracianna, especially because they never had the chance to say good-bye.

That was why I went to Paris maybe—to say good-bye in person.

She could hardly believe the resilience she saw in all their faces.

"Are you well enough to come to the barracks tonight?" Anja asked the next day, when she saw Constance walking again in the little potato room.

"Yes," Constance said. All afternoon she battled her fear to give up the safety of the room. *Gracianna would not be so afraid! Gracianna. . . .* Her regret was deep about how she had thrown away a relationship that meant so much.

When the dinner shift was over at 10 p.m., Anja took Constance's makeshift bedpan (a pot they made soup in the next day), cleaned it, and they walked out, arm-in-arm, to the latrines.

"Listen at the toilets," Anja explained. "The day's information is spread among prisoners from here, since the guards do not go in there because of their fear of 'catching a Jew disease,' and fear of filth in general. The latrines are the 'newspaper,' of the camp. News and especially rumors get spread right from inside the toilet. So keep your ears open."

She added, "Oh, and it is sometimes the only place for family members to see one another, so you will see a lot of hugging and crying. Just so you know."

Constance soaked in these lessons.

Anja went on, "All of us prisoners are allowed to go two times per day—once in the morning and once at the end of the day." She told her to expect latrines that were built as a long bench over a trough—one that you could see pigs feasting from in any other setting.

Gracianna would not be afraid!

Chapter 19

TARGET NUMBER ONE

$\mathscr{B}$etween serving customers, Gracianna knew the target would soon be identified.

Juan stopped into La Maison only for a moment at the beginning of dinner service to show his support. Fontaine wanted Juan nowhere near the operation. "Outside" is all he was told. Ostensibly, it would be because he was emotionally exposed and would probably act erratically and not allow Gracianna to focus on her task. He nodded toward her and left. As he walked, he wondered if she had really joined La Résistance for Constance, as she told him, or was eager to seek revenge for the terrible injustice that had been foisted upon her.

Late that night she had told Juan, "I will support La Résistance, now," while they lay still in bed, even though she had already told Fontaine she was in.

She reminded him about the chance to leave for America by Christmas—but she could "call the whole thing off," she had assured him.

"I think about Constance all the time," Juan said, looking at her. "I do every moment, you know it. I hope she knows it."

I have a choice, but they are making me do this. Is it right?!

She was scared.

He paced in his mind.

Still, he had not told her Mikolaus' words of marriage, the need for a lover and a fighter in a marriage match. He did not need to encourage her. He was unsure how to square his feelings for a wife who is a central figure in this drama dilemma. Juan had no choice but just to stand back.

Steady, Gracianna told herself through the night. *Patience.* Her crew would be working alongside her. Everyone would be watching every move without being obvious. She knew she could "see" the operation room now. She felt it as if the room was a living organism. Her sight and hearing were hypersensitive; she worked on appearing natural, smiling, listening, bending just so before her prey and always watching, always with Constance in the back of her mind.

The crew stole glances as the bartender secretly gestured to her—*he is our man.* Everyone acknowledged the appointment except Gracianna, who probably could have pointed him out to the bartender upon his entry several hours early.

So this is the poor bastard. He will be mine tonight.

Everyone knew whose operation this really was. Gracianna was already in the zone.

She could feel the room and every emotion was on her radar, even just a smile or a look. She was in charge of the room she was working, all the while meekly delivering a typical service.

In the summer after a sizzling-hot day it could drizzle outside late in the evening from the humidity and heat inversion. Inside, Gracianna could see and feel the electricity in the smoky room. Petals of song notes hung in the dense air from the Victrola. Living was easy for the German soldiers, especially these men. Fontaine had made it clear that most soldiers who came here were the elite. Their privilege was obvious. Anything they wanted they could have, as if it was their right. Their pay was converted to depressed francs, so they could live well with a coin going far. Drink and extra attention were afforded whenever they needed a few restful moments for any pleasure that could be derived away from the war work.

They are just Hitler's sheep, she thought.

With all the stories they told, Gracianna guessed many of them must enjoy the brutalities they perpetrated—which made fire burn in her.

For soldiers, their next moment could be their last, so these men needed no prompting to live large.

"Here, for now!" they would cheer with their toasts.

Again, she stole a sly glance at the target.

A clash of entitlement and humility fused when the officer of the evening was identified.

How could he be so handsome?

But pale. His skin was whiter than the others, translucent, near albino and, to project his Aryan right, his beard shaved closely away. Against this contrast you could see the color of his eyes and his steely slate uniform were identical.

She sensed that he was the alpha. The officer laughed last at everything. He seemed intelligent and, if possible, he was the most smartly dressed. There was something sharper and more precise about him than the rest. His haircut crisper. His uniform more severe. His jawline cut and his other features chiseled. His eyes were pool-true blue, an icy-cold blueness. His voice was strident when he spoke and all looked, listened and laughed, even if what he had to say was not significant.

He was alpha, for sure, and dangerous. It was now obvious why he was the mark for this night. His laugh was muzzled as was his smile—if you could call it that with the crinkle in his mouth; depending on the light he was either devastatingly handsome or very unattractive. The mannerisms of this officer of the evening were curt in contrast to the jovial and Italianesque animated soldier to his left. The animated one was drunk, but our man was even drunker, though his eyes could still be seen through thin slits. His steely blues were beery and bleary—but he was still in control. He would tell you so if asked. She had shrugged, tilting her head with a smile.

She was sure he had looked her over from the outset, and he dimly continued to notice Gracianna all evening as she serviced the table over the hours. Drinks, more drinks, and more. Then food, well prepared (sans sauce, the way the new neighbors preferred it), and simply served with steam rising as plates were set down. Then wine with dinner. Cheap wine now, since the singular goal was only to wash and stimulate and sustain the pre-meal buzz and better complement the food. The taste of the wine was inconsequential now. This was good because the house could buy the dregs and serve the lesser of the lesser wine the later and later it got.

The chef had refused to use his best fresh spices for the pigs, and Dom' had gotten into a long lecture with Marceau about not poisoning the food. Marceau wouldn't have done it; well, he would have with Gracianna's egging. Anyway, there was too much to do and that form of mayhem was "unpredictable."

"I am doing enough," Dom' had said, and that was the end of that.

The volume in the room increased as the evening continued. As the lesser wine flowed, the grander the gestures and stories and voices and expectation of the evening became. Beer eyes became royal wine eyes and the jubilant could now see any thrill they wished for.

"Nothing is far away!" one soldier exclaimed.

In wonder of the evening, the officer of the evening stood up and walked to the toilet with nary a hitch. Gracianna watched with the realization: he is alive. He is a man. His eyes may be droopy, his tongue loose, and he may not be so drunk after all.

The conversation continued with stories and jokes and lies. "*Noch einen drink* [Another drink]?"

Gracianna brought more low-quality wine. One chubby man pushed it away.

"I am in a haze," he shouted, pink-faced, "but even I know this is piss!" He drank some from the glass. "It is over. It has no acid. It's flabby and pasty!"

The delivery of poor wine seemingly gave the fat man permission to lean into her a bit and reach out his fat mitt to touch her. He laughed greedily and she sneered and he turned deliberately to swat her as she moved away, but she had seen this sleazy move hundreds of times. He easily missed her. Another man made his move toward her with his hand and arms, but she had seen him ogling her from miles away. He missed by a wider margin, and they all began to laugh at him.

As she circled the table to pour for another uniformed soldier, he asked her to bring something new.

"*Digestif!*"

She was back now with Cointreau from the confectioners, Adolphe and

Edouard-Jean Cointreau, a triple sec liqueur, as Gracianna's inside joke unfolded. Since their stomachs might be turning, she wanted to add bitter oranges to the mix, adding to a righteous soon-to-be hangover. She sploshed the triple sec into the tiny glasses.

When she got to the chubby man, Gracianna was startled when he threw the triple sec to the floor and thrust his empty glass at her to refill. The others followed suit. This was just a game for them now, round and round she went—*fill my glass and I will waste it on the floor.*

Her cheeks burned, knowing what a sticky mess it would be.

They were downing their digestif as Gracianna made the full circle over again. As the first recipient guzzled his entire glass, she slowly continued around the table until she ended with our officer, her assignment.

He looked up at her in their first full view of each other, so close, and then he subtly reached toward her; it may have been just the glass in his hand, but she knew better. It was *the reach.*

It was a fine balance to evade yet not to evade, to let his hand brush just a little—to evade just enough that he would know she might be interested in something more—but careful that no one else would notice. It was important not to let the other soldiers know that she was receptive to him, or there would be accusations when he was found dead.

He gave her the international nod for "more," and Gracianna poured. This was an innocent look to everyone, but it was not innocent to men and women who know when a deal has been reached.

She had not even needed to wink. As she turned to the bar, she could feel his eyes on her backside. As she rounded the corner of the bar, she caught his final look and they exchanged a private smile.

He is baited, so the special rose of his eye could back off now. Keep pouring the drinks, and wait for all to leave and him to stay. This was the plan.

She knew the second act was not far away. Could it be that he tells them to leave and proclaims his victory in advance, or fakes a reason to come back after leaving? Her assessment was that he would declare victory and tell them he will be along in an hour or so, and to wait up so he could share the story of the spoils with them.

Then, after dinner, "Port! Now port!"

The conversation and drinking continued with "war" stories about women. They boasted of deeds from times gone past, like all men eventually do.

"Will they never leave?" Marceau whispered more than once to the other man working the bar, while they smoked behind the kitchen near the garden.

There was more drinking. Then he reached for her again.

She startled and so did the crew. She withdrew. Juan was nowhere to be seen, but she knew he was outside nearby, pacing somewhere, probably smoking more and more. The target got up and headed to the toilet.

Everyone on her team was tensing.

Three a.m., the typical time—five, then seven minutes went by and the man had not come back out. Eleven minutes went by—the time it takes the least drunk soldier to look to the door to wonder where the missing party is. Twelve, for him to look again and the second man to look, too. At thirteen minutes, the first would normally consider getting up to look, but at fourteen minutes, the officer finally appeared. He was still alert except for his belt, flailing and askew, wiping his mouth while momentarily leaning on the toilet door. Gracianna briefly stared at the Army-issued gun on his belt.

How is he still sharp? the crew all thought.

He was still able to manage the drink, Gracianna admitted. With the poor quality wine she gave him, even the combination of heavily sauced food and the port, she wondered how he could maintain his composure *and* arrogance. She wondered how motivations well hidden by day appear so easily with drink at night.

Patience . . . but will Fontaine and his people hide his body well?

The gunshot?

The GESTAPO?

It was a churn of confusion, and she stood breathless for a moment. Suddenly and in unison, most of them stood up to leave. Her officer went to the door, watching Gracianna with his thin-set eyes.

A soldier joked with him, "*Ein letztes getränk* [One last drink]?" He drunkenly waved him off. His mates stumbled past unconcernedly as they headed out the door to smoke. They all knew they were in the same condition.

His mates began to pace—one outside, then two—and peeked in, "We are leaving." Then there were four outside, and one in the toilet. Her officer leaned on the front door to steady and preen himself. Two more went outside and said, "Let's go."

It is up to him to determine how to lose his friends.

As the entire soldier party left, the target followed them to just outside the door. They called to him, "*Komm oder nicht—wir sehen uns bei der besprechung* [Come or don't, we will see you at the briefing]."

Gracianna could not see him. *Was he gone? He must come back.*

The empty bar became very quiet and, as he stood just outside the door wavering, the last two couples got up and left on cue. There were hugs and kisses from couples, and "*au revoirs*" and light jackets and scarves, and lights going off in the kitchen and bartenders instantly pushing glasses and cloths across clean bars, while all looked at each other to see what Gracianna would do. Within four minutes, the place was dead, with music turned down and lights lowered as well. The "last" bartender went out as Gracianna headed to her "office" for supplies. It was all an act. She knew her fellow resisters were still close by.

Marceau, relieved, passed the officer coming back in as he walked out and made it clear, "you are on your own," as he gestured to the officer, "no more drink." The officer waved him off as inconsequential. Marceau just gave him the "I'm tired, do as you wish" wave.

The office door was open and a single light hung from the ceiling.

Did he not understand I was interested and meant for him to stay? What did I do wrong?

She was sorting towels and making no noise, except for a slight humming sound. Then the eyes in the back of her head said there was company. She turned, *expecting* him to be in the doorway, and there he was, lighting a cigarette.

Juan, pacing outside, had seen it all. The officer had left with his friends, walked nearly around the corner, *relief!—NO!* He came stumbling back two minutes later. Juan's straight-line view made him want to scream.

Yet, Juan knew Fontaine's men were in their places.

The officer leaned against the office doorjamb and said something to her in German. She replied in French. So he spoke in English, "I could not take my eyes off you all night."

She replied in English, "I did not notice."

"Did not notice?" he laughed in disbelief. "We will be together tonight."

As she peered at his wedding ring, she said, "How very romantic . . . I do not see your flowers or chocolate. Did you call my father and ask for his permission? Are you a single man?"

She channeled the Russian tart she'd lived with at the dorms, and it came easily. She tried hard to make him understand that she was making this a matter of virtue.

"So, my flowers and chocolate," she said with a waiting smile.

"You are full of questions, aren't you, flower girl? I like that. You have a lot of energy. I have energy, too, let me show you. . . ."

Gracianna could see the heat growing in his cold, hazy gaze. She allowed her eyes to help his interest grow.

"You need more than energy to be with me, my friend. . . ." she barely had turned when he was on her.

She did not expect the force by which he was there.

"Stay calm," Fontaine had told her again and again. *"Stay calm, and then disarm him."*

So, she had laughed. "Wait, wait, I have something for you . . . relax and enjoy it." He stepped back for a moment as she insisted on closing the discreetly padded door to the small room. It occurred to her: *never again will this atrocious man force himself on another innocent woman.* Then, he was on her again. She pretended she wanted to take off his jacket, going after his buttons as he went after hers. She wondered if real love or real lust was ever truly this frenzied. She slid her arms under his, around him, as his hungry mouth tried to find hers. She turned her mouth—the one that not even Juan had kissed—and then calmly and deliberately unsnapped the state-issued killing machine from his holster.

He didn't notice.

She reached for the gun . . . *where is it!?* But, it *was* there, and in an instant **BANG!** he crumpled to the floor. Eyes closed.

Done.

The next mission, two weeks later, was at another location, and even easier.

The third, back at Maison, did not end so neatly. That night, Juan knew something must have gone wrong. He paced quickly in the alley under the window of the back room where the deed was set. It was taking too long and he wanted to rush in, but the sentry Hawkeye looked at him coolly from his perched position overhead. The target that Gracianna had lured into her back room this night was taking his time; he had opened the window and curtain while smoking with a drink in his hand. He was moving back and forth, and she was obviously having trouble getting him still to finish him. Fontaine had said before it was too dangerous to have another gun in the room, one for her—"Two guns is just a mess waiting to happen. No, it has to be his issue. Use his. You can do it."

Now, with the curtain open, it was possible for Hawkeye to see inside the spacious room, from the building right across the alley.

Nothing was happening, so he quietly climbed down the fire escape to the alley.

"What is happening," begged Juan.

"The curtain is open, but I couldn't see anything," he said, which had been obvious, "I heard their voices, and some laughing, then some rustling, then quiet. I strained to hear and to see in the window, but I am too short. I am the wrong man for this post."

There was a short landing outside the window, and Juan suggested if he piled a couple of boxes, Hawkeye could stand on them and see in. Juan intended to be ready to run up the stairs and refused to climb up onto the boxes himself.

Just then, he could hear a struggle occurring and hastily set up the boxes to stand on. As he grappled to the top, he heard Gracianna choking and trying to scream as the man laughed in defiance. Hawkeye finally reached the slightly opened window.

Flash.

BANG!

WHOOSH. Splatter flew onto his face. He started and fell off the box to the landing and then onto some boxes below—only a four-foot fall.

"I'm shot!" he shouted to Juan—but it was soon apparent that he had not been shot and would not die.

There was a silence as Hawkeye wiped his face.

I AM ALIVE!

But Juan was gone, up the stairs into Maison.

Juan, along with Marceau, who beat him to the door, saw Gracianna standing over the lifeless soldier with the gun in her hand, the flash gone from her eyes, now just staring, looking, wondering, and breathing heavily.

Men were already doing their cleanup duty as Juan stood outside the room.

Hawkeye had gotten back up and was now peering through the window. *"God bless her."*

HONK! HOOOONK! HOOOOOOOOONK!

Gracianna was not very happy with Fontaine even though she felt compelled to do her duty. Yes, she knew what to do. It seemed the right thing to do, but she still felt sick about it and kept feeling like she had been coerced somehow. Yes, she had her own reasons to continue, but killing to get to America was not one of them.

They would clean up after each time. "No news of Constance," he would always say.

Then, "We are moving you back to La Maison shortly, but we are taking a small break, a week or so off. We need to go cold now," he had said. It was a directive.

Dom', of course, would be happy that his Gras' was safe and back at her Maison.

However, the Gestapo investigation had heated up again and Fontaine was very nervous to go back to where it all started. "We are cold now," he kept saying. "Everyone just stand down. Nothing will happen until I give the order. Does everyone understand?"

Gracianna could feel the instinct deep in her now. She knew there would be many more acts and that she would be moved from arrondissement to arrondissement, exploiting the Germans' insatiable penchant for women, young mothers, the weakest ones, young girls, and prostitutes. "Horizontal collaboration" was the order of the day. The number of prostitutes was impossible to estimate since so many women joined the ranks. Even some of those who were married started working *"pour faire sa fin de mois* [to make the end of month]," to pay bills.

Thousands of prostitutes were working either in *bordels* [brothels], in their apartments, on the street, or freelancing in bars. Even though, for the French, the prostitute symbolized the German domination of French culture; it was just another rush of injustice flung in the face of everyday France.

Prostitutes everywhere had had a laissez-faire attitude toward casual sex with Frenchmen, before the war was amplified. When the occupiers started to partake, the French *men* didn't like it.

"These whores are ours," said the common man under his breath.

They are very "helpful to the cause," as Dom' would say to Fontaine.

Prostitutes were the perfect cover and eased the explanation of disappearing officers.

"He ran off with a sexy French maid," to Italy or North Africa, everyone was coached to say. Plus, investigating German officers were purposely presented with the most beautiful women during investigations to "push" the undeniable possibility that desertion was plausible and they were reminded with every waif that passed by. The Gestapo was all men, and the risk of running away with a beauty, likely, even crossed their minds.

Witness interrogations lasted longer than usual as these pretties played their part, "convincing" investigators that they had "seen" certain behaviors that became more and more believable as time went by. It helped that there were "sightings," real and fictional, of officers with their French sparrows in Rome and Milan and other faraway lands, where there was little chance of the war. They had taken up the good life. Stories were everywhere. Pictures of Nazi servicemen that had gone AWOL "materialized," which added to the fodder usually heaving in the bosom of the next investigation.

Every soldier dreamed of the possibility and wondered to himself after a few days leave: *Would they really miss me or come after me if I did not come back? After all, the war will not last forever, and I will be forgotten—won't I?*

La Résistance was forthright in helping to "push" at every moment this possibility of deserting. It may have helped men actually give up their arms under their own volition—not many, but even one was a lesser force to fight. The constant stream of investigators had these suspicions in place, but they also knew there were Résistance forces at work, and thousands of men and women had been picked up for subversive actions, many just for acting suspiciously. Tens of thousands, maybe hundreds of thousands of resisters from various organizations—loose, imagined, or organized—were in jail, in hiding, or in exile.

This resistance cell, however, was very well oiled. There was simply no indication that any of these civilians were involved, and the Germans, knowing something was amiss—could not find a reason to suspect any particular person.

The investigations continued, but it appeared that at least one and maybe two of the missing had fallen drunk into the River Seine and simply couldn't be found.

"Yes, officer, I was walking on the Pont Neuf with my grandmother just before sunrise, we go to church right around the corner from here, right over there," pointing to the bridge. "See there? Well, we heard a loud splash. There was no one around. But we did hear singing, officer; yes singing—like a man who was maybe inebriated? Is that possible? Could he have fallen in? It was so dark and foggy that we could not see a thing. We called out but then imagined it could not have been a man falling into the water. Could it have been, officer? A man?"

It was all just an elaborate trap by now. Starting with a simple wooing—just a look or a smile, really; as soon as the party atmosphere ended and the door closed, the staff seemed to disappear as they became alter-shadows, just out of view. Then it was time for Gracianna's final act, then the disposition, and then the investigation.

She could feel the walls of a prison around her as much as Constance. Her mind went to Constance every time. Gracianna felt the rage as the café door closed on those nights and her "weakling" team's faux "*au revoirs*" were said. They acted limp but were prepared to leap. She just said, "*au revoir finis*" to herself, and went to work.

I know the war will be over someday, and that good is going to win over evil. I will do what I can.

She felt she was doing her part as a remover of darkness. She believed strongly in the movement and wanted to see freedom in every depressed French eye she passed. Gracianna tried to send a signal to each passerby, "*We are going to win this. One important officer at a time.*"

Gracianna had come to accept the accidental harmony of her duty.

Juan, as silent-promised, was nearby but never in the room—usually outside smoking and nervously waiting to see if his wife would walk out alive. They never said a word about it. Never touched. They never spoke of it. Each just did the job.

And she performed hers again and again. It just happened. Powerfully.

The week ended with no missions, and it had gone by slowly. Gracianna was restless with the cleaning. She heard more stories of Nazi callousness as she served them night after night without the rhythm of the chase. Lately, also, it seemed that Juan was growing away from her. He said little.

"I am a lover," Juan would joke with a warm smile and open arms, inferring that she was the fighter in the duo. Gracianna, however, found it hard enough to be worthy of love at any time. How could she enjoy love at a time like this?

He really isn't joking.

She is so affected by this entire trauma. I understand, but will we ever touch?

Her heart resisted.

She'd learned already that there were hundreds of nuances to her new mission. It was much more than the look and the smile at the soon-to-be-departed, the glance and the hello. It was a certain body language, a confidence, a walk, a nod. She could not describe her skill, newfound thanks to the Russian girl.

I guess I learned something from her flirting with Juan after all.

She had done everything perfectly, aside from it being a close call the last time. She had communicated what was necessary to Fontaine but never mentioned the fear that would grip her once she was alone with the soldiers. She had made her best effort to stay calm and never let anyone know her terror. On the outside, she was perfect and she knew it. She followed the rules and was an active participant—she had even helped with the planning, explaining in the smallest detail to Fontaine and the crew how she wanted certain preparations done and whom she hoped would be where.

She said, "I do not want to have anything to do with the target choice. That is out of my hands."

"Leave it to us. You just stay focused," Fontaine had said. Fontaine knew that having Gracianna involved in choosing a target was out of the question. He wanted her to stay on task because it was difficult enough to pretend to be a slack woman, let alone to put her finger on the trigger.

He warned her, "Sometimes, the most obvious choice is not so easy to find. We must research, prepare, be very cautious. And be prepared for variations. Stay calm."

Still she had no word of Constance. How Gracianna would sometimes have liked to take matters into her own hands! She constantly pestered Fontaine for information about Constance. She knew he could find out *something*.

"I'm looking into it."

Then, as if to break her out of her deep thoughts, Fontaine showed up. He walked into the little no-name café a few blocks away from La Maison where she had been working and cooling off that week and said, "Go here this afternoon. We are back on."

Butterflies!

So, two hours later at a cozy restaurant about twenty blocks from Maison, Gracianna walked in as if she had worked there for years.

She was welcomed with barely a look. She instantly found an apron, put a scarf on her head to cover her hair and sat down to look over the short menu. The proprietor and another man sat down next to her without fanfare and, as if routine, explained that a certain officer had been coming in for the past few days and that they knew for a fact he was supposed to go on leave the next day. This was the perfect situation! The team could ensure that an officer-decoy "got into a taxi" at the end of the evening, he would be seen by many, and voilà! The real officer would be gloriously gone.

As the evening preparations clinked and folded, and the tables were placed along, the sun began to set and patrons spilled into the café. The miniature, marble-topped café tables and spindly chairs hosted a garden of activity. Smiling and lost notions and whispered plans passed in hopeful dreams of escape among the patrons. Things picked up early at this new eatery and it was busy.

A hand was raised from a table, and Gracianna efficiently approached to serve them. It was another beady-eyed German officer with a lovely French-woman in a sparkling dress, who reminded her of Mrs. Latour, and also of Constance. Always, things reminded her of Constance. She thought of how happy Constance had said she'd been with Rousseau.

Poor Rousseau. Dead. And I am the cause of it.

The couple was talking and laughing with enjoyment and twinkling eyes already, when she asked for their order.

"*Le meilleur vin de la maison, s'il vous plaît* [The best wine of the house, please]," the woman said to her in perfect French, and turned with a smile to her Nazi beau to dive back into his blue eyes—but he was not smiling anymore. Apparently, he had wanted to order a different wine—it was hard to tell, as he was speaking to his lady in staccato German. His date was more than apologetic, and Gracianna offered a different wine, but still the man gave the woman trouble about it.

"This is how you start things?" he seemed to demand of his date, completely ignoring both women's appeals. His eyes were dark, his shoulders tense. The woman tried to laugh and charm him to no avail.

Gracianna could feel her hackles rise in defense of the hounded woman. What was she doing with this beady man, anyway? She was lovely! Perhaps she was a prostitute. It was her grin that most grated on Gracianna's nerves. Was it a fake smile, the way she tried to laugh off the officer's angst? It seemed the woman had endless patience to reassure him, like a child. It was concerning. *Who is this girl? Was she smart enough to understand that many lives were hanging in the balance? That many families would be hurt by this man?*

Finally, Gracianna could not wait for the argument to end and moved to the next table. She bustled around to keep everyone happy. Her crew—the bartender and a busser—were dancing with her to catch up. They helped out a bit doing extraordinary things, like taking a wine order or bringing food to a table to allow her to catch her breath. Still, the Nazi and the French lady were arguing quietly, in tensed voices.

At one point, hearing a pause in the room, Gracianna looked up to see the Frenchwoman stand and drop her shawl to reveal a nude shoulder with lines that any Hollywood actress would admire. In an attempt to take the sudden attention away from herself, she quickly walked to the toilet. Gracianna figured that even her former flirty Russian roommate couldn't have delivered that move. Once again, everyone's eyes fell on the French beauty as she returned to her table and Gracianna wondered, *what was that all about?*

The proprietor, she did not even know his name, caught Gras' in one of her many kitchen stops and said, "*La femme est une résistante* [The woman is a resister]."

Gracianna realized they had used the beauty to ensure the officer arrived that night, but was confused about what was happening.

"Is *she* my accomplice?"

He shrugged, "*Oui.*"

She didn't like the idea. Her team was tight. They all knew what to do. What if Beauty did, or said, the wrong thing? How would Gracianna manage that? She got angry.

Returning to the couple's table, Gracianna poured the wine and was disappointed to notice that the Nazi now had another complaint against his date, that the man's tense attitude was starting to make other customers uncomfortable, and that the woman was continuing to try and soothe him in the most degrading way. That's when Gracianna became furious.

On her next trip in the kitchen she exploded, "*Où sont mes plats? J'ai des clients qui ont faim. Qui va m'aider? Je ne suis pas heureuse* [Where are my plates? I have hungry people. Who will help me? I am not happy]." She did not care if everyone in the place heard.

Although hardly anyone in the kitchen knew Gracianna, it was not hard to gather that the outburst was uncharacteristic, because everyone in the front room had heard every word. But it seemed to break the tension that had been building, and cause some laughter out there.

Gracianna could not laugh.

The back of the house jumped to attention and even her Beauty backup was at attention.

Gracianna received a sprinkle of applause as she exited through the swing-out door with an armful of *hors d'oeuvre* plates dangling from her slight form. Her entry back into the dining room was more dramatic than even the look-at-me catwalk of the girlfriend of the evening.

Even the Beauty clapped and instantly regretted it as her insufferable date found something else to complain about, not letting her laugh it off lightly.

As Gracianna professionally brought the plates to the tables, she noticed that the couple had finished with the one bottle and she simply nodded to the bartender to deliver another.

She turned to take a customer's order, noticing his little table had no food or drink—just the menu.

"The debilitating food shortages and rationing throughout France do not seem to affect this café's offerings," the man said in English, handing her the menu.

Gracianna looked at him and was surprised at how handsome he was. "Yes, the menu changes every day, based on what's available from the local markets. Plus we obviously have excellent black market connections, so you can be sure we are working for the Germans," she joked quietly. Maybe it was a stupid joke, but he laughed.

She liked his teeth, his easy smile.

"We have fresh fish, and rounds of cheese and certain wines that are uncommon around the city. The vegetable of the day—I'm sure you have heard of *le rutabaga*. Are you from the university?"

"No, no," he chuckled, "far from the university. Those days are gone. I am German."

She felt a chill. But, there was a flicker in his eye and she was sure he was intelligent. "Well, you had better watch out, then, I might poison you." Her eyes sparked, half-joking because she didn't believe he was German. He spoke perfect English, but she could hear his accent.

He laughed as if it was all a joke and ordered, "Fine Bordeaux." Yes, he had nice teeth.

Suddenly, the French Beauty at the table with the difficult officer stood up and shouted in her native language, "*Je ne vais pas* [I will not]!" She gathered her shawl angrily. "I do not care if you go on leave in the morning, I will not spend the night, I am not that way, and you will not drop it, so—GOOD-bye, *Muller!*" She emphasized his name for everyone to hear.

The Beauty gathered her shawl and stormed out, with her cheekbones high despite sudden and real tear-tracks, to the glee and applause of most of the group—well, certainly to the women in the room.

Gracianna joined in the couple claps that dissipated the instant Muller's eyes swept over her. Then, he made some announcement in German in regards to the fact that, all day, the lady had struggled with his German, and he had struggled with her French—"It was very frustrating!" Just when there was maybe a little sympathy for him, he called the French girl who'd left, and women in general, some ugly names that made him unredeemable.

She ignored him while backing into the kitchen and letting out a long sigh of relief. Although no one had told her, and she realized why, the accomplice had been a masterful idea and she actually smiled about it.

A long time after he had cooled down—he was just pestering the other customers, some in German—Gracianna was still hot about how he had been acting. She felt a deep loathing. She'd been bred to not feel kindly toward invaders and dominators. Her Basque instinct was to fight against them.

So she did what she knew she should not do and wagged over to his table. Bend. Pour. A graze of eye contact.

Muller caught her meaning easily.

"Yes, the wine is fantastic," she said loudly. This made Muller know clearly with a look and subtle body language that their affair was to be their secret.

Muller could understand how it would look bad for everyone to know. He gave another chuckle as she walked away.

The trap was set. The cover in place.

Pour.

Pour more.

Stronger now.

Smile secretly.

The night quieted as the music quieted, and finally all the couples and customers—most, if not all, who were in on the game—were bleeding out of the café. A new bottle of wine and a shot was miraculously placed on our hero's table, and Gracianna saw the bartender raise his glass to the officer as they both downed the drink while standing at a firing-squad distance from one another.

Thus, Muller stayed. A pheromone of magnetism kept him seated as he stared openly at Gracianna, with her scarf removed, her unusual hair visible with its barrette.

Then—quiet.

Alone.

Muller looked at her in wonder a bit, as she straightened the flowers in the deserted, semi-dark café where some candles were still burning.

Looking him square in the eye, she said in English, "Too bad about her, but it must be my luck. I'm sure I can save your evening."

"Fantastic!" He was unsure why this good fortune was his, but he was officially on vacation now and things always look the darkest and then brighten the moment before going on holiday.

"I am so happy to meet you." Then, in his affected German-French accent, he bowed his head a bit (then built the courage to use his French even though it did not stand up), "*Enchanté* [Enchanted]."

Gracianna could not really feel flattered, but understood the attention was reasonable. A car headlight streaked across her face from the window and the light danced through a maze of crystalline to frame her smiling eyes.

"Look, how you are glowing," Muller said. He could not help but enjoy the view as any another, and the last, late couple passed by the open door outside.

"I must do my few duties—now enjoy yourself. Maybe we can talk a little later? It will only be ten or twenty minutes. You will wait?"

"Yes, you do that. Yes, of course, *ma chérie*. Do what you need, now hurry. I will wait. I am on leave tomorrow and maybe we can have some fun before I go. I seem to have been graced with another chance tonight."

"You *are* a very lucky officer," she said as she playfully about-face pivoted, smoothly locking the door with them both inside.

Less than 10 seconds later, on cue, the bartender peeked into the dining room from the back to say, "I am leaving, I am tired." He nodded and half-winked at Muller and walked out the back, closing the door, opening it, and then closing it harder.

It was only a moment before the lieutenant stood up, and pulled at his uniform. He caught himself to find his legs and ended up at the wall in the kitchen, just as Gracianna turned off the light. He nearly fell into her and she caught him and rolled him into the kitchen corner, all in one move.

He hung there moon-grinning in the half-dark. She looked him directly in the eye. He continued leering. She smiled. He closed his eyes for a moment in anticipation of vacation as her hands caressed his chest. She had opened his holster at least ten minutes before.

She waited a moment for the car to honk outside.

One honk, he blinked his eyes open, two honks, and then three, a long, hooooooooooooooooooooo***bang!***ooooooooooooooooooooooonk.

Just like that, it was over.

No more tension.

She flipped the light twice and then off again, and started checking his pockets.

Tonight she felt like an accidental resister, but one who was powerfully bound by her profound duty.

The prospect of being alone or without Juan was unbearable!

OH!—dear Constance.

I pray for you!

OH!—dear Constance.

Do I even know myself anymore?

Who is Gracianna now?

She promised herself that she could not change because of these damn acts. *They are just necessary now, and after the war I will forget them.* "*Je le promets* [I promise]."

Chapter 20

COPING WITH WAR

Juan was not happy when they got home that night. Gracianna could tell, because he went straight to the little table with his woodcarving projects. For a moment, she lingered at the door.

"I do not know what has come over you," he said, but she said nothing.

Over the next few days, Juan was agitated. He could only think of protecting Gracianna.

He slept uneasily.

Once, late at night, when she was sleeping, he gently removed her hair from her face. Her small chin was so stubborn, and his eyes lingered on her. He watched her and thought about how far they had come, and how far they might go.

He was not sure he was strong enough to continue watching what she was doing. She pretended she could handle anything, but he had heard her sob sometimes at night, quietly trying to fight the pain. He knew she did not want him to reach for her. They never talked about the pain. She would not let him hold her.

I wish she knew that she could cry as I hold her.

Looking at her in the Paris light, in their apartment, finally finished for the night, in their bed, he on *his* side and she on *hers,* so close but not close enough, Juan sighed deeply and was surprised when Gracianna turned to him with a sleepy murmur. They'd had a couple bottles of wine when they got home, and she was drunk.

However, he welcomed her, and they pressed together and kissed for the first time. He melted. She just went to sleep.

He suppressed his true emotion. He was not sure if he was strong enough to handle what she was doing.

There, holding her in the night, Juan realized that Gracianna was compelled to stubbornly fight for what she believed was right. Crushing her close and smelling the lavender in her snowy hair Juan knew he was not ready to die, but he would keep fighting on the sidelines—mostly fighting to keep Gracianna alive and safe.

I will be right there when she needs me.

She wanted to fight for Constance; he wanted to save Gracianna—whether or not she wanted him to.

The next morning, it was as if it had been just another "separate" night. She was up and pulled the curtains with a *snap,* and went to cook breakfast.

Sigh.

Juan knew this was to be her way. She would never mention it and he would just be there. She knew it. He knew it. He wondered how long he could be happy in this situation. Christmas was so far away. He wondered if Gracianna would ever open up. He wondered if he was wasting his time with her, but his heart rebelled at the thought.

At the railroad that day, Juan's mind wandered. His foreman queried, "*Où êtes-vous, Juan* [Where are you, Juan]?"

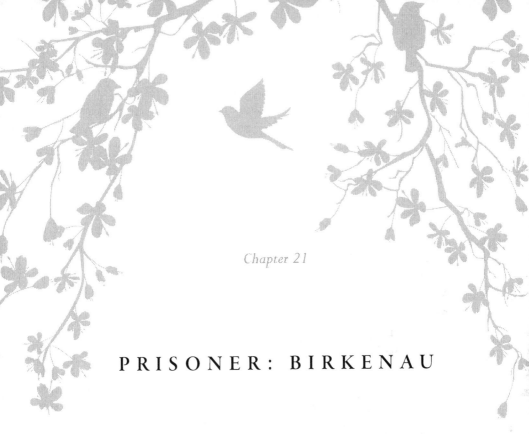

Chapter 21

PRISONER : BIRKENAU

"Where are we? What is this camp called?" Constance asked Anja the next day. She knew she was in Poland but had no idea where.

"It's Birkenau." The camp was one of the satellite concentration camps of Auschwitz, which was placed virtually over the top of a small village called Brzezinka, miles outside Krakow, which was four hours from Warsaw.

Auschwitz!! No!

Anja told her how the villagers had been taken from their homes at night before the homes were demolished, most burned, and right before their eyes. Those who protested were unceremoniously killed. Villagers in the nearby Oświęcim, a suburb of Zasole, suffered the same fate. Anyone not associated with the concentration camp was removed from within a 40-square-mile radius—the camp's *Interessengebiet* [interest zone].

Constance thought, the more she knew about the camp, the better. Maybe the thought was fleeting, but it crossed her mind, like anyone incarcerated, that she might have the chance to escape by some sliver of luck. Mostly, though, she found herself concerned with what was going on in her immediate world, with the women of the Auschwitz kitchen, and so she watched carefully and listened to Anja.

The commanders had their choice of women. It could be very subtle at times. A simple look to an overseeing soldier sent the message: *Bring her to me later.* In most cases, the woman was returned to the dorm a few hours later—sometimes the worse for wear. Sometimes not. Sometimes they never came back. The kitchen was overridden with raging hormones—some mutual.

She saw how some of the women gained favor and special treatment by taking a lover in the form of an ordinary soldier. Diana, the pretty girl, had taken a few lovers, it seemed. She enjoyed using the men's lust against them, making them jealous of each other. She created soap operas of who liked whom, with one goal. She was always announcing that she would work her way up in the ranks—work her way out. It was a dangerous game that the others did not pretend to participate in.

One morning, there was a frightful fight. The whole kitchen watched, Diana with her eyes wide and her hand over her mouth, as two German soldiers ferociously beat one another.

The rumor was that Diana, the beautiful Gypsy, apparently performed a love-specialty in a way that was in demand by multiple soldiers. Lately, she had been busy all the time with some man or another and was very rarely at work anymore, which was too bad because she did not mind cutting the onions.

Now, shocked by the scene, Diana had nothing to say. One of her paramours was jealous of the other, and she had succeeded in inciting them to hurt one another—but that was not really her mission. It had never been this serious before. Still, it was delicious for the girls to watch the men turn on one another. These bastards were hurting one another—*over one of us!* It was a tiny victory that lasted the length of the fight.

Even Constance had enjoyed it, and afterward it made her sick to think she had sunk to the level of their captors, delighting in brutal violence. The seesaw of emotions, from glee and giddiness to self-loathing and punishment, took its toll. Finally, the hatred of the Nazis won out over Constance's self-hatred, and she embraced their infighting with hope. Still, she kept her face hidden and her presence small around any man.

Anja introduced Auschwitz to her once Constance was walking better.

On one tour, Anja explained, "The barracks for the women, at least, are weather sealed. A Jewish architect in residence at the camp drew the plans. He used the materials from the area and oversaw all the buildings—and he slyly made the places as water- and wind-tight as possible, having been through a winter here before the barracks were built. It's terrible!"

Constance wanted to know more about the men's barracks, so Anja told her, "The sleeping barracks where the hard labor crews live were converted from old horse stables. The stables floors had turned to dirt from years and years of horse droppings. The shiny brass rings for tying the horses are still on the walls and horse hair is snagged all over the wooden edgings. It smells like a barn, I have smelled it!" It smelled like frozen dirt, even in the summer, with a stale, musty-still air that was heavy on the nose, like when hard mineral-filled water is on the palate.

"There is one potbellied stove per barrack with barely any wood to burn in the harsh winter. Once, a whole group of men who were roommates were executed for burning some of the wood of a bunk bed for some heat. And these horrific Polish winters have the men fighting for the warmer top bunks in order to at least live through the night, and not freeze to death in the coldest lower bunks. But even the lower-downs find a way to live—three or four men will huddle together to stay alive. The strong ones, the ones who have the say about being on the top bunk, carefully choose their high-bunk sleeping mate and, in return for the privilege, keep each other warm. They call it 'taking a wife for a night' and try to laugh about it."

Constance's heart went out to the prisoners forced to work in the camps. The stretching of the physical limits of men's and women's bodies alarmed her. To imagine, working so hard in the day, only to be so cold at night. She felt a chill come over her. What she would do for a wool blanket, already! And the men! She could not help but think of Rousseau—to imagine he had also been taken, to imagine him curled up with some man in the winter barracks after slaving all day.

"What is their labor?" she had to ask.

Anja explained that she'd heard a rumor that on the other side of the camp they were building something at the end of the train tracks—near the men's hard-labor barracks, which was filled with all the men that were in the best condition to work. It was to be some sort of large, underground facility—probably a bomb shelter of some sorts.

"And all of us women, I heard there are about 20,000 of us so far, live in section B1a, in separated quarters on this side of camp."

The number was unimaginable to them both.

Anja explained that this side of the camp was for the service workers and the guard soldiers that lived here, too. "Here" was "Auschwitz II," which included a camp for new arrivals and those to be sent on to labor elsewhere, a Gypsy camp, a camp for holding and sorting stolen goods, and a women's camp.

Constance told Anja she was surprised at the barracks in B1a. "But, I am very surprised at the lack of supervision and the amiability of the guards we have encountered, like the one who gave you that cigarette."

"Overall," Anja said between puffs, "the guards in our area are well taken care of by the women. Most of the girls consider the kitchen work a comfort job, compared to working out in the mills or on the train tracks, so each party takes care of the other in this godforsaken place. They give us some due and we give them what they want. Do not expect them to be kind—don't get me wrong. Sometimes, they are very, very brutal and firm—especially when a superior is around."

Anja knew it all, lowering her voice, ". . .but one time a guard apologized for the treatment he had given a woman. We suspect it was because she was his prison girlfriend and he liked the way she treated him. You never know what will happen, Constance. You will see moments of forgiveness and much horror. There are twenty thousand women here to choose from, but the guards will find one or two women they really like and stick with them. It also works the other way around, I've noticed.

"Our kitchen troupe represents some of the few women whose hair is not sheared. It is because the camp commander can see us through the kitchen window and he doesn't want to be reminded we are in prison, I think."

Anja never spoke of her relationship with Herr Meyer, so Constance did not ask.

She listened to more of Anja's rumors and news. One rumor was that the Russians were near and everyone needed to hold on just one more day. Occasionally, there was rapid gunfire outside the camp—early in the morning and late at night. Because the prisoners were together in their dormitories at that time, word would spread like wildfire. "The Russians are here!"

It was hysteria to the degree, Anja told her, that someone who needed to believe it so much would run out of the dorm, in bare feet in the middle of winter and head for the barbed wire fence to be the first to see the liberators. Only to be shot down in front of everyone. Sadly, it was a typical scene that would have been horrifying, had it not been so common. Everyone would stop for a moment and then go back to work.

Constance dwelled on how desensitized she was becoming to the casual cruelty that was now in her daily kitchen life. Always, a new train would come, one after the other, into the center of the camp each day. So many people were getting off, an endless stream being moved to the other side of camp. Did they have men building new residences all the time? The rumor was that they were being killed—forced to dig their own graves and then pushed in to die, suffocated by being buried alive by others who had just arrived. Still, here it could be a blessing to go straight to the grave.

She knew death could be preferable, because Anja had told her all the rumors. There were rumors about people who went to the infirmary—that at night you could see the lights blaze and then flicker and then hear horrific screams. The rumor was that the Nazis were performing evil, supposedly scientific, tests on prisoners—men, women, and children of every race.

Anja told her about the rumor of a club of Nazi soldiers—the Saturday Night Club—that raped Jewish men in front of their wives and families in order to extract information about what was really happening in the camp. Once they discovered who was pilfering an extra slice of bread, who had stolen a piece of apple, or who had snuck a note out of the camp, they would rape the women and sometimes the youngsters and then kill everyone anyway, so no one would know of their systematic sodomizing.

She heard about the family camps—whole families that had been relocated to the camp, and the thought made her want to weep. Constance was reeling with all this information. Anja had continued with barely a breath, "Others quickly start rumors. Rumors are rampant in the death camps. Some are stupid! Some are lies started by the enemy. Some turn out to be true or come true."

A few weeks later, Constance could see and appreciate the cage she was in. The German's prisoners had managed to build hundreds of buildings, probably 300 as far as she could estimate, but she could not see the entire camp. There were housing, administrative, and infrastructure barracks and buildings. She estimated that within an area of about 350 acres at Birkenau there were 12 to 13 miles of ditches dug by the prisoners to drain off water and dreams—most of the ditches were probably to capture any expectancy of positive hopes and run them off; 16 miles of barbed-wire fencing to prick thoughts of escape; over 10 miles of roads for a soul to walk, but only to the next evil.

She could see it all now—this camp was a machine that had been built to bring people to an end, that was sure—but it was not so clear in the moment.

Death is probably preferable.

NEW POTATOES

Under Anja's tutelage, Constance got busy. She was no chef but she had cooked a thousand meals as a young girl. She did not particularly enjoy the cooking and the chopping, but she soon became known around the kitchen.

"You could make an onion taste like a strawberry if you had the right ingredients!" Herr Meyer would say in wonder.

Constance had figured out that the Basque palate liked food that was a bit different than the dishes others might be cooking. She found the Eastern European girl to be monochromatic in her cooking style, so Constance teamed up with a French girl and they were off and running with new food ideas.

And she took some pride in her work, too. "No, write 'lamb' on the menu," she had told Herr Meyer, in regard to the Basque *paella*-type dish she was making (without fish, but *ram* was what they had and it was acceptable).

"But it is not lamb!" Herr Meyer complained. "It is not even a sheep; he is a *goat*—and a very old, hard-worked ram at that."

"But ram *rhymes* with lamb," she pointed out sweetly.

"You like your words, don't you dear!" Herr had noticed.

One of the camp higher-ups was so pleased with Constance's "lamb" meal that he ordered a small flock of sheep to be brought to the camp to be tended by the prisoners. The word was, some soldiers, upon being told what to procure, had found a flock hidden away on a nearby farm and rustled them at gunpoint from the owners—but getting the sheep to obey had been a laughable matter. Well, they finally had managed, and suddenly there was a small flock of sheep outside the kitchen.

Being Basque, Constance had much to say about the care of the sheep, and a way of chiding that was wearying, and soon a livestock pen was born. She grimaced at the irony—cages within cages. She swore to the sheep that she would do her best to protect them and treat them well, until it was time. At night, sleeping with Anja, she would think of how the sound of sheep and the smell of potatoes reminded her of life in the Pyrenees. It could have been so peaceful . . . it was horrifying to realize that her life was more peaceful here, at Auschwitz, than during her childhood, where constant berating, the continuous comparisons to her perfect sister, and the secret beatings had been normal. Oh!—but vile acts were happening all around her every day, just nothing yet against her. She had learned how to fade into the wall, stuffed her dress to look drab, and showed her chipped tooth prominently.

Tucked in next to Anja, Constance's mind wandered to many things at night after a long day in the kitchen. She thought of her sister often. It was too painful to remember the past, their harsh words, so she hoped for the way it could be in the future—how she wanted to be with Gracianna.

One night, Constance woke to screaming in the next barrack. Her mind went to Gracianna. She missed her so much but knew she would never see her again. *But I need forgiveness and need to forgive myself for being so dreadful to her—I was jealous and took her for granted. Gracianna, please forgive me. . . . I love you and admire you so much.*

The next morning in her little food supply room she noticed a lone, shriveled potato clinging to life. The spud had sprouted a bud, and it was the only sign of life for miles. In the potato, she saw the resilience that she had seen in the many prisoners around her. It clung to life, drawing on its own resources to live. It was like her and everyone in the camp, because it lived despite its wretchedness. The will to live seemed almost unconquerable, and she held the spud in her hand with care and hope.

Then, Constance noticed that the eyes of other potatoes in the pantry could see a chance for life, and those spuds had sprung buds as well. The sprigs came out of sympathy, or maybe it was the warmth in the room; she did not know.

I have an idea!

Where Constance came from, potatoes were a staple. She knew a bit about potatoes. She and Gracianna had learned that Basque sailors began to cultivate potatoes along the Biscay coast of Northern Spain around the end of the 16th century. Spanish conquistadors exploring the New World had observed the Incan Indians in Peru growing and cultivating potatoes in about 200 B.C., and brought this "strange plant" home where Europeans received it with *fear*. The poor potato was shunned for years because it was from the same family as the deadly nightshade plant. But the potato had eyes, gave life, and could see its life-giving future—and might even bring it to this shameful environment.

She wondered, *could I start a small patch of potatoes for special meals? They would be fresher than the old potatoes coming from the intermittent train deliveries, and they would be "just right."*

By now, she knew she should go straight to Herr Meyer; after all, he *was* the camp's official chef to the commander.

After a few days of her charm, Herr Meyer said, "fine! But do not take up any room, and do it quietly."

Voilà!

Constance knew exactly what to do even though it was late in the growing season; single potatoes in water would not do. For once, she had her grandmother to thank. Anastasia had started the potatoes and made the girls care for them. They had grown them in straw! They used to work some composted manure into the ground lightly, then place potatoes on top of the ground, place a bed of straw over them—maybe six inches—and water them every day.

Just like at home, as the potatoes grew, she would add more straw. She used some thin, long logs as bed boards to keep the straw in place. Constance found a small space near the sheep pen for this life-bed. She knew to keep a good thick layer of straw over the developing potatoes to keep them from getting sunburned and to hold the moisture in. The manure helped too.

Since potatoes need a lot of water while they are blooming, she diverted water twice a day with her bucket, and more people were becoming curious. This made it difficult to be a wallflower.

Once, she explained to a passing child who wandered by that, as soon as the leaf stalks died off, she would stop watering, scrape away the straw, and collect the gems. Then the little boy was coming back every day, sometimes with a friend.

She explained to the kitchen girls how it was just like home, sort of. "I harvest the 'tiny' potatoes only two weeks after the plant flowers—typically, you would wait another week for a real 'baby' potato. At home, we would store our potatoes, spreading them out, unwashed, across the top of the straw for two or three days to allow the skins to thicken. But," she showed them, "the skin is thick enough now." She figured her own skin was thick enough now for all of them, and an extra minute early to enjoy these—her own crop—was necessary.

They had liked the lesson very much, so she continued to tell them about how, after she harvested, she'd work the straw into the soil lightly and cover it all up with another layer of straw so the bed would be ready to work the next winter. But they had not liked the thought of staying for another year.

It forced Constance to consider the future possibilities, rotating the potato beds. One area should only be used for at least a season before working more manure into it and planting another crop there. The thought of another season at Auschwitz was not pleasant, but it was a possibility she had to accept.

One day, patting the straw in the late-day sunshine, it occurred to Constance how happy this made her.

How can you be content at a time like this? Grand-Mère Anastasia's voice seemed to ask her.

One day, a curious soldier came by and poked the bayonet of his rifle under the straw to see what was going on. He came up with a speared tiny potato and smiled broadly, saying something that Constance thought was "grandmother" and she smiled, hoping he would leave her alone. He didn't. He came by at the exact same time each day to watch the progress. It was very distracting.

It was a good lesson for her to never be caught off guard. She realized that life at Auschwitz was possibly as good as it could be—no better. Her monotony did not include enduring one painful moment after another, as she heard others working in the camp did. Cooking, cleaning, preparing, and serving meals was a godsend compared to what she saw and heard from the dining tables!

Mostly, camp command officers and guests—sometimes high-ranking

Jewish elders—were invited to join the meals she helped prepare. Besides the horrifying stories and occasionally seeing brutalities firsthand, Constance loved her job and came to be fond of Herr Meyer. He was calm and kind and a very good chef. She learned much from him and he seemed to genuinely enjoy learning from her. He also spoke some French, and he would practice with her sometimes—usually just food names and some such words.

From pestering Anja, she learned that Herr Meyer had actually been a prisoner in Germany, but somehow had been assigned to the camp as the head chef. There was speculation about his crime; everyone had a history in the camp, and his was rumored to have been murder. There were no details. No one knew, but no one was going to ask him, for fear of losing a wonderful job.

Constance decided it did not matter if Herr was a "murderer." She was a "shoplifter," supposedly. Who knew what was really true? What she saw in front of her seemed to be a good man. It made no sense to fret or cry over the past anymore. There was nothing she could do about the situation that had accidentally slipped her into this hell, but make the best of it.

Besides, even though Auschwitz was probably teeming with some real criminals, at least Constance was not here because she was Basque or Catholic. Somehow, she knew this would have felt much, much worse.

She was keenly aware that, despite any feelings of happiness, this was a dangerous land—this land of wolves—and she must continue to be very, very careful.

The soldier with the bayonet was alarming. He was showing interest in the patch but that could change in a moment.

Over the waning potato season, Constance honed her perfect survival instincts, learning the ins and outs of her world that was full of death and life and invasion, ever watchful and always listening. She remained faded into the scenery; evaded and dodged; hid; slipped and slinked away; made herself small; and dressed in ways that never revealed her ankles, wrists, or neck and appeared as unattractive as possible—never brushing her hair and rarely washing it—only when she could not stand it herself. Most women's heads were shaved but those in the kitchen were allowed to wear their hair longer since they served officers and guests. She purposely wore loose-fitting clothing that did not match, plus she also cut her hair badly and grew her bangs long in her face. Eye contact?—never! She could not be like Anja or Diana, and just go "visit" some soldier, or submit if some soldier took an interest.

Only if it means to save my life—or Anja's life. That is all.

She would never stop for a rare cigarette with the girls who would talk to the soldiers on break behind the kitchen sometimes, even if they seemed friendly. When she was walking with Anja, she would still not make eye contact with anyone. She could never trust a Nazi again. She had learned that one the hard way.

Zero attention!

So, it made her very nervous—this soldier with the bayonet. She did everything to be unattractive, walk awkwardly and limp when he was around, stoop in an old-woman's way. Hide her beauty, hide her grace, hide, hide, hide. Still, the potatoes bloomed. Anja and Herr Meyer were admiring them from the kitchen porch one afternoon, and Constance grinned at them with her chipped tooth, letting the little happiness of the moment in.

Thank you, grand-mère.

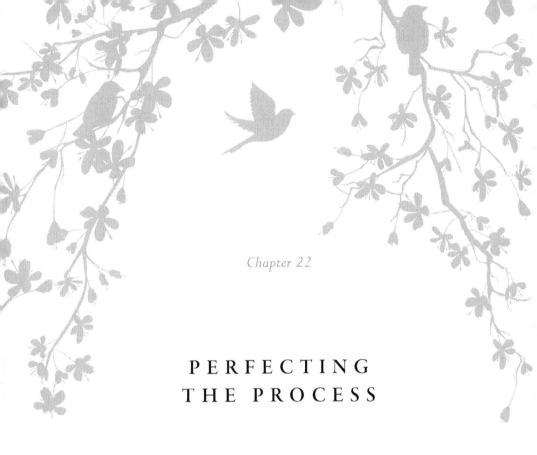

Chapter 22

PERFECTING
THE PROCESS

Through the season, like her sister, Gracianna sharpened her instincts for survival in occupied Paris. There were reports of death camps that were inundated with Jews.

Gracianna knew she had to be very careful to not draw any attention to herself—except from the target that Fontaine had arranged.

Her poise emerged. Fontaine designed it all to ensure no suspicion came her way.

Gracianna submerged her Basque fire so that she could accept Fontaine as the leader, but she continued to badger him for information on Constance.

"Constance, what of her? Please help me get information? A letter? Is she alive? Or . . . is she. . . ." she would insist. "The winter is coming!"

Finally, Fontaine produced some documents and stood over her late one night as she poured through lists of thousands of names of prisoners that some underground agents were able to steal.

So many names!

She learned to scan quickly, until she questioned herself and reread the list. Then, she would read the names once again. Fontaine never told her to hurry. He just stood there. Yet he refused to encourage her, because he thought her Constance search was a fool's effort.

Only that morning Fontaine had obtained the lists for Gracianna to review, when he also received the intelligence about Muller and his record. Now Fontaine understood the significance of the target that Gracianna had taken out. Muller was a "big fish" and it felt, with this one, as if they were making a difference.

"Is that it? Are you sure? Do you want to look at the list once more?"

"No. *Merci*. I do not see her. Nothing. No, I am sure."

He had given a little by trading for a small portion of an Auschwitz prisoner manifest and she continued to give a lot for it. But she was grateful to him. Gracianna realized she filled a niche in the chain, as she was hitting her stride in fulfilling her mission. Everything was going perfectly.

If not me, then who? Another girl would not be as strong. She would just be French, yes, she would probably be much more beautiful, with shiny hair and nice lips and tiny hips and a coy smile. But she would be missing something—Basque-ness. It was something that was needed at this time and in this place. It was a gift she was compelled to give.

As Juan walked her home that early morning he tried to put the whole thing in context, "The Gestapo would torture you, you know, any little thing could go wrong and you would be gone from me." Juan's complicity in something he thought was wrong was obvious as he tried to reason with her.

"I have accepted that we have everything to lose in this fight and even that I may be endangering you. This is my sacrifice for what I believe in. You do not have to do this. You are fighting by my side. We are doing it together. That is your choice. I have this inside of me. You know it has a hold of me and it won't let go. I have to give everything, Juan. You understand. Please . . . go or . . . stay. You decide. But I would rather you stay. No more talking about it."

It seemed every week that Gracianna was constantly moving back and forth between the venue du jour. The places she was shuttled to for the operations were always dingy and rat infested. With dirty floors, every one of them, they were nothing like La Maison.

Disgusting.

Marceau would do the floors of La Maison when she was away. He hated it and his hatred was apparent in his work. She did not fault him. Instead, she always and relentlessly carried out her assignment again, then again as they moved her to each place. Back and forth. Sometimes, she and Juan would sleep at their place, sometimes at a safe hotel across town.

In a turn of heart, Fontaine now suggested Gracianna take a silencer smuggled from the UK. He said, "It is too dangerous to rely on being able to disarm the target and use his gun. We have had some close calls."

"No. If I have that I will always think of it. Best to stay with what I know. If I get in trouble, you are all close." He didn't like it but there was no talking to her, "I'll leave it in the tool shed in the garden under the trunk anyway. Not much good it would do you but . . . "

She was his star and he needed her. She was finding herself. She felt more open, more aware, and more attractive. Her confidence was turning her from near-hubris to feeling comfortable with her situation. "Your little girl is growing up," Fontaine had told Dom' with a sly grin, but he said it with pride.

She realized that the officers were accustomed to bend-over service; working on her knees allowed her to easily get them off guard at the most crucial moment. Sometimes, they would even close their eyes! But, they were invariably in a place in their heads where they were transported, distracted, and unaware of the danger that could befall them.

"After all, Gracianna is slight," Fontaine laughed, looking down on her. "You are. You must admit. They think of you as the weaker sex! You are half their size!" Looking away he proclaimed, "She is beautifully plain. She is—oh no! Basque!" Then, pretending his hand is a gun, "Bang! It is too late!"

She did not think it funny. Fontaine, normally serious, occasionally tried to make light of what she did, but she did not appreciate his jibes. Her life now was much more serious than before and filled with deception.

How did I get here?

She was like a small handsome flower, dangerous but able to attract. She learned to feign seduction. Of course, she never let them kiss her. She was always in control of the scene. After the time when she had been choked, she hated herself for losing control. She knew she had looked away and knew why. She disliked chaos. It wouldn't happen again. She learned the hard way not to allow any room for error. Her sharpened instincts were guiding her now. It was a perfect fit.

She'd learned to pretend she was about to be subservient herself as her target unbuckled his pants. Doing so achieved two important things: first, it offered her ready access to the object she needed; also, his opened trousers offered a perverse form of self-protection, putting him in a compromised and awkward position to help tangle him so that he was unable to grab his weapon.

Then, in a sound-padded room: *Bang!*

The perfectly creased uniforms, the ominous and badging epaulettes, the moth-eaten woolen uniform, the ribbons of achievement dangling near her nose as they would bend over her, all proved worthless at this moment.

BANG!

Once, always once, with perfection, and it was over.

Oh, she would occasionally hear a whisper among the actors in this play . . . everyone had his part. They would often talk about her performance right after the act. She could hear resisters saying, "Oh! He is a heavy one," as they carried him out. "He was ready to be happy but now he is sad." Once they said, "She missed," apparently a reference to the fact that early on, Gracianna had begun shooting the men in their forehead—ostensibly, "right between the eyes." It was probably based on the "pattern" that had started from the beginning. It was significant for many reasons. It created a stunning word of mouth among the resistance that Gracianna's way of operating had become her calling card. She was becoming a legend.

Hawkeye had teased her once, "How can you miss at this close range?" Of course, he had to point out that one kill had taken two shots to do the job. Hawkeye was not the only one who had laughed.

In reality, the men did not want to think about the dirty act that she was performing at close range, so close it would be hard to miss. The man "she missed" had turned his head at his last moment—only because he was looking for the drink that she had poured for him and she could not wait to get it done. No one would ever know this because she never spoke of it to anyone. The time for speaking of the details had passed. She reasoned that if she did not speak of them, it might be possible that they did not happen.

After the second time, Juan was always on the scene. It turned out that he would assume the job of cleaning up Gracianna afterward—to "handle" her, change her. He would not enter the room; he could not bear it. He would put her back together when she stepped out of the room. He had always prepared damp towels. He would warm them if he could, except once, and he apologized for it—profusely. It was as if the round or the fight was over, and the trainer was primping his fighter, preparing for the next round.

From her corner, he calmly said encouraging things to her, "You did good, really well," "it is over." He always said, "I am here to take you." "You are safe now."

"See me?" he would say as he bent to put his cheek next to hers. "Here I am. I will take you away from this now." She never looked at Juan afterward. He never tried to look her in the eye either.

Juan always gave himself the sign of the cross just after the muffled shot. He would always have a change of clothes for her. Almost always, he would have a new blouse, or sometimes an overcoat. He would simply unbutton his wife's blouse and replace it with another cotton blouse. None of the men on cleanup duty ever looked. They had a job to do. Everyone was doing what he needed to do after Gracianna did her job.

Like a dresser in the theater responsible for quick changes between acts, Juan performed his duty. They button "up the wrong side," he would always say, and she would glance down and see what he had brought her and know what he meant. He was wiping the perspiration from her face and then unbuttoning and buttoning with octopus hands, working feverishly, but they weren't like the hands that had groped her only moments ago. She stood there like a mannequin, lifeless, wooden.

Juan had come to do this task out of love for his wife and out of fear for her life, but she was desperately and serenely detached.

She gazed away toward a land only she could see. She stood, lifeless, except occasionally she shook her head, always in agreement.

Juan never asked a "no" question, only "yes" questions.

She was just like the boxer, M. Dom' would say, "albeit, a very small fighter," whose eyes and body seem to be in Bilbao, but whose mind is really in Pamplona.

The men in her operation did their jobs after Gracianna the boxer delivered the knockout punch. And afterward, as Dom' would say with piety, "And now the serious cleanup begins."

Gracianna knew that they, the sympathizers, were all there behind her, intent to support the operation. They were strewn among the crowd—in the bar and at the tables, couples sometimes, their job just to leave on cue. They wanted to do something. Others were on the street outside and out back in the alleyway, smoking and talking, at the apartment next door, in cars around the block. They were actually like wolves, or like vultures lying in wait, in sheep's clothing, supposed drunkards, talkative bartenders, unimportant and stupid Frenchmen who had allowed the new regime to run over them like a weaker race. What the superior race failed to notice was that the stupid French were waiting to pick the carcass clean and then, in the final act, make it disappear. Into the darkness. Make it all disappear they did, with ready alibis. They were alibis filled with imperfections that led to success.

Selecting the target had to be done with precision. The choice fell on Fontaine, and no one really knew about all the intelligence he had available to him. It came to him in oh-so-many ways. It was clear he was meticulous about the choice.

"Always leave just a little room for error," he said repeatedly.

Rarely was a target chosen randomly. It would always be someone in particular. Fontaine would sic her on the most strategically important targets. She imagined the ones without stripes were communications technicians or couriers; she wasn't sure, but knew they must be important and that there was a bigger plan, and she just needed to do her job. One of the "weaklings" on her crew would be the one to identify the officer of the evening and offer him a free drink. That was the signal. It was a cruel joke, a last supper of sorts. (Other officers were subsequently offered free drinks that evening, so as not to allow that little extra attention to be called out in an investigation.)

Then, Gracianna would catch his eye. It was almost too easy. "*Sie sind hübsch* [You are handsome]," was all Gracianna had to say quietly in German.

Then it was just all over. The German officers were well known for running and exercising in their briefs on the streets of Paris, their fine bodies in contrast to the Frenchman's average physique. It was not a secret that French waifs were attracted to them. The Germans were not shy about trying to take advantage of the opportunity so easily given to them.

In her field, however, was a wolf wanting a lamb but finding a wolf. Gracianna was intent on taking a life to save lives and, maybe somehow, her sister's life.

It was always only a matter of time. The lingering at closing—miraculously everyone would clear out—and she would barely look over her shoulder as she moved upstairs, downstairs, or to a back room. The chosen officer would usually be drunk, his eyes transfixed and flushed with lust. He would often insist that he would stay and have "one more drink" when his party was ready to leave.

Her job was to transfix the target, but so that no one in his party would see her doing so. It sent the powerful signal to the officer to keep this a secret rendezvous. This was between them. Only he and she knew this was going to happen and he needed it that way, and so did she. It was like a mind trick that hypnotized the man, who was in the hands of a skilled practitioner; though it was artless and banal, it was proven over and over through the ages. Now, though, the game was being played for a different prize-ending.

It was like creating a magical illusion, and then delivering the coup de grace.

She was part of a bigger organism working toward the same end. The information team would gather intelligence; the communication team would get the word out. Every pre-planned scene was synchronistic and tightly integrated. They would get the precise word to the right place at the right time—unless their purpose was to confound communications—by taking portions of messages from the enemy and mixing them up or ever-so-slightly altering one little item such as the time or date, changing it from 9 a.m. to 9 p.m., from July 6 to July 8. They would intercept packages and messages and mix them up to confound discovery, and jumble messages with the greatest of ease. They would hear and see things through espionage and old fashioned eavesdropping, and pass the treasure to the information analysts who would convert it to intelligence and to action.

La Résistance worked like ants, operating twenty-four hours a day, with well-conducted jobs. The procurement group would swipe material needed for operations: cars, alcohol, radios, and weapons. The expediters—they are the fixers—they get people to the right place at the right time, whether they are dead or not. Usually it was the lifeless ones they were known for cleaning up. They whisked away the mess with blinding speed and integrated the disappearance "just right" so it became, usually, the runaway of a decorated officer.

Usually a woman was suspected—a whore—and there were plenty of them who would gladly take a ticket to North Africa or America or some-where out of the war scene in return for acting as the shill for the operation and for Gracianna. Gracianna knew the women of course—she would often see the ladies—the stragglers walking awkwardly in impossible shoes on her way home. They would exchange "*bonsoirs*," even though it was very early in the morning, with little real eye contact on Gracianna's part. Ironically, the unknowing prostitutes often called out to Gracianna, "Get home or a man is going to get you."

They laughed, but all the ladies knew they wished to trade places with her instead.

The expediters were mostly visible to Gracianna. They were setting up the mark, and the first in the room right after work was done.

With this same precision, the expediters, like production designers, would carefully choose the locations—establishments with basements and large rooms that could be fortified to muffle sounds of the ambush—and identify the places that needed extra soundproofing. One by one the officers were "pushed" into the room and picked off.

"The push!" Fontaine had explained, "It's a technique of the carnival workers, who will get the last dime out of anyone. It's like herding." He looked at her and Juan.

He explained how carnival workers in P. T. Barnum's circus had per-fected it. Disguised as customers in the crowd, they would call out ques-tions to the barker, and laugh and insinuate that they could not wait to see the for-pay spectacle. Some would even "pay" and walk in, hooting and hollering from inside as if in amazement at what they could see right behind the canvas. This endorsement paled next to the physical urge that the crowd felt to follow the early shills—for another force was really at work. Carnies working the back of the crowd would elbow and "push" with their hips and shoulders; forward, forward, forward into the real customers in front of them, who would in turn push the customer in front of them, like domi-noes. Once the first was dropped, the rest fell in unison, with less glittery jingle in their pocket as they hit P. T.'s cash extrication tent.

Not realizing the push was *the push*, Dom' would say, "Gracianna, together, we are pushing for something for all of us. Something bigger."

She never felt alone. Working with La Résistance, she was learning how to orchestrate the push precisely—as one force. It was collective body language and they perfected the dance. A light was turned off in the back, always the signal. Someone, maybe a chef, would call "*Bonsoir,*" and others would call back. Doors closed, bags were opened and shut in exaggerated ways. The bartenders would start to "put away" glasses and put bottles back up on the shelf to signal "closing." And Gracianna played her part like a sharp-shooter. Once the spider's web was set, her job was singular and solo. She never wanted to talk about it with anyone, no matter how Fontaine tried to debrief her. How could she tell him how terrified and angry she felt inside? The sick details of the man, of the act? The killing was her cross to bear.

Every time, it was a clean sweep. Smile discreetly, glide, strut, point, disappear, greet, smile, grab—and Pop! With minor variations, every operation was the same. "Always allow for variation!" Fontaine would warn her.

She did her job again and again. It just happened with efficiency now.

She did not like looking at them, in the eyes, when she shot them point blank. What mattered was that he was gone and unable to potentially rustle an innocent woman from her life to a concentration camp ever again. In an instant, gone. For a reason, killed—a reason she believed in.

Every night it was the same.

Smile,

glide,

strut,

point,

disappear,

greet,

smile,

grab,

and

BANG!

Smile at the *special someone* that night.

Glide past him, with ease and intent.

Strut with just a bit of "she" in the movement.

Point out where she would be later.

Disappear at the end of the evening, and make her way to the waiting place and wait. And wait . . . and then . . .

Greet, "Well, you figured out my little game didn't you?"

Smile. Simply. Coyly. Intentionally. Invitingly.

Grab the gun, while he is distracted or indisposed.

BANG!

Smile, glide, strut, point, disappear, greet, smile, grab, *BANG!*

There!

Done.

She reasoned she could not extinguish the soul of a man after all. Graci-anna had come to this nature of things and rationalized the balance of war.

Someone could kill him the next day. He was in the war after all, wear-ing the uniform; he must have a reasonable expectation to die.

Even if she did not want to, if she did not persist, things might be out of order. She had her own reasonable expectation to die. It did not occur to her that she was putting herself in harm's way. After all, Constance had done nothing, and she was harmed and may be dead. So, fighting for her made sense, and the fairness of it all coalesced.

NOT FAST ENOUGH

"It is not enough," Gracianna said to herself while alone, as winter arrived in a frightful rain one night—studying another pile of prisoner lists with names to scour through. "I can't do this anymore." Constance was no closer, and there was an endless sea of occupying faces. The war was no closer to ending. Constance seemed unreachable. Wave after wave of occupiers came, took apartments, took girlfriends, paid for or not. They took part, but she could not take them all.

This work. It does not seem to stop anything or accomplish much.

At the end of the night, Gracianna reflected, what she was doing was humble work—and frustrating, infuriating even. And exhausting. The only thing that really seemed to be getting accomplished was that Christmas was coming closer, and Juan seemed to be getting farther away.

Why would he stand for this? We are married but not really. He waits for me.

So there was Juan. Always in the background. Always ready and never interfering with operations. He was not allowed to get any closer than the boundaries set by Fontaine.

Juan just smoked in the alley with the others. Sometimes, Gracianna would see him pacing alone, his Basque legs wanting for the high mead-ows—she could tell. She wished she could give him what he wanted: a normal life. The tension was grinding them both now. Once they could easily speak of these things. Now, there was something in the way. They did not speak about it. They were trying to accept each other, but Gracianna could see the imbalance in the way.

"Yes, we do it your way," he had always said. "For now," he had begun to add, lately.

She knew he could not be patient with her forever, that perhaps her heart-flower could not open to his feelings fully. It had never opened for any man—other than the university man in her dreams. *I want to love him. Why can I not let it be?* She knew she had turned to Juan at night once, but never since.

"The barrel is filling," Juan would say with a smile, of their tin money box for America.

"Time is running out," Gracianna would say somewhat sadly of it filling. The thought of Constance left behind always gave her butterflies and a sense of urgency.

She would look out the window over Paris and wonder if she would ever make it overseas. It reminded her that her mother had told her once as a child, "Your grandmother and I could always look out the same window without ever seeing the same thing."

She knew what that meant now.

Gracianna and Juan looked out the window and saw two different things. She saw duty and the loss of Constance. He only saw Gracianna in his future. *Is he just my puppy dog?*

When Juan was on the street or in the next building waiting for the eventuality of the evening, he felt tied up. His emotions burned like spitting sparklers inside his stomach and throat, throwing off hissing flickers. Waiting reminded him of what it was like being a teenager again; he felt his emotions so raw, right under his skin. As an adult he lost, like all adults do, the recollection of the intensity of teen feelings. Like feeling in love, just like the first time he had seen her there across the room, like it was yesterday at the church rectory where they were going to sing Christmas carols when they were young; feelings like a tide of attraction that he could not understand. His thoughts went everywhere at a frantic pace with the waiting. Here was Juan waiting, his wife fighting her own battle for righteousness and virtue . . . *And here I am thinking of myself. What is wrong with me?*

"Ridiculous!" Juan had said to Hawkeye one time in the puddled alley while waiting. "What is wrong with us—what husband and wife do this!?"

"My wife and I do," said Hawkeye, directly.

ANOTHER NEW TARGET

Fontaine and Dom' came to see Gracianna at their apartment that bristly day; it was unusual, but this assignment briefing would take place back at her home base, La Maison. This was understandable because most cafés were not far from Maison, but in different neighborhoods just outside the typical resting spots of the command crowd. After working the long day thinking up ways to brutalize the populace, the officers needed to find refreshment close to their host headquarters, Le Meurice. There were different cafés all the time and in some variation, but it was essentially the same operation.

"He is important, Gracianna," Fontaine said. "He's a colonel. Kohn. This is it—no more."

"I will do my best," she chided.

Colonel Kohn.

Dom' was there and said, "We are nearly finished. You will leave us soon my dear. I am proud of you. I know you and Juan will leave soon. I miss you already, dear. Thank you."

She said, "You are a patriot, Dom'," knowing he was feeling melancholy, always wanting to do more.

She had always known the time would come, but it had come so fast, too fast. *Constance!*

When Gracianna arrived at La Maison that evening, the clean floor surprised her. "It seems the world goes on without me," she said to Marceau with a wink.

"Good to have you back," he said.

Yet it was nice to be back, after "working" at various other cafés in Paris. Only, a little sad to think that soon, she would be away—from Dom' and Fontaine, Marceau, and Hawkeye, and the others.

But oh! Constance! Maybe I need to stay to learn what I can of her?

Tonight would be for Constance.

The target had been chosen and everything was moving swimmingly. Gracianna fixed her gaze on the man as she approached his table. He was talking to another officer, both men in uniform. Her instincts were rattled. He was a stately officer with something. Something special. Gracianna could not put her finger on the difference, but she instantly knew he was something else.

Trusting her instincts, she slowed as she approached his table, fingering the empty drink tray so no one would think it too odd if they looked up. But Kohn was not looking.

He is supposed to be looking. They always look.

Instead he was listening, sitting forward with his hands folded on his lap, very carefully attending to the speaker—it seemed as if he were catching some news: listening, leaning in. Concentrating, Gracianna tried to catch what was being said: "Auschwitz."

She caught it like a thud.

Constance is there!

A chill seared through her. *Auschwitz* came with stories too horrific to believe, but she had to listen. She knew that Constance was there, because of the manifest that Juan had "borrowed."

"Auschwitzzzzzz . . ."

They were laughing!

Gracianna seethed silently while picking at her tray and "speaking" to the decoy couple at the next table—they were talking to her but she was listening to him. She could tell he was important from the symbols on his uniform—Fontaine had explained them all, what they meant. It occurred to her he would be the highest-ranking officer she would ever take down.

She recognized him as a German who traveled. As he entered the café she had heard him poorly pronounce a Polish word but had passed it off. His peers looked upon him admiringly. Now she could piece it together.

In German she could make out that he said, "*Gefangener und transport* [Prisoner and transport]."

Gracianna's heart leaped. As she listened, she became sure that he had the power to move people around—at Auschwitz?! She was transfixed and confused, and voices and music now sounded shrill. Her lingering was cut just right by a call for her. "*Oui, un moment . . .*" She hardly cared about them. Nothing mattered but this. She picked up her tray and listened.

A bite bit through her insides. This officer had a key to the Birkenau Concentration Camp near Krakow. It was one of the satellite concentration camps in Auschwitz for criminals to be "reeducated," and for Jews, supposedly, to be given hard labor. It was where Constance had been sent.

But is she alive?

She heard it again. "Auschwitz."

The word floated again and again, landing on her chest in ghastly blooms.

Suddenly a trace of hope was inside of her.

Kohn noticed her and called her over, and asked her in perfect English if she would fetch him a glass of Bordeaux.

"Bordeaux?" Gracianna asked. The real question—*he speaks to me in English?*

He must have heard one of the kitchen staff speak to her in English briefly when he entered over two hours ago.

Their eyes had met when he came in—only for a moment. He looked at her confidently, not down at her. There was something very hard about him, but she saw a glint of tranquility? It seemed impossible that this man was at peace with himself. She could tell he was ruthless. Yet—he carried it as an obligation. She could see or at least feel he was not a bad man inside. It was an understated look; she saw a glimmer of faith. She used her sense, of these things she felt in people. Though she was going to kill him anyway.

There was something else about this man, and her brain rattled trying to think.

"*Oui, du Bordeaux,*" Kohn said and smiled.

With the flash of his perfect teeth, the recognition triggered. He was the customer she had told about the rutabaga at the cozy restaurant, where the Beauty helped her out recently.

He had been wearing plain clothes and was friendly.

He'd joked that he was "German" and she a "poisoner." It was unlikely that he would recognize her because her hair was hidden that day and she had been wearing thick glasses that Fontaine had given her.

Bordeaux.

She almost said these flash-thoughts aloud to him spontaneously, but at the last second, every muscle froze. *Dakien guztia ez derrala* [Don't say as much as you know].

"*Oui, Bordeaux,*" she said then and bumbled away, her head spinning. "The first look is very, very important—the most important!" she learned it from the Russian girl. She always made the connection on the *first look*.

She stopped cold.

He knows about Auschwitz transports.

She stole glances toward the colonel throughout the night, *to see if he was looking*, but he did not return any of them.

Am I not pretty enough for him? Does he not recognize me?

Gracianna was alarmed to find him so handsome.

He is stupid then, if he doesn't understand he can get me!

Still, her attraction response troubled her as she looked at him admiringly.

Is this how it feels, when men see a beautiful woman? Are they so easily disarmed? I suppose I should know.

Gracianna refused to be disarmed and thought of Constance.

The target, Kohn, hardly noticed her at all, except for his Bordeaux order earlier. He never looked at her for very long when she was at the table. There seemed to be no opportunity to make a connection. This was uncommon for the flirt-dance that usually ensued, and Gracianna was not sure what to do.

Allow for variation.

Yet, when it was time to go, finally, after many desperate moments in Gracianna's heart, the colonel told the other officers that he would stay behind for one more drink. It was unexpected.

Everything feels wrong, yet he asked to stay?

The outcome would be the same, no matter what the path. He could get to his *home* whatever way he wanted, she thought, as long as he gave her the 45 seconds she needed to maneuver him to the compromising spot after he had just one or two more drinks.

He sipped while she cleaned. It was late and on cue. "Patrons" filed out. She noticed he remained quite upright and sober even after drinking all night.

He watched, tapped his finger deliberately to a tune, and even raised an index finger on the high point of one song, as if he were the maestro to an orchestra of empty chairs.

In English he said, "Come here. Sit. What is your name?"

She looked straight at him, not seeming surprised, "Gracianna."

"Where are you from? You are not French. I can hear your accent is . . ."

"I'm Basque."

He chuckled knowingly, "Basquo? Well, that describes it all?" and he laughed heartily.

She was unsure if he was laughing at her or complimenting her heritage, so she gave him a twisted look.

"What, Gracianna?" he reached toward her to move a dangling hair from her face, but stopped short. She looked closely at his clean manicured hand as he self-consciously withdrew it.

She wondered, *What is he doing?*

"So, Gra-ci-anna," he sounded it out. "I have read of the Romans and your people. I am a student of conflicts and know the famous of many battles, Carol the Great, the Reconquest. I admire the Basque for the way they fight and work. It is obvious you work very hard. You are a rebel, I can see it. I like that about you," he said as he briefly looked her over.

"And you? A fighter?" she asked.

A shadow came over his eyes and he took a long drink. "Eh, sometimes, but it is not my life." He gave a shrug.

A shrug? Not my life?

Gracianna was perplexed.

Why is he telling me this?

Yet, a shrug also meant more. Hope sprang in her. "Well, I see that you are an important officer. And you know my people? Can I get you something else? Anything? I really need to work," it all spewed out of her in a soup of words.

She was confused and not thinking well; she did not know what to say or what she was saying. He wasn't behaving appropriately—or was it she? A flick-glance toward the bar, and she could see Hawkeye looking at her sternly: *What is happening? Why are you walking away from him? Take him to the back now!*

She stopped cold.

"So, may I get you something else? I need to close. I must go," she stood up, looking back briefly as she walked.

As if waking suddenly, he said, "No, no, sorry to have kept you." He stood up, twisted on the inky heel of tall, shining black boots, without leaving a mark, she noticed, pulled at his perfectly pressed jacket and made for the door.

She stepped out of the back room to see him, and he said, "Come here." She did not want to go but could feel his energy drawing her.

He opened the door as she approached. He pointed. "You see that hotel?

I am staying there. You see that room? The top on the right? That is my room. Mademoiselle Chambon is at the desk—I will tell her to let you up if you ever decide to. Since you are a learned woman, you may want to come see my books on the Roman Empire. If the light is on, I am awake. It was my pleasure to meet you, Gracianna."

She watched him walk away. Two of her compatriots poured in after she turned down the light, "What happened?" they wanted to know.

"He is different," she said.

She sunk into the chair he had been sitting in—she could feel his heat on the seat and now on her seat and it made her jump. "What?" and the two men laughed, "A ghost?"

Juan had entered and wondered what was going on.

"Let's go home, Gras'."

She said, "I am not finished."

"I think we really need to go," he said against her protestations.

He took her by the arm, flung her coat over her shoulders and walked her out. She glanced up at the hotel window.

The light was on.

A few nights later, Colonel Kohn returned. Alone. With some papers and books.

There was much laughter and frolicking that night from the weekend customers—and many, many drinks. Kohn ordered a small meal and two glasses of Bordeaux. He barely looked at her when she tripped while helping the bartender pick up a mountain of glasses that had spilled. She turned red with embarrassment and could not help but catch his eye and was surprised to find some solace there. He left as she was on the floor.

Why could she not get this right?

Always with his nose in a book!

She admired how studious he was. She wished she had been able to go to the university. It reminded her of when she used to read all the time. It seemed so long ago.

I miss reading. Studying.

What had become of her dreams?

Constance. . . . America. . . . Juan. Fontaine!

"Relax," Fontaine said, after two more nights had passed when Kohn appeared. It was a total of four nights with no result, because the man never stayed.

"He is a smart one," Dom' told her. "You watch out for him." Gracianna was humiliated as much as intrigued.

"There is a new operation," Fontaine said on another night and began to tell the location, but Gracianna said she had started something and wanted to finish this one, no matter how long it took.

Dom' told Fontaine that night, "You know she is like a pit bull and won't let go."

"I know," Fontaine said and winked.

"It runs in her family," Dom' snickered.

By now, La Résistance had pieced together a better picture of Colonel Kohn and was resigned to "take weeks to get him, if necessary." They knew from information sourced from across the street that Herr Kohn was a Nazi colonel in the Wartheland (Polish) division and that he was born outside Frankfurt, Germany. He studied at Universität Freiburg as an engineering scholar, and could not hide his love for history. He always had books with him, and many work papers. When Gracianna heard the name of his university, it spoke a lot about him. She surmised that he surely drank a lot of beer in his "uni" days and that he came into contact with many French *and* Swiss people, girls especially, since Freiburg was close to two borders. This helped Gracianna understand what she supposed was his more liberal nature.

The hotel night manager confirmed that he had papers with an "Auschwitz" seal on them; a maid had seen them in his room one day. The day manager had heard him speaking with another officer in the lobby as they both waited for a colleague, and those little bits were added to the treasure trove of information that was put together each day.

Finally, the colonel came around again, and Gracianna's easily distracted support crew was instantly reengaged. According to them, Kohn was almost a "fixture" by now, but they settled into a rhythm of waiting for him to play along. "She has never let us down before," said Marceau with a nod toward Gracianna. "It will just be a matter of time until we get busy cleaning up after her, tonight, tomorrow, next week . . . whenever."

Kohn was always in a perfectly pressed uniform, always with a book, this time with another officer to entertain. Gracianna did not wait on them, but while she passed, she heard Kohn say to his man, ". . . that is the Basque that I told you about."

Gracianna froze.

"She has no fight in her," his tablemate said sarcastically.

Gracianna turned, flipped her pure hair, and said, "Don't underestimate me." She looked boldly at Kohn before swaggering away. Both men backed up, feigning fear and nervously laughing. Kohn, though, quickly realized that he was genuinely unhappy at her display of defiance, especially in front of his colleague. She could feel his eyes singe her as she went into the kitchen.

Dinner service was wordless.

He left with his friend without a nod.

Later, she was up in the office straightening up and turned, feeling someone was there. He was standing in the doorway.

"I did not expect you to come to see me in my room."

She looked at him, not thinking tonight would be the night, but she knew her backup was out there.

"I brought this for you," he said and he handed her an old book, "*The Dictionary of Greek and Roman Geography*. I marked a page," he motioned, "it is the story of Crassus, the young leader sent by Caesar to win Aquitania."

"Yes, that is a region of my ancient country."

"But your people gave in to him."

"Yes, they did but we kept fighting and never stopped. Yes, I know something of this story . . . but . . ."

"But what?"

". . . I would like to read more about it."

"Well, I thought you would. Enjoy this. I will be back to see you soon."

"Wait."

He swirled on his heel expectedly with a smile, "Yes, Gra-ci-anna."

She just blurted it out. "*My sister* . . . her name is Constance. She is in your prison—Birkenau. I would do anything if you helped me. Help me help her, that is."

He scowled now; he had heard it a hundred times before. "How do you know of me? Why would you think I could help you?"

"I heard you say, '*Dobry wieczor* [Good evening]' in Polish; you said it to that officer the first night. I heard them say, 'Auschwitz' to you too. You are a powerful man; I just know it. You are, aren't you?"

"Well . . . ," he said, not softening, but curious.

"I can tell you," pulling a paper from the pocket of her apron—she paused as if embarrassed, then not. As he looked intently at her, she excitedly put the paper on the table and they both looked at it as she read:

"Constance Marie Arrayet Rousseau, Basque, Le Marais, Paris, for stealing, on this date," as she pointed to it. "Guilty. Sentenced to two years hard labor in Auschwitz—two years for stealing they said, but she did not steal anything . . . but she is in Birkenau. In Birkenau. Auschwitz, Number Two."

He nodded knowingly.

"She is innocent—it was a mistake—an officer, a bad man did not like her—she was beautiful, is beautiful, she probably did not smile at him. He accused her and then, one of yours," she puffed, "he picked her up for stealing. She did not steal. She did not steal," she said choking back tears.

Hopefully, looking up at him, she said, "Can you help me?"

Curiously he said, "Help you . . . help you what? Get a letter to her? I do not even know if she is there."

Confidently, "She is there, I know it."

Smartly, "Well, you have this all figured out then, don't you? I assume you had some help finding that out?"

Steadfastly, "I do not want to get her a letter."

"What do you want then?"

Out of nowhere she announced it. "I want her out."

"Out!?"

He laughed out loud. Hard. "Once someone is in they do not come 'out!' What are you thinking—I know you are stubborn but I did not know you were an imbecile!"

"Imbecile? Do not call me that," she was angry—angry like when Bettina had seen her in the ranch kitchen before. She rose up on her toes, reached up with her right arm and slapped Colonel Kohn hard across the face.

Stunned. He stood there.

"So, I suppose you want to send me to Auschwitz now so I can be with my sister? Well take me then if you must, I am ready," she said as she assumed the position with her hands out for handcuffs.

Angry and confused, his hand went to his face and he felt the heat of her ferocity on it.

An involuntary tear formed in his left eye and he blinked. Then he laughed, laughed like he laughed the first night they met, and then laughed some more. "Oh! Basquo! I remember you now! You wanted to poison me," he said and he reached out and slapped her hard across the face.

Stunned, she stood there.

Angry and confused, her hand went to her face and she felt the heat of him on it.

Then she laughed with him and laughed like she had not laughed in months and months.

They both laughed and then she reached out for him and slapped him hard.

Stunned again, he stood there. They both laughed harder.

She unexpectedly realized that the gentleness in him was her weakness, and he accepted that her strength was beginning to draw him in.

Gracianna's partners were outside waiting.

What is she doing in there? It never takes this long.

All the other routine acts usually started with the "pop." But tonight they could hear *laughing* coming from inside.

Confused and wide-eyed, the backup watched Colonel Kohn walk away with his collar turned up. He was seen putting a paper in his breast pocket as he strode across the street to his room. They rushed in when he was out of sight, expecting to find her dead.

She was not dead. She was whistling. Happily working. Whistling. "What . . . ?" she looked at them deadpan.

"What happened?

"I let him live. He will be back tomorrow. I will do it then. It was not right."

She was back mopping the floor, the music now on and the clarinet wailing. The clean-up men were incredulous. She had missed him again.

Juan, watching from across the street, waited. When she came out, he was there. They walked home side by side in the dark. They walked up the stairs.

Unceremoniously and silently they got in bed. They lay far apart. After a while, neither knew the other was awake. Gracianna was thinking of one thing that one of her "maid mafia," who worked at the nearby hotel, had told her: "I heard that if a letter had the "seal" of officers of a certain rank or above, that the order would not, 'could not' be questioned. Anything can be made to happen if you have such an order with a seal."

Gracianna prayed for Constance and for herself. She did not pray for Colonel Kohn.

Lord, help me help Constance.

FONTAINE'S WARNING

"What the hell are you thinking? We are at war!" Fontaine roared at Gracianna the next morning in the kitchen at La Maison. "What are you waiting for? Shoot the bastard! Of course, do the right things. Take your time and be safe, but we have been in place for many nights now."

"You are comparing him to easy targets. He is different. *And* it takes time to develop information!"

"In-for-ma-tion? You are forbidden to develop information in this operation! Haven't I made this clear! You don't understand the implications of this man disappearing."

That evening, Colonel Kohn was there when she arrived at work, uncharacteristically late.

It was quiet that night and getting quieter, with just a couple bartenders sorting the evening's receipts. He had no idea they were hangers-on waiting to clear his mess.

He stayed all night. The moment the last man left, she resolutely sat with him at his table.

"Have you considered my sister? Constance Rousseau. It might be Constance Arrayet. Constance Arrayet Rousseau."

"I will look into it."

"Thank you," she was lifted cheerfully and she jumped up, whimsically and uncharacteristically kissed him on the cheek, and could not help but half-skip once. She had never skipped.

"Did you like the book I brought you?"

"Yes, I like it very much," she said from behind the bar. "I have been reading it but I am very busy at night as you know, and tired in the day. I can barely make it here at four o'clock in the evening and be rested to work."

"You work too hard," he said.

"I'm curious," she said and thought quickly, "why do you like the Basque?"

He lit up again.

"I told you I am a student of strategy. Like the early Basques, you know, the Sotiates."

"You know Sotiate?" Gracianna asked, amazed.

"Yes, of course."

She was perfectly hooked and he could see it. So he explained. "Well, it was before Christ. . . ."

Christ?! This Nazi said 'Christ'—and what will be next?

". . . this tribe of early Basques—they were miners—copper miners. And they were against the Romans! The invaders! The miners fought for freedom against the strong army. But they could not beat the militia on land, no matter if the Roman leader was a very young man . . ."

"Crassus—'Boy General,' his men called him," she finished the sentence.

"Yes. So they dug tunnels. This was the Sotiates' specialty. . . ."

"Tunnels," she completed him.

". . . and they nearly lived *underground* and attacked from below. They knew their way underground well, in the mines, your people."

"As I recall," she said, "they planned to draw Crassus into an ambush."

On the table, Kohn placed the salt and the pepper and the knife just so, and began an elaborate demonstration of strategic moves using them.

". . . and then their infantry was placed in this position where they could attack the Romans as they passed through this valley. The Sotiates used their strong cavalry to lure the Romans in. . . . Right . . . here."

Gracianna watched in admiration.

"Then Crassus fell into the trap. The Sotiates' cavalry attacked the Roman column while they marched right into the trap about here," pointing to the napkin he had placed as the valley, "but their cavalry was defeated, and then . . ."

"Actually," Gracianna had to interrupt. Taking the salt and pepper, she corrected the placement of them on the table. "This is how it happened, as I remember." Soon, they were debating with the salt and pepper shakers, arguing over their versions of history.

"Please, give me the knife, let me show you," one would say to the other, wishing there was another knife nearby to use.

"But we still surprised them and surprised them from underground . . ." she emphasized.

"Yes, they, you," looking at her square in the eyes, "your people were crafty" he tried to explain.

"Not crafty. We are a thinking people, strategic!"

"Yes," with a broad smile.

A deep chill now.

Marceau and Hawkeye looked at each other astonished.

Finally, Gracianna stood back, crossed her arms, and said, "*Zu hor eta ni hemen* [You there and me here]."

He wanted an explanation, and he wanted to know more proverbs.

"It would take all night to tell you all the proverbs," she said and dropped her eyes. When she looked up, she knew he had caught her meaning. There was the slight sympathetic feeling. Finally. It registered in his eyes and a small spark jumped between them.

This is the time to back off. No, I can't.

"I think I could talk with you all night," he said and smiled.

Gracianna smiled bashfully but did not answer. She tried to control her pounding heart, not let it show how she was playing for more than a simple end. Something was between them and Constance hung in the balance. "Uh, sorry, can I get you anything else? I need to close—I mean, clean. I must go," she stood up to walk to the back, pausing briefly as he quickly moved toward the door.

Stopping, he gracefully twisted again on planted boots and said, "They lost."

"What? Who lost?"

"The Romans annihilated them. The Sotiates." He grinned and purposefully closed the door with another pull and twist of the handle.

In the kitchen, two of her backups poured in after she turned down the light, "What happened with the salt and pepper?" they wanted to know.

"The operation is back in motion is what happened." She stepped into the garden to catch her breath. She could see Juan through the fence.

She waved, "*Go home,*" to him.

Gracianna stood on the stoop of the café that night looking up at Kohn's window. She saw his shadow moving inside. She couldn't look away.

I feel drunk with anticipation for the first time since Constance was taken.

BACK AGAIN

He was back late the very next night—he was obviously looking forward to seeing her.

He watched cars roll by out the window until she was free.

Hawkeye and Marceau's eyes rolled as they seemingly faded into the background and excused themselves to their nearby posts feeling another night of wasted time was upon them. There was a chill outside that night.

Gracianna graciously said, "I like the book. Thank you."

They talked for hours. He was a gentleman and she could tell their chemistry was colliding, but cautiously figured his "gentleman" could change at any moment. He glinted with his very slightly German-accented English. It was just so. He did not speak French, Basque, Italian (well, a little), Spanish, or Portuguese as she did, but they shared English. Her German had been improving but she preferred not to admit it—nor for him to know it.

Only once did he make a measured move toward her. "May we dance close?" he asked as he stood reaching for her waist. She refused.

Quickly he sat, not used to being turned down, and changed the subject. Yes, she was right, he felt it best for them to continue to get to know each other. Clearing his throat he said, "I had a thought," he left it out there like an anchor.

"What is it?"

"Once when I was in the university I had the chance to visit the South of France. It was beautiful . . ."

At the same time, they said it: "The Riviera," and they both laughed.

She bloomed, and he caught that she was in favor of the place.

"I have always wanted to go there."

He said, "After the war, I have been thinking . . ."

"But the war just started," she said. "It can't be over soon . . ."

He interrupted and said sharply, "The war *can* be over! *As soon as we want it to be over.*"

She stood up, defiant. "You cannot make it end that fast. People's lives are at stake, they will not fold that easily. We will fight and don't you forget . . . there is America!"

He jumped to his feet, "Ha! America! They will not come to help. You, you, French . . ." and then he stomped out.

"I am Basque—"she screamed after him. "Ahhhhh!"

The door rattled without latching and bounced to a stop, still open.

He is a barbarian. How could I think he was any different? He is a Nazi and . . . a man. He can only do harm. That is it. No more!

Her hopes for Constance were dashed, as well, and her hope for ending her mission struck. She would lose all credibility with Fontaine, with her support group, with Juan, with Constance, Oh! Constance! She had nothing to give Fontaine tonight and nothing to show for her idiocy. That was it—she knew she should quit.

One of her handlers peeked in the window and she nodded him off. The men left and she got to work fluffing the room back together. She would be out early, she figured.

As she soaked the mop she realized how stupid she had been.

"I am an imbecile."

A few minutes later the door handle turned and then turned again. The door opened.

She dropped the mop and ran to the colonel and they embraced.

"I am sorry," they both said.

"I am so sorry," he said. "The war does this to people."

"It makes people too stupid."

"Too frustrated."

"Too frustrated, the food is bad," she said with a smile.

"And the wine," he said, "is worse," she said.

"Sad," she said.

"Lonely," he said.

"Sit," she said.

They smiled and sat again. She jumped up and went to get a bottle of dreg wine. She poured the long 'Gras' pour' into a tall glass and they sat knee-to-knee, and talked.

"So, tell me about the Riv-i-era . . ." she smile-sounded it out.

Leaning forward, he gently took her hand and said softly, "Oh! It is so beautiful. The Mediterranean breeze is easy and the sunset bounces off Italy and onto your skin. It absolutely glows. I would like to see your skin glow," he said, "from the sun."

She sighed as he placed his hand on her cheek and she embraced his hand with hers.

He had something on his mind.

She had one thing on her mind.

"So . . . Constance?"

"Yes, yes," he chuckled.

"Has anyone ever been released from Birkenau?"

"It has happened."

"Oh! Constance, Constance, Constance . . . I am so happy."

"Yes, Constance, I will look into it tomorrow."

"No, please don't look into it. The letter. An order. Please put the paper in the typewriter. Tell your manservant. . . ."

"He is my assistant—how do you know he serves me and that he is a—"

She went on without a breath, "Tell your manservant—assistant," she acknowledged, "to put the paper in the typewriter and type it out, 'Please return Constance Arrayet Rousseau to Paris,' signed, the very important and powerful colonel."

"Yes, yes," he smiled.

"She was picked up in the Le Marais arrondissement four months ago, here in Paris."

"Yes, yes, yes, Gracianna, do you think I do not know this? You have told me a hundred times. . . . You know, when I was young I never thought I would be in this place. I had dreams of being an architect, but my father wanted me to be an engineer. I did become an engineer."

"I bet you are a fine one . . . but . . ."

". . . but. . . . What?"

"You would have made a better architect."

He wasn't sure how to take what she said, and motioned at her, asking why.

"There is something about you. It is hard, like an engineer, distant and calculating. Sad and mean. Yet, there is an intellectual as well—yes, very smart. You see things that other people don't see. Like me. There is something, something warm and sincere, very deep down there about you too." He nodded knowingly and approvingly. "That emotion would have served you well as an architect."

"Send your father a letter and tell him you have quit the army and are going to become an architect . . . in, in Paris, or Milano."

"Ha! Milano? You are too kind. Are you coming with me?"

"No. This you need to do on your own." Yet, as she turned him down, something occurred to her.

He is THE one—the one that I imagined, in my girlish, late-night thoughts. He is educated, handsome, and I knew it in an instant—instant understanding, an instant sensing of me. He knows me, can talk to me about things of the world. He wants more—more of the things I want. He wants me.

He wanted her. She knew it and he knew.

She leaned closer.

He said, "You are a dreamer you know, aren't you?"

She caught herself recognizing that he was not an architect, and leaned back into reality. "How many deaths are you responsible for?"

Confused, he leaned back. "You should never ask anyone that, ever. I am doing what I need to do to get out of this war. I'd rather be at the Riviera with you."

"No, no, you are right. I am sorry. Really. I should never have asked you that." She realized she was treading on the Devil's ground, and Constance's life was dangling in the balance.

"I must go." He stood up and walked to the door . . .

"No, stay."

Please stay with me.

"PLEASE STAY"

Gracianna took his hand.

Much time had passed after she convinced him to remain a little longer. Finally she looked at the clock in her little office and nearly two hours had already gone by.

"It is much too late," she yawned, "I am sorry to have been short with you earlier."

"I was going to say the same. Time flies with you," he said as he got up.

"I am really leaving this time," he said, turning away. Then he turned back, troubled, his eyes looking away. "Gracianna? Seriously, I do not think I can make the order, really—it is impossible."

He turned away again and just walked out.

Crushed.

I should have finished him the moment I saw him. What was I thinking? All that for nothing.

Gracianna walked downstairs, sat on a perfectly dusted stool, pulled her apron to her face, and cried. She could smell his clean cologne on her apron. She cried harder.

As the colonel walked across the street toward his room, he passed one of the fighters carrying a bottle of wine in a brown paper bag. The resister was shocked to see the officer emerge unexpectedly and pass by—Kohn had slipped past them and into Maison without Gracianna's support team seeing him. They had gotten too lax and were not watching closely enough. The resister waited until the officer disappeared and then peeked into the dining room to see Gracianna crying.

Kohn did not come the next night.

Nor the night after that.

Hope was low.

TONIGHT?

To everyone's astonishment, on the fourth night, he walked right into La Maison Cossette like he owned the place.

Gracianna was instantly high.

Why does he come back in here if he is not trying to help me? Her heart started. *I know I am using him for my own good. I am using all of them for my own good.*

Her Résistance team was now grousing and Fontaine, who had come to

La Maison to see the colonel for himself, had little to keep them motivated. He was beginning to look weak and he knew it. He had had enough and decided that he was going to strongly assert himself and that *tonight* was it for Colonel Kohn.

The colonel sat. He ordered the usual. He and Gracianna acted a bit more than just acquaintances but it was clear they were uncomfortably playacting. It was if they were lovers trying to keep anyone from knowing. Tonight: cordial, familiar, but not warm. Everyone knew this was an act. So did the actors. She was tense, but did not really understand why Kohn was tense.

"I will be away. But back soon with five colleagues from out of town in two weeks from tonight, for dinner. I want something special."

"From out of town?" Her head tilt asked, *where from?*

"Berlin."

"So do you have other powerful colleagues coming to dinner with you?"

"Why? You think you have a better chance to get them to write you a release order than me?"

"Maybe," she radiated.

"Well, you are very clever and witty and you might get the letter, but not the seal. That does the trick with no questions asked."

"The seal?"

"Yes, my little Basquo, an order is no good without a seal, my seal. So, you must be very good to me to get it."

"Well, I could get any of them to write a letter for me and seal it! Besides you said it was impossible for you. You know, I could get it out of each one. Do you want to see me try?"

"Ha! Yes, well, that would never happen, but they are coming—you can try it. I'd like to see you try."

"Besides I *have* been good to you." She grinned.

He smiled.

"Berlin is very beautiful I understand?"

"Why, yes, it is. . . . Do I need to make a reservation?"

"No, you just tell me how many and I will organize it for you."

He held out five fingers. She held out her smaller five and said, "I can get five sealed orders." He smiled. She smirked and, of course, he enjoyed that look.

"And tonight?"

He said, "I want to, but I just can't stay. I'm sorry, I am leaving—"

"Leaving?"

"Don't worry, I will be back in two weeks . . . "

He stood up, straightened his uniform, and said, ". . . but I may," lingering, "have a gift for you soon."

Again he disappeared.

Gracianna got a chill. Any thoughts of finishing the mission were gone. *The letter. The order. The seal. Constance!*

FURIOUS FONTAINE

Fontaine was furious! And stern! He even reminded her for a moment of her grand-mère.

"What the hell are you thinking? What is going on with you?"

She declared, "I am not sure what is going on with me. Maybe it is just *inside me—*"

He did not want to hear whatever that meant, and went on and on about Gracianna and her stubborn way. Juan heard it all. Dom' was there too. They found it hard to disagree but said nothing.

"You are using this system for your own gain! You have used us! You have taken advantage of me and Dom' and everyone! You have endangered the operation! Am I not right?" He was near his wit's end and had decided that this night he must end her time as a resister. "This is it, Gracianna! You are out!" he burst. "Finie!"

The blood drained from her face. She had known she was at the end of a tight rubber band, which could snap back in her face, but she had not expected it to break.

"That is not fair!" Gracianna argued. "For all I have done, all I *can do* for the resistance!" She tried to defend herself.

"You are using Constance for your own good! You *can not* save her!" Fontaine halted back.

"What they did to her is evil. And you protect them from me?"

Although he said he did not want to know, Gracianna had given Fontaine tiny shreds of information to keep him as an ally.

A train is leaving at around this time.

A commander is making calls to Auschwitz and complaining he was not getting information fast enough.

It was nothing really.

But today she added the gem, "I found out last night that he is hosting five officers from Berlin in two weeks. Here at La Maison! This has to be valuable information."

Fontaine stopped in his tracks. In one step he was reengaged. "Did he tell you this, about the officers?"

"Yes," she held out her tiny fingers. "Five officers from Berlin." She explained how she had not even been trying to get the information. "I think it might be easy to find more, inform—"

"I have told you! I forbid it, Gracianna!!" Fontaine began pacing. "Why do you not understand?! He is a smart *and* very evil man! I cannot carry the burden of what may happen. I am carrying enough!"

"Let me help! Let me help the resistance! For Constance!"

"You are done," he said. But she knew he didn't really mean it. They were all losing patience with her and she knew it. She couldn't wait to act anymore. Fontaine pressed her to take the officer or, as he said, "we will move you permanently." She barricaded herself and said, her voice stern, "I will open this entire operation if you do not allow me to get what I want." Fontaine was always a bundle of shaking nerves. His brethren called him, *agité* [shaky].

"As much as I believed in this cause, I am not interested in dying."

"What are you waiting for? Tell me. . . ." he demanded.

She broke down, "the first night, when he arrived, I heard him speak Polish to another man. I used to have some Polish roommates; I understood him. I knew he was from the German border region. They were also talking about trains to Auschwitz and prisoners. He is a senior officer—I knew he had something to do with that place—and we now know he has power there and he is the most senior officer we have ever seen. What else do you want? He has access and," she snarled it defiantly, "he wants me."

Fontaine understood her reasoning before she even started. He had had his suspicions, and he did not like where this was going.

"I *am* saddened by the war, Gracianna. I am angry, like you!" he roared. "My fellow professors, many Jews, have been taken and tortured for information they did not have. This operation is my way to pay back what they have given to me—belief in my work, striving for what I believe in—love, friendship, loyalty, respect. I owe this to my colleagues. My payment is to resist, like your payment! But being a resister will never erase what they have done!

"I am haunted by the image of a rifle butt to my dear friend's head right in front of me! You do not comprehend the danger! The impact—I can still hear that blow echoing in my ears even now—especially at night. And the image of a university professor, my friend, dragged away with his toes pointing downward, wearing shoes that were cobbled by his father—he left skid marks on the waxed classroom floor.

"This! This, Gracianna, is my constant reminder of how anyone's path could be the same. You cannot lose self-control! You cannot! Who knows when this war will end? You must have some patience when you are reaching, for you are reaching for things that are very difficult to achieve—some say impossible!"

Gracianna's cheeks burned in shame, but still she said what her heart felt. "But, but, she is my sister!"

Fontaine flushed and said tightly, "*Constance*, I am sorry to say," pausing, "is not worth the failure of our entire operation. She is only one of many thousands we are trying to help."

"But—"

"*I* am in charge here! You do not drive this operation; I do! The world does not revolve around you and your goals, Gracianna. You must do as you are told. You are a single soldier in a filthy war where you do what we need. We are all just mice taking crumbs, and you are hoping to steal the entire piece of cheese because you think you are so crafty. You are dreaming! And it is a dangerous dream for everyone around you—it is not just you who could be caught in the trap. Do not be so selfish! You do not understand the torture they can inflict on you, Gracianna—on us! They will get every last detail out of you! Every single one!"

"And you? You are not a dreamer?" Gracianna's eyes flashed bright and defiant, "Yes! I *want* the entire piece of cheese. Yes! I want something for myself. Yes! I deserve it and Constance deserves it too."

"You don't even know if she is alive."

"She is alive! I know it! All the missions I have completed for you—I have done it for her! And I have gotten nowhere for her—I have not helped

Constance. You think I am not terrified?" her voice quavered. "I need to be brave! And . . . careful—"

"Gracianna!"

She hated it when he used her full name.

"If this comes up one more time, you are finished. You will be out, out, out, for good, for the sake of La Résistance."

"I can help!"

He held up his hand. "You have perfected this game, I told you. We are grateful for your services. I promise, we will not forget—"

"I can do better! But picking off a Nazi here and a Nazi there, how the hell does this really help? There are a hundred to take his place. A thousand! I do not feel we are making a difference, or getting any closer to ending the war. You know it! We have no control. Are we really making any difference? . . . Well? Are we?"

"You have no patience," he snapped. "Yes, we are making a difference," he said. "*You* have made a difference." Then, more softly, "You have to give up on her. She is in God's hands now."

"She is in the Nazi's hands! I cannot give up! I will not—never!" She could not help her tears or rage.

"You are too hot," Fontaine said. "You are too attached to this now. And you are thinking too small."

He looked out the window and said nothing. Slowly, he started laughing. Finally, they struck a deal for her to never go renegade again, if he would select another target by the end of the month and step up his search for Constance.

"Only one more chance, Gras', that is it!"

He walked away from her.

Gracianna smoldered. Finally, she stole a glance at Juan and Dom', but they would not look at her.

"I am going to get her out," she announced as Fontaine hit the door, but he did not turn around, only waved his disgust behind him like a cardinal waving off a venial sin. "You are silly," he muttered. "She is silly, silly, silly, Dom'. Only one more chance, Gracianna, that is all you. . . ." He trailed off, as Dom' followed.

"Don't call me that! I know he is coming with all those officers from Berlin soon. Tell me *that* is silly."

"That is good," he called waving at her. "Take this time off. Recharge. We all need a break. Until he comes back. But finish it next time, or else."

*A*s Fontaine readied for bed that night he thought of the friend taken by the Nazis. He crossed himself.

He knew all the resisters' sins would be atoned for. He estimated, *one more day on this officer or another is just delaying the inevitable. Eventually we all could be killed. Or, we could just ease into our new German life and stop resisting.*

As he drifted, he had one more thought. *I need to explain to the men to keep helping her anyway,* so he could quell any rumbling. *I do not need explanations. She is better than ten men. It is possible women can be better than men.* He thought errant thoughts now. *One teacher that I respected was a woman. I wonder where Madam Manou is now. She would be sad about the war if she were still alive.* Thoughts extinguished. Sleep. In his dreams, he smoldered.

*G*racianna sat alone in La Maison.
I am going to get her out.

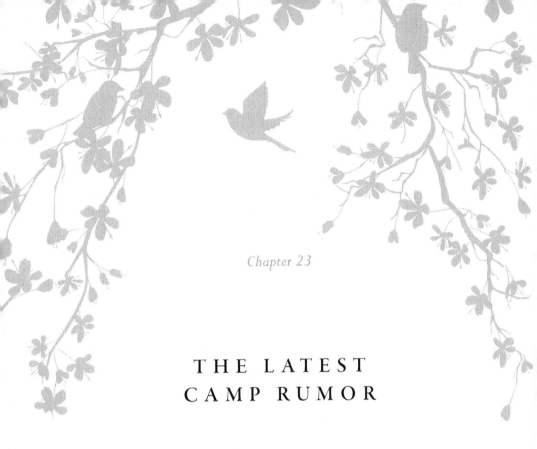

Chapter 23

THE LATEST
CAMP RUMOR

Fille de Pommes de Terre [Potato Girl]. That was her name now.

Constance's potato patch had exploded and she ended up with a space about ten times the original size, once the first sprouts came. Before long she was making every kind of potato dish. Her favorite was Basque shepherd's pie.

Every Basque child eats this many times before they can walk, and virtually every patriot reveres this dish as the national meal. Constance made the dish her new avocation, thinly slicing some potatoes, adding the plentiful onions, wild parsley that was found growing nearby, salt, some pepper, and a bit of goat's milk. She would crack raw eggs into a bowl with the milk and mix them, then pour the mixture over the cooking potatoes. After allowing some minutes for it to coalesce, she loosened the food from the sides of the pan like a master bricklayer, with a trowel-like wooden spatula. Because she did not have bacon to crumble on top, she dripped some goat belly fat that she had saved for this occasion over it all, plated it, and served it piping hot for the camp commander and his minions. Constance never went out to serve them herself. She was terrified of the bastards.

As she would prepare the meal, Anja would help and keep her updated on the latest camp stories.

One afternoon: "The latest camp rumor is that we are lovers!" Anja giggled, her eyes teary with onions.

Constance laughed too. It was true that they had grown very close. Although Anja had not been there much longer than Constance, she seemed a veteran and Constance leaned on her and hid behind her as much as possible. She would watch Anja and follow her like her shadow, listening and learning quickly.

"But others are close and I do not hear this about them."

"But you do not go with the men."

"But you have a lover—two!" Constance tried to joke.

"No—Herr and I are not lovers. I do . . . other things for him because I love him in some way. And the other man, he is not my lover—he is a smelly pig!"

They were referring to the frumpy soldier with the lazy grin who would come by now and then. He was smitten by Anja, who was pretty enough, with a nice figure.

"How did you meet your soldier?" Constance was curious.

"It was accidental!" Anja explained how when a certain soldier would come around looking, he usually came around looking for a certain girl. Anja just happened to be in line for inspection, when a soldier that she had fancied and that she hoped would choose her, didn't. The next solider, "Herr Frumpy," had chosen her instead. Now, he would come around once a week or so and bring small gifts, a dried apple, and a ribbon, probably something stolen from another poor woman. Anja would roll her eyes and reluctantly make the walk across the street, where he would take her to a nearby office and force her to do what he needed. He was glassy-eyed when he would bring her back and she was shamed, her hair inevitably and unmistakably mussed.

Constance vowed to never be "the extra girl" caught hanging around when another girl wasn't there. She took great pains to keep to herself invisible. There were many women, but if any man tapped her on the shoulder, she would not be able to say, "No." So, luck and numbers were all she had in her favor. She would hide behind the other sheep, ever pushing to be in the center of the flock.

"I could have escaped the tap," Anja admitted, "but I see Diana and some of these girls who service soldiers and get extra rations—sweet apples and dried apricots, bread, and sometimes *chocolate* and cigarettes and even wine. Plus," Anja lowered her voice to a whisper, looking around first, "I have a silly idea that I could convince him to send a message to the outside, or even sneak me out!"

The thought had not occurred to Constance, and she suddenly wondered whether featuring her well-chipped tooth was so smart after all. Sure, the chances were nil, but there is something about a ray of hope that shines and beckons.

Smiling, Constance finished by saying, "I would trade the cigarettes for wine," and winked.

As time wore on, the rumor continued to grow that Anja and Constance were lovers. At first, it was a lark. Of course, how could one not think that? They had become virtually inseparable. Constance was enamored with Anja. Needed her. They would talk, walk together, and hold arms. Of course, they slept together and huddled close to keep warm, but every girl slept with another girl in the barracks. They were constant companions. They needed each other. They loved each other.

Constance reconsidered, thinking maybe she should not have let Anja cut her hair. She missed the warmth of her natural scarf. However, she was terrified of attracting a man. Many people knew Anja had given Constance the bad haircut and it fed the rumor. It had seemed a good idea at the time. Then, Anja had wanted a haircut. Despite Constance's efforts, Anja thought it looked "cute." Now, with their matching haircuts, it seemed there was no way to set the rumor straight.

However the latest talk at the camp was just the beginning. "Do you know about Anja today?" Diana had whispered to her over the kitchen island. It hurt Constance that Diana was talking about her friend. But she knew it was just a rumor. Anja told her everything.

One day, after a slow start—Anja seemed to be feeling faint and was just not acting right—Constance said, "What is it? Are you not well?"

"It's nothing."

It was not long before Constance found her friend dry heaving behind the kitchen near the sheep pen.

Leaning on a little tree, Anja looked up at Constance with wet eyes, mouth in pain, "I'm pregnant."

The rumor was true.

The blood drained out of Constance's face. "What will you do? What can *I* do?"

"To try to have the baby is suicide, and the baby will be killed too. I might live if I get an abortion."

Anja started weeping.

"I have heard they drown the baby right in front of you! To send a message!" The questions that inevitably come at any of life's inflection points came to Constance's mind:

What have I done?

How should I act?

How will I act?

What should I do?

"Are you sure? Maybe you just have the flu?"

"I have had children. These bastards killed them. I know I am pregnant. It is that bastard's child."

"Oh no, Anja."

"Once I start to show, I will be singled out and both the baby and me—we will be slaughtered! And I can think of worse that could happen."

Constance could not imagine what worse could be. "We will do what we have to do," she tried to say firmly, though she had heard the disgusting stories of backroom abortions. She had never thought it would happen to Anja. But it was happening all throughout the camp.

"What do we have to do?"

"Tonight, at the latrines—I will see the woman known as 'The Doctor.' Constance, come with me?"

Constance could not say no. That night, they waited for the Doctor in the toilet. As they waited, Anja nervously told Constance about the woman. "She is very popular. She is an experienced Jewish doctor that can offer advice on all types of illnesses and abnormalities. And she also performs abortions."

Since arriving, the Doctor was known to have done so for nearly two hundred women. Many were permanently disfigured as a result. At least ten pregnant women and their babies had died. Everyone knew she would keep terminating hundreds more pregnancies. Although in some cases she did nothing, since rampant malnutrition did its work. Miscarriages were the typical outcome.

The rumor was that the soldiers (and maybe the command) had given the supplies to the Doctor, because they did not want the word to get out that they had made a prisoner pregnant. It was nonsensical to the women, however, since they knew the guards would barely get a slap on the wrists if they were caught. A reprimand meant maybe having their vodka ration cut for a week for letting it happen, or for not having the discipline to demand only oral sex. The Doctor was performing a service for the camp. She was valuable. The supplies made sense.

"But maybe, at least, that means the abortion will go smoothly, with so much practice." Constance offered.

Anja laughed bitterly. "I will probably die," she said fatalistically.

"Stop it. Never talk like that."

They continued to discuss the subject until the Doctor arrived. She had a big bun of dark curls on her head, a nondescript potato sack for a dress, and she spoke competently. They brought her up to speed in no time.

"I haven't had my period for at least a year, but I know I am pregnant."

"How do you know then?" Turning to Constance, "and *who are you?*"

"I am her friend. She has been dizzy and vomiting the past few days."

"I have had children before. They are dead now."

"And this is the exact same feeling?"

". . . yes."

"Where do you work?"

"In the command kitchen."

"Get me some rations. It is not a question. Fruit. Bread."

"Yes, of course. Can you help me?"

"Yes, tomorrow night. Later than this. If you can, drink some alcohol or something to knock you out a bit. Drink as much as you can beforehand. It will be painful and you will need to decide . . ."

"Decide what?"

"Decide how to get rid of the baby, of course."

"What are the choices?"

There was a long sigh from the Doctor, then after a lifeless look at where her watch used to be, she took Constance aside and explained the options. Constance's hand automatically went to her mouth as she gasped. She vomited macerated carrots and cabbage in her mouth, but she held it back.

When Constance recovered she said, "I can't imagine these choices."

"Bring me some alcohol too, if you can get it," and then the Doctor was gone.

As Anja and Constance walked out, Anja begged her to tell her what the choices were. The women held each other as they asked permission to walk across to the path back to their dormitory.

"Listen, all these so-called choices are dangerous! I cannot—"

"Tell me, damn it!"

Constance breathed deep and said it straight, the same way the Doctor delivered it. "Piercing of the fetus with a knitting needle inserted into the uterus and through the cervix . . . being punched and kicked hard in the stomach . . . staying outside all night until you are near hypothermic."

Anja dropped to her knees in the middle of the road as she listened to her sickening options.

This was one time that Constance's way with words failed her. There was no other way to put it.

Anja nodded at probably the most painful choice . . . and it was decided. The next night, Constance and Anja went to the last place in the world they wanted to be.

Constance propped the tipsy Anja into the latrines.

There were many tears and much pain. Only eye-rolls from the Doctor, however. "Hush," she snapped, "be a woman!"

Constance nearly carried Anja back to the barracks after it was over.

The baby was aborted. Anja had excruciating spasms all night.

By the next night, it was obvious that Anja was not recovering. She was pale, sweating, and delirious with fever.

Constance got her to the kitchen early the next morning.

"She does not seem to be recovering," Constance told the knowing Herr Meyer, as he came with fresh, hot, damp towels and soup. "She does not look well and she keeps bleeding."

Anja's eyes opened and she turned to Constance with tears. "Barbaric," was all that she could say. "My insides have been mixed. I cannot imagine what so many women are going through. These are women! Oh! My children!"

Of course, Anja was now in the storeroom and was missing her shift working in the kitchen.

Twice, the frumpy soldier came by, sniffing around for Anja. Constance and Herr Meyer would distract him. On the fourth day he came calling, after looking for her for the past two days. "Where is she?" He was angry. He knew somehow. Herr Meyer stood back as the big man bulled his way through to the back room.

He found Anja dying in the potato room. He was shouting loudly and no one in the kitchen would dare to go in.

Anja made it through the door as he continued to berate her in German. She was nearly doubled over in the wet, cold kitchen. Then he slammed her head off of the steel countertop and dropped her to the floor. She was out cold.

The soldier dragged Anja out by her short hair. Herr Meyer stood there with the kitchen knife, hand trembling. The scene became strangely quiet. Constance panted and sank back out the doorway, eyes wide.

The others watched the slow-motion explosion unfold.

Suddenly, Anja woke, frantic, a rag doll. Constance locked eyes with Anja as she reached toward Constance for safety and mouthed, "I love you." They both knew there was nothing she could do. With tears washing her face, Constance could only blow her a soft kiss.

As Anja was dragged out, her screams were muffled first by the swinging doors, then by the next set of doors, then by the doors of the office next door. After that, they could hear nothing.

Anja never came back to work. Her name was not brought up. The women were certain her soldier raped her one last time before ensuring she was gone.

The offending soldier was transferred to another area of the camp and never seen by the kitchen girls again. Anja's disappearance was just another reminder to Constance: that there was no God, on one hand, but that Anja had helped her find an inner balance.

Constance was angry.

It was an anger that could be very dangerous in a place like this, and she struggled to quell the beast pulling at the reins. Then, the irony struck her.

I had to come to hell to find myself.

THE CAMP COMMANDER

Sunday morning, Constance wept into the shepherd's pie.

Herr Meyer appeared and came quickly into the galley. "You have been requested by the commander! He wants to see you now!"

Constance involuntarily put her hands to her hair and tried in vain to find a mirror and to be sure her face was dirty, but Meyer pulled her out by the arm. She held her breath as they went out through the kitchen door.

The officer was eating the shepherd's pie, biting deliberately and then, a broad smile. "This is delicious!" he said, as he looked her over. "So you are the Potato Girl from Basque Country. I have been hearing about your farm. Good!"

Constance was alarmed to hear her reputation had preceded her and was growing.

What a mistake!

She stood in front of the commander without looking him in the eye. Many guests from Berlin were in the room. They were mostly talking to one another and were oblivious of the girl and the commander. They had come to see the progress—and to visit the prison brothel. The brothel was primarily set up as an incentive for well performing male prisoners, but an occasional visitor was served in private. It could not have been more prominently located, at Block 24 near the main gate. Even German prostitutes could come and go, and use the brothel for their own business.

She hated to be around all the men. They looked right at her, it seemed.

I never want to end up in the brothel—six or eight men a day with a voucher—a voucher! To spend 15 to 20 minutes with me? Oh! Even if I am treated well.

She stood with her tiny stomach stuck out as far as she could.

In German, the commander said, "*Der Geschmack davon ist hervorragend. Ich möchte es jeden Sonntag zum Frühstück haben. Danke Kartoffel-Mädchen* [The flavor of this is outstanding. I want to have this every Sunday for breakfast. Thank you, Potato Girl]."

She smiled to expose her chipped tooth, and stole a glance at him, then instantly looked away. He was perfectly shaved, she noticed. She especially liked his smile.

An underling walked up, "Colonel?"

He smiled, warmed slightly, and then waved Constance off, turning to his business just after he looked her up and down once again. She smiled and half-curtsied. He shot a glance to Meyer. She nodded a sarcastic "thank you" to Meyer for passing her nickname along. She shuffled away with a slight "*Merci*," and back to the kitchen she spilled.

The other girls were fawning and asking what the commander said? "Isn't he handsome?" They said. "The colonel is so powerful. We have all dreamed of him."

"If he took you, you would be made," cooed Diana enviously.

They all laughed hysterically, then Meyer came in the swinging door. They instantly became quiet.

Meyer was not sure how to take things. "It seems you have made a friend," he said to Constance.

Walking tensely through the swing-door, she decided she would use every trick to repel him, and, in the future, tone down her spices.

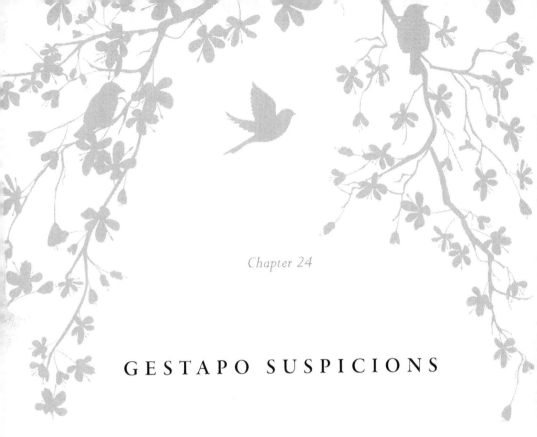

Chapter 24

GESTAPO SUSPICIONS

*H*umbled by Fontaine, Gracianna had accepted the diversion of two weeks of lying low, since Kohn was going to be away. So, she got to work at the Petit Café, in another neighborhood, with Juan behind the bar. When she opened the messy broom closet, Gracianna sighed at the mess.

Constance . . . but she snapped back.

Then he came in. The first customer of the day. A soldier, of course. He just walked in, picked up the menu, and sat. Alone, in the empty room, in his uniform, with the menu.

She gave him a moment to look over the menu. Occasionally, some high-ranking officers would come from a nearby hotel around 4 p.m. for a light meal and two or three beers, before returning to the evening's strategy dinners. He was a bit early to be one of them, but she did not think much of it, until she noticed him looking at her curiously.

It was unnerving, how he kept staring at her, as if he wanted something.

When he looked toward the window, Gracianna saw a long scar on his neck, and recognition rattled in her brain but would not surface. Her instincts told her something was wrong.

"Something is wrong," she told Juan in the back. "I think he knows me."

Juan peered out the diamond-shaped kitchen window and saw the very tall officer with his back to him. He instantly got on the phone to Fontaine. While he was waiting for someone to pick up the line, he spread the word to the cooks to pass the word. "On your toes, everyone," he quietly told them.

As each man produced his own gun, he told Fontaine, "It's trouble. We might need to take him—here—in the day."

Fontaine ordered, "Do not take him! Do not do anything! I am sending Hawkeye immediately."

Juan tried to take the soldier's order, to protect Gracianna, who kept busy with her back turned and would not make eye contact with the officer. But—the officer asked for her.

"He wants *you* to take the order," Juan said to Gracianna. There was nothing else he could do.

At the table, Gracianna's eyes froze. It was obvious he was different—*Geheime Staatspolizei* [Secret State Police].

Her blood ran cold. The man was Gestapo. She pretended not to care. "Some food or drink for you, Monsieur?"

"I know you," he peered down his straight nose.

"Didn't you used to work at the café across from headquarters at Le Meurice? Yes, I have seen you there." He said it coolly.

"La Maison?" Gracianna forced herself to laugh lightly. "Oh, I work at many places, here and there. That is not an important job to me, with that fat Frenchman owner who loves his cheese and smells like it. These French!" She tried to make it us versus them. "I am Basque," she explained.

"Ha!" the officer howled and said in German, "I agree, I know just the fat man you mean. These French, they are insufferable."

"I'm sorry, I do not speak any German. Just a few words," Gracianna lied. Just when Gracianna started to relax, he just stood there and stared at her with cold eyes.

"There has been trouble around there, missing officers. Soldiers. What do you know of that?"

Her blush was real. "Me? Men? No, no, no," she wagged her finger and exaggerated her accent slightly, "You have me confused with someone else. I know nothing about how to treat men. Just ask my grandmother, I am very traditional," and she tried to step away shyly. She picked up some silverware from the nearby table to bring it into the kitchen.

"Come here!"

She turned slowly.

"What is your name and where do you live?" he asked in French and pulled out his notepad.

"I do not understand."

"Shut up!"

He stood over her and sneered. "*What is your name and where do you live?*"

"Bettina." She did not know why that came to her lips, but it was too late now. "Bettina Etchebarren, from arrondissement number two. She began to spell it for him. E-T-C-H . . ."

"Shut up!"

His eyes, swept over her. "I know you. I will find out where you have been. Identification. Identification!"

Just then, there was an enormous crash in the back—like a hundred plates hitting the ground. Gracianna thought Juan was brilliant, but the soldier snapped into action, and in the next second peered through the kitchen door with his hand in his jacket, likely on his gun.

Juan had his back to the door, picking up the dishes.

The fewer faces he sees, the better . . . I hope I do not get shot in the back.

He could feel the officer's eyes raking him, but he just continued to stack the broken dishes, thinking.

Apparently satisfied, the officer snapped on his heel. He shot Gracianna a withering glare and slipped out the door. As he passed the window, they were eye to eye until he was out of her sight. *We should have shot him. I must get a gun,* Gracianna told herself.

When she turned back to Juan, his eyes were blazing.

She beat back, "What? He can't hurt me."

JUAN'S MOVE

Juan and Gracianna lay in bed in the dark, the blankets separating them as they did every night. He thought he knew what she was thinking.

She was thinking about Kohn, how he had not come back to Maison for many weeks now, and that the trail had run cold. She wasn't allowed to come to La Maison anymore. Even the Gestapo had stopped coming around.

Even lying still, Juan could sense her restless thoughts.

One night: "It is difficult to let go," Gracianna told Juan. "It is difficult to accept that I have done enough."

She had tried everything and gotten—nowhere! She had not told Juan, or anyone, about Kohn's "maybe" offer. Isolated in her anxiety, she waited.

The next week he did not come in. Nor the next.

Résistance intelligence had lost sight of him once again. Gracianna's network also failed her. No one, not a maid, not a taxi driver, not a doorman, had heard from or seen him. Gracianna had asked everyone she trusted, but there was no news about him.

She imagined that everyone thought she was a prima donna but it was hard not to think of Kohn's kiss. They had kissed many times the night she convinced him to stay. It stood between her and Juan, though she didn't tell him. Yet Juan knew Gracianna was thinking about the officer, and he wasn't sure she was thinking of him because he could help Constance.

Night after night, the silent emotional curtain was drawn between them. One night, Juan decided he had had enough. He told Fontaine, "It is over. Gracianna is not Dom's girl, or your girl. She is *my* girl. She is not coming back."

Fontaine would miss Gracianna but didn't need her. He had been grooming another girl, "My Tall Beauty," he called her, and did not complain when Juan insisted that he provide the money and papers now for their passage. Later, Fontaine—a man not bent toward feelings—put one hand on Juan's shoulder as he gave him an envelope with the forged documents and cash.

"*Merci.* There will be two men waiting for you at the river dock. You know where it is. They will secretly deliver you to a stop or two, and then to London along with some others. You will set sail from there."

Juan went to Maison to see Dom' and tell him his decision.

An exhausted Dom' wept openly. "Bring her to me, I have not seen her. I want to see both of you before you leave."

"I will try. I know she will want to see you. But you know how she is," Juan joked.

"Yes, she is just like her mother," Dom' revealed. "She is very special to me, Juan."

Juan left. No one had ever spoken of Gracianna's family. It seemed odd.

No matter, he had things to do, since he decided he was going to insist she leave with him now. Gracianna had done her share for the war. To save them, passage had been secured on a ship headed to New York from London on December 26th. However, they needed to get to London first. That meant they needed to leave Paris on Christmas night.

Gracianna visited a sick friend during the day on Christmas Eve, so Juan had little time to make all the arrangements. He organized everything and was not going to take no for an answer. He did it all in the hope that she would see they needed to move forward. Without her permission, he packed only the essentials, and gave the furnishings away to the new girls in the dorm. He withdrew their small nest egg from the bank and added it to the money that Fontaine had provided. It was enough for a fresh start.

Then it dawned on him. *What if she won't go?*

When she returned to the apartment to open gifts that evening, it was in a shambles.

"What is happening, Juan?"

"It is Christmas Eve and my gift? We are leaving and never coming back," he told Gracianna. "Gras'—I have them. The tickets. It's over. I love you. We are leaving tomorrow night! Like you wanted."

A small murmur, "Oh! How did you?"

"Never mind."

Finally he just blurted it out to Gracianna, "I know you are conflicted—I am too, but I am going to America the day after tomorrow. We sail from London." Puffing his chest a bit, he said, "It's now my dream."

It was a gamble he had to take, losing Gracianna. He could feel the gravitational pull of Constance. He understood it.

More silence.

"Someday I would like a family," Juan announced quietly, "and a wife who holds me in the night. Will you come with me?"

He had never been so direct. There was no answer.

Finally, tears filled her eyes and she cleared her throat twice and then said, "I think so. I don't know."

"You should do it only if you want to. Not because you think you should. This, I thought you would know. Do not mind for me. I want this more than you now. We both know it. I am not happy like this. With everything that has happened. We are not the only couple to be torn apart by this bullshit. Things happen sometimes. It is all right, Gracianna."

The bed was always cold when they got in or on it. They both stared at the ceiling as he waited for her answer anxiously. They heard sounds of sporadic gunfire "popping" far away. Even after a long while, they each knew the other was awake. Still, she could not sleep.

Finally, it was early on Christmas Day. Juan had all of their belongings all packed—and in their bed, isolated by a wide divide, Gracianna seemed to surrender.

"I have done what I can," she said, and finally turned to him, moving under the blankets, past the "curtain" between them. He was warm from the fuzzy wool. She smelled like lavender.

"I will come with you. It is what I should do."

His heart boomed.

"You did more than anyone could have done. Fontaine will miss you. He arranged everything for our trip. Tonight, it's the boat to London and then we sail for New York tomorrow. I have the documents. We have to be at the dock near the fishmonger tonight. Yes, Fontaine was impressed with you."

"Stop teasing, Juan."

Since it was Christmas morning she wanted to surprise Juan with a cake. She dressed carefully. Gracianna placed her Biedermeier flower cameo just so. It was still morning, before 8 a.m. She went to the patisserie and returned with Juan's favorite, Gâteau Basque, a combination of cake and pie, stuffed with pastry cream, flavored with almonds, anise, rum, orange-flower water, and Armagnac. Her mother used to add extra Armagnac to make it really moist inside. Well, this dry bomb was as close as a Parisian could come. In any event, it was a surprise.

She saw that Juan was happier than he had ever appeared to be, and at one point he reached for her but they both knew it was too soon.

"I want to see Dom' today," she said, "before we leave. I need to say goodbye."

Someone knocked on their apartment door.

"Marceau!" They were happy to see him, but soon their smiles faded with his dark look.

"A message. It came to La Maison this morning. I have not told anyone." He handed a letter to Gracianna, said "Merry Christmas," and jogged away.

The letter was unmarked. It was a handwritten note for Gracianna.

Juan sank as she read it out loud.

"Meet me at La Maison at midnight tonight." It was from Colonel Kohn. She looked up at Juan.

"But the boat leaves for London at 8 p.m.. There are others going too. We can't hold everyone up," Juan said. He could see the flash in her eyes. He threw up his hands and grabbed up their tickets.

"I am going to be on that boat, Gracianna. If you want to stay, that is your choice." He stuck his ticket in his pocket and handed the other one to her. "I am going to the dock early tonight."

Crossing the threshold he looked back over his shoulder and said, "I think you are in love with him!"

"I am not!" Gracianna shouted. "He is a Nazi! I know I don't love him, because. . . ."

"Because why? Because you don't know how to love?"

"I do not! I cannot! I don't know why!"

Juan closed the door. He was gone.

Oh, Constance!

Maybe he will help me?

Chapter 25

THE LAST NIGHT

*J*ust before midnight on Christmas Day, Gracianna stood in her little office upstairs in La Maison. She had taken a taxi to the dock that night at 7:30 p.m., and nearly leaped from the moving car as it passed. She couldn't see the boat or Juan or anyone. She wanted to explain to Juan what she felt she needed to do. But he knew it. It tore her up inside. She knew he had sacrificed everything for her, for Constance.

Yet, her thoughts turned back to the place she had worked so hard for Dom' and for Fontaine for so long—her office-workroom. Soon, Kohn was at her doorway as promised. He just appeared again as she dusted some glasses. She knew if you were careful you could quietly make it up the stairs, if you knew where the weak steps were. Now, with Kohn in the doorway, her senses snapped to attention. He was in plainclothes. Strange. He was as handsome as ever, and his eyes were bright. She sat and folded her hands in front of her.

"So Colonel Kohn," she said warmly, hoping she did not appear anxious. He said, "Let's go across the street."

"No," she blurted.

"Well, I mean let's have a drink at the bar in my hotel first. . . . Why are you so, so nervous?"

"I have missed you!" was all she could think to say.

He smiled broadly, mischievously. "I have something for you." He made her wait for a long time, his hand slipping into his jacket.

"Did you give the order? Write the letter?"

"Yes."

"And seal it?"

"Yes, dear. I did it for you. For us. And he patted the breast pocket over his heart, finally withdrawing the precious, sealed letter. He pushed it back in his pocket as if it were nothing—a mere symbol of his power.

Gracianna's knees shook.

"I cannot thank you enough! Oh! Thank you, thank you. My sister means so much to me. I owe you so much."

"That is not all I have." After another mischievous smile and a dive for his other pocket, his hand slowly emerged with some paperwork.

"These are my resignation papers," he snapped them on the desk. "My severance pay. I have quit. My commission has ended."

His eyes glinted, ". . . and there are two train tickets for the Riv-i-era, then Milano!"

Gracianna's heart was pounding. Her throat closed.

"Have I redeemed myself in your eyes, Basquo?" he asked.

"I feel like a hero again. Writing my resignation letter and quitting. It is a fresh start! I am going to follow my dream—I want to be an architect! You make me alive. We'll start all over! We'll travel far away from this war. See all the things we love to read about! You, and me, together—we are *perfect!* It is all so right, isn't it?" he asked.

It does sound all so right, doesn't it?

"Uh . . . yes. Yes. Yes. Yes," she said with more conviction each time as if convincing herself. She looked down, "Yes . . ." her voice fell off.

He smiled, puffing proudly.

"Maybe not," she whispered as it occurred to her.

"Excuse me?"

"Well, yes," she said so brightly at first and then less convincingly, "it sounds right but . . . no."

"No!?"

"No," she said quietly.

"NO WHAT?," he barked.

"I . . . have changed my mind."

"What," his voice broke. "It can't be. I can't believe we. . . ." Kohn was stunned. "It's that *boy*, isn't it?! Ha! He will never make you happy—never give you things . . . forget him. He is just a goat shepherd. You deserve more, and you know it. I can love you better! Give you a better life. You will live! I have money for us."

Juan is what I am grateful for.

"No. I don't want you. I don't want this now. I can't."

"How can that be? You will throw everything away to run off with some shepherd?" He stared at her. "He cannot love you like I can—he is not deep enough. Not smart enough!"

"He is not a boy. You and I, we never had anything real!" she backed up.

"How can you say that?"

"How could I ever love you? I love my husband; I know it. I could never have been with you. You are not real. This, it is not real. You just needed an escape, and I am your excuse."

"Husband? Not real? Excuse me? I have quit my command for you. *That* is real! You ingrate."

Then he said, more hotly, "I have done everything you wanted me to. Everything for you! You used me! You Basque bitch! You must think you are very clever for a stupid mountain girl."

"Apparently you underestimated me, Colonel, and you underestimated my roots."

"You must be kidding! All of this to get one whore out of my camp?"

"I am not a," emphasizing the B's, " . . . *B*asque . . . *b*itch," he sneered as she continued, "and my *s*is-*t*er is *not* a whore."

She knew he was not armed. *I am civilized*, he had once said.

Gracianna came prepared. She produced a gun and pointed it at him.

"Put it down," he said, regarding her calmly. Suddenly, his head cocked as he realized who she was. "It is you," he said with wonder. "You all along. The missing men. It is you, isn't it, Basquo?" Kohn laughed. "It seems that *I* was the honest and heroic one in our relationship. But it really wasn't a relationship, was it, Gra-ci-anna? Put it down, I said."

He rushed her. Other officers had been either so shocked or in the throes of lust that they never even noticed her draw their own gun . . . but he saw her do it in slow motion. He grabbed her, and as they crashed to the floor, her gun slid but was pointing at them, just under the bed.

He was strong. His hand grabbed her wrist and he instantly twisted her around. He was behind her, his broad shoulders overshadowing her small, strong body. His free hand reached for her waistband.

He turned her and squeezed her so hard from behind that she whistled involuntarily as the breath blew from her lungs.

Whistle!

He threw her to the other side of the room and headed toward her now. She began to whistle—low and long.

Kohn stopped for a moment, amused. He knew there was no one. He thought she was whistling as an expression of defiance. She glanced at the gun on the floor.

She whistled this time louder—her Basque-ness coming to her aid like it had for her father. He had fallen in the mountains once and strained his ankle badly. They both had whistled long and low together for half the day and finally someone came from over the hill. She had not whistled like this since she was a young girl. It was a low forlorn signal of hopelessness.

If I live, I will be thankful for each moment that I spend, for everything.

Kohn reveled in the revenge of her humiliation.

She leaped and tried to push past him.

He blocked the door.

He threw her up against the wall with great force and she fell to the floor. Her breath knocked clear of her.

He landed on top of her, his hand at her throat, his mouth next to her ear as they rolled on the floor. She reached under the bed for the gun as he whispered, "There was never an order. I would never write an order for your whore sister. I know she will rot in hell."

Gracianna passed out momentarily at the sound of the gunshot and then her eyes burst right back open. This time she was not the one who had pulled the trigger.

She had not been shot.

He had.

She felt sorry for him as she watched him step backward and fall to his knees, shocked. There was a moment, when they looked at each other—*really looked at each other*—and each of them accepted the truth of the moment.

Kohn half-turned and saw the shooter.

Juan stood stoically inside the doorway. The "river" Luger was still outstretched and pointing at the kneeling man. The gun was the one from Gracianna's first kill. Juan had never disposed of it.

With his last breath, Colonel Kohn slid to Gracianna's feet.

Juan seemed to have a way of holding onto the right things. The way he held on to Gracianna. The same way he held onto the knowledge that, as stubborn as Gracianna was, he could never get on that boat without her.

It crossed Gracianna's mind, *Fontaine would be furious if he knew Juan did not throw that gun away. Thank God.*

She looked at Juan then at the dead man and reached down and unbuttoned his suit flap with one trembling hand and retrieved the envelope from his breast pocket. She knew it would be there.

She opened the envelope and removed the official parchment paper. It just fell open. His seal was unbroken. The order unbreakable.

"He loved you. . . ." Juan said.

She looked up for forgiveness.

"I love you so much, Juan."

"Juan? Never ever tell her."

He just nodded.

The light flickered.

"Come with me," Juan whispered. Fontaine and other men had gathered outside the door. She had done it. Completed the mission. Fontaine touched her shoulder as she walked past.

She hugged Dominique and cried as he said, "Now go my child. I love you."

Fontaine raised his eyebrows at Dom', as if to say, *your daughter is our hero.*

Chapter 26

QUIET TEARS

"Constance," said Herr Meyer flatly, "come here now."

"Yes?"

"You are being released." There. He had said it right in front of the entire kitchen staff.

"Don't joke. . . ."

"I am not joking," he panned.

All the girls cried out. They knew Meyer would never talk of such a thing if it were not true.

"Oh my God. This is true?" Diana squealed.

It was easier for Meyer to be angry. He knew he was stuck in that bare kitchen until the bitter end.

"Follow this man and go to the office." He handed her the order, the prominent seal on top.

"I don't understand. . . ." She turned in disbelief toward the girls, and he snapped, "Do it, now."

Diana took off her best sweater and put it over Constance's shoulders. She squeezed her face and kissed her on both cheeks.

Each girl kissed Constance in silence.

There were no smiles. Only envy.

Meyer was sick about it. He knew she would be shot as soon as she got out of sight.

This is all a ruse. He was sure of it. *I try to care for them, really. God, please help me save them. They are my girls. I am responsible for them. I watch over them and I cannot let one stray. Why take this one? She is beautiful and calm. She deserves to live.*

It was frigid as she walked past the barbs and the guards and the *HALT!* signs to enter the warm office.

Warmth!

Without ceremony, a box with new clothes was handed to her. She was given a shower. A car was waiting. *Hurry.*

She had no idea what was to come.

Her ignorance was blissful.

Constance had heard that the few "freed" prisoners were killed when they got far enough away from the camp. Sometimes the camp guards let someone out to refresh the hope of freedom amongst the prisoners. When you are *that* prisoner, however, freedom is not the first thing on your mind.

After the driver closed the door, he exited several gates and the staff car drove on and on, making her feel sick from the motion.

After thirty-five minutes, they stopped at the train station: *Cracow.* The soldier got out and opened the door. He helped her to the platform and bought her a ticket. He handed her the stub and a small box. He reached in his pocket and gave her some change, his money, and then walked away without a word.

Onlookers watched, unsure what they were seeing. No one spoke to her. *Could it be she was a prisoner from THE camp? Not possible.*

The train arrived 15 minutes later, as Constance held on to the bench for stability.

Only when she confidently grasped the boarding rail of the train did she begin to weep. Although she was stronger now, she was overcome and she needed help to board.

"Wait a moment," a man from behind her put down his packages and helped her.

He accompanied her to a seat by the window and then went back to get his things. He came back and sat right across from her and could not take his eyes away.

As the train jerked forward, he motioned to her by pulling up his sleeve . . . and touched the inside of his blank forearm motioning for her to do it.

She raised her sleeve to expose the mark. Tears instantly welled in his eyes and he involuntarily fell toward her and embraced her. They wept.

As they passed the first station he finally leaned back, wiping his eyes. Then he promptly fell asleep, from the swaying.

She stared at the sleeping man. He reminded her of an old friend. She opened the small box that the soldier had given her and she cried again. It contained an apple, some bread, and a small piece of Swiss chocolate. She recognized it from the base cafeteria.

It was his lunch.

She cried without tears as she watched the fields pass by. She cried at every barn. At every blade of grass. She wept but could not sleep.

When the man awoke he could not speak to her. She never said a word to him. He gave her his own jacket, despite the biting Polish cold; it was new with fur around the hood.

The reunion was a miracle. Fontaine had arranged for a private room in the Paris station, outside the eye of the Nazi guards, to ensure Constance made it all the way home. Everyone was overcome. The sisters shed quiet tears. They had no words. Words were not necessary. Juan's friends helped gather Constance to take her home.

In the car, Gracianna told her, "We are going to the Rousseau house, your house, it is empty. Those men killed Rousseau. He died the day after you were . . . taken."

Constance just nodded and put her head on Gracianna's shoulder.

She was not shocked. After what she had seen in Birkenau, news like this was just another day in the kitchen.

Gracianna saw the faraway look and prayed for her sister's health.

Lord, help me bring her life again? Notre Père [Our Father]. . . .

Gracianna was by Constance's bedside for the next twenty days. She helped her sister get back on her feet over the next couple of weeks. They would sit in the garden and take short walks, and then they started to cook together again.

There was not much to say, except, "I know you and Juan are waiting until I am better to leave for America. I am so grateful. I never stopped thinking of you. I am so sorry for that stupid argument and all my selfishness. I am sad for Rousseau."

"Hush, no, I am the one that has been so stupid. *I* am sorry. I love you so much, Constance. I never stopped praying for you, Juan too. We miss Rousseau too."

"I love you so, so much too."

Even though they both shed discreet tears, Constance only asked one question over and over: "Why have I been released?"

"A miracle," Gracianna would say.

"All I can think of is that it was some sort of administrative mistake."

She did not dwell on it. She grieved for the friends she had made, and prayed for every last one of the souls in the death camp.

Fontaine was the one to realize miracle.

He made sure the order with the seal was on the train to Auschwitz in the early morning after Colonel Kohn's death. It was dated on the last day of the colonel's commission.

Fontaine arranged to have it immediately delivered to the Auschwitz administrative office through a well-placed mail courier. It was just another order to the soldier working that morning. He processed it and executed it before the Nazi command was the wiser. The order was efficiently executed.

Marked above her wrist, Constance decided to move back to the Basque Country, alone, to live in the house where she had been raised by their grandmother. After her convalescence, she knew that she had taken advantage of Rousseau, and that the city life was not right for her. Constance had promised herself that she would help Basque children learn that every human is the same, that every man is equal and deserves to be free, and that God is necessary in every life.

Years later, Juan remarked, "Anastasia would have sold everything she owned, the house, the animals, and the ancestral lands, to travel to Poland to get to the gates of Auschwitz and try to get Constance out . . . any way she could. She would have been shot and died trying to save her." And then, turning to Gracianna, "or you."

Days before Constance was ready to leave for Baigorri, Juan found Gracianna in Rousseau's house making soup for Constance.

"Gras'? Fontaine has arranged for us to get the fishmonger boat to London. To catch our ship. I have them. The tickets. . . ."

Gracianna looked up with a towel in her hand as she wiped the counter.

Juan whispered, "This is over. I love you. You were dying inside, but I am taking you back. We are going to America now."

"I love you so much, Juan. But Constance. . . ."

"No, don't worry. You know she does not want to go. She is going home. I have made arrangements for Marceau to take her back to the mountains."

"Marceau? Yes, he will take care of her. Yes. Good. Thank you. Thanks to dear Marceau."

Aurrera begiratzen ez duena, atzean dago [Those who don't look forward, stay behind].

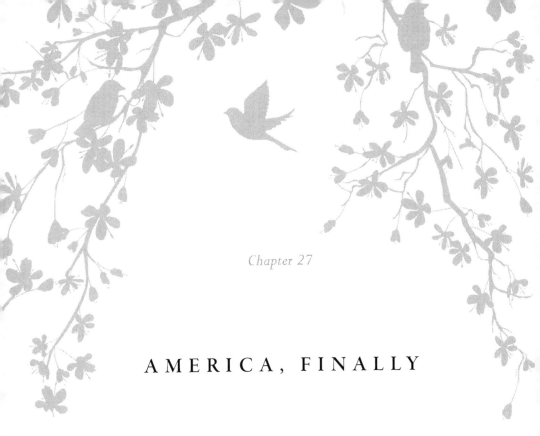

Chapter 27

AMERICA, FINALLY

*U*pon entering the country, their name, Laxague, was Americanized and became Lasaga. Their Basque was dropped with the scratch of a pen.

Juan became John.

Even though it had been *her* dream, John was the one who decided that they would move to the United States and live in Santa Barbara.

Eventually they bought land in Gaviota, just above the "California Riviera." It was a ranch where they could run thousands of head of sheep. It was what he knew. What they both knew. John needed Gracianna to feel safe, away from the war. With it behind both of them now—with children and his serious wife with dishwashing bubbles on her hands, he smiled sometimes.

Gracianna never spoke of the war again.

But she did speak of being thankful.

I understood it to mean that giving thanks is our only way to show gratitude for each gift we are given.

Constance came to visit the United States once in the late 1950s. She stayed for two months, and the sisters laughed and walked in the park and visited. They always stayed in touch by letter.

Only remaining photo of Gracianna and Juan (John) Lasaga,
Santa Barbara County, years after coming to the United States.

John and Gracianna never spoke of the war again, but it was always between them. They loved each other as much as a couple could after such an emotional holocaust. After years and years of never talking about it they were like a long bridge with two buttresses, two enormously strong tower foundations linked by the bridge, but unable to really be one.

John and Gracianna opened a bar in Santa Maria when the herding got too strenuous. They had no one to pass the ranch to since none of their three now-grown children had an interest in the tough herding life.

The Gaviota ranch overlooked a pass that could have been like the one the Romans tried to get through to conquer the Navarre Basques. It was above the waves of the Pacific as it licked the warm Santa Barbara shores, like the Riviera that Gracianna dreamed of as a young girl.

In the days before they were to sell the ranch, John was on the range just like the old days. He wanted to feel the sun on his old face and hear the sheep once again. The bleats were calming. They were like a song of joy and of home. He had been away with the dogs and herd for a few days and would still be out for nearly a week more, but he had arranged for Gracianna to meet him with lunch on the seventh day—a rare treat. Juan had left a message for Gracianna about where he would be, just like when they were younger.

Since Gracianna had never learned to drive, she was driven up the winding hills to a meeting point by her daughter, Ann. Ann stopped the car and, in the distance, she could see her father waiting in the clearing below the crest of the hill. They both waited as John came slowly down the hill, just like Gracianna had remembered him doing all those years before.

Then she said to Ann, "I will be back in a bit. Why don't you leave your old parents alone for a while?" Gracianna got out and walked toward him as Ann drove off.

They were both transported to the time when he had been waiting for his supplies and Gracianna had arrived. This time she brought a blanket, spread a picnic, and they just sat next to each other and looked out over their world. It was the first time they had really looked at each other in years.

"Just this one night, Gras'."

Gracianna smiled, "*Oui*, Juan."

Ann had come back and was waiting, but Gracianna waved her off and called, "Come back tomorrow."

Gracianna stayed with Juan and lay against him as the crickets scratched a happy saw. He touched her and brought her close. She pushed next to him against an oak tree and pulled the blanket over them.

AUTHOR'S AFTERWORD

After reflecting on the legacy of powerful values and a powerful woman, we arrive here.

This is the story I have pieced together from bits I've picked up from my family, some of my own memories, memories of memories, and well known family stories and interviews.

The rest is how I imagined my great-grandmother would have acted, based on my observations of her worried mind; controlling tendency; and pensive inward-looking gaze; and also of my perceptions of her joy, sadness, and beliefs.

When recalling memories from your youth, sometimes pieces come to you over the years. They get woven together, re-woven and woven again until something starts "to be." These are my recollections, facts, and beliefs, starting with my childhood, converted into my what-I-came-to-believe story. It took nearly fifty years for me to understand it myself.

Until recently, I never fully understood how much World War II, Hitler, the Auschwitz-Birkenau death camp, or French freedom resistance had impacted my family and me.

The Basque have a saying, "*Aldi luzeak, guztia ahaztu* [With the passing of time, all things are forgotten]."

But this will not be forgotten. Gracianna's sister miraculously did live through Birkenau, where it is estimated that between 700,000 and 1 million people were gassed, hanged, or shot.

I needed to tell the story about my lifelong belief of how that gun had gotten into my grandmother's nightstand.

I wanted to convey my understanding of her values and what they meant to her, and what they took from her and what she gave us. I believe these values were always on her mind, never far from her always-moist, pursed lips and French-accented thoughts. I wanted to understand her values and convictions and compare them to now-values, and I wondered, "What might today's generation believe in so strongly that it would cause them to act so desperately. . . . What is it that is so important that each of us would act upon it, based on our values, beliefs, and attitudes today?"

I wonder how distant we are from acting meaningfully.

I attended Cardinal Newman High School in California, on the kindness of friends or hardship scholarships. I was unable to go to college. Yet I was left with a powerful, persistent, and an ever-seeking curiosity. Unfortunately, my spiritual side was one-dimensional. For example, I did not know what a "Jew" was until I was eighteen. As a kid, I had never heard of Islam, met few blacks, and lived mostly in financial and emotional distress.

But *gratitude* stuck with me throughout the years, from "Grandma Lasaga." I did not understand what gratitude was until I was in my forties. When I was young, she used the word "thankful" in a powerful way.

She spoke to me as an adult, I think, hoping that this message would stay with me; and maybe reassert itself when I was able to understand. It did.

So, I *needed* to bring Gracianna and her values to life, while revealing their meaning in mine.

All these years later, my family, the Amadors of Sonoma County, started Gracianna Winery as a way to express the hand-me-down gratitude of Gracianna. Now folks from all over the world share our Sonoma County wine with their friends and family.

The analogy to winemaking is not lost on my family and me.

Shepherding families, like winemakers, know it all starts outside, in the field. A shepherd would "trail" his flock of one-to-two thousand sheep, where he would feed and water the herd in the summer. His job was to manage a huge number of lives in an enormous space, just like a vineyard. Shepherds loved these animals and knew each by sight. The shepherd had responsibility for the herd year-round, during the busy and active spring and summer, preparing for the slaughter—but also through the dreary and lonely winter and rains.

A single herder and dog could manage thousands of animals. It was a thankless existence. This is reminiscent of the modern-day vineyard manager, "herding" thousands of vines filled with life through unbearable heat and driving rain. Whether it is the vineyard manger or the herder, however, each knows it is all in the journey to grow and foster the very best you can.

Gracianna, the shepherd's wife, would prepare simple but gracious meals that included wine, a food staple as necessary as lamb. Her meal presentations, filled with thanks, were drawn from the heritage of thousands of years of satisfying hungry herders and families with sustenance. This effort was delivered with grace, and is what today's descendants aim to keep alive.

Money was tight for John and Gracianna when they were running sheep in the lush hills above Santa Barbara, especially in the months before slaughter. As practiced for centuries by European shepherds, the Lasaga's would offer "chits" in the form of coins, good for a certain number of sheep as an IOU (abbreviated from the phrase "I owe you") to pay for goods and mercantile, to hold them over until the herd was sold off again the next season. "Good for 50 sheep" was on one side of the coin, establishing the value. "J. Lazaga," probably misspelled, was on the other, establishing the debtor.

My family cherishes the single remaining coin of the five hundred minted that our great-grandparents used.

My wish is for much grace, graciousness, and gratitude in your life— from Gracianna, my great-grandmother, to you.

IOU for 50 sheep; privately minted during
Juan & Gracianna's struggles shepherding in America.

ABOUT THE AUTHOR

TRINI AMADOR is co-owner of GRACIANNA WINERY, a "fruit-first" craftsman's winery in the Russian River Valley of Sonoma County. The winery was founded on the principles of his great-grand-mother, Gracianna Lasaga, the subject of this book, who would prepare simple but gracious meals that always included wine—her meal presentations were delivered with grace and gratitude, and that is what today's descendants aim to keep alive through their world-class wines.

For the past fifteen years, Amador has also been a principal at BHC Consulting, which specializes in brand strategy, research, and insights development. Global brands like General Electric; Microsoft; AT&T; Yahoo!; Mattel, Inc.; Google; Jack Daniel's; and Rodale, Inc. have benefited from his counsel.